"IZZY! STOP!"

She ignored the command and swung the blade again. A big gloved hand reached out and shoved her back.

"Gods-dammit, Izzy! It's me!" He yanked the hood of his cape back, revealing his handsome face and dark blue hair. Some of it in braids with leather strips, feathers, and small animal bones tied throughout. "It's Éibhear."

"Yeah," Izzy answered honestly. "I know."

Then she pulled back her arm and threw the sword she held directly at his head.

More from G. A. Aiken

DRAGON ACTUALLY

ABOUT A DRAGON

WHAT A DRAGON SHOULD KNOW

LAST DRAGON STANDING

THE DRAGON WHO LOVED ME

And find her stories in this anthology

SUPERNATURAL

Published by Kensington Publishing Corporation

How To DRIVE A DRAGON CRAZY

G. A. AIKEN

ZEBRA BOOKS
KENSINGTON PUBLISHING CORP.
http://www.kensingtonbooks.com

ZEBRA BOOKS are published by

Kensington Publishing Corp.
119 West 40th Street
New York, NY 10018

All Kensington titles, imprints, and distributed lines are available at special quantity discounts for bulk purchases for sales promotion, premiums, fund-raising, educational, or institutional use.

Special book excerpts or customized printings can also be created to fit specific needs. For details, write or phone the office of the Kensington Special Sales Manager: Attn. Special Sales Department. Kensington Publishing Corp., 119 West 40th Street, New York, NY 10018. Phone: 1-800-221-2647.

Zebra and the Z logo Reg. U.S. Pat. & TM Off.

ISBN-13: 978-1-4201-0890-3
ISBN-10: 1-4201-0890-5

First Printing: September 2012

10 9 8 7 6 5 4 3 2 1

Printed in the United States of America

Places and Inhabitants
of the Dragon Kin World

A

Addolgar: Bercelak the Great's older brother.

Aidan the Divine: A gold dragon and a Mì-runach warrior.

Ailean the Wicked: (aka Ailean the Whore) Father to Bercelak the Great.

Alppi: Eldest son of Eymund Reinholdt. Dagmar's nephew.

Angor: Mì-runach legion commander.

Annwyl the Bloody: Human Queen of the Southlands, mate to Fearghus the Destroyer. Lives on Garbhán Isle. Nicknames: Mad Queen of Garbhán Isle, Blood Queen of Garbhán Isle, the Blood Queen.

Aoibhell: Teacher/philosopher when she lived, did not follow any god. Dagmar follows her teachings.

Arzhela: Goddess of light, love, and fertility.

Austell the Red: Éibhear's friend when he was still a recruit in the Dragon Queen's army.

Ásta: Kyvich legion commander.

B

Bercelak the Great: Mate and consort to Queen Rhiannon, father to the Queen's royal offspring.

Borderlands: Territory between the Southlands and the Desert Lands, houses the salt mines.

Bram the Merciful: Branwen and Celyn's father. Mate to Ghleanna the Decimator.

Branwen the Awful: (aka Brannie or Bran) Izzy's cousin and captain in the Dragon Queen's army.

Brastias: Morfyd's human mate. General Commander of Annwyl's armies.

Briec the Mighty: Adoptive father to Iseabail the Dangerous and birth father to Princess Rhianwen; mated to Talaith, Daughter of Haldane; second born son and offspring to the Dragon Queen.

Bryndís: Second in command in the Kyvich legion.

C

Cadwaladr Clan: The royals' "poor" relatives, the Cadwaladr Clan are warrior dragons used by the Dragon Queen to protect her territories.

Caswyn the Butcher: Mì-runach and a black dragon.

Celyn: Cousin to the Dragon Queen's royal offspring, Branwen's brother, and one of the Queen's Personal Guards.

Centaurs: Half-human/half-horse, able to shift to fully human, and are revered and, in some instances, feared by the dragons.

Chramnesind: God of earth and pain. Also known as The Sightless One.

Claiming: The ritualistic branding performed between dragon couples upon mating for life.

D

Dagmar Reinholdt: (aka The Beast) Gwenvael's mate, daughter to Northland warlord The Reinholdt, Steward to Annwyl the Bloody, and Battle Lord of Garbhán Isle.

Dai: Horse to Iseabail the Dangerous.

Dark Plains: The home of Garbhán Isle and the human Southland Queen.

Desert Lands: The southernmost territory inhabited by the Sand dragons and the warrior race of humans.

Devenallt Mountain: The home and royal court of the Dragon Queen and her consort.

Dragon Queen's Personal Guard: Handpicked warriors whose calling in life is to protect the queen with their lives.

Dragonwarrior Trials: The trials performed by soldiers from the Dragon Queen's army to move into the upper echelons of the Dragonwarriors. In order to become an officer in Her Majesty's army, one must be a Dragonwarrior.

E

Ebba: Centaur and royal nanny to the twins and Princess Rhianwen.

Éibhear the Contemptible: Fourth-born son, youngest off-spring to the Dragon Queen and Mì-runach Squad Leader.

Eirianwen: Human goddess of war and death. Mate to Rhydderch Hael.

Elisa: Nolwenn Elder and Izzy's great grandmother.

Eymund: Dagmar Reinholdt's eldest brother.

F

Fal: Brannie and Celyn's older brother.

Fearghus the Destroyer: First-born son and eldest off-spring to the Dragon Queen, first in line to the royal throne, mated to human Southland Queen, Annwyl the Bloody.

Fire Dragons: Southland dragons ruled by one queen, the ability to breathe flame is their natural weapon.

Frederik Reinholdt: Eighth-born son of Fridmar Reinholdt. Dagmar's nephew.

Fridmar Reinholdt: Dagmar's brother.

G

Gaius Lucius Domitus: Iron dragon and the Rebel King from the west.

Garbhán Isle: Seat of power of Annwyl the Bloody.

Ghleanna the Decimator: Branwen's mother. Bercelak's sister. Bram's mate.

Gwalchmai fab Gwyar, House of: The Dragon kin's royal name.

Gwenvael the Handsome: (aka Gwenvael the Slag) Mate to Dagmar Reinholdt, third-born son and fourth-born offspring to the Dragon Queen.

H

Haldane: Talaith's mother.

I

Ice Lands: The ice-covered lands far north of the Northlands.

Imperial Guards: Sefu city guards.

Iron Dragons: Silver fire breathers that separated from the Southland dragons centuries ago and moved to the Quintilian Provinces and Western Territories to rule over the human Sovereigns.

Iseabail the Dangerous: (aka Izzy) Daughter of Talaith and adoptive daughter of Briec. General in Annwyl's army. Chosen champion to Rhydderch Hael.

J, K

Keita the Viper: Second-born daughter, fifth-born offspring to the Dragon Queen. Bound to Ragnar and a Protector of The Throne.

Kyvich: Powerful witches of the Ice Lands, sworn enemies of the Nolwenns.

L

Layla: Captain in Sefu's Imperial Guard.

Lightning dragons: Northland dragons, one-time enemies of the Southland dragons, they are broken up into Hordes run by Dragonlords.

M

Macsen: Izzy's dog.

Meinhard the Savage: Northland dragon and Ragnar the Cunning's cousin.

Mì-runach: Beserker warriors who only take direct orders from the Dragon Queen. Only the most difficult and deadly warriors are sent to the Mì-runach.

Morfyd the White: First-born daughter, third-born offspring to the Dragon Queen, a powerful white witch, and vassal to the human Southland Queen.

N

Nolwenn: Powerful witches of the Desert Lands, sworn enemies of the Kyvich.

Northlands: Snow-covered, barren territory run by dragon Hordes and human warlords.

O

Olgeir the Wastrel: Deceased father of Ragnar the Cunning, former enemy of Queen Rhiannon.

Outer Plains: Small territory between the Southlands and Northlands.

P

Pombray: Visiting royal.

Q

Quintilian Provinces: Main city of the Western Territories run by the Iron dragons and human Sovereigns.

R

Ragnar the Cunning: Dragonlord Chief of the Olgeirsson Horde, bound to Keita the Viper.

Rhiannon the White: Dragon Queen of the Southlands.

Rhianwen: (aka Rhi) Human-dragon daughter of Talaith and Briec, younger sister to Izzy.

Rhona the Fearless: Lead blacksmith in the Northlands, mated to Vigholf.

Rhydderch Hael: God and father dragon to all. Mated to the human goddess Eirianwen.

S

Samuel: Izzy's squire.

Sand Dragons: Dragons of the Desert Lands with sand as their natural weapon.

Sefu: Major Desert Land city.

Sethos: Iseabail the Dangerous's birth father, deceased before her birth.

Shalin the Innocent: Mate to Ailean the Wicked, grandmother to Bercelak and Rhiannon's royal offspring. Name eventually changed to Shalin, Tamer of Ailean the Wicked.

Snow Dragons: Ice Land dragons broken into tribes, the ability to breathe snow is their natural weapon.

Southlands: Main territory of Rhiannon the White, Dragon Queen, and Annwyl the Bloody, human queen.

Sovereigns: Human inhabitants of the Quintilian Provinces and Western Territories beyond the Western Mountains.

Spikes: Nickname for the Ice Land white dragons.

T

Talan: Annwyl and Fearghus's dragon-human son. Twin of Talwyn.

Talwyn: Annwyl and Fearghus's dragon-human daughter. Twin of Talan.

U

Uther the Despicable: Mì-runach and a brown dragon.

V

Varro: Gaius's human general and friend.

Vateria Flominia: Iron She-dragon and the daughter of the late Overlord Thracius.

Vigholf the Abhorrent: Lightning dragon, brother to Ragnar, mated to Rhona the Fearless.

Volcano Dragons: Dragons born and raised deep in the Black Mountains near the southern Borderlands, they spew lava as their natural weapon.

W

Western Horseman Tribes: Nomadic slavers who live on the Western Plains, outside the Southlands, and near the Western Mountains. They are the sworn enemies of Annwyl the Bloody.

X, Y, Z

Zachariah: Izzy's grandfather on her birth father's side.

Zarah: Izzy's great grandmother on her birth father's side. Former commander general of Sefu's Imperial Guard.

Chapter 1

The orders from their queen had been direct and to the point: Stop the Ice Land dragons from regrouping and attacking the Northland dragons on their coast.

The Northlanders had been holding their own for years, pushing the Ice Land dragons, called the Spikes, back to their territorial lines and holding them there. Yet the Mì-runach were the ones who stopped the Spikes from ever really gathering enough forces in one place, at one time, to push their way back into the Northlands and putting the dragon warlords' territories at risk.

It had not been easy, though. Not for them. For they were the Mì-runach and they were all Fire Breathers trapped in one of the harshest lands known to dragon or gods. The Ice Lands with their hard winters and their even harder people. But that's why the Mì-runach had been sent here. Because among their own, the Mì-runach were considered hard and harsh. They didn't belong. They were the outcasts, the troublemakers, the pit fighters. They were the ones you didn't want setting up camp near your cave, but if you'd run out of options . . . then they were the ones you called.

They were the ones who killed. For their honor. For their queen. And because they were all really bloody good at it.

Mì-runach Legion Commander Angor landed on the mountaintop and watched his troops move in. As he'd trained them, they moved quick and quiet. Dragons they might be, one of the largest beings in the world, but that didn't mean they had to stomp everywhere. Not like the Spikes who let their snow-and-ice storms hide their presence. But the Mì-runach didn't let storms or being outsiders or anything else get in the way of their queen's orders.

Angor smiled a bit when he saw a flash of blade and then, as if from nowhere, a blue claw caught the Spike leader's head by the hair and yanked it back. A broadsword rammed through the neck, cutting off the Spike's chance to do anything but look stunned.

The Spikes, who had been rallying around their leader to begin their flight into enemy territory, froze, blood splattering their white and silver scales. Then the Mì-runach attacked, coming up from under the ground where some of them had been hiding for days.

He watched and waited while his troops decimated the Spikes. It didn't take long. They'd been trained not for battle but for massacres. That's what they did best. They struck with no warning, no negotiations, no prisoners. There were only sixty-six of them total, but they could do—and had done—the work of a full-size legion. They were the Dragon Queen's deadliest weapon and were hated and feared amongst the dragon world—and for very good reason.

Angor sat back on his haunches as his squad leaders landed in front of him.

"We're done," one of them reported. "And I sent out my team to strike down any stragglers."

"Good. We'll be heading back to the south in a few days."

"Really?" another asked, but he wasn't the only one thinking it. The queen had kept her Mì-runach in the Ice Lands off and on for years, but it wasn't for him or the rest of the Mì-runach to ask. Merely did as they'd been ordered by their queen.

"Really." He jerked his head to the side. "You lot. Get ready to move out for the night. Wait," he said to the one who'd killed the Spike leader. "Not you. Not yet."

Angor waited until the others had gone back down the mountain before turning to the dragon he'd trained himself.

To be honest, he'd had no hope for this one when he'd been forced on Angor nearly a decade ago. He'd been uselessly angry and astoundingly bitter. He'd refused to do even the simplest of tasks and put himself and his brethren at risk more than once during important assignments. But Angor had been able to see past all that rage and he'd kept the young dragon close to him and trained him hard from day one. Beat him when necessary, praised him when deserved. And now . . . ?

And now he was the most heartless, vile, and murdering bastard many of them had ever had the displeasure of knowing, and the most loathed dragon in all the Ice Lands.

For he was Éibhear the Contemptible, a Southland prince, and one of the dreaded Mì-runach Squad Leaders. He was also blindingly loyal, incredibly smart, and as close to a son as Angor ever had since he and his mate had never wanted offspring of their own.

The only problem with the royal? He read a lot, which Angor thought added to a lot of his problems. Who needed all those bloody books anyway?

"What do you need?" the blue dragon asked.

"We've stopped these Spikes from moving into Northland territories and meeting up with that young leader from the Ice Land tribe. But I want you and yours to go in, strike that leader down, so that them Spikes will understand this ox shit is over."

"Right."

"Just your squad. The others will come with me."

"Got it."

"You'll find them near that territorial line by them Mountains of Depression or whatever."

The Blue chuckled. "I think you mean the Mountains of Pain and Suffering."

"Yeah. Whatever. You go. You kill the leader, end this. That way we can head home without worrying about it."

"Consider it done."

"Then you can go back to your kin, Éibhear the Contemptible. You go back and see your mum."

The dragon stopped, blinked. "What?"

"Go home. See your mum."

"Um . . . why? Is something wrong?"

"Other than you being an ungrateful son? No."

"Ungrateful? I've destroyed dragon after dragon in her name."

"You enjoyed it."

He shrugged. "That's true."

"It's been ten years. Your mum should see you."

"I see you're still drawn to my mother."

"I am loyal to my queen. Do you know why?"

"Please not this story again," the Blue begged.

"Because when that bastard father of yours wanted to have me executed for insubordination—"

"That was probably because you'd come after him with an axe when he gave you an order."

"—your mum said no. She saw me worth. For that I'm loyal to her until I breathe me last. So take your ungrateful blue ass and go home."

The Blue studied Angor. "So you're kicking me out then?"

"Once Mì-runach, always Mì-runach, boy. You should know that by now. But you can't avoid your kin forever."

"I haven't been avoiding anything." He gave a small smile, showing one side of his fangs. "Not anymore."

"There's truth to that. So go home. See your mum. Make her happy. For me." Angor turned from the younger dragon, moving toward some Ice Land oxen he'd seen earlier. Watching his warriors kill always made him hungry.

"And my squad when we're done in the Northlands?" the boy called out. "Should I send them on ahead to meet you?"

"Don't you dare. Take those mean bastards with you. No other squad will have them anyway." He flicked his claw in the air. "Go home, Éibhear the Contemptible. See your mum. See your kin. Spend some time with those who raised you. Think of it like a holiday. Then remember why you left in the first place, and return to the Mì-runach. We'll be camped near the Western Mountains. Waiting to do what we do best."

"Kill?" the blue dragon asked Angor.

"Some would say," Angor muttered on a chuckle. "Some would say."

Chapter 2

Éibhear the Contemptible—once called Éibhear the Blue—walked up to his squad. The Mì-runach were broken up into four-to-six-member squads. Angor was commander of them all, but it wasn't a job any of them envied.

For one to become Mì-runach he not only had to be a mighty fighter, he also had to be a vicious, heartless bastard who couldn't take basic orders. Although they'd been around for centuries in different forms, usually brought together during a specific war or battle, the Mì-runach really had come into their own when Éibhear's grandfather, Ailean—the shining example of a dragon who couldn't take orders but made himself worth the trouble during a battle—joined. Of course, they didn't have a name then; instead, they were just known as those "unreliable, heartless bastards" who were too good as warriors to dismiss completely but too much of a bother to force some poor commander to have to tolerate while trying to manage scores of other soldier dragons during a heated battle.

In the Dragon Queen's army, not taking orders made a Dragonwarrior a dangerous liability. But among the Mì-runach, where one's strengths were used to benefit, it made that soldier a useful servant of the queen. For the Mì-runach handled that which many would not. It took some time for Éibhear to figure out exactly what that made them, but he finally did. . . . They were a death squad.

Like they'd just done with the Spikes, the Mì-runach would sneak in during the cover of night and slaughter soldiers in their caves. Or they'd burrow underground and strike in the middle of a battle, killing the leaders and then decimating the rest of the army, if necessary. Many dragon soldiers in Her Majesty's Army considered this type of fighting dishonorable. But to the Mì-runach, who needed honor when there was ale? And pubs? And females to entertain? Who needed rank and orders and rules and a bunch of daily tasks when they could sleep all day and drink all night until called to do what they did best?

It wasn't rank and power that kept the Mì-runach returning to battle day after day, night after night. The gods knew, it would never be rank. It was the love of blood and battle and destruction. It was knowing that they were the ones their Queen's enemies feared because they had reason to fear.

"Well?" asked Aidan the Divine, a Gold whose royal family hailed from the Western Mountains.

"We're heading out for one final task in the Northlands."

"Oh?"

"Aye. Kill Spike leader Jorgesson's son, since the boy seems to think he can take his father's place."

"Which he probably thought he had to do because we killed Jorgesson."

"True. Once we're done with the boy, we're heading to Dark Plains. Angor wants me to go home for a bit."

Aidan blinked, dropping the dragon whose neck he'd just crushed. "Home? You?"

"Why do you say it like that? You've been away from your kin longer than I have."

"I loathe my kin as they loathe me." Aidan slammed his fist into the Spike on the ground although it seemed unnecessary.

"You seem to like yours, but I'm not sure you returning home will make that better or worse."

"I do like them." Éibhear thought on that a moment. "Well, the females. I like the females . . . mostly."

Uther the Despicable, a cranky Brown from mountains near the port cities, grunted and snarled—as he snarled at most things—"And what are we doing while you're playing happy families?" He gritted his fangs and pulled on the legs of the Ice Land dragon he held in his arms. The screaming during this was a tad unpleasant. "Joining another squad?"

"After what you lot did last time?" Éibhear asked.

"That was not my fault!" Caswyn the Butcher argued, yet again. "He shouldn't have tried to push me around. I may not be some fancy royal, like you and pretty boy over there—"

Aidan grinned. "I am so very pretty."

"—but that don't mean some Red bastard can just walk all over me."

"By 'walk all over me,'" Éibhear cut in, "do you mean ask you to do your job?"

"Didn't like his tone, did I?"

"So you tore his arms off."

Caswyn's head lowered a bit, his black wings bristling. "Don't much like your tone either."

"Yeah, but you already tried to tear Éibhear's arms off," Uther reminded him. "You were in a coma for weeks."

"It was more a deep rest."

Éibhear rolled his eyes and said, "You all will come with me."

Uther's head snapped up. "Will your sisters be there?"

Imitating his eager tone, Éibhear quickly replied, "They will! And so will my father!"

Uther's face fell. "Oh."

Reflective, Aidan stroked his chin while pounding his back claw into the head of the Spike lying in front of him. Again . . . still seemed unnecessary as that Spike was already quite dead.

"How *did* your father not become Mì-runach? He seems ruthless enough."

"Oh, he is," Éibhear agreed. "But he can take orders."

"Aaaaah," the others said.

"So if we go with you," Caswyn asked. "What do we do?"

Éibhear shrugged. "It's Garbhán Isle. There'll be drink and pussy. What more do you need?" Garbhán Isle was the seat of power for the human queen of the Southlands, Annwyl the Bloody. Insane monarch and mate to Éibhear's eldest brother Fearghus, Annwyl was adored and loathed in equal parts, but to Éibhear she'd simply become one of his sisters.

"Nothing," Uther said. "But that makes me sad."

"But first we take care of the Spikes leader in the North-lands."

His squad groaned.

"What?"

"I'm tired of snow and ice," Caswyn complained. "I'm tired of shades of purple and white. I want to see grass again. And trees. Birds that aren't crows."

"We won't be in the Northlands long. Just long enough to do a little killing. You lot like killing. Remember?"

"I do remember. But *you* seem to have forgotten that the Northlanders hate you," Aidan reminded him.

"Not more than the Ice Landers do."

"Only because you haven't been there for the last decade. Trust me, if you had, they'd only hate you more."

"I want to see my sister Keita. As far as I know she's still with Ragnar in the Northlands."

"A little elegance among the barbarians." Aidan sighed. "I guess that's worth something."

"So finish killing this lot," Éibhear said, gesturing to the Spikes trying to crawl away. He really had to work on that with his team. They disabled, sometimes tortured, then killed, but the disabling and torture were just time consuming. They needed to kill faster so they could move to the drinking and females quicker. Honestly, one would think they'd know that already. "Then we head out."

Éibhear turned, saw a Spike fighting with one of the other squads. He pulled his sword and headed over to assist. Aidan caught up to him.

"Oy," his friend said.

"What?"

"You know what might be waiting for you back at Garbhán Isle, don't you?"

"The loving warmth of my mother, the admiration of my father, and the caring of my dear brothers?"

"Are you going to be serious about this?"

Éibhear chuckled, then rammed his sword into the side of the Spike. It was an easier way to attack an Ice Land dragon since they had those bloody spikes going from the top of their heads, down their spines, to the tips of their tails. He twisted the blade while using his free claw to push the Ice Lander down by the side of his neck.

When the dragon took his last breath, Éibhear pulled out his sword, nodded at his fellow squad leader, then faced his friend. "Yeah. I know what might be waiting for me."

"And?"

"And nothing. That was a long time ago . . . for a human. Besides, I apologized."

Aidan frowned. "When? You haven't seen her in nearly ten bloody years."

"Remember? I sent her a letter."

"Oh. The letter. Right." Aidan looked off. "Yeah. I remember. The letter."

"Although she never did answer me. Rude cow."

"Yeah. Rude."

"But I'm sure she's over it. There was a healthy amount of groveling in that letter. She likes groveling."

"I'm sure she does."

"So there's nothing to worry about." Éibhear patted his

suddenly quiet friend's shoulder. "We'll go. We'll spend some time with my kin. Then hit every pub between Garbhán Isle and the Western Mountains as we go to meet up with Angor and the other squads. It'll be a lovely holiday that we richly deserve."

Aidan finally looked at him. "But first the Northlands?"

"First the Northlands. Deal with the new Spikes leader for those poor Lightning bastards."

"Can we call the Northlanders that when we see them? I'm sure they'll just love it."

"Then I'll check in with Keita before we head south."

"Check in with Keita while still in the Northlands? Sure that's wise?"

"Come now," Éibhear dismissed his friend's worry. "It's been ages. I'm sure Ragnar's forgiven me by now."

"Right." Aidan snorted. "I'm sure he has."

"We challenge you," the Spikes' leader had called out, bright white wings extending from his back, white spikes going from his head, down his spine, to the tip of his tail, white and silver hair braided up like a horse's mane touching the ground. "Let's decide this now and end it."

So it had been agreed. The Spike's champion against theirs. But there were rumors coming in from Ragnar's spies that all this was merely a fancy ruse. The young leader's idea to get the Northlanders to think the war was over and head home, so that this leader's troops and another Spike's legion could come over territorial lines and into the Northlands unmolested. Because unlike the Spikes, honor was all to the Northland dragons.

And it was true. Honor was all, but not stupidity. Ragnar had already sent word to his contacts in the Ice Lands to stop the second army from crossing into their territory by any means necessary. Knowing that was being handled allowed him to enjoy the champion contest currently going on in front of him.

Ragnar studied the dragon his champion was facing. He was bigger than anything Ragnar had ever seen, easily the size of two castles. Around his neck he wore a necklace made of smaller dragons' heads and his scales had hardened into an armor of its own, the sound of his heavy breathing rattling the nearby trees. Ragnar wasn't even sure the dragon could fly anymore. All that weight combined with the stiffness of his scales . . .

"Gods," Ragnar's cousin Meinhard whispered next to him. "It's a cannibal."

"A what?" Ragnar's brother, Vigholf, asked.

"A cannibal dragon," Ragnar clarified. "He eats his own kind. That's what makes him look like that."

The cannibal thrust his battle lance, aiming for their champion's shoulder. There was great power behind that move. Enough to tear open a hole in a small mountain. The lance flashed in the early morning suns as the champion caught that lance in his claw, held it.

Tugging, the cannibal tried to pry it free. He became frustrated and roared. He held out his other claw and someone tossed him a sword. He caught it, swung for the champion's neck. But the claw that held the sword was caught and held.

Strength battled strength as each male pushed back against the other, but neither budged. Yet the cannibal had no patience; he leaned in, opening his maw. The champion didn't wait for whatever the cannibal had planned. He unleashed his own flame first, the stream hitting deep inside the cannibal's throat, choking him. The cannibal released his weapons, and stumbled back.

The champion dropped the weapons and went for his own. A battle axe and a warhammer. He wielded both at the same time, swinging on the cannibal before he had a chance to snap back. The hammer hit him first, ramming into his head, knocking him to one side. The axe followed, attacking the same side, connecting with his shoulder. The blow knocked the cannibal to the ground, trapping several dragons beneath him.

The champion flew over to him, landing hard, and battered at him with both axe and hammer, hitting him mostly in the face and neck and chest until the cannibal roared his rage and rose, knocking the champion off him. He dragged himself up, the champion scrambling back, trying to move out of his way.

Taking in a deep breath, the cannibal again opened his mouth wide, about to unleash a weapon that had nothing to do with steel.

"Shields!" Vigholf yelled out, and they all brought their shields up or stepped in behind a comrade's.

Ragnar watched the cannibal release neither lightning nor flame nor water nor any of the other weapons that every dragon had within it. But acid. The only other dragon with acid as its natural weapon was the Immortal dragon. The Immortals had been given their weapon by the gods, but it was said that those who ate their own were cursed with acid as their weapon. Stomach acid.

The acid sprayed out, shields sizzling as the hard steel was struck, a large ball of it hurtling toward the champion.

The champion grabbed a shield, lifting it to protect his face and chest, the power of the acid shoving him back, burning through the metal. He dropped the shield, raised his gaze, and charged at the cannibal again. But he suddenly pulled back as another dragon, one covered in the pelts of dead animals, such as Ice Landers were known to wear, dropped between their champion and the Spike's.

Ragnar looked between his brother and cousin, but they seemed lost as well.

"The trap?" Vigholf asked.

If it was, it was a tragically premature trap. Ragnar still had a full army out here, ready to fight.

The cannibal opened his mouth, ready to unleash more acid, but the mysterious dragon dressed as a barbarian Ice Lander suddenly turned and struck. He rammed his lance into the open mouth of the cannibal, halting his ability to unleash his acid—at least for the moment.

The cannibal was battered to the ground, the stranger using only his giant forearms covered in leather gauntlets. He then raised an oversized steel axe up and over his head in one fluid movement, bringing it down with a mighty force into the cannibal's giant neck, hacking through those thick scales. And he kept hacking until he'd separated head from spine.

The stranger picked up the head by its hair and held it high for all of them to see, slowly turning once so they could get a good look. Then he pitched it to the ground at the claws of the remaining Spikes, chuckling when the head bounced up and hit the Spike's leader in the snout.

The stranger turned from the Spikes and faced Ragnar and his kin. Talons reached up and pulled the hood of the fur cloak from his head so that braided blue hair spilled out, pieces of leather and animal bone weaved throughout the strands. Just like the Ice Landers wore.

"Maybe this Ice Lander wants to immigrate," Vigholf suggested. "Not that I blame him. . . . Are those bones in his hair on purpose?"

"I think so. Perhaps it's a fashion thing. Like Keita and her dresses."

"Maybe the Ice Landers *make* you wear bones in your hair."

The Ice Lander walked over to Ragnar and stopped. "Oy."

Surprised by his familiar tone, Ragnar frowned, but he quickly caught hold of Meinhard's arm to stop his cousin from pulling his battle axe and chopping off the Ice Lander's head for rudeness to the Dragonlord Chief.

"Yes?" Ragnar asked.

"Where's my sister?"

Ragnar frowned again. "How the hells would I know?"

The Ice Lander blinked. "What did she do? Leave you?" He shrugged. "Well . . . you did last longer than most."

Completely confused and annoyed, Ragnar released his cousin's arm so that Meinhard could take the whelp's head and they could finish this bloody battle with the bloody Spikes and get on with their bloody lives! But a female voice behind them stopped Meinhard from striking.

"Éibhear?"

Ragnar glanced back at Rhona the Fearless, Vigholf's female, as she moved through the crowd of soldiers, removing the helmet she'd made herself as their lead blacksmith. Most blacksmiths didn't involve themselves in battles, but Rhona was such a damn good soldier, Ragnar didn't complain. Vigholf certainly didn't either—he knew better.

"Éibhear's here?" Vigholf asked. "Where?"

She pointed at the Ice Lander. "Right there."

Shocked to his core, Ragnar looked first at his brother, then at his cousin . . . then at the boy. The useless, ridiculous, love-sick boy that they'd summarily dismissed, briefly respected, then had no longer been able to tolerate until the blue dragon's father had him assigned to some other unit within the Dragon Queen's army.

Mouth hanging open, Vigholf shook his head, and Meinhard muttered, "It can't be."

"Éibhear?" Ragnar asked again.

"Yeah. My sister?" he pushed.

"What?"

"Keita. Remember her? Gods, how long ago did she leave you?" he snapped, annoying Ragnar again. *Rude whelp!*

"She hasn't left me, you worthless little sh—"

"Then where is she?"

Vigholf, his mouth still hanging open, pointed toward the mountains where they'd left Keita with a battalion of soldiers to protect her.

"Good." Éibhear looked behind him. "Mì-runachs—with

me." He walked into the crowd of Northland soldiers, patting Rhona's shoulder as he passed. Ragnar watched him for a long while until another Fire Breather dressed in the fashion of the Ice Lands stood in front of him. This one held out a blood-covered white dragon head to him. "You want this?"

Without thinking, Ragnar took the head of the one-time Spikes leader, wondering when the young leader had been killed, since less than a minute ago he'd been quite alive.

"You know the scariest part of all this?" Vigholf asked as he stepped aside to allow the three other Mì-runachs to follow Éibhear.

"What?"

"Since we last saw him, that blue bastard actually got *bigger*."

Keita lay stretched out on the floor, a book on the topic of poisons in front of her. She went through each kind, trying to find which could best be used to poison the water supply of the Spikes. She longed to return to the warmth of her Southland home for a little holiday, but these constant battles with these ridiculous Ice Landers had made it impossible. Honestly, these Northerners! All they did was fight! Constantly! It was like living with her Cadwaladr kin all the time.

She turned another page. "Oooh," she sighed, when she saw a root that might be perfect for what she needed. But before she could read further, she heard one of the soldiers who guarded her cavern give a warning cry, then the sounds of battle.

Keita quickly got to her claws and swiped up some Ved bark. If necessary, she could force it into a dragon's mouth and end him quite quickly.

An Ice Land dragon stalked through the cavern entry.

"Keita," he said, his voice indescribably low. She was shocked that he knew her name.

The dragon moved toward her, but she quickly raised her empty claw, halting him. "You'll never take me alive!" Then she thought on that proclamation a bit and added, "All right. You *can*, of course, take me alive. But most importantly, try not to damage this face." She lowered her head a bit and looked up through her lashes. "Or these beautiful fangs." Then she smiled.

The dragon leaned back from her, a look of disgust on his face. At least, it looked like disgust. Hard to tell with all that blue hair in his face. Wait . . . shouldn't his hair be whiter? Or silver? Or something that easily melded in with the snow-covered world of the Ice Lands?

"It's me, you little idiot," the invader said.

She crossed her forearms over her chest. "I can say with all honesty that I've never fucked an Ice Lander before. And I'm not about to start now!"

The invader closed his eyes, sighed long and deep. "It's me . . . *Éibhear.*"

"Éibhear who?"

He threw down his blade. "Your brother!"

Keita's arms slowly fell to her sides and her mouth opened as she stared at the dragon in front of her. Then she exploded into laughter that rocked the cave walls.

"How do you forget your own brother?"

"Don't blame me!" Keita argued around her hysterical and, to be honest, quite annoying laughter. "How was I supposed to recognize you when you look like the lowest barbarian known to dragon or gods?"

"I've been in the Ice Lands for a decade, you snobby cow! I had to blend."

"Well . . . blend you did."

Disgusted, Éibhear turned to go. Sorry he'd ever come.

But before he could take more than a step, Keita grabbed his forearm and caught hold.

"I'm sorry." Although she was still laughing. "I'm sorry." She stepped in front of him and wrapped her arms around his chest. "I'm so glad to see you!"

"Really? It was a bit hard to tell."

"You have grown quite a bit, baby brother." Her head fell back so she could look up at him. "I can't even get my forearms around you! You're gargantuan!"

"I'm not that big."

"Hopefully you've finally stopped growing or you might cover the world, my handsome, majestic brother."

"You'll not fool me with your centaur-shit platitudes," he muttered, even as he put his own forearms around her and hugged her tight. "No matter how sweet you may act. I know the truth about Keita the Viper."

"Of course you do. You're a prince of the mightiest dragons on earth. I'd expect no less." She rested her head against his chest and sighed. "So . . . what brings you here?"

"Come to kill some cannibal dragon for the Northlanders, then I thought I'd go home for a bit. Since I haven't been in a while."

He felt his sister tense against him. "You're going home? Now?"

"Aye."

"Huh." She pulled away, moved around him. "Does Mother know? Or Fearghus and the others?"

"No. Why?"

"Oh . . . well, I think that there's some very important assignment they need you involved in."

"What assignment?"

"Not sure of all the details, but I'm certain I can find out. But I think you'll need to take care of that first before you return home."

"Really?" Éibhear slowly turned so that he could keep his sister in sight.

"Aye. I'm sorry, love. I know how much you want to go home and see everyone. I'm sure this assignment will take no time at all."

"How long, do you think?"

"Two . . . three weeks at most. Then you can be home and we can all spend some time together."

"You're lying, Keita."

Keita gasped and spun around to face him. "Éibhear! How could you say something like that to me? *Me?*"

"Because I know when you're lying. And you're lying. There's no assignment. If there was, my commander would have told me about it. So then my question becomes, why don't you want me to go home? After ten bloody years?"

"Of course I want you to go home. Go! Ignore your duties. I'm sure everyone will be very happy to see you, little brother."

Éibhear crossed his forearms over his chest and tapped one talon of his back claw. "Tell me, Keita"—and he knew he was practically begging because he was so damn annoyed—"tell me this has nothing to do with Izzy."

"What? Of course not! That's a ridiculous thing to even ask. What would Izzy have to do with anything?"

Again, he knew his sister was lying. This had everything to do with Izzy.

Little Izzy the Dangerous. At least that's how he'd thought of her when he'd first met her. She'd only been sixteen then. Pretty but awkward. All long legs and gangly arms. And a child. Even worse than that—his niece. No. Not by blood. But his brother had taken Izzy's mother as his mate and the entire family had accepted both mother and daughter as their own. Something that wouldn't have been a problem if Izzy had just stayed that awkward, gangly child. But she hadn't, had she? She'd kept growing, getting stronger and more beautiful nearly every day. Something that probably wouldn't have been a problem if his kin had just left the whole thing alone.

But they hadn't then, and it seemed they wouldn't now.

"Izzy?" Ragnar said as he walked into the cavern, Meinhard and Vigholf behind him. "Is he going to pick her up instead of us?"

Keita flinched the slightest bit, but Éibhear saw it . . . and smirked.

"Oh, I'll pick her up," Éibhear quickly offered, not even knowing where the hells the woman might be and not remotely caring.

"No, you will not," Keita said, panic in her voice.

Vigholf pointed outside the cavern. "What did you do to the guards, boy?"

"They got in my way," Éibhear explained before refocusing on his sister. "And why wouldn't I go to get my dear niece?"

"Because I said so."

"Did you actually tell the guards who you are?" Vigholf continued on.

"Didn't feel like it. And I don't think 'Because I said so' is really a good enough reason for not letting me do you this favor."

Keita's eyes narrowed on Éibhear and Éibhear narrowed his right back.

"Maybe you could have just asked them to check with your sister before you attacked them," Vigholf suggested.

Letting out a sigh, Éibhear yelled out, "Aidan! Are they still breathing?"

"Aye. They are." The three Mì-runach entered the cavern, Aidan stopping to lean against the entrance wall with one shoulder. "And they still have all their parts. That's pretty good for us."

Éibhear looked at Vigholf. "Happy now?"

"Not particularly."

"We will take care of my niece. You can just head home," Keita insisted.

Éibhear couldn't help but laugh a little. "Are you really trying to keep me away from her? After all this time?"

"It's not just me, brother, and we're doing it in Izzy's best interest."

"Oh, come on, Keita. That was a long time ago. And I apologized."

"And when did you do that? You haven't seen her in ten years!"

"Five years ago I wrote her a letter and apologized."

"Uh . . ."

Éibhear looked over his shoulder at Aidan. "Uh . . . what?"

Caswyn looked at Aidan, and asked, "You didn't tell him?"

"Tell me? Tell me what?"

"It never seemed the right time."

"What never seemed the right time? What's going on?"

Aidan stared at Éibhear and finally admitted, "We burned your letter."

Keita gave a shocked laugh as Éibhear faced his comrades. "You did *what*?"

"Don't get mad. It was in your best interest."

"How was burning my letter to Izzy in my best interest?"

"We could have let it be sent instead."

"Females hate that," Uther felt the need to explain. "A letter. If you can't say it to her face, then you shouldn't bother."

"So we'll go pick her up," Aidan said, winking at Éibhear. "You can tell her to her face on the way to Garbhán Isle."

Éibhear looked back at his sister. "Guess I'll be picking up Izzy. So we can talk."

Keita's eyes crossed. "Why must you be sooooo difficult?"

"It's in the bloodline."

"That's no longer a good enough excuse!"

Éibhear reached over and stroked his sister's cheek. "I'm

glad to see you're well, sister." He turned, headed toward the exit. "Where can I find Izzy?"

"You'll find her in the Blathnat Forests fighting the ogres," Ragnar replied.

Éibhear stopped, glanced back at the Northland Dragonlord. "Because she'll ask . . . why am I taking Izzy back to Garbhán Isle?"

"I still say you shouldn't be taking her—" Keita began to protest again, but Ragnar covered her snout with his claw and nodded at Éibhear.

"Have a good trip. We'll see you at Garbhán Isle in a few days' time."

Not only did Éibhear realize that Ragnar didn't answer his question, he also kind of knew that the Lightning *wasn't* going to answer his question. No matter how many times he asked. So why bother? Instead, he headed off to track down Izzy and do what he thought he'd done five years ago.

Once Éibhear and his entourage of dangerous friends were gone, Keita slapped her mate's claw off her snout and spun to face him. "Why did you do that?"

"I don't see the problem, Keita."

"Of course you don't." She swept her claw at the idiot Northland males. "None of you do!"

"Where's Éibhear going?" Rhona demanded as she stalked into the cavern.

"These idiots—"

Vigholf frowned. "What do you mean '*these* idiots'?"

"—sent Éibhear to pick up Iseabail."

Rhona stopped and faced Vigholf. "You did what?"

"It wasn't me. It was Ragnar."

Ragnar sighed in disgust. "Your weakness sickens me, brother."

Vigholf shrugged. "I do what I have to in order to get through my day."

"You lot," Rhona said, sneering. "You Northlanders forget nothing."

"Don't know what you're talking about, Rhona."

"This is still about that cousin of yours missing his wing and horns, isn't it?"

"That was a long time ago," Vigholf stated. "Nothing we'd ever . . . cling to."

"Although it would have been nice if he'd at least apologized."

"You bastards," Rhona sighed, shaking her head. "All of you . . . bastards."

"I don't know what you're all talking about," Keita snarled. "And I don't care. I just can't believe you were all so bloody stupid!"

"The boy's no longer a hatchling, Keita," Ragnar argued. "So I'm unclear why you're acting like he is."

"But Izzy—"

"Is definitely no longer a child. Not anymore. So stop trying to protect her from your brother."

Keita sat back on her haunches, crossed her forearms over her chest, and challenged, "And what makes you think it's *Izzy* we're protecting?"

The three Northland males smirked and Ragnar said with so much false innocence, her back fangs ached. "Oh . . . was that your concern?"

"Told you, cousin," Rhona sighed, heading toward several crates of ale. "Bastards. All of 'em."

Chapter 3

As human, in their Ice Land fur capes that hid their faces and chain-mail leggings and shirts, the four Mì-runach stood on the ridge overlooking the valley caught between a half-ring of mountains and a vast forest where a battle raged on.

"I didn't know we'd have to fight our way in," Aidan complained. "I was hoping we'd swoop in and swoop out."

"That won't be happening today."

A battle cry sounded from beside them and Uther turned, gutting the male running at them with his blade and tossing the body back several feet.

Éibhear sighed. "That was one of Annwyl's men."

"Oh." Uther shrugged. "Sorry."

"Annwyl's troops are in red and silver. The enemies are ogres, which means their skin is in varying shades of green and they're not human. So it shouldn't be too hard to figure out."

"Why are they fighting ogres?" Caswyn asked.

"Annwyl had to fight ogres once in a pit fight. Now she hates ogres."

"Interesting woman, your human queen."

Éibhear walked a bit until he found a path leading down the ridge and right into the battle. As they walked, not really engaging in the battle unless threatened, Aidan asked him, "So which one is the infamous Izzy?"

"Can't you tell?"

"I can tell." Caswyn stopped, pointed at a warrior woman riding on a black steed, her sword flashing as she gave orders to the men surrounding her.

Aidan laughed. "Not even close."

"Why not? She looks like a proper soldier, leading a queen's army into battle."

"That's the problem. Éibhear's never been interested in anyone doing the 'proper' thing."

"Then who?"

Aidan looked over the battle, then finally smiled and pointed. "Her."

They all looked where he pointed, but all Éibhear could see was a group of ogres beating on something with their clubs. Then there was a scream and a shield came up from the center of those ogres, pushing them back. And from the midst of all that green flesh, she stood. Tall and proud. No longer the young girl he'd met so many years ago, nor the young soldier he'd walked away from.

Now she was something different. Scarred, bruised, and covered in blood, she shoved her long shield forward, knocking a few more ogres out of her way. From her left, another ogre swung at her. Izzy raised her arm, caught the club in her hand. Snarling, she yanked the weapon from the ogre and turned on him, kicking him in the gut. The shield was yanked from her, but that just freed her to grip the club in both hands. She swung it, knocking an ogre to the ground; then she brought the club up and over, bringing the spiked head of the weapon down onto the ogre's face.

Screaming, she ripped the club out of the skull and took out another attacker. That's when Caswyn looked at Éibhear. "Yeah. Aidan's right. That's gotta be her."

* * *

Iseabail, Daughter of Talaith and Briec, Human Princess by Mating of the House of Gwalchmai fab Gwyar, and General of the Eighth, Fourteenth, and Twenty-sixth Legions of Annwyl the Bloody, Queen of Garbhán Isle and Dark Plains, ducked the flint axe swinging for her head and brought the club she held up between the legs of the ogre trying to kill her.

He squealed and dropped to his knees. Izzy tore the spiked club up and out of the ogre's body, then brought it back down on his head, now that he was closer to her height.

It had been a bloody, ugly war for the last two months, but Izzy hoped an end was near because she believed she was finally getting her chance at the ogre leader. Once he was dead, the rest of his army would fall.

So she took down another ogre, ducked a flint axe aimed at her head, and crushed a kneecap with a well-placed kick, all in the hopes of finding that damn ogre leader.

"Iz!"

Izzy heard her dragon cousin's screamed warning and was able to move out of the way in time to avoid the ogre attacking from behind, but the blade of his flint axe cut across her arm. The wound began to bleed almost immediately and she knew she'd have to get it sewn up. But she refused to worry about that now. Not with the ogre leader finally in her sights. She could see him about thirty feet away. So very close.

Izzy spun, swung the club, and slammed it into the neck of the bastard behind her as he tried to run away. He went down face first and Izzy pulled out her sword and rammed it into the back of the beast's head.

"Izzy."

She heard her name called again, this time by a much different voice from her cousin Branwen's, but she had to ignore it as she was being attacked again. *Gods, the ogres just keep coming.*

She blocked the flint mace aimed for her face by using the club she still held in her left hand and cut the thick arteries inside the ogre's thighs with her sword. She spun and slashed her sword again, cutting a throat, then spun again and swung, but her blade was stopped by an obscenely large battle axe. She knew the weapon was not an ogre's. They only used flint weapons and although deadly were often crudely made. This was a well-made weapon forged by a true blacksmith.

So Izzy struck at the knees with the club she still held. The heavy flint made contact and there was an angry snarl from beneath the heavy fur cape that covered the face and body of the axe wielder.

"Izzy! Stop!"

She ignored the command and swung the blade again. A big gloved hand reached out and shoved her back.

"Gods-dammit, Izzy! It's me!" He yanked the hood of his cape back, revealing his handsome face and dark blue hair. Some of it in braids with leather strips, feathers, and small animal bones tied throughout. "It's Éibhear."

"Yeah," Izzy answered honestly. "I know."

Then she pulled back her arm and threw the sword she held directly at his head.

Éibhear knew that because of his size, it was believed he was quite slow. *Lumbering* was a word he'd often heard used by those seeing him doing nothing more than standing. Yet at that moment when he saw the short sword coming right at him, thrown by a woman who clearly knew what she was doing, Éibhear would say he'd never been so grateful that everyone was wrong. He was fast. Very fast. And it was that speed, being able to drop to the ground in seconds, that really saved his life.

Once he hit the ground, he looked up and saw that Izzy was running right at him. He wasn't sure if she was coming to finish him off or just kick the shit from him, but the thought of batting her away or blasting her with his flame—stupidly—never entered his head.

He would never know why.

When Izzy reached him, she snatched his short sword from his belt and leaped up, one foot landing on his shoulder. She used that foot to launch herself, lifting her body and spinning in the air. Éibhear turned over and watched as Izzy raised the sword that most human males couldn't lift and shoved it into the nine-foot ogre that had stood behind Éibhear. He'd been so focused on Izzy, he hadn't even been aware of the big bastard wearing a human skull on a chain around his neck.

But even with the sword buried in the top of his head, the ogre wasn't dead yet. He was snarling and snapping at Izzy as she hung there, and that's when she spoke to the green bastard. Éibhear had no idea what she said, but he was positive the ogre did. And the words were so guttural, so vile-sounding that he knew she was speaking the ancient language of the ogres.

When Izzy finished, she released her hold on the sword and dropped to the ground. With one good kick to the ogre's stomach, she knocked him on his back and walked around until she was able to look him in the eye. Gripping in both hands the club she still held, she raised it above her head and brought it down once, smashing the ogre's face in.

It was then that Éibhear realized this must be the ogre leader because all the surviving ogres stopped fighting and began to turn and run back toward the mountains in the distance, probably to choose another leader and regroup. Izzy seemed to know that as she yanked Éibhear's blade from the dead leader's head.

"All of you!" Izzy called out while walking back toward Éibhear. "Don't let them reach the caves. Kill them all! *Now move!*"

Izzy stopped by Éibhear's side, looked him over. "Why are you here?" she asked.

"To bring you home."

"Can't." She dropped the blade over his stomach, Éibhear barely catching it before the blade possibly cut something vital. "Not done."

She turned away from him, dismissing him without a backward glance. "Lieutenant Alistair." A full-human male rode up to her.

"General!"

"Rally the men. Pull several to get the wounded to healers. We'll deal with the dead later. I want those ogres meeting their green-skinned ancestors in hell before the moon's high in the sky. Do you understand?"

"Aye, General."

"Go."

He rode off and another female rode to Izzy's side.

"Fionn. How are we looking?"

"Good, Iz. But there's still some fight left in the South Valley."

"Take a contingent and strike them down."

"Your arm, General," the woman, Fionn, pushed.

"Yeah, yeah. I know, Colonel. I'll deal with it." She laughed, waved the woman away.

Then, without even looking at him again, Izzy walked off, leaving him lying there.

"I don't know why you look so shocked," a voice said from beside him and he looked up into the face of his cousin Branwen. "What did you expect her to do? Drop to her knees and suck your cock right here?"

Well . . . it had crossed his mind.

Chapter 4

Izzy walked into her tent, her squire right behind her.

"What do you mean you don't know?" Samuel demanded. "How do you lose a two-ton animal?"

She shrugged at his question, amused by his usual outrage and annoyance. Reaching for a carafe of fresh water, she added, "She went off with Macsen."

"You let our horse go off with that vile, disgusting beast? *Alone?*"

"That's my dog you're talking about."

"I don't know what that thing is, but it ain't no dog I've ever seen." Sam looked her over and winced. "For someone so good at fighting, you do get hit a lot."

"You know, I could have you flogged for insubordination *and* being a right prat."

"Really? And who are you going to get to replace me?"

"Well—"

"That's what I thought." He unbuckled the leather straps holding on her steel breast plate. "You'll need another one of these before you return to combat."

"Well—"

"I'll take care of it. Marcus still refuses to deal with you."

"For a burly blacksmith, he's awfully sensitive."

Sighing in disgust, Sam added, "And someone will need to sew up that arm. I'll get the healer." He headed to the exit but stopped before walking out and glared at Izzy. "Don't move until I return."

Of course, when he turned his back, Izzy began to shimmy, stopping when he looked at her over his shoulder.

She could see him trying not to laugh and she winked at him before he walked out to get her fresh armor.

Stretching her tired shoulders, Izzy first poured herself a mug of water to drink, then another to pour over her bleeding arm. It hurt, and she was becoming concerned about the amount of blood she seemed to be losing, but then she decided that instead of worrying about that, she would pour herself a mug of ale. Perhaps the ale would help the wound.

With drink in hand, she headed toward her favorite chair, her mind already plotting her next moves to finish off the ogres in this region while simultaneously attempting to force out the image of one big, blue, idiot dragon flat on his back and looking gods-damn delicious.

The bastard. What was he doing here anyway? After ten years of never seeing him, he suddenly appeared. Back in her life. How bloody annoying!

She turned, about to drop into her chair when she abruptly realized she was no longer in her tent. In fact, she could be wrong, but she felt relatively certain she was no longer in her world but rather in the most beautiful glen she'd ever seen. But she wasn't alone.

"Hello, little Izzy."

Slowly, Izzy turned and faced what was behind her. And what was behind her was a god. A dragon god, specifically. With black scales, twelve horns on his massive head, and long black hair streaked with every color in the dragon pantheon. She wished she could say he was an ugly demon from the underworld, but he was, as always, beautiful.

"Your arm," he noted, pointing a talon at her wound.

"You're losing much blood." When she didn't say anything, he drew his talon down her arm and she knew immediately that he'd healed her.

"Better?" he asked. When she didn't respond to that either—"Izzy? Have you nothing to say to me?"

Did she have anything to say to him? Well, since he'd asked . . .

"Where is she?" Éibhear asked his cousin and, in answer, Branwen crossed her arms over her chest, pursed her lips, and snorted.

"I want an answer, cousin."

"And I want a longer tail, but we can't always get what we want, now can we?"

Éibhear's eyes narrowed. His cousin had passed the Trials three years ago, officially making her one of the elite Dragonwarriors. And since then, it seemed, she'd become quite the snobby cow.

"Maybe you'd like me and my mates to tear your human camp apart until I find her?" Éibhear asked. "Because you know I will."

"Your mates," she sneered. "The Mì-runach."

"The tone seems unnecessary," Aidan joked.

"Shut up, royal."

"Éibhear's a royal, too."

"He's kin so I overlook the flaw."

"I'm not a royal." They all looked at Uther and he shrugged. "Well . . . I'm not."

Brannie sighed and focused back on Éibhear. "What are you doing here, Éibhear?"

"That's for me to discuss with Izzy."

Brannie's pursed lips returned, one foot tapping. Knowing how stubborn the females in his family could be, Éibhear grabbed one of the human soldiers by the throat, ignoring the man's panicked scream, and held him up in front of his cousin's face.

She snorted. "If Izzy wants to see you—"

Éibhear tightened his grip and the soldier began kicking and trying to pry Éibhear's fingers off his throat.

Disgusted, Brannie snarled, "You have become *such* a mean bastard."

"Izzy. Now. Take me to her."

"Put him down first."

Éibhear flung the soldier away and gestured for his cousin to move. She did, but not before tossing over her shoulder, "You've become just like your father!"

He stared after Brannie. "Well, that was just *mean*."

"And then," Izzy went on while pacing in front of the god, "you not only impregnated Annwyl against her will, but you also deserted her when she needed you most!"

By now Rhydderch Hael had rolled to his back, his gaze up at the big sky, annoyed sighs echoing throughout the world he'd dragged her to.

"I mean, who *does that*?" she demanded. "And *then* you planned to take Annwyl's twins away from her rather than bringing Annwyl back from the dead, which we both know you could have done, but when my dear sweet Aunt Dagmar pissed you off, you tossed her *and* the children into a pit with Minotaurs!"

"You know, Izzy, my memory's excellent. I remember all—"

She pointed a finger at him. "You wanted me to talk . . . so I'm talking!" She began to pace again and continued, "And *then* . . ."

* * *

Éibhear followed Brannie into a tent, but he took one look around and raised his arms. "Where the hells is she?"

"I don't know."

He tilted his head and she held up her hands. "I'll find her. I'll find her." She pushed past him. "Mean," she snapped before she walked out.

Letting out an annoyed sigh, Éibhear walked around the tent. It seemed Izzy was still a messy female. She had weapons *everywhere*. And every kind. She didn't just have one battle axe, but battle axes from all the different armies she'd faced off against. Plus an array of long swords, short swords, curved swords, serrated swords . . . the woman liked swords. Blood-and-gore-covered clothes littered the floor and lots of missives from her queen and other generals in Annwyl's army were scattered about. Yet there was only one book, on the floor, right by the head of the bed. It was a history on the first war against the Iron dragons in the west led by Éibhear's royal grandfather.

Crouching down, Éibhear flipped the cover open and read the inscription.

For Izzy. Thought you'd like to read how it all began. Thank you for everything. You'll always have my loyalty and I'll always have the memory of you challenging a head-licking wolf. ~Gaius

Gaius? Gaius the Rebel King from the west? Éibhear briefly remembered being introduced to the Rebel King a few hours after he'd killed the Rebel King's bastard uncle, Overlord Thracius. But at the time, Éibhear had been so filled with rage and pain about the loss of his friend, Austell the Red, he wasn't sure he'd know the dragon if he tripped over him in the market.

But, more importantly, why was the Rebel King sending

books to Izzy? Especially when Izzy rarely bothered to read? And not only books but books with rather affectionate and strangely bizarre inscriptions.

Head-licking wolf?

Éibhear heard approaching footsteps but knew from the sound that it wasn't Izzy or his cousin. The tent flap was pulled back and a human male walked in.

"Izzy, we need to talk about . . ." His words faded off when Éibhear slowly got to his feet and stood to his full human height.

"Oh," the man said, staring up at Éibhear. "I was, uh, looking for the general."

"Not here."

"Do you know when she'll be back?"

Éibhear shrugged.

"Oh."

"I can give her a message." Especially since he was curious who this man was.

"No. I'll just wait."

"Okay. We'll just wait." Éibhear crossed his arms over his chest and stared down at the human male . . . and he kept staring.

"And not only that but then you—"

Before Izzy could go on, Rhydderch Hael rolled to his stomach and bellowed, "*By the love of all that is me, shut up!*"

Izzy gazed up at the god, working hard not to smile or outright laugh.

Closing his eyes, he took in several deep breaths.

"And yet," he finally said, much more calmly, "after all this time, you still manage to irritate the living fuck out of me, Iseabail the Dangerous."

"You asked me if I had anything to—"

"Yes, I know!" Another deep breath, eyes still closed. After some thirty seconds or so, when he was once again calm, he said, "I am well aware what I said to you, Izzy. And I know over the years I've disappointed you."

"Understatement."

Violet eyes snapped open and locked on her, and Izzy quickly focused on a tree in the distance.

"As I was saying, I know I've disappointed you, but you still owe me a blood debt."

Izzy returned her gaze to the god, surprised. "Blood debt?"

"You made a promise to me."

"When I was sixteen."

"Your mother's life for your commitment to me," he reminded her.

"You were the one who killed her!" To this day Izzy still sometimes woke up in a cold sweat from the nightmare of seeing her mother sacrifice herself to Rhydderch Hael to save Izzy. A price Talaith had willingly paid—so how could Izzy do any different?

Yet Rhydderch Hael waved all that away with his claw. "Nitpicking. I restored your mother's life."

"You haven't changed at all, have you?"

"Iseabail, I'm a god. I don't have to change. For anyone. *Ever*. That's the wondrous beauty that is being a god."

"And you can take your wondrous beauty and shove it up your godly as—"

"*Iseabail.*"

"She's been gone a long time, eh?"

Éibhear, who hadn't stopped staring at the man, grunted in reply.

"Maybe she went to track down ogres with the others."

Another grunt.

"Maybe I should come back later."

Minor grunt.

The man's gaze moved around the tent in an attempt not to look at Éibhear. "Soooo . . . you're a friend of Izzy's?"

No grunt, instead Éibhear narrowed his eyes and the human male took a step back.

"How could you think I would not one day call in this debt?" Rhydderch Hael asked, appearing truly perplexed. "You still wear my mark on your shoulder."

She glanced at the dragon brand that he'd burned into the flesh of her upper bicep all those years ago. "I just assumed it was there permanently whether you planned to use me or not. Besides"—she shrugged—"it's a nice-looking thing if you like dragons. I like dragons. Just don't like you."

He let out a breath, slowly shaking his mighty head. "You've always played a dangerous game, Iseabail, Daughter of Talaith."

"Hence the name. And I don't like to be betrayed. I don't like those I love to be hurt for some god's amusement. Sorry if that bothers you. My disloyalty."

"You are hardly my only concern, Iseabail."

"Then what do you want from me?"

"You'll find out soon enough."

She rolled her eyes. "Don't play this game with—"

But before she could finish, he flicked his claw at her and she was flying.

"Why don't I go?" the human male said, trying to keep the tremor from his voice.

"Why don't you?"

"Yeah. I'll . . . uh . . . yeah . . ." He quickly walked out of the tent and Éibhear grinned.

After all these years, he shouldn't enjoy doing that sort of thing . . . but he did.

Still . . . where the hells *was* Izzy?

Thinking he should go track down his cousin, Éibhear was reaching for the tent flap when he heard from behind him ". . . game with me . . . arrrggghhhh!" He spun around at the scream.

"*I bloody hate when you do that!*" Izzy yelled up at the tent ceiling.

"Where the hells did you come from?" Éibhear demanded, knowing he would have heard the woman come back in if she'd snuck in under another part of the tent.

But he must have startled her because Izzy snatched the small blade she had holstered to her thigh, spun, and threw it at Éibhear's head. He jerked to the side in time to avoid the damn thing impaling his nose, but the blade tore across his cheek instead, leaving a healthy-sized gash.

Fed up and bleeding, Éibhear barked, "Izzy! It's me!"

And Izzy barked back, "Yeah. *I know!*"

Brannie rushed in to the tent, dark brown eyes blinking wide. "Izzy? Where did you come from?"

"Out, Branwen," Éibhear ordered his cousin, and Izzy looked at Brannie, watched the dragoness begin to get irritated with her kin.

"I don't take orders from you, Éibhear the Blue."

"And I"—Éibhear placed his huge hand over Brannie's face and forced her back out the tent—"take orders from no one!"

"That was just rude, you big bastard!" Brannie yelled from outside the tent.

Éibhear faced Izzy. "Why do you keep throwing things at my head?"

"It's such a large target—"

"Izzy."

"Why are you here, Éibhear?" she asked, frustrated. The conversation with Rhydderch Hael . . . it annoyed her. It had been more than a decade since she'd heard from him. It used to bother her. For years, when she was a child, Rhydderch Hael had been with her. She'd been taken from her mother at birth by a bitch goddess and it was Rhydderch Hael who'd protected her. He'd sent three loyal human soldiers to save her, to watch out for her. For years Izzy and her three Protectors had traveled around the Southlands, the god's voice in her head, sometimes in her dreams, promising that one day she'd be with her mother again. And he'd kept that promise. Izzy had loved him then. Not just as a god, but as someone who cared for her. But her mother had tried to warn her. Tried to tell her that the gods were never to be trusted. Izzy hadn't listened, though, and now Rhydderch Hael wanted something from her. What that was . . . she had no idea. But she wasn't looking forward to it, she knew that much.

So having Éibhear here when she was already irritated, looking annoyingly adorable with those damn warrior braids in his blue hair, but acting pushy and demanding, did nothing but piss her off.

"I was sent to get you," he explained, watching her closely. Probably confused as hell. Good! Let him be confused. "To bring you back to Garbhán Isle."

"Why? I've heard nothing from my mother or Rhi," she said, mentioning her baby sister.

"I was just told to bring you back."

"By who?"

"Ragnar."

Izzy groaned at that. "Oh, gods."

"What?"

"If you heard from Ragnar, he heard from Keita who heard from Morfyd or Briec, which means—"

"Tell me this ends at some point."

"—Mum and Rhi are going at it again." She shook her head and walked over to the large, plain wood desk that was covered in maps and missives and weapons. "I don't have time for this."

"You don't have time for your mother and sister?"

She faced him. "You have nerve to talk. When were you home last?"

Instead of answering her direct question, he pointed at her arm and asked, "Your arm . . . it's healed rather quickly."

Now she didn't answer him. The last thing she needed was for Éibhear the Blue to know about her conversation with Rhydderch Hael. Gods . . . what a mess that would be.

"I'm not going back to Garbhán Isle, Éibhear."

"You're not?"

"If it was important, Annwyl would have sent messengers for me. So my mother and Rhi will have to work this out on their own or wait until I'm done here."

"Until you're done doing what?"

Izzy focused on the map spread out on the table, looking for places the enemy might hide. "The Queen wants the ogres wiped clean from this region. And that's what I'm going to do."

"All right then."

But instead of leaving, Izzy looked up to see the big bastard take off his fur cape and toss it onto a nearby chair. Then he began to remove the many weapons he had strapped on his body.

Fascinated—gods, was he getting naked? And would she mind?—Izzy walked around the table and leaned her butt against it, arms crossing over her chest. Éibhear removed the majority of his weapons until he finally was able to drop onto her bed and stretch out with his arms behind his head, incredibly long legs crossed at the ankles.

When he closed his eyes and let out an exhausted sigh, she finally asked without rancor, "What the battle-fuck are you doing?"

"Me?"

"Yes. You."

"I'm Mi-runach. I don't stop until I fulfill my duty."

"Which means what exactly?"

"That until you're ready to go, I'm here with you. By your side. Attached to you until I can deliver you to Garbhán Isle."

"Attached to me?"

"Aye."

"Like a parasite?"

"I prefer loyal companion. But don't worry." He smiled up at her. "You'll get used to me."

Somehow, Izzy doubted that.

Chapter 5

Princess Rhianwen, Daughter of Talaith and Briec the Mighty; Granddaughter of Dragon Queen Rhiannon and Bercelak the Great; Sister of the feared General Iseabail the Dangerous; Nolwenn Witch by birth; Niece of Morfyd the White, Fearghus the Destroyer, Keita the Viper, Gwenvael the Handsome, Lady Dagmar, Beast of the Northlands, and Annwyl the Bloody, human Queen of Dark Plains; and future great artist of the Southland realm, sat in the forest doing what she loved best. Drawing.

Rhi loved getting away from the castle when she could, spending some time on her own. Especially when outside royals staying in the guest homes had the whole house buzzing with activity—for the servants—and annoyance—for Rhi's kin. Auntie Annwyl didn't like outsiders or royals, so both combined . . .

But that was all right. Because the visiting royal, Lord Pombray, had a son of seventeen winters. And he was quite handsome and tall. He was human, but Rhi was at least *half* human. Her mother was a Nolwenn witch and her father a mighty Southland dragon prince. It wasn't easy being made of two completely different species—many believing it was an abomination that she and her twin cousins even existed, though that wasn't something Rhi allowed herself to worry about—but there were definitely benefits.

For instance, Rhi's superb sense of smell allowed her to scent Lord Pombray's son nearly a mile back. He smelled very good, so she didn't mind much.

Glancing around, Rhi quickly swiped her hands down her hair and fluffed out the edges of her gown. Then she picked up the board she'd pinned a piece of parchment on and pretended to sketch while simultaneously looking serene. She knew she looked serene because she often practiced in the mirror in her room. She'd found that boys responded better to a serene countenance than to an angry, kill-everything-in-my-way one. A major reason why Rhi's cousin Talwyn had pretty much given up on boys in general.

"Princess Rhianwen?"

She slowly looked up, smiled, and nodded her head at the young royal. Not even eighteen and he'd already begun to grow a very nice beard and he had such a handsome smile. He stood before her now with his arms behind his back and what looked to be his best clothes on. "Lord Albrecht." She carefully lowered her drawing to the ground. "Is everything all right?"

"Oh, yes, yes."

"Do you have everything you need? Are your rooms satisfactory?"

"Oh, they're wonderful. And so large."

"Our guest house is quite popular among our visitors because of the size." And because it meant the visiting royals weren't forced to put up with Rhi's kin at every meal. Her father and his brothers were bad enough to human royals, snarling in the mornings and basically ignoring them in the evenings. But it was Annwyl the Bloody, Rhi's aunt and the Southland's human queen, who made it near impossible to have royals, human or otherwise, staying within the queen's castle for any length of time. She had little patience for outsiders, trusted few, and when she threatened to remove someone's head, she often meant it. So Rhi's Aunt Dagmar had had a large guest house built on Garbhán Isle for any visiting royals. It was a small castle that was equipped with its own staff and human guards. Once the house was finished, royals were more comfortable traveling to Dark Plains for important meetings with their queen. Something Rhi could easily understand.

"The queen believes in providing visitors with a lot of space."

Albrecht nodded, glanced off. Rhi waited. No use in rushing him.

"I didn't mean to interrupt you," he finally said.

"Oh, you didn't really. I was just sketching. I like to come out here where it's quiet. It can get so busy in the house."

"I'm sure."

When he appeared at a loss for words, she prompted, "Would you like to join me for a bit?"

"Um . . . yes. Yes, I would."

He started to walk toward her, but stopped. He blinked and suddenly brought his arms around, a bouquet of flowers in his hand. "I nearly forgot. These are for you."

"Oh! Those are beautiful!" She held her hands out and Albrecht was leaning down to hand them to her when a stream of flame torched the gorgeous blooms and had the poor boy screaming like a small animal.

"*What do you think you're doing, boy?*" Briec the Mighty's voice boomed across the glen.

"Father!"

"Quiet, Rhi!" her father ordered, while he stomped through the trees. At least he was in his human form. She had the distinct feeling Albrecht would have soiled himself if Briec the Mighty had faced him while in his silver dragon form.

Her father pointed at the boy. "What makes you think you're worthy of my perfect, *perfect* daughter, you worthless human? Now get from my sight before I have you turning on a spit for my evening meal!"

Holding his singed hand, Albrecht bolted off and Rhi got to her feet.

"Oh, Father!" She stomped her foot. "*How could you?*"

Face blank, her father shrugged, and asked calmly, "How could I what?"

Talaith, Daughter of Haldane, sat on the big table in the dining hall and watched one of her sisters-by-mating pace in front of her. Matching the woman step by step, as always, were two of her well-trained battle dogs.

"I don't know why you're getting so upset," Talaith said again.

"Because I should have said no. To think I actually *agreed* to this!" Dagmar Reinholdt, Steward to Annwyl the Bloody and Battle Lord of Garbhán Isle, stopped and faced her. "I should have said no."

"But you didn't. So suck it up already."

Steel-grey eyes narrowed on Talaith behind round spectacles. "You're not being very sympathetic."

"I didn't know I had to be." Talaith tossed up her hands. "Look, I'm sure it'll be fine. Your nephew is one blood relative. How bad can he be?"

"You met my father. That should tell you something."

"I liked your father."

"Which disturbs me endlessly."

Talaith took Dagmar's hand. "It'll be fine."

"You're right, you're right. I'm panicking over nothing." She pulled her hand back—Dagmar never liked to be touched except by the children and her mate, Gwenvael—and took a deep breath. In that instant, Dagmar Reinholdt had put herself under control again. It was something that Talaith absolutely envied about the small Northlander. Her ability to keep control. It was a skill Talaith didn't have when she became angry enough and Annwyl never had in the first place.

When Talaith had first seen Dagmar Reinholdt, she'd dismissed her as a sad, plain woman that the hedonistic Gwenvael the Handsome was hoping to fuck. In her plain gray gowns and fur boots, and with a gray scarf on her head, it seemed she was just some old maid. Oh, how wrong Talaith had been. There was nothing sad about Dagmar. Instead, she was fascinating and terrifying all at once; her time in Annwyl the Bloody's court had allowed her to flourish.

Being the power behind the crazed throne was a role that suited Dagmar very well, but having even one member of her own blood kin coming to the south was setting the poor woman's teeth on edge. It was the first chink in Dagmar's armor that Talaith had seen that had nothing to do with Gwenvael.

"So . . . how is your day?" Dagmar asked, trying to calm herself as she waited for the arrival of her kin, which should be any minute now.

"Not bad. But, as you know, sister, that can change in a—"

"Mum!"

"—second."

Sighing, Talaith slid off the table. A few moments later, her youngest daughter ran into the Great Hall, tears streaking down her face. But even all that sobbing could not take away from Rhi's natural beauty. She had the brown skin and long curly hair of Talaith's Desert Land bloodline, but like her father, her hair was a gorgeous silver and her eyes a vibrant violet.

Rhi threw herself into Talaith's arms and openly sobbed against her shoulder.

"What's wrong?" Talaith asked, worrying something terrible had happened.

"Ask Daddy!"

Talaith's fear disappeared and she immediately looked over at Dagmar. Together, they both crossed their eyes and waited.

"I don't know what you're getting so upset about," Briec complained as he stalked into the hall behind their daughter. "I was saving you from a life of misery and boredom."

"What did you do now?" Talaith demanded of her mate.

"Why do you have to say it like that?"

"Because I know you so bloody well."

"He was just trying to hand me some flowers!" Rhi sobbed out. "And you burned him!"

"You expect me to let some worthless low-born human get near *my* daughter? You don't really think I'd let that happen, do you?"

"But I like him!"

Briec rolled his eyes. "I'm sure he's a very nice boy who will one day get a very nice girl and they'll have very nice babies together. You, however, are a royal princess of the House of Gwalchmai fab Gwyar and you will *not be involving yourself with riffraff!*"

Bursting into tears, Rhi again buried her face against Talaith's shoulder.

"I don't know why you're getting so hysterical," Briec complained. "You sound like that crying boy!"

"Both of you stop." Talaith pushed her daughter back a bit, looked into her tear-streaked face. "Who was trying to hand you flowers, Rhi?"

"That idiot," Briec answered for their daughter.

Rhi glared at her father. "He's not an idiot! Albrecht is a perfectly nice—"

"Albrecht?" Dagmar faced Briec. "You burned Lord Pombray's son?"

"He was trying to hand her flowers. We all know where that will lead."

Dagmar's hands curled into fists. "By all reason, what is wrong with you?"

Briec shrugged nonchalantly. "Nothing. Why?" And Talaith knew that he truly didn't understand why everyone was so concerned.

"You'd best get Morfyd," Talaith told Dagmar before the woman could find a way to remove Briec's scales while he slept. "She can heal the boy."

Dagmar headed toward the exit but stopped long enough to glare at Briec.

"Why are you looking at me like that?"

The Northland female snarled at Briec and stormed off.

"I don't know why everyone is so upset. Did any of you really think I'd let some ludicrous *boy* get close to my perfect, perfect daughter?"

"I am *not* perfect!" Rhi argued. "Why do you keep saying that?"

"Because I've graciously decided to overlook any minor flaws you may have gotten from your mother. Tragically, those can't be helped and I love you in *spite* of them."

And if Rhi hadn't caught Talaith's arm and held her, Talaith was positive she would have ripped the smug bastard's nose off!

"My brother did *what*?"

"What part of that statement did you not understand?" Dagmar demanded of her mate's Dragonwitch sister, Morfyd.

"But . . . but why?"

Dagmar sighed. "Apparently young Albrecht gave Rhi flowers. I think he's smitten."

Morfyd fell silent, eyes briefly gazing off, before she replied, "Well . . . that was clearly a bad idea. He's not all that handsome."

"Morfyd!"

She refocused back on Dagmar. "Don't yell at me."

"Don't make me! Rhi is a lovely girl. Boys will be show-ing interest. That doesn't mean your brothers can go around burning them all."

"Of course not. But still . . . my father—"

"Is not known for his rational thought when it comes to his daughters. It's why I've never questioned the decision to name your Brastias general commander of Annwyl's armies. The mere fact he's survived this long with your brothers and father in close proximity says much about the man's survival skills. That being said, Rhi will continue to grow only more beauti-ful as the years go by and I cannot afford to have this reign known for its dragons burning every young man that comes near her."

"This reign? Don't you mean Annwyl's reign?"

"Morfyd!"

The Dragonwitch held up her hands. "Calm yourself. I'll have him healed by nightfall. I don't see why you're so upset," she muttered as she headed toward the guest house. "I was only saying that Briec wasn't necessarily irrational during all—"

And that was when Dagmar stopped listening. Instead, she rubbed her now throbbing head and tried to think of how the rest of her day was going to go. But as she stood there, fingers against her temples, she knew someone was stand-ing behind her. She wasn't always so observant, but like the time she'd been out alone in the woods surrounding her father's lands and she'd sensed a hungry wolf watching her from a nearby boulder, Dagmar always knew when a preda-tor was close.

Slowly, she turned, and looked up at her nephew, the son of Annwyl and Fearghus.

"Talan."

He smiled. Gods. Such a handsome boy. Unbelievably handsome. With his father's eyes and his mother's face, streaked brown hair reaching massive shoulders and as tall as his Uncle Gwenvael's human form. But, like his twin sister, there was something about Talan. . . .

"Auntie Dagmar."

Although it had been disturbing that the twins spoke so little as children, Dagmar could say that when they did begin to say more . . . it wasn't any less unsettling.

Of course when they'd just stand there and stare . . . things weren't much better.

"Is there something you want, Talan?"

"There's a caravan of rough-looking, grunting males. I'm assuming they're your kin since they're not dragons."

Dagmar snorted a little. "Yes. That does sound like my kin."

"They're heading through the gates now. Should I send someone to deal with them?"

"No. I'll go."

He nodded, but his gaze lifted, locking on something behind her. Dagmar looked over her shoulder and clenched her fists in order to keep from snarling.

"They've been chummy lately," she blandly remarked, trying not to sound concerned.

Talan shrugged and walked off, reminding her that the twins only seemed to speak when they felt like it.

Although she knew she had to get to the main gate, Dagmar stood her ground until her niece and Talan's twin sister, Talwyn, nodded at the woman she was walking with and headed over to Dagmar.

"Auntie Dagmar."

"Talwyn." Her niece, like Talan, was tall and beautiful, with pitch-black hair and her mother's green eyes. But she constantly hid that beauty under hair she rarely combed, dirt she rarely bothered to wipe off, and a perpetual glare that could scare hell's demons.

Dagmar glanced over at the woman walking away. But she

wasn't just a woman, was she? No. She was a Kyvich from the Ice Lands. One of the warrior witches who was so powerful and feared that even the gods called on them only when absolutely necessary. Nearly sixteen years ago, they'd come to Garbhán Isle to protect the twins while their mother was off in the west waging war against the Sovereigns. At the time, Dagmar had been grateful, but she'd also been wary because the Kyvich were rarely born into their rank. . . . They were taken from their mothers, usually before they were even two winters old. But, on rare occasions, they had been known to take older girls. Although Talwyn was now eighteen winters, she also had a mighty strength. Her fighting skills unmatched by anyone except the most seasoned warriors. Meaning she was exactly the kind of warrior the Kyvich would want.

So seeing that the Kyvich were lurking around her niece made Dagmar feel nothing but discomfort.

"Did Commander Ásta have anything interesting to say?" she asked Talwyn.

"No."

Dagmar, as always, waited for more, but after all these years, one would think she'd know better.

"Talwyn," Dagmar finally said, "should I be concern—"

"Aren't the barbarian horde at the gates?" her niece cut in.

Unwilling to delve into how Talwyn knew that the Reinholdts had arrived without actually seeing them, Dagmar asked, "Can't you just call them family?"

Talwyn looked at her through the mass of black hair that constantly fell into her eyes and bluntly admitted, "Not and mean it."

Snorting a little before she could stop herself, Dagmar nodded. "Fair enough."

Without another word—she talked less than her brother— Talwyn headed to the training ring for more weapons practice than anyone would ever need, and with a heavy sigh, Dagmar headed to the front gate.

Although Dagmar and Gwenvael visited her aging father as often as she could manage, even bringing Talaith and Annwyl with them on occasion, she'd never had any of her family here at Garbhán Isle.

But her father had written her himself. Well . . . he'd dictated a letter himself to the assistant she'd handpicked for him. And her father had made this request. How could she turn him down?

She couldn't. So she had to suck this up, as Talaith had told her.

Dagmar headed toward the courtyard, getting there just as the sons of her brothers arrived on their large Northland stallions. The oldest, Alppi, eldest son of Dagmar's eldest brother, Eymund, dismounted his horse and stood before Dagmar. He nodded his head . . . then stared at her, frowning just like her brother often did when he was confused.

"Aunt Dagmar . . ." His frown worsened. "I . . ."

"You . . . what?"

"Thought you'd be old by now," Alppi's younger brother informed her. "But you look the same . . . don'tcha?"

Dagmar wouldn't bother explaining the gift of long life similar to that of a dragon's, which had been bestowed upon her by the Dragon Queen when she'd committed herself to the queen's son Gwenvael. Instead, she simply replied, "I'll look like this long after all of you are dust and forgotten."

Her nephew stared at her a little longer before Alppi shrugged and said, "Yeah, whatever. Got anything to eat?"

She pointed toward the guards' mess, not even considering sending any of them to the Great Hall, where, most horrifying of all, they might catch sight of sweet and unattached Rhi. The vision of the bodies of her many nephews, burned beyond recognition, being returned to her brothers woke her up some nights.

The rest of her nephews dismounted their horses and

followed Alppi. All except one, who seemed to be struggling with the concept of removing himself from the back of his steed.

Dagmar walked around until she stood next to the boy and his horse.

"Hello, Frederik." Frederik Reinholdt, eighth-born son of her brother Fridmar. And, as her father had less than kindly said in his letter, "Resident family idiot."

The fourteen-year-old boy glanced at her, nodded. "Aunt Dagmar."

"Need some help?"

"No, no. I'm fine."

She didn't really believe him, so she motioned over one of the squires who'd come to take care of her nephews' horses. But as the squire moved in to assist, Dagmar had to take a quick step back just as Frederik slipped from the horse and hit the ground hard.

"Ow," she heard him mumble.

And Dagmar barely kept in a long, pained sigh. Gods, what had she agreed to?

Chapter 6

"You have to go."

"I can't. I've made a—"

"Out," Izzy ordered.

Éibhear shrugged. "Make me."

"Make you?"

Gods, she sounded annoyed. Not that he blamed her. But her annoyance combined with the scent of blood, dirt, and death that she was covered in, was rather enticing.

Iseabail the Dangerous was definitely not the girl he'd left behind all those years ago. Tall and powerfully built, her bare arms showed the hard years of life in the human queen's army, from her strong, well-defined muscular physique to the scars he could see on any exposed skin. But her beauty—that had not changed. Instead it had merely sharpened, becoming even more powerful.

Even now, pissed as she was, all he could see were large, light brown eyes glaring down at him, while shoulder-length, wavy light brown hair framed a sculpted face, cheekbones sharp, dimples temporarily missing because she wasn't smiling. Her lips were full and rather—if he did say so himself—pouty; and her once-sharp nose was no longer as sharp now that, he'd guess, it had been broken. Perhaps more than once.

But that bit of imperfection only made her more beautiful, as far as Éibhear was concerned.

"Éibhear—"

"I'm not leaving."

Izzy grabbed one of his hands from behind his head and pulled. She kept pulling too, while Éibhear lay there and let her.

"Gods be damned! You weigh as much as my bloody horse!"

"Only when I'm human."

Snarling, she tossed his arm back at him and he barely managed not to hit himself in the face.

"Out!"

"I'm with you until this is over, Princess."

"It's General, you big bastard."

"Calling me mean names will not change anything either."

"I should just slit your throat and be done with it."

"But then I'll shift back to dragon and ruin your bed."

Her eyes crossed and she turned from him just as the tent flap was pulled back. One of her soldiers walked in, but he stopped when he saw Éibhear lounging there.

"Should I come back?" he asked.

"Only if you want to lose a body part." She glanced at the human. "Did you find Dai?"

"He was with Macsen, as you said."

She faced the man. "Where's Macsen?"

"Outside."

"Let him in."

The man glanced at Éibhear and back at Izzy. "Are you sure?"

She shrugged, headed back to her desk. "It's his tent too."

"Macsen," the soldier called out. "Macsen!"

Izzy had a man? It couldn't be a husband. That, he was sure, his kin would have told him. But a man she lived with? Another soldier? Well . . . good for her. She should have a mate. Someone she felt close to and could rely on. Aye. That was a very good thing indeed. Because he was sure that Izzy would pick someone loyal and worthy of her.

Éibhear again placed both hands behind his head and waited for this "worthy male" to enter, but he only had a moment to hear extreme, heavy panting before something large and furry charged through the tent flap and launched itself directly at Éibhear's face.

Izzy watched the animal she'd found bloody and dying three years ago crash chest first onto Éibhear the Blue's face.

Macsen was not a trained battle dog. He was definitely not one of Dagmar's carefully bred canines. Instead, Izzy had found him after a battle. He'd been only a puppy, his battered body curled into the hollow of a tree trunk. Whimpering and shuddering, he'd been a pitiful-looking thing that Izzy simply couldn't ignore. Covered in open wounds, he'd also been missing part of his left ear and his eye had been so damaged it was still nothing more than a milky white spot in his head. She'd picked his shaking body up and brought him back to her tent, tending to him herself. She'd cleaned and cared for his wounds, fed him by hand until he could eat on his own, and kept him warm at night by letting him sleep by her side. And, as each day passed, the puppy had grown stronger and, she soon realized, bigger. Very big. Big enough that she'd wondered if he was actually a dog or some other beast she was unaware of. Wolves weren't as big as Macsen. His fangs were longer, his bite stronger, his fur shaggier, than any canine she'd ever seen. Yet he was blindingly loyal to her, fought with her in every battle, and protected her horse when she or Samuel could not.

And woe to any who dared enter her tent without permission.

But to Macsen, it must have seemed that Éibhear was there with permission because he didn't bother to attack. Yet he was annoyed that someone other than Izzy was in his space, which meant he did what he always did to males that he felt didn't belong.

"Gods!" Éibhear demanded, trying to push Macsen off. "What is that smell?"

"Oh . . ." Izzy smirked. "He must have gotten into the beans again."

"He does like beans," Samuel added, his hand under his nose to block out the smell. Considering all the hard years Samuel had done in the military, forced in by his father when he was barely nine, it always amazed Izzy that he couldn't tolerate a few farts from a dog.

Then again . . . it seemed that Éibhear couldn't either.

The dragon threw Macsen across the room and tried to sit up, but Macsen only scrambled back to his really big feet and launched himself again at Éibhear's head.

By now, Izzy had her hand over her mouth, her body shaking as she hysterically laughed, Samuel leaning against her, his laughter ringing out.

"Don't just stand there, woman! Get him off me!" He threw Macsen again, but, as was Macsen's way, he merely bounced back and came at Éibhear once more. That was the thing about Macsen, the thing that many enemy soldiers had learned over the years . . . Macsen didn't go down easy and once down, he didn't stay down. It simply wasn't in his nature.

The dog was just going for Éibhear again when Fionn stepped in, motioning to Izzy.

"What?" she asked once she stood next to the woman.

"We have a problem."

When Éibhear finally had the dog pinned to the floor he realized that, except for the animal, he was alone.

Feeling something gnawing on his booted foot, Éibhear looked down at the dog. At least, he felt sure it was a dog of some kind. At the moment, it was trying to tear off the thick leather.

Éibhear pressed down harder and, instead of calming down, the beast only became more irritated, fought harder. Impressed, Éibhear lifted his foot and the dog scrambled away, before spinning around to face him and squaring off again.

Studying the thing's size, Éibhear leaned down a bit and asked, "You're not a god, are you?"

With a snarl, it launched its body at him and Éibhear swung his fist, knocking the dog across the tent and out the back.

Satisfied, Éibhear sniffed the air and followed Izzy's scent. She hadn't gone far. Only a few feet away from her tent, surrounded by her officers. A small contingent of soldiers stood at the ready, and another officer was on his knees, two soldiers guarding him.

Éibhear walked up to Aidan and the others.

"What's going on?" he asked, keeping his voice low.

"Your general thought she'd killed the ogre leader. She hasn't."

"A decoy?"

"Aye. The ogres were tipped off by him there." He nodded at the soldier on his knees. "Then while the general and her troops were fighting the decoy, he went into a nearby human town, grabbed one of the local girls off the street, and—"

Éibhear held up his hand, not needing to hear any more, and turned to watch this play out.

But then he remembered this was Iseabail he was dealing with. *Not* Annwyl. For if it were, the bastard's head would be rolling right by Éibhear's feet at this moment.

Instead, Izzy, although clearly disgusted, turned to her officers and began discussing "laws" and "rules" and what this worthless bastard did or did not deserve based on his dishonoring his role as a soldier blah, blah, blah, blah, blah!

Gods! Was she joking? Why was she wasting her time and, most importantly, his own?

Unwilling to wait a second longer, Éibhear looked at Aidan and motioned to the soldier with a tilt of his head.

Aidan frowned; then his eyes grew wide. He immediately shook his head, never one to just take his damn orders. So Éibhear focused on Uther. The only problem with Uther was that he was a little slower to grasp things, mostly because he was easily bored and didn't always pay attention. By the third, adamant tilt of his head, Uther blinked and said, "Oh!" He chuckled. "Sorry."

Shaking his head, Éibhear stood back and waited.

Although two of her officers wanted a hearing, the rest just wanted the soldier's head removed so they could focus on the ogres. Izzy didn't mind bothering with the niceties—when they had the time—but they now had the ogre leader's correct location, so at the moment, they really didn't.

She nodded at Fionn to keep an eye out in case any of the soldier's comrades might try to intervene, while Izzy began to pull her sword from its scabbard.

She almost had it clear, too, when she heard Brannie say, "Uh, Iz?" mere seconds before the betraying soldier's head and part of his shoulder tumbled past her legs, landing a few feet away.

Everyone fell silent, her officers refusing to meet Izzy's gaze. Because they knew. It might take much to piss her off, but once she was . . .

"What just happened?" she asked her cousin, unwilling to turn around.

"Uhhhh . . ."

She was about to demand that Brannie say something

besides "Uh" when Éibhear appeared in front of her. "Now can we go?" he asked, grinning.

She almost had her sword out of its scabbard again, when Brannie stepped up, shoving Éibhear away with one hand and taking firm hold of Izzy's arm with the other.

"To the caves," she ordered the officers, steering Izzy toward her horse. "We track down the ogres and finish them off tonight. Now move!"

"What is going on?" Izzy demanded while mounting her horse, which Samuel was holding by the reins.

"I was going to ask you." Brannie settled into her own saddle, her horse patiently waiting for her. "What did he say he wanted?"

"He said he has orders to bring me back to Garbhán Isle."

"Is there a problem?"

"I haven't heard a word, but that could just mean the orders are coming from someone other than my mother."

"You're not going to go?"

"If it was important, Annwyl would have sent a proper messenger, not that idiot. No. I'll go in my own time, Bran. Not because Éibhear the Annoying tells me to."

"So," Éibhear said, suddenly appearing next to her, his hand resting on her boot. "How long will killing this ogre leader take? Can we leave then?"

Snarling, Izzy shook the dragon's hand off and clicked her tongue against her teeth. She spurred Dai forward and headed toward the caves and away from Éibhear the Annoying!

"What are you doing?" Aidan asked.

Éibhear shrugged. "Annoying her until she does what I want." He glanced at his friend. "It's worked before."

"With Izzy?"

"No. But it's worked with others."

Uther, wiping off his blood-covered blade and placing

it in its sheath, stepped beside Aidan. "So what are we doing now?"

"I'm bored," Caswyn complained. And when they all stared at him: "What? Was I supposed to lie about that?"

"Yes." Éibhear watched Izzy's troops ride out. She and several battalions were going straight into the caves, but in case it was a trap, she had the rest of the legions surrounding the caves and coming in from the forest.

A wise move since ogres were not to be trusted.

"Ogres aren't easy to kill," Aidan remarked. "And the real leader will be much more of a challenge. So this could take some time."

Éibhear placed his hands on his hips. "Well, that's not going to work for me."

Chapter 7

The flint axe came down hard, smashing another human's head. The Leader felt nothing as he did it. These humans were nothing to him other than more skin to make into his kilts, more teeth to give his favorite breeder, and more blood to make his ale.

He'd brought his troops to this human village looking for food, breeders, and slaves. They'd done well this hunting season, cutting through this swath of countryside, leaving a trail of blood, death, and misery behind. That's what he did best. What he enjoyed doing every season.

But then those human troops had shown up and he'd moved inside this cave, sending out his fighters to engage the humans. When that grew boring, he'd sent out one of the stupider fighters to pretend to be him. That one would die and then, when the human soldiers thought the worst of it was over, he'd reemerge and finish them. A good plan, even had a human to help because they'd given him some gold. Gold only meant something to humans; it meant nothing to ogres. Only meat and blood and death meant anything to them. Only battle and war meant anything to the mighty ogres.

His plan had been working well, too, but then that traitor

was found out and the human soldiers had tracked the rest of his troops to these caves.

But he had no intention of dying now. Not at the hands of these weak humans with their fragile skin, tiny size, and fancy armor and weapons. True warriors didn't need all that armor to cover their body. True warriors fought without it.

"Blood Leader!"

The Leader looked up to see a human female walking toward him. She'd used his proper title in his language to call his attention. She wore little armor but had many fancy weapons. She was tall for a female but brown of skin. Strange. He'd never seen that before. But she was sturdy, strong. She'd make a good breeder.

Too bad he'd have to kill her instead.

The Leader lifted his axe and challenged with a nod of his head. The human strode toward him, short sword brandished; then she was charging him flat out.

Lip curling, the Leader swung his flint axe. The woman, fast considering her size, ducked his weapon and came charging at him again. She made no sound as she charged— no warning battle cry, no scream of rage. She simply ran at him with her short sword at the ready.

He swung the axe again, but the woman leaped up, her foot colliding with his chest. She shoved herself off and spun, bringing the sword around and down against his neck. The woman was surprisingly strong, her sword cutting past thick green skin and taut, layered muscle, burying itself there.

The Leader staggered, his blood spurting from the wound. But he wasn't dead. Not yet. Not for quite a while. It took much effort to kill his kind, but he sensed she already knew that. Knew this wouldn't be an easy fight. *Ahhhh. A true challenge. How nice.*

He lifted his mighty flint axe. This axe was only wielded by the leader of the tribes and he was the leader. The strongest, the meanest. He'd made sure everyone knew that when he'd eaten his firstborn whole. It had proved his point and had been no great loss. It had been a female after all. Just another breeder.

How could killing this human be any harder?

His axe was coming down again, aimed for the human woman's head, but as he nearly reached her, she raised her arm, caught hold of his weapon's handle and held it.

She held it. Held him. Growling, he tried to pull the axe from her, but she held it. He knew he hadn't weakened that much. Not enough that this human *female* could stop him from holding on to his weapon. The weapon that made him the Leader. But she held tight, eventually yanking it away.

The Leader reached for her with his bare hands, enraged that she'd dare take his axe. But she stepped to the side and swung the axe up, over, and down, cutting off his arm that was closest to her.

The Leader gazed down at where his arm used to be, and that's when she kicked him in the back of the leg and dropped him to his knees.

Around him, he could hear his troops dying, screaming to their gods. He'd give these humans none of that from him. Not now, not ever.

The human stepped close, studied him. The Leader sat back on his heels, his life's blood pouring out of him.

She lifted her booted foot, pressed it against his chest and shoved him to the ground.

"You can't be that big a fool," he snarled at her in his language, knowing she'd understand. "To think I'd die so easy."

With the arm he still had left, he reached over and grabbed a club from the body of one of his dead. Grabbed it and was swinging it toward her with the intent to break her leg and then her head.

But something wrapped around her waist. Something long and scaled and blue. One second she was above him, raising his own axe to finish him off, the next she was pulled away and the Leader looked up into the face of the biggest dragon he'd ever seen. He didn't know there were dragons that big.

The beast took a big breath in and even before the flames covered his body, he knew *this* would be the thing that killed him.

The flames burned hot and removed his flesh and muscle and, as darkness surrounded him and the dying screams of his troops filled the cavern, the Leader heard the dragon say to the human female, "So can we go back *now*?"

As soon as Izzy's feet touched the ground, Brannie quickly threw her arms around her cousin and held her. She held her tight because she knew that Izzy killing Éibhear probably wouldn't be overlooked by the rest of the family. Most likely.

Although Brannie knew for a fact that her mum, Ghleanna the Decimator, would completely understand when she found out that Éibhear had gotten between a warrior female and a kill. There were just some things one didn't do among the Cadwaladrs and that was a big one.

But Brannie understood that Éibhear was too self-absorbed to have a death wish, so there had to be another reason he was doing all this.

Determined to find out what that was, Brannie carried Izzy away from Éibhear and the other Mì-runach. She stopped by Fionn, Izzy's next in command. When she released her, Brannie immediately saw that Izzy was way beyond mere anger. She could tell because Izzy hadn't said anything. She hadn't done anything. She was simply standing tall and straight like a statue. Not a good thing. The last time Brannie had seen Izzy act like that, an entire army had been wiped out. It hadn't been pretty then, and it wouldn't be pretty now to see the same thing happen to blood kin, so Brannie knew she had to handle this.

Something strong and powerful grabbed Éibhear by the hair and yanked him around.

"What the bloody hells are you up to?"

Éibhear gazed at the female cousin yelling at him. "Did you just do that?" he asked, fascinated.

"Who else?"

"Gods, you're strong. Ever think of joining the Mì-runach?"

"Unlike you lot, I actually obey orders from all my commanding officers, not just my queen. So I don't think I'll fit in too well."

"We follow orders from our commanding officers," Aidan argued while squeezing the head of an ogre until it popped like a grape. "Or at least from Angor. We simply do it in our own time and in our own"—he shook his claw to get rid of the ogre blood and flesh—"way."

"Fascinating," Brannie sneered before turning away from Aidan. "I asked you a question, cousin. Now answer it."

Huh. His cousin had grown pushy over the years. He might find that annoying at some point.

"I have a duty to get her home," he said.

"By getting in her way?"

"She's being difficult. If she'd just do what I told her to . . ."

Branwen held up her hand. "Just so you know," she said, "you sound exactly like your father."

Hurt, Éibhear asked, "Why are you being so mean?"

"Because that's exactly how you're acting. You're following right behind him. Just like your brothers did. You going to demand a blood debt now, too, just like Briec did with Izzy's mum?"

Éibhear thought a moment and asked, "If I do what do I get out of it?"

She reached for his hair again, but Éibhear stumbled back, warding her off with his claws. "All right. All right, I was just kidding."

"What do you really want, Éibhear?"

"Just to take her home. That's what I committed to."

"And?"

He shrugged. "And a chance to say I'm sorry."

"This Celyn shit? *Again?*"

"I promise, I'm not here for that. I swear," he insisted when her eyes narrowed. "I just want to say I'm sorry and be done with it."

"That's all?"

"That's all. Talk to her for me?" He lowered his head a bit, fluttered his eyes. "Please?"

"Och. That was just appalling, Éibhear. Although you're obviously *not* following in Gwenvael's footsteps because *he* could have pulled that off!"

Brannie stomped back to Izzy's side, her tail impaling fleeing ogres as she passed. She'd shifted when she'd gone to find Éibhear. Not for safety from the ogres but because she wanted to look him in the eyes when she spoke to him.

Once near Izzy, Brannie shifted to human and grabbed the clothes she'd left at her cousin's feet, quickly pulling them on.

"Well?" Izzy demanded before Brannie even got her leggings on.

Brannie glanced up, her lips slowly curling into a smile. "What?"

Grabbing her chain-mail shirt, Brannie stood tall, slipping her arms inside the protective garment. "His orders are to get you home. And, as Mì-runach, he's committed to that. There'll be no deterring him."

"Why are you smiling?"

She pulled the shirt over her head and down her torso. "He also would like to take this opportunity to apologize."

Confused, Izzy asked, "Apologize? For what?" When Brannie's smile only grew . . . "Good gods! That was ages ago. *Ages!*"

Brannie, now dressed, retrieved her weapons. Laughing, she said, "I know. But for some reason he feels the need to say it."

"After all this time?"

"No matter his royal lineage, cousin, Éibhear the Contemptible is still a Cadwaladr male in his heart . . . his soul."

"Which means what?" Izzy turned and used her long sword to impale an ogre that had been coming up behind her.

"It means that he won't be satisfied until he gets what he wants."

Wiping dark green blood from her face, she again faced her cousin. "To apologize? Can't he just do that and go? I assure you I can make it to Garbhán Isle without his or his friends' help."

"Come, Izzy. You know better. You've lived among my brethren." Brannie grabbed the blade from Izzy's grasp and swiped it through the air. Izzy ducked, the blade missing her head by inches, but the ogre who'd been running up to them from the left was cut nearly in half from left hip to right shoulder. "You know the way of things, my cousin. An apology is only part of it. He seems to believe he wants forgiveness. That's what I saw in his eyes."

"And?"

She handed the blade back to Izzy. "And I say you give it to him."

"And he'll leave me be?"

"Oh, no." Brannie giggled, sounding like a small child rather than the feared warrior dragon she'd grown into. "Ease is not something a Cadwaladr male understands or knows how to deal with . . . which is why you should give him as much ease and forgiveness as you can stomach."

Izzy shook her head, her own smile blossoming. "You are a callous cow, Branwen the Awful. A cruel, callous cow . . . and I adore you like the suns."

Branwen shrugged, black eyes twinkling, "And I you, cousin, for together we are a true blood-filled nightmare— which I find nothing but entertaining!"

Using his fist, Uther bashed ogres into flat green disks. It was fun and killed some time.

"There has to be an easier way for you to get women," Aidan told Éibhear. Aidan was stepping on the ogres while Caswyn was swiping at them with his tail. But Éibhear was just standing there . . . waiting.

"What if she still says no?" Uther asked.

"We should just take her," Caswyn offered.

Aidan stopped crushing ogres to ask, "Take Izzy the Dangerous?"

"We're four dragons. She's one human female. How much trouble can she be?"

Aidan smirked at Éibhear. "You're a much better story-teller than I."

Éibhear looked at Caswyn. "When Izzy was seventeen, she—with the slight help of her mother—killed Olgeir of the Olgeirsson Horde. When she was nineteen she fought against the Kyvich witches and lived to tell about it. When she was twenty-and-five, she survived in the Sovereign fighting pits and buried a dragon's axe into the back of Overlord Thracius, one time ruler of the Irons."

Caswyn blinked. "Oh."

"And she's been marked by Rhydderch Hael himself as his champion."

"All right then."

"So, just a thought," Aidan added. "You may not want to piss her off."

"You mean like Éibhear does?" Uther asked.

Insulted, Éibhear snapped, "I'm trying to be helpful." And it only pissed him off more when they all laughed at him.

"Oy!" a voice yelled up at them and they all looked at the human female standing beneath them. She stood tall, a blade in each hand, and covered in ogre's blood. She showed no fear—Dragonfear or otherwise—of standing before four giant dragons who could easily crush her. And, Uther had to admit, he could see what Éibhear found so intriguing about her. Although there was always something about a female with a sword, wasn't there . . . ?

"We leave in the morning, when the suns rise," she told them.

"Well—" Éibhear began.

"Shut up." Izzy pointed one of her swords at him. "I'm not talking to you."

"Again?"

"You are a true idiot, Éibhear the Blue," she snarled and walked off.

"You really have a way with the females," Aidan told Éibhear.

And the blue dragon smiled. "They do like me."

Chapter 8

As Izzy had ordered, they left the next morning before the suns were even up. But she'd refused to fly when Éibhear refused to carry her horse *and* her dog. He knew better than to ask the others to carry the two animals. Dragons were not beasts of burden and Izzy, of all humans, knew this.

Brannie, however, managed to find the four Mì-runach horses that were not only strong enough to carry the weight of a dragon male in human form, but also willing to carry a dragon at all.

They traveled for hours until midday, when they stopped in a wooded area for a quick meal. While they pulled out dried meat from their travel packs, Izzy walked off with that monstrosity she had the nerve to call a dog. That thing had run by Izzy's side all morning and didn't even appear winded.

And no one thinks that's strange?

Since they had some time, Éibhear followed Izzy, tracking her down by a freshwater stream. Her dog was busy splashing around, trying to grab the fish, while she crouched beside it taking in palms-full of water.

"Sure he's not a bear?" Éibhear asked loudly, not wanting to sneak up on her. He was tired of getting things thrown at him. . . . How did Gwenvael put up with that sort of thing constantly?

"He's a dog," she replied, shaking off her wet hands. "I promise."

Éibhear crouched down beside her and she sighed.

"What do you want, Éibhear?"

He let out a breath and plunged forward. "To apologize."

"For killing the ogre leader? One of my troops? Or for not taking 'no' for an answer?"

"Uh . . . I didn't know I had to apologize for any of that."

"You didn't . . ." She shook her head and stood. "Forget it. Just forget it."

Éibhear caught her hand. "Don't go."

"Why should I stay?" She snatched her hand away. "I don't even know what the mighty hells you're apologizing for, and to be honest, I'm not sure I'm in the mood to find out."

Éibhear stood. "I'm sorry, Izzy. I'm sorry for everything."

"Even that time you yelled at me in front of my mother about that dagger I borrowed from you?"

"Borrowed? You stole that damn . . ." Éibhear stopped. He would not let her goad him into one of these ridiculous arguments they'd been having since they'd met. "Izzy—"

"Or that time you told my father that Gwenvael was taking me flying behind his back."

"Your mother made it clear she didn't want you flying."

"Or that other time you—"

"All right!" Éibhear blew out a breath. "Gods, woman! I'm trying to apologize."

"Yes. For *everything*. Perhaps," she suggested, "if you narrowed the scope of your all-important apology."

"Fine. I'm sorry about what happened between you, me, and Celyn."

"Which was what exactly?"

"Now you're just tormenting me."

"You mean like you did after you found out I'd been sleeping with Celyn so you beat him bloody just before calling me a whore in front of your kin?"

"Yes," Éibhear reluctantly admitted. "Like that."

"Do you know because of what you did there are still at least three of your aunts who call me the whore who got between cousins?"

Éibhear stared down at her. "You expect me to believe you allow any of my aunts to keep calling you a whore?"

She shrugged. "Perhaps after a few knife fights at family dinners, they no longer say the words . . . but they're thinking it. And then you," she snarled. "After ten years you simply have to apologize? You have to dredge up the past?"

"As a matter of fact, Iseabail, I did apologize earlier."

"Oh, really? Was I *there* at the time of this apology? Because I don't remember it."

"I apologized in a letter. But my comrades, Aidan and the others, they burned it."

"A letter? You apologized to me in a *letter*?"

"It seemed like a good idea at the time."

"And when was this letter *not* sent?"

"Five years or so ago."

"I see."

"Look, Izzy, I know you don't believe me. But I am sorry about what happened. I really am."

She studied him for a long moment and he waited for what had decidedly become an acid tongue over the years. But then Izzy smiled, patted his shoulder, and said, "And I accept your apology, Éibhear. And thank you for it. It was very kind."

And with that . . . she walked off.

Éibhear watched her for a moment. "Wait."

She stopped, faced him. "Aye?"

"That's it then? You forgive me?"

"Of course I do. Why would I cling to the past?"

"I'm not saying you should. It's just . . ."

"Just what?" She walked back to his side. "It's over, Éibhear. You've apologized. That's all that matters. Besides, I wouldn't hold that against you as I would never expect you to hold such things against me. We were young . . . foolish. It's the past; let's leave it there." Concern showed on her brow. "But you should know that Brannie tells me Celyn may be coming to Garbhán Isle in the next few days. I hope you two will make up as well if you haven't already. He's your cousin and family is all, Éibhear. Never forget that." She turned and headed back to the others. "I'm so glad we're all done with that." She spun on her heel, facing him as she walked backward. "Although I wish I could have read your letter. I'm sure it was beautiful."

Then Iseabail was gone and Éibhear was left with nothing but what even he'd call his own paranoid thoughts and a mass of wet fur and muscle that was flying at his head and knocking him out completely.

"What did you do?" Izzy asked her dog while she worked so very hard not to laugh. And gods, did she want to laugh.

But in answer, all Macsen did was roll to his back, paws up in the air, overly long tongue hanging out of his mouth. That was not a pretty sight, but she loved it just the same.

Izzy returned to Éibhear's side, crouching next to him. She leaned over and looked into his face. "Éibhear?" She tapped his shoulder. "Éibhear?" She cringed and glanced back at his dog. "He won't be happy with you, Lord Sneak-Attack."

She brushed the hair off Éibhear's face and studied his forehead. He had a bit of a knot there, from when he'd hit the ground, but she doubted there was any real damage done. According to her mother, the males in Éibhear's bloodline had notoriously hard heads.

Resting her arm on her knee, Izzy pointed out, "At least

you're still devastatingly handsome, you letter-sending bastard." She shook her head and looked at Macsen, who was now right next to her. "A letter? What am I? His granny?"

Macsen leaned over Éibhear's head, drool pouring on the dragon's face.

Many of Izzy's troops had asked her why she'd kept the dog around. He smelled, he drooled, he ate things he really shouldn't; plus he snarled and snapped for no obvious reason, and had bitten off a hand or two because those particular hands had gotten too close to his food bowl or a rotting carcass he'd dragged back to camp. But Izzy always rewarded loyalty and Macsen was loyal. Blindingly so.

Éibhear coughed and grimaced, his hands wiping at his now wet face. He lifted his head, silver eyes narrowing on Macsen, then her. "I hate that dog."

Izzy, trying to comb her fingers through Macsen's always-matted hair, laughed. "The feeling is mutual, I think. But don't worry, he'll get used to you now that we are friends again, you and I."

The dragon sat up, growling low at her words, but Macsen backed up a bit and growled in return, fangs bared.

When she saw Éibhear's brow lower, she quickly warned, "One flame touches this dog and you *will* be sorry."

"Then get control of it."

She laughed and stood. "Yeah. Right."

Still laughing, Izzy returned to the others.

Éibhear watched Izzy walk off—laughing.

What in the holy hells was going on with her? He didn't believe for a second she'd meant any of that forgiveness she'd so gallantly laid at his feet. Not the Izzy he remembered. Was she merely trying to placate him? Why? She wasn't known for placating anyone except maybe his . . .

His brothers.

Disgusted at the thought, Éibhear got to his feet and used the bottom of his fur cape to wipe the dog drool from his poor, defenseless face.

Izzy always placated his brothers, especially Briec and Fearghus. And then, of course, there was his father, Bercelak. Izzy was the reigning queen when it came to placating his father. But Éibhear wasn't his father, nor his brothers. He didn't want to hear what Izzy *thought* he wanted to hear. He wanted the truth. He wanted . . . well, it didn't matter. He just knew he didn't want *this* . . . this centaur shit of platitudes.

Family is all? Really?

Deciding they weren't nearly done with this whole thing, Éibhear started to head back to the others. But before he could take the first step, he noticed Izzy's dog charging right at him—again—teeth bared, eyes wild.

Gods, really?

"Everything all right?" Brannie asked, her voice low so only Izzy could hear.

"Of course. All's forgiven." Then she grinned. "Family is all, you know."

Brannie briefly closed her eyes before stating, "Oh, that's *brilliant.*"

They giggled until Éibhear's comrade Aidan walked up to them. "Everything all right?"

The females nodded. "Aye."

His light eyes narrowed a bit, but Izzy, sensing that Aidan was much smarter than the other two Mì-runach accompanying Éibhear, glanced around and called out for her dog.

"Macsen? Macsen!"

"He's coming." Éibhear walked out of the woods.

"What do you mean he's coming?"

"Give him a second." He stepped back and she watched as Macsen happily dragged a large bear into the clearing.

"Oh, not again," Brannie sighed.

Aidan blinked. "Again? How often does he attack bears?"

"He likes bear," Izzy admitted.

"It came up behind me," Éibhear explained, "and this one went for him like a bone."

Brannie pointed at the bear. "Macsen took that down by himself?"

A valid question. Macsen enjoyed challenging bears, but it was usually Izzy or her troops who ended up taking down the bear so that the dog could eat his full.

Éibhear walked closer, leaned in, and whispered, "Not really. I could see the bear was not happy and about to tear the dog apart so I just sort of"—he shrugged—"punched him while the dog wasn't looking. Bear's out cold. We should probably go before he wakes up."

"Why are you whispering?" Brannie whispered.

"Just look at him." He glanced back at Macsen. "He's so proud of himself. I couldn't take that from him."

Brannie rolled her eyes and walked around her cousin, slinging her pack over her shoulder.

"What?" he asked when Izzy continued to stare at him.

"Nothing." She started laughing and couldn't stop, walking after her friend. "Nothing at all."

Chapter 9

They traveled late into the evening, finally stopping in a valley another few hours away from Garbhán Isle.

As a group, they silently ate dried beef and bread, pulled out their bedrolls, and went to sleep.

The next morning, when Éibhear woke up, he was alone. Since he found no signs of blood or body parts, he assumed everyone was alive somewhere.

Éibhear ate more of the dried beef and bread, already thinking about the food he'd get once he returned to Garbhán Isle. It was something he'd missed greatly while living mostly in the north. Although the Ice Landers did use some interesting seasonings and well-cooked, rich food was the one indulgence they allowed themselves in their harsh world. Still, it's not like he could enjoy that Ice Lander home cooking very often when he and his squad spent much of their time buried under ice and dirt, waiting for the right time to strike at some unsuspecting tribe leader.

Aye. It would be good to have a bit of a holiday. It would be good to see his kin . . . well, it would be good to see his mother and the mates of his brothers. That would be good.

Once he finished eating, Éibhear discovered he was no

longer alone, but his company was only that damn dog. Where exactly was everyone else?

The dog circled around, finally sidling up to him, his eyes on the remainder of Éibhear's beef.

"I should let you starve," he told the beast. "Just for the snoring that you tormented us with last night, I should let you starve."

But he ended up giving it a few pieces of beef instead. Simply because he didn't want to hear Izzy complain if the dog died before they made it back to Garbhán Isle. He really didn't want to hear her complain.

"Where is everyone anyway?" he asked the dog once he was done eating.

It jumped back like a rearing horse, spun around, and ran a few feet away, came back, stared at Éibhear.

Deciding it wouldn't hurt to follow, that's what Éibhear did. The dog led him up a steep incline until he found his fellow Mì-runach standing at the very top beside a large tree and looking over the other side to the land below.

Without saying a word, Éibhear walked up behind them and stood. They were tall, but he was taller and he only had to go slightly up on his toes to see what they were looking at.

One look at the lake beneath had Éibhear dropping back on his heels and shaking his head in disgust. Disgust! These bastards!

"You know," he barked at them, enjoying the way they all jumped a bit, "that's my brother's daughter you're eyeing, you disgusting bastards."

Uther frowned. "I thought she was your cousin."

"Oh, oh." Caswyn punched Uther in the shoulder, his gaze still locked over the ridge. "There she goes again."

All three refocused on the lake and Éibhear felt his lip curl, fangs starting to ease out of his gums. How dare they! She was his brother's . . .

Brannie flew up past the ridge they all stood on, black wings extended from her back, black scales shining in the early-morning suns, and his comrades watching every move she made.

"Look at that tail," Uther sighed.

"I think it's a little short," Aidan complained.

"You're all watching Brannie?" Éibhear asked. "Really?"

They didn't bother answering him since they were still busy staring at her, but he didn't really see what they seemed to see. She was just . . . Brannie.

His cousin flipped over and dived back toward the lake. Éibhear heard Izzy squeal and he looked over the edge to see her trying to swim back to shore.

Brannie landed in the lake hard, the water exploding out and sending Izzy racing to land. Éibhear was convinced she'd drown or worse, but by the time she rolled naked across the ground, the water retreating, she was laughing hysterically.

"You mad cow!" she yelled around her laughter.

Brannie was laughing, too, while floating on her back in the still-sloshing water.

Izzy managed to sit up. She seemed completely comfortable naked, and he understood why. She was perfect. Long body, powerful legs, strong shoulders, and scars across her back, torso, chest, and even her inside thighs. Yet she still moved with grace and strength, getting to her feet easily and stretching her entire body, her arms high over her head, muscles rippling.

"Should you be staring at your niece like that, *Uncle* Éibhear?" Aidan asked him while Uther and Caswyn continued to lustfully gawk at an unsuspecting Brannie.

"Piss off," Éibhear growled, moving around the bastard he sometimes called friend.

"Gods, look at the breast scales on her," Uther muttered about Brannie.

Still disgusted and pissed off in general, Éibhear rammed the big oaf's head into the tree he stood next to before heading back to camp. "We're moving out in ten minutes."

Izzy was trying to reach the clothes that Brannie had annoyingly put on a high branch.

"You are such a bitch!" she yelled at her laughing cousin, who was back in her human form, dressed, and running back to camp.

Izzy jumped again, hoping to reach her damn leggings without being forced to climb the damn tree. The vision of her splayed naked across that branch did nothing but make her feel uneasy.

Her fingers nearly touched the leggings, but she just missed them, growling when her feet again landed on the ground.

She was eyeing the tree, trying to figure out the best way up, when an incredibly large arm reached around her and grabbed her clothes. Her first instinct was to cover herself with her arms, or at the very least cover her tits. As her mother had always warned her, she'd been a late bloomer. Now she usually kept her chest bound around her troops. But she didn't want to give Éibhear the satisfaction of seeing her embarrassed. So she planted her hands on her hips and smiled up at him.

"I think," he said, "that you need to remember you and Brannie aren't alone on this trip."

"Why do you think she put my clothes in the tree? She knows your dirty friends were watching." Izzy took the clothes from him. "Thanks."

"Perhaps you two have spent too much time together."

"Aunt Ghleanna has said that more than once." Izzy

dropped her clothes and began to get dressed with Éibhear right there. He frowned but didn't say anything. He also didn't turn away. "She says I'm a bad influence on her daughter. Me. A bad influence on Branwen the Awful. I'm not sure how she comes to that conclusion."

"Probably because you get my cousin drunk and she just wakes up in the middle of your insane centaur shit."

"That could be part of Ghleanna's argument." She finished pulling her chain-mail shirt over her head and shook her wet hair out.

"You know," Izzy said, stepping closer to Éibhear and placing her hand on his chest. "I'm so glad we made up and that we've put the past behind us."

"Uh." Éibhear looked down at her hand and then at her face. "Yeah. Me, too."

"Now we can be the proper uncle and niece that the family has always wanted us to be."

The dragon blinked, his body going stiff. "Uncle and niece?"

"*Proper* uncle and niece. That must be such a relief for you. Not to have some child running around trying to stroke your hair." She laughed a little, patting his chest. "Thank you for being so patient with me back then. It must have been very hard."

"Well, no, it was—"

"Don't worry about it. It's the past. Now we're family. Kin. My wonderful Uncle Éibhear." On a whim, she went up on her toes and kissed him on the chin since she couldn't quite reach his cheek without more effort.

Then she walked away and headed back to camp. She was almost there when Brannie stepped out from behind a tree and yanked her over.

Her friend stared at her. "*Uncle* Éibhear?" she whispered. Izzy chewed her lip. "Too much?"

Bent over, silently laughing, Brannie shook her head and leaned against Izzy. "You're the best, you evil bitch!" she managed to squeal and whisper simultaneously. "The best!"

Then the friends held each other and laughed until Éibhear and the Mì-runach called for them so they could return to Garbhán Isle.

Chapter 10

"No. Absolutely not."

Talaith got up and followed Briec while he stalked around their bedroom.

"I think you're being unreasonable," she told him.

"I'm being a father."

"No. You're being *your* father."

"Well, you don't have to get nasty," he tossed back at her, looping around the bed again.

"Just let her spend the day with him. He must like her if he's still willing to after what you did."

Briec stopped and spun around to face her. "Of course he still likes her. She's perfect. She's—"

"Your daughter. Yes. Yes. We all know. Which means that you should understand exactly how stubborn and difficult *your* daughter can be when she doesn't get her bloody way."

"She's too young," he now argued.

"She's sixteen, Briec. Not a dragon sixteen either, but a healthy sixteen-year-old girl who likes a boy. There's no shame in that."

"You want her involved with this . . . this . . ."

Talaith crossed her arms over her chest. "Human?"

"I was going to say cock-haver, but human covers it, too."

Rubbing her eyes, she paced away from him. "All she wants is to go into town with him. Do a little shopping and have luncheon at the tavern. Not become his wife."

"No."

"I've already discussed it with Brastias and he says he'll go with them. You know how protective he is of his niece."

"Then why can't I go?"

"Because now when that poor boy sees you, he pisses himself. So that's not a good idea."

"Weakness! Why should *my* daughter be around someone so weak and useless?"

"You could stop her if you'd like—"

"Good." He headed toward the door. "I will."

"Just like my mother stopped me. Izzy is evidence of how successful that was."

Briec stopped with his hand on the doorknob, his entire body tense.

"Do you really want to be called 'grandfather' by some byproduct of Lord Pombray's bloodline?"

Her mate shuddered at the thought and Talaith bit the inside of her mouth to stop from laughing. When he didn't move, she walked up behind him and wrapped her arms around his waist. She rested her cheek against his back and said, "The Pombrays won't be here for long. Let her do this. Just one day, then they'll secretly flirt until he leaves."

"And Brastias will—"

"Keep a very close eye on them. I promise."

"And if you're wrong about all this?"

"You'll be able to lord it over me from now until our ancestors take us home."

He nodded. "As long as you understand that last bit."

* * *

Izzy pulled her horse to a stop beside Éibhear's and, like him, gazed down into the town below. Past that town she could see Annwyl's castle, where the sight of dragons circling the tall spires of the building always told her that she was home again.

"You all right?" she asked.

"Aye. Just thinking about how long it's been since I've been back here."

"Sure you don't want to see your mum first? I know for a fact she's missed you greatly."

"How do you know that?"

"Because she said, 'I miss my son greatly.'"

He snorted a little, but the smile was there. "You don't really go for general euphemisms, do you, Izzy?"

"I don't even know what that means, so I'll go with no. I don't." She adjusted the reins in her hand. "I can take your horse for you, if you want to head to Devenallt." Devenallt Mountain was the seat of power of the ruling Southland dragons and where the Dragon Queen, Éibhear's mum and Izzy's grandmum-by-mating, lived in safety.

"And be forced to see my father at the same time?" He shook his head. "No. I think I'd rather deal with my brothers first."

"I wouldn't worry," she teased. "I'm sure they didn't even notice you were gone."

"Thank you. That's very nice."

"Just getting you ready for the rest of the family. Isn't that what nieces are for?"

Éibhear rolled his eyes. "We're not back here again, are we?"

"Oh, dear old uncle." She patted his cheek ever so gently. "You dear *old* thing. You know you're my favorite old uncle."

"Vicious cow," Éibhear muttered under his breath. "Heartless, vicious cow," he amended.

Laughing, Izzy spurred her horse on and headed toward home and whatever waited there for her.

* * *

Éibhear watched Izzy ride down the trail toward home. Brannie pulled up next to him, giving him a quick once-over. "Going to Garbhán Isle looking like that, are you?"

"What's wrong with how I look?"

His cousin sighed, shook her head, and followed after Izzy.

He watched them for a bit before he snarled, "And where do you lot think you're going?"

"To the pub," Aidan answered for them all.

"You're not coming with me?"

"I know your brothers, which should answer that question. And Cas and Uther have heard your tales over the years, sooooo . . . no. We're going to the pub. Get drunk. Get some pussy. Maybe gamble a bit. Good luck to ya."

His comrades continued on down a path that led to the closest pub, leaving Éibhear alone. It wasn't until now that he'd bothered to think much on how difficult this could possibly be. His kin, both the royal side and the Cadwaladrs, didn't think much of the Mì-runach. The royals avoided them and the Cadwaladrs thought of them as crazed dogs to be unleashed in battle when you didn't care what the outcome might be. Éibhear had once thought the same thing . . . until he'd become one. Until he realized how important the Mì-runach were to the survival of their kind. But he knew better than to try to convince his kin of any of that. Dragons rarely changed their minds unless forced to, and Éibhear was no longer as tolerant as he once had been.

Still . . . it had been ten years. He was no longer the hatchling they'd adored, nor the unhappy adolescent they'd had little patience for. Instead, he was Éibhear the Contemptible, Squad Leader of the Mì-runach; Hated Southlander of the Ice Land Dragons; and Destroyer of Sixteen Ice Land Dragon Tribes—a number that outranked all other Mì-runach.

When he realized none of that would matter to his siblings,

he briefly debated following his mates to the pub. But Éibhear knew he couldn't avoid this forever. Avoid *them* forever.

So he tapped the sides of his horse with his heels and the animal moved forward, taking Éibhear home—and to whatever awaited him there.

Dagmar went out of her way not to react when she heard Briec the Mighty imperiously inform his daughter that he was "allowing" her to spend an afternoon with Lord Pombray's son. Instead she kept her head down and her smile to herself.

Although she greatly doubted the relationship between the boy and Rhi would go beyond some innocent flirtation, she knew it was important for Rhi to get away from her overprotective father, uncles, and cousins for a bit. Dagmar didn't want the same life for Briec's daughter that she'd had. Having to lie, connive, and quietly make things happen in the background while the men took all the credit was no life for any female. And now that Dagmar had gone years being trusted with the security of these lands and the politics of the Southlanders, she couldn't imagine going back to the life she'd lived in the north.

This was especially true when she saw her brother's son wander into the Great Hall. Poor, confused idiot. He'd been here for several days and yet he seemed baffled by everything. People talked to him and he stared at them mindlessly. She even noticed that Frederik's brothers and cousins paid little attention to the boy. Clearly the men of her family had already given up on him. They weren't comfortable with men as smart as Dagmar—and yes, she knew she was smart . . . definitely smarter than any male in her family—but they had no use for males too stupid for basic conversation who were also completely unable to handle a sword or mace or any other weapon. And the boy couldn't handle any weapon. He was as bad as Dagmar, and that said much.

Which was why she knew that her nephews would ask her to keep Frederik for a while. Reason forbid the big bastards should try to deal with the tragic idiot themselves. Instead they'd try to pawn him off on someone else. Well, Dagmar had no intention of letting that happen this time. She *refused* to play these ridiculous games with her family. Still, for now, she'd have to tolerate the boy. It was the least she could do for him.

Biting back a sigh, Dagmar motioned him over, but he only frowned. So, she snapped, "*Frederik.*"

He made his way over to her, but slammed his leg into the table before he sat down in the chair next to her. She was convinced the boy must be covered in bruises from all the things he walked into during the day.

"Morning, Auntie Dagmar."

"Morning, Frederik. Do you like your room?" she asked, falling back on the boring patter she used with most royals.

"Yes, yes. It's very nice."

"Good."

When she couldn't think of anything else to say to the boy, she went back to reading her missives from several of the ports Annwyl's troops controlled and trying to block out Rhi's excited babble. Shame Keita wasn't around. She'd love all this discussion over gowns and what one girl should wear to walk into town and go shopping with one boy.

"Nothing revealing," her father warned.

"Daddy," Rhi chastised.

"Do you want the boy to live to see the birth of his children with some other boring human female, or do you want to be crying at his funeral pyre? Your choice."

"*Daddy!*"

Dagmar was shaking her head and quietly chuckling when she sensed *them* nearby.

She lifted her head and found Talan sitting on her right, eating the buttered bread she'd had on a plate beside all her papers. Talwyn sat cattycorner from Frederik—who still hadn't noticed anything—her feet on the worn wood, her bright green eyes watching Rhi and Briec at the other end of the table.

"Mornin', Aunt Dagmar," Talan murmured around *her* food. Only eighteen and his voice was no more than a low rumble of sound. It had been that way since he was twelve. Something that still disturbed her a bit.

"Talan."

"Anything interesting in there?" he asked, trying to see the documents she was reviewing.

Dagmar placed her arm over the parchment, stared her nephew directly in those black eyes. "Nothing for you to see, I assure you."

His grin was disturbingly wicked for someone so young. A smile that his sister only had when weapons were involved.

"What's all this about?" Talwyn asked, motioning down the table with her apple.

"Rhi is going to be spending the day with young Albrecht."

"What?" Talwyn looked at Rhi. "Oy!"

Rhi let out a breath and Dagmar knew the girl was steeling herself. The connection between the twins and Rhi was unbelievably strong. But the arguing . . .

Gods. The arguing.

She slowly faced her cousin. "Aye?"

"What's this about the Pombray brat?"

"This has nothing to do with you, Talwyn. Stay out of it."

"I won't stay out of it." Talwyn looked to her uncle. "And you're all right with this?"

"I've given my permission."

"What's wrong with you?"

"I have to admit," Briec said, "I liked it better when you didn't speak."

"Back off, Talwyn." And that came from Talan. Brother and sister looked at each other and Dagmar instinctively leaned back in her chair. Of course Frederik, oblivious as always, leaned closer to the table so that he could study the plate of food one of the servants had placed in front of him. *What exactly did he expect to see? Besides eggs and slabs of meat?*

"Stay out of it, Talan."

"Leave her alone, sister."

"You don't tell me what to do, *brother*."

"If she wants to spend time with Pombray—"

"You may think it's quite all right to stick your cock in anything that moves—"

"What does my cock have to do with anything?"

"—but I don't trust Pombray or his son and I won't have her spending time with any of them."

"It's none of your bloody business, sister. Lay off."

"Make me."

Rhi stamped her foot, her frustration evident and clearly growing. Once again, her cousins' bickering was getting between her and her enjoyment. Something she'd grown less and less tolerant of the last couple of years or so. "Both of you, stop it!"

But it was too late. Brother and sister had locked on each other, both of them getting to their feet, hands moving toward the weapons they kept on them at all times.

"I mean it," Rhi tried again. "Stop it!"

Dagmar quickly got out of her chair, her papers held against her chest. But as she started to move away, she realized Frederik was still sitting there, toying with some bacon. Completely oblivious. She was reaching for him when a large hand she knew so well reached past her, grabbed the boy by the back of his cotton shirt and yanked him from the chair.

Dagmar stumbled into the wall, nodding her appreciation up at her mate, who still held the boy in his arms.

"I leave you alone for five minutes," he quietly joked.

She pressed into Gwenvael the Handsome's side. "I know. I simply can't be trusted on my own."

"Tragically weak female."

He winked at her, but then the twins were up on the table and charging each other, short swords unsheathed.

Rhi slammed her foot against the ground again and screamed out, "*Stop it!*"

And, her mouth open in shock, Dagmar watched as Talan was flung into the wall and Talwyn flung right across the Great Hall and out the doors.

"Huh," Gwenvael said. "That's new."

Dagmar shook off her surprise and quickly said to Frederik, "You didn't see any of that. Understand me?"

"Didn't see what?" the boy asked.

Dagmar wanted to believe Frederik had caught on quickly, but she actually knew he was just painfully clueless.

After they stabled their horses, Brannie had headed off to one of the nearby lakes where many of her dragon kin camped whenever they came to visit or protect Garbhán Isle. According to Éibhear, the three other Mì-runach had stayed in town to spend time at one of the pubs while Izzy and Éibhear walked to the castle.

They were cutting through the courtyard, nearing the steps that would take them to the Great Hall, when Éibhear abruptly stopped, his head tipping to the side. Izzy stopped as well. The dragon had the best hearing she'd ever known and if he thought he heard something—

His arm slipped around her waist and he yanked her out of the way just as a loud bang echoed out from the Great Hall and something exploded through the doorway.

They watched that something shoot past them and slam into one of the nearby buildings. When it landed, Izzy sighed. "Talwyn."

"Good gods!" Éibhear exclaimed. Then he added, "She's gotten tall."

"That she has."

"Do you think Talan did this?"

"I don't know. I usually find them entangled in a pit fight, not throwing each other around."

They became quiet and that's when Izzy realized that Éibhear's arm was still around her waist. She looked down at his arm and then up at him. He smiled at her until she murmured, "Someone's a naughty uncle." Then he couldn't release her fast enough.

Izzy was just about to head over to her cousin to check on her when Rhi stumbled down the first few steps of the Great Hall. She took one look at Talwyn and Rhi's hand covered her mouth, her eyes wide in shock. That's when Izzy knew who'd done this.

Grateful, for the first time, that she'd come home when she did, she quickly turned and headed toward the Great Hall.

"Rhi," she called out and her sister looked down at her with their father's eyes. Bright violet and beautiful, long silver hair framing her gorgeous face, brown skin perfect, soft, and completely unscarred.

"Izzy?" Rhi burst into tears. "Izzy!" She charged down the steps and Izzy met her at the bottom. Her sister dove into her arms, sobbing uncontrollably as Izzy held her.

"It's all right. It's all right," she soothed, patting her back.

"I've killed her!"

"You have not." Izzy glanced back and saw that Éibhear had gone over and scooped up his niece, carrying her back to the stairs. "See? She's fine."

Rhi lifted her head and Talwyn waved a little, smiled. "I'm fine. I promise."

But Rhi only sobbed louder, resting against her sister.

With a shrug, Éibhear carried Talwyn back inside. Once they were alone, Izzy asked her sister, "What is it, Rhi? She's fine."

"She's not fine." Rhi looked up at her sister with all that painful earnestness she couldn't hide. "She smiled. Izzy . . . Talwyn smiled!"

Inconsolable, she gripped Izzy harder, sobbed louder, and all Izzy could do was pat her sister's back and sigh.

Éibhear walked into the Great Hall but stopped when he saw Briec sending a wounded male off with one of the servants. And if that wounded male was Talan . . . well, like his sister, the boy had matured into quite the human specimen.

The girl in his arms suddenly tensed, green eyes looked up at him and narrowed . . . dangerously. Just like her mother.

"Who are you?" she asked.

"Don't you know?"

"If I knew, I'd not have asked." She sniffed. "Dragon."

Impressed, he answered, "I'm—"

"Éibhear?"

He looked up, smiled at Dagmar Reinholdt. "Hello, Dagmar."

"Éibhear!" She dropped papers onto the table and ran to his side, throwing her arms around his waist.

"You can put me down," Talwyn muttered.

"You sure?"

"I'm sure." He could hear that sneer in her words. He wondered if she sneered at everything. Something told him that yes, she did.

So Éibhear released her. She landed on her feet, but then she stumbled back and dropped butt first to the floor. Instead of helping her, he hugged Dagmar.

"I'm so glad to see you." She stepped back and looked him over. "Although I'm not sure about this look you've got going here."

"I've been in the Ice Lands for ten years. What did you expect me to look like?"

"Not like this. But we all work with what we have access to, I guess."

"What are you doing here?" another voice barked.

Éibhear looked to Briec, who stood glowering at him. "And I missed you, too, brother."

"I didn't miss you."

Éibhear crossed his eyes. "Of course you didn't."

"Where's Rhi?"

"With Izzy. We came here together."

Briec glanced over at Gwenvael, stared, then looked back at Éibhear. "Oh," Briec said. "Great. She'll be fine with Izzy." Then he walked off, heading farther into the castle.

Dagmar reached for Talwyn. "Why don't I get her to Morfyd?"

"Thanks, Dagmar."

"Of course. I'll let her know you're here. She'll be so happy to see you." She smiled up at him. "I'm so glad you're home, Éibhear." And he knew she meant it. Meaningful, since she rarely meant anything she said when speaking to royals.

"So am I."

Éibhear watched Dagmar take Talwyn up the stairs to the bedrooms before he moved to Gwenvael's side. "Hello, brother."

"Éibhear." Gwenvael looked him over. "Nice hair."

"Thank you. I do try." Éibhear motioned to the human boy who was walking back to the table and picking up his plate.

"Who's that?"

"Dagmar's nephew from the north." They silently watched the boy head off . . . somewhere. Éibhear had no idea where.

"Not the brightest thing, I'm afraid," Gwenvael muttered when the boy was gone. "But I guess he's family."

"True. True."

The brothers faced each other, smiled; then Éibhear

caught hold of Gwenvael's hair and rammed him head-first into the wall.

"Let's go find the rest of the bastards, shall we?" Éibhear asked, as he dragged his unconscious brother down the hallway by what the idiot insisted on referring to as his "long, luxurious golden locks."

Chapter 11

Izzy knew that walking would calm her sister down, so she took her to one of her favorite places. A stream surrounded by trees and large boulders.

She sat Rhi down on one of the smaller boulders and took out a clean cloth from her travel bag. She wiped the tears from her sister's face, then held the cloth to the girl's nose.

"Blow," she ordered.

After a few hiccups, the girl did as she was told.

"Now what happened?" Izzy asked her.

"They just wouldn't stop bickering. Either they're bickering out loud or in my head, but it's constant. And Daddy just told me I could go shopping with Albrecht and—"

"Who's Albrecht?"

"Lord Pombray's son. He gave me flowers the other day and Daddy nearly burned his hand off."

Izzy's laugh was out before she could stop it and violet eyes flashed in anger.

"It's not funny, Iseabail! He was terrified!"

"I'm sure he was," she said around the laughter, unable to stop.

Rhi stood and began to pace. "You're as bad as Daddy! The two of you!"

"You know how Daddy is."

"He won't let any man near me if they're not family."

"Man? Human, dragon, god, or centaur, if it's male and not blood, Daddy will burn the poor bloke to the ground."

"I'll be a virgin forever," Rhi sobbed.

"Good."

The sobbing abruptly stopped and her sister stared at her. "What do you mean 'good'?"

"I mean good. I mean fucking complicates everything."

Rhi's lips twitched, a smile fighting its way forth while her cheeks and forehead turned bright red. "*Iseabail.*"

"And *good* fucking can ruin your life. So stay a virgin forever. You'll be much happier that way. Besides, do you really want to be the one to cause all those deaths?"

Rhi's smile faded. "What do you mean?"

"When Daddy gets his claws on whatever poor male sets his sights on you . . . there will be death. Death after death after death. All at the talons of one wonderful but terribly arrogant silver dragon who adores both his perfect, *perfect* daughters."

Her sister's smile returned, but Izzy couldn't help but think there was also some relief there. As if she'd thought Izzy had meant something else.

"Gods, I wish he would stop saying that. It sounds awful."

"I like that he thinks of me as perfect. Despite my hysterical mother's questionable bloodline."

Rhi sighed, shook her head. "I truly don't know how she hasn't killed him yet." She blinked, her hand covering her mouth. "I can't believe I said that. That was a horrible thing to say about Mum and Dad!"

Izzy gazed at her sister. "Whose family do you think you belong to?"

* * *

Éibhear tracked Fearghus and Briec down in the war room. Using Gwenvael's head, he pushed the door open and walked in, tossing Gwenvael next to the big wood table they sat at.

Fearghus and Briec glanced down at a groaning Gwenvael, then immediately went back to their conversation as if they were still alone.

"We have to figure out a course of action," Briec said. "It can't go on like this. I feel things building."

"Mum suggested—"

"*No*." Briec looked pointedly at Fearghus. "Absolutely not. Rhi adores Mum and I won't have her turned into a tiny Rhiannon."

"Then maybe you shouldn't have named her after her."

Briec snarled. "I did *not* name my daughter after Mum!"

Éibhear stepped close to the table. "Oy!"

The two males stopped snapping at each other and slowly looked over at Éibhear.

"Is there something you want?" Briec asked.

"Do you have bones in your *hair*?" Fearghus asked.

Ignoring Fearghus's question, Éibhear asked, "Don't you have something to say to me?"

Briec thought a moment then answered, "No."

"Why are you here?" Fearghus asked.

"My commander thought it was time I came home to visit my loving kin."

Fearghus frowned. "Which is who exactly?"

Briec laughed and Fearghus shook his head. "No. I mean, who's your commander?"

"Why does that matter?"

"Because I want to know if I can trust his decision to send you back here."

"His decision to . . . what?" Éibhear took a moment before asking, "You lot had me sent away?"

"It was in your best interest."

"But mostly our best interest," Briec clarified. "You were becoming a right prat."

"And Mum would have been mad if we'd beaten you to death."

"So you lot had me sent to the Mì-runach?"

"That was Dad's idea."

"We suggested the salt mines," Briec explained. "But Dad was afraid the rest of the troops would turn on you because of your incessant whining and inability to follow orders."

"Sending you to the Mì-runach was," Fearghus reiterated, "in your best interest."

Éibhear pulled off his fur cape and tossed it onto a nearby chair.

"Gods," Briec gasped. "The bastard's gotten bigger."

"I stopped growing five years ago."

"Not soon enough."

"Let me ask you," Éibhear went on, determined to understand all this. "Sending me away . . . that didn't have anything to do with Izzy, did it?"

Gwenvael looked up from where he still lay on the floor. "It took you *ten* bloody years to figure that out?"

His brothers burst out laughing and Éibhear walked close to the table Fearghus and Briec sat at. He raised his fists and slammed them against the hundred-year-old, thick wood table. It broke into three distinct pieces and crumpled to the floor.

His brothers looked over the mess until Fearghus said, "I'm making you tell Annwyl you broke the war room table."

Izzy put her arm around her sister's shoulders. "Tell me what's wrong?"

"Everything!"

Izzy closed her eyes so that her sister didn't see her cross them in exasperation. Gods, had she been this *dramatic* when she was sixteen? Izzy doubted it. Her life had been so serious up to that point, how could she be dramatic?

Taken from her mother right after her birth, Izzy hadn't met Talaith again until she was sixteen. In the years before that meeting Izzy had traveled the countryside with three soldiers she called her Protectors. Men who'd left their lives and families behind just to protect Izzy from the goddess Arzhela and her followers.

For years those followers had hidden the fact that they'd lost Izzy so that they could keep control of Talaith. It had worked too, until Briec the Mighty came along and changed everything for mother and daughter. He'd fallen in love with Talaith, making her his mate. Or, as the dragons called it, Briec had Claimed Talaith. And from the very beginning, Briec had treated Izzy as his own daughter, without question, without doubt. To a girl who'd never known her birth father, Briec's unconditional love had meant so very much.

"Can we narrow 'everything' down to something manageable?" Izzy asked.

Rhi dropped her head, the back of her hands wiping her cheeks and eyes. "What if I'd killed her?" she whispered.

"Killed who?"

"Talwyn."

"With that hard head she has?"

Rhi pushed Izzy's arm off and stalked a few feet away before facing her. "I'm not joking, Izzy."

She really wasn't. Rhi was truly distraught, fingers twisted into knots, her entire body shaking.

"But you didn't kill Talwyn. I saw her, luv. She's fine."

"But I could have."

"And I could have killed many over the years, but I haven't. Mostly."

"It's not the same, Iz."

"What's different?"

"I have no control." Her hands fluttered around. "Over any of . . . of . . . *this.*"

"Your Magicks?" Izzy moved closer. "What did you mean to do to Talwyn and Talan?"

"I didn't want them to start fighting. Again. For once Daddy was being reasonable and they were ruining it. So I only wanted to push them away from each other. Just a few feet."

"And they went flying."

"Talwyn got the worst because she pissed me off the most . . . and she was closer to an open door." She covered her face with her hands, but Izzy could still hear her words clear enough. "And if it had been anyone but Talan and Talwyn, they probably would be dead. Their brains dashed—"

The sobbing started again and Izzy went to her sister, pulled her into her arms. "It's all right, luv. I'm here. I'm home. We'll figure this out together."

And her sister gripped her so tight that Izzy knew she owed that big blue bastard for insisting she come back.

Dammit.

Talaith had gone to a nearby village to see a woman who would be giving birth soon. All was going well, but it was the woman's first child and she was, not surprisingly, nervous. Besides, Talaith wanted father and daughter to work these little issues out on their own. Briec had to learn to listen to Rhi, and Rhi had to learn to stand up for herself without tears and foot stamping. Although Talaith was no royal, her daughter very much was. And, truth be told, if she could learn to manage her father, gods knew she could manage *anyone.*

Dismounting her mare, Talaith nodded at her armed guards. "We'll return to the village tomorrow. Sometime after first meal. I'll see you then."

"As you wish, my lady," said the older guard. He took

the reins from Talaith and headed to the stables with his companions.

Briec had insisted on Talaith having guards if she was going to be "gallivanting all over the land helping others birth more future running snacks for my kin." Not exactly how Talaith would put it, but she had laughed.

She headed up the stairs to the Great Hall, hoping not to find father and daughter in yet another screaming-crying match. That did nothing but give her such a headache. But when Talaith walked through the big doors, she stopped and gazed at her twin nephew and niece. Morfyd was busy sewing up a gash on Talan's arm and Talwyn had a block of ice from the kitchens pressed to the side of her head.

"What the hells happened?"

The twins looked at each other and then away. "Nothing," they both muttered, which meant it had been something. If it was nothing, Talan would gleefully make up some lie to start trouble while Talwyn would wander away, bored.

Talaith took a quick look around. No Rhi. No Briec. Not liking that at all, she stalked back toward the war room, where Briec and Fearghus had been spending much of their time lately. And not even thirty feet away from the door, she could already hear the bloody fighting!

Éibhear had finally gotten Briec in a nice chokehold after knocking Gwenvael out completely and possibly breaking a couple of Fearghus's ribs. He was about to twist Briec like a piece of rope when he heard footsteps approaching. He knew from the lightness of the steps that it was definitely not Annwyl. And the quickness told him it wasn't Dagmar. That left Talaith and Morfyd.

He scented the air. A human female. Talaith.

Lifting Briec up, he tossed him across the room, trying not

to smile when his brother hit the wall, then the floor, gasping out, "*Bastard!*"

Then he smeared some of the blood from a cut on his head farther down his face and quickly sat on the floor. He'd just rested his back against the wall when the war room door flew open.

Talaith took one look around, her dark gaze finally resting on Éibhear. She frowned, probably confused by his Ice Lander look.

"Éibhear?" she finally asked.

"Talaith," he said softly.

She gasped and rushed to his side. "Oh, Éibhear! What did they do to you?"

"Us?" Briec demanded, trying to pick himself up off the floor—and failing. "*You're blaming* us *for this?*"

"Quiet, lizard!" She studied the wound on Éibhear's head. "You poor thing. I can't believe your brothers did this to you."

"I'm all right, Talaith," he said . . . weakly. "Really."

"Let's get you out of here." She took his arm and he let her help him off the floor. With one hand on his forearm, the other on his back, Talaith led Éibhear through the door. Although he did manage to look back at Fearghus and Briec—not Gwenvael, since he was still out cold—and smile.

And that ball of fire that slammed into the wall right outside the door but missed him and Talaith? That only managed to make him smile more.

Izzy decided more walking was in order for her sister because exercise always calmed Izzy when she was upset. But she'd forgotten that her sister . . . not much for exercising. Less than five miles in, she was already whining.

Stopping to face her, Izzy asked, "Are you panting?"

"Think we can slow down a bit?" Rhi asked, her hand pressed to her chest. "Maybe you can carry me?"

"Aren't you a little young to be so . . . weak?"

"Could you say that with any more distaste?"

"Aye. I could."

Izzy heard footsteps approaching—many footsteps—and she pulled her sword, motioning Rhi to get behind a large boulder. And, as she'd been trained, Rhi followed orders without complaint.

Soldiers wearing the armor of the Elite Guard came through the trees. They were younger men, and their unadorned shields told Izzy they were still in training. In other words, they hadn't yet left Garbhán Isle to be royal escorts.

She also doubted they had any idea who she was because she didn't recognize them at all.

Plus, she didn't have on her military armor, nor her bright red surcoat with the Queen's crest of two dragons. Instead, Izzy only wore chain mail, worn leather boots, a dark brown cape, and every weapon she could fit on her body.

It was the weapons that probably worried the young soldiers. The one at the head of the small group called out a warning and the soldiers dropped their shields so they created a sort of wall.

"Speak!" one of them demanded. "State your purpose!"

Izzy? she heard her sister whisper in her head, as if these human males could hear her as well. They couldn't and Izzy shouldn't be able to either, but Rhi had been talking to her this way for years, sometimes over a thousand leagues away. It was something that took Izzy a while to get used to.

It's all right, she assured her sister. *Stay where you are.*

Izzy took several steps toward the soldiers and they immediately pulled their weapons, their bodies tensing behind their tall shields.

Gripping her sword in both hands, Izzy pulled it back and readied for her attack, the soldiers following suit.

"Hold!" a voice ordered and the soldiers were pushed aside as a warrior walked past.

The red-headed soldier urgently said, "My lady—"

"*Stop* calling me that," the Queen of Garbhán Isle ordered her men.

"Sorry, my . . . uh . . . Annwyl."

Annwyl the Bloody crossed her arms over her chest and gazed at Izzy. "You dare come to my lands and challenge my guard?"

"They look like they need a challenge. You'd be better off with a loyal squire. Someone young, perky, and good with your horse."

"Perky?" Annwyl laughed. "You were never perky, you lying harlot!"

Izzy shrugged. "It depends on your definition of perky."

"My definition is *not Izzy.*" Grinning, Annwyl walked toward her, arms thrown open. Izzy slid her sword back into her holster and threw herself at Annwyl, the pair hugging and laughing.

"I'm so glad you're home," Annwyl said. "It's been ages."

"Ten moons is hardly ages."

"It is to me." Annwyl stepped back, looked her over. "A new scar. From a battle axe?"

"Angry raccoon in my tent."

Laughing again, Annwyl gripped Izzy's forearm and Izzy turned her hand to grip Annwyl's. And, as Izzy often did, she used her thumb to trace the outline of the mark burned into Annwyl's flesh. A brand placed there by Annwyl's mate, Fearghus. The dragon's way of Claiming his partner for life. Annwyl wore her brands on both forearms—and, Izzy had found out while she was Annwyl's squire, on her inside thighs—Talaith wore hers on her lower back, and Dagmar's was right on her ass. Something the family still teased her about. Yet of all the brands Izzy had seen on her mated kin over the years, it was her grandmother's that Izzy secretly envied. Rhiannon's went from the base of her foot to just below her chin, winding around her entire body as a small dragon would. And when Izzy was younger, dreaming of the day some dragon worthy of her would Claim her as his own, she'd planned on a similar mark.

"Gods, I missed you, Iz."

"And you."

Annwyl turned to her guards. "You lot, this is Izzy. But you can call her General Iseabail of the Eighth, Fourteenth, and Twenty-sixth Legions."

Color drained from the soldiers' faces, their eyes growing wide.

"General, sir!" said the one who'd been speaking from the beginning. "We apologize, sir. We didn't know—"

Izzy waved all that away. "I didn't announce myself and I'm not wearing our colors, so I'd expect you to err on the side of caution when it comes to protecting our queen."

"Thank you, General."

Annwyl hugged Izzy again, then asked, "Why are you here?"

Izzy pulled back, gazed at her queen. "I was told I was requested."

"Requested? By me?"

She shrugged. "I really didn't know, but I knew it wasn't Mum because she usually contacts me herself if she needs me to come home." As a practicing witch, her mother was able to talk to Izzy directly using only her mind, just like Rhi could, the distance between them meaning nothing. But, and Izzy appreciated this, her mother didn't contact her that way often. Instead she wrote to Izzy regularly to fill her in on the day-to-day events of life at court and saved contacting her through her mind for emergencies and such.

"Well, I didn't send for you. I wanted you to concentrate on those ogres."

"It's been handled. Their leader is dead. I left my next in command to round up and execute any stragglers."

"Good. But that's honestly all I've needed from you the last few months, Iz."

"I didn't send for you either, Izzy," another voice called out.

The queen blinked, her gaze still locked with Izzy's. "Why is your sister hiding behind that boulder?"

"At first it was for safety. But now I can only imagine she's hiding out of fear of telling you the truth."

"The truth?" Annwyl sighed, her eyes briefly closing. "What did the twins do now?"

"Nothing!" Rhi rushed around the boulder, her hands twisting together in front of her. "It was my fault. I promise."

"It's never your fault," Annwyl said.

"But it was this time. I . . . I overreacted."

"Which meant The Girl was doing something."

Rhi stomped her tiny foot. "You always accuse her! And it wasn't her fault!"

"You do always accuse Talwyn," Izzy reminded Annwyl, making sure not to laugh when her queen rolled green eyes skyward.

"Fine," Annwyl said with a very heavy sigh. "It wasn't The Girl's fault. You just overreacted to . . . nothing?"

"It doesn't matter. I overreacted. Badly. I think I hurt her."

"Hurt her how?"

Rhi used the tips of her fingers to comb loose silver curls behind her ears. "I used Magicks to . . . to . . . throw her and Talan. He hit the Great Hall wall, but Talwyn went out the door and into the buildings across from the courtyard."

"I see." Annwyl stared down at her niece, her face very stern. "And tell me true, Princess Rhianwen . . . did my daughter's hard head damage my wall?"

Izzy snorted and quickly looked off. Rhi, however, was typically appalled. "Aunt Annwyl!"

"What? It's a valid question. You know that girl's head is as hard as her father's. Do I need to call in the stone masons again?"

"I don't understand this family!" Rhi charged before she stalked off. Poor thing . . . she stalked off often around her kin.

"Nicely handled, my liege."

"I still say it was a valid question. Stone masons cost money, you know."

Talaith was gently wiping blood from Éibhear's head when Rhi stormed into the Great Hall.

Talaith turned, watching her daughter head up the stairs.

"What's wrong?"

"This family is ridiculous!"

Shaking her head, Talaith went back to her task, muttering low, "I've been warning her of that fact since birth. Yet she always seems so bloody shocked."

"I can hear you!" Rhi yelled from the stairs, startling them both.

"She flounces quite well," Éibhear noted when his niece disappeared in a flurry of pretty pink satin and silk.

"Your brother always tells me I taught her how to flounce, but I've caught Keita giving her lessons several times."

"It's definitely a Keita flounce, with a bit of me mum thrown in."

Talaith chuckled and dunked the cloth she held in a bowl of water, squeezing the material to get out the excess liquid. While his brother's mate had her head down, Éibhear watched Izzy walk into the Great Hall with Annwyl. Izzy saw him before Annwyl, her eyes growing wide at the sight of him, then narrowing suspiciously. He grinned and her eyes narrowed more. But when Annwyl turned toward him, he quickly changed the grin into a wince and placed his hand to his head.

"Éibhear? Is that you?" Annwyl rushed to Talaith's side. "Gods! What happened to you?"

"Those idiot brothers of his," Talaith complained. She again pressed the cloth to his head.

"What is wrong with them?" Annwyl petted his cheek. "You poor, poor thing."

Behind the women, Izzy's mouth dropped open and she gawked at him.

"It's all right," Éibhear said, lowering his eyes to look more sincere and to give himself a moment to get control in the face of Izzy's outraged expression. "I'm sure they didn't mean it."

"They just don't deserve you as a brother," Talaith nearly snarled.

"I'll go talk to them," Annwyl said. But she cracked her knuckles. "Right now."

Izzy cut in front of Annwyl, forced a smile. "Why don't *I* talk to them? Daddy listens to me."

"You want my sword?"

Izzy blinked. Hard. "No. I don't think that's necessary. To talk to my father and uncles that I adore."

"You want me warhammer then?"

Deciding not to answer Annwyl, Izzy turned and faced her mother. "Hi, Mum."

Talaith went up on her toes and hugged Izzy tight. "I'm so glad you're home."

"Did you send for me?" she asked.

"No." Talaith stepped back. "I didn't. Why?"

"Ragnar said she was wanted home," Éibhear explained.

"That didn't come from me."

"Dad?"

"You'll have to ask him. I'm not talking to him right now."

Izzy cringed. "Again?"

Lips pursed, Talaith turned from her daughter. "He's in the war room."

Izzy headed off, but as the other women focused back on

Éibhear, Izzy turned on her heel and shook her head at him in disgust. Too bad for her that only made him laugh a little.

After getting Gwenvael off the floor and fetching cold cloths for her father and uncles' heads, Izzy asked, "So Mum has been right all this time. . . . You *do* continue to fight with him."

"He started it," they stated in unison and Izzy rubbed her forehead with the tips of her fingers.

"That's pathetic. You're his wiser and older brothers . . . and Gwenvael."

Gwenvael smiled. "I missed you, too, Iseabail."

She kissed the dragon's golden head. "And I you. But I still don't know why I'm here."

The three dragons looked at each other and back at her, then shrugged.

"Why are you here?" her father asked.

"Didn't you send for me?"

"No."

Fearghus cracked his neck. "Last we heard, you were killing ogres. Why would we stop you from doing that? We know how you enjoy it so."

"Ragnar said I'd been sent for. At least that's what he told Éibhear." She briefly studied the males. "And why were you fighting with Éibhear?"

"He didn't like what we had to say about why he was sent to the Mì-runach."

"Although, he was lucky," Briec argued. "It could have been the salt mines."

"Did sending him away have anything to do with me?"

"Sending him away?" Fearghus shook his head. "Of course not, Izzy. We'd never do that."

"Good."

"But *keeping* him away? Aye. That we did."

Izzy winced and had to admit, "That doesn't seem fair to him."

"Perhaps, but it seemed easier that way," Briec sighed.

"Easier for whom?"

"For me. Was I not clear on the importance of *me*?"

Izzy smiled at Fearghus and Gwenvael. "I love my daddy."

Briec sniffed. "Of course you do."

Éibhear grabbed an apple from the bowl on the table, shaking his head as he bit into the fruit.

"Ragnar didn't tell me who asked for her," he said around the bite of fruit in his mouth. "Then again, I didn't ask."

Annwyl, who was sitting on the table and ramming the wood with a dagger, demanded, "How could you not ask?"

"By not opening my mouth and speaking."

Her eyes narrowed. "You and that sarcasm."

"I was actually just being honest."

Talaith checked Éibhear's head wound again. "That ointment I put on there should help heal this by tonight."

"Will it leave a scar?"

"Do you care?"

"Maybe. If I'm left hideous, will you still love me as you do?"

Talaith folded her arms over her chest. "Who says I love you now?"

"You do . . . with your *eyes*." Talaith and Annwyl laughed, and Éibhear, grinning, reached blindly over for another piece of fruit. But what he now held in his hand didn't feel like an apple. More like a melon . . . covered in chain mail.

Confused, he looked over and realized that he'd inadvertently taken hold of Izzy's right breast. Even worse, his three brothers stood behind her, all of them focused on where his hand met her chest.

Éibhear raised his gaze and met Izzy's. They stared at each other, with Éibhear's hand still . . . there.

Izzy raised a brow and asked, "You just going to leave it there?"

"Well," he answered honestly, "it is comfortable."

That's when Gwenvael slapped his hand off and Briec and Fearghus began pummeling him, slamming him to the table. He didn't have to look to know Izzy had walked away.

Chapter 12

Izzy grabbed some clean clothes from her old room and went down to one of the lakes to take a bath. She scrubbed herself clean in the cold water, trying not to think too much about having Éibhear's hand on her. It surprised her, the effect that one touch had had on her. Surprised and annoyed her. She shouldn't have any feelings about Éibhear's hands being anywhere—except maybe a slight loathing.

Izzy went under the water once more, hoping the cold would make her forget everything. It didn't.

But as she walked to shore, she smiled at the woman serenely waiting for her by her clothes.

"Lady Dagmar," she greeted.

"General Iseabail."

"Something wrong?"

"There is some . . . *thing* in my dog kennels. Eating metal, wood, and rocks. And shitting. *Everywhere.*"

"Is he shitting metal, wood, and rocks? Because that would be fascinating."

Prim lips pursed, Dagmar tapped one toe and Izzy giggled.

"I hate that thing, Izzy!" Dagmar finally exclaimed, laughing with her. "Hate it."

"He is loyal and I love him. You said the loyalty of a dog is all."

"I lied," the Northlander told Izzy flatly. "He's ugly. He farts. *Constantly*. He drools. He's always dragging that giant penis of his around!"

"How is that his fault? And what am I supposed to do about that? Force him to wear doggie leggings?"

"Well, do something because the first thing he did was escape from his run and then try to mount every one of my in-heat bitches he could get next to."

"Was Mum upset about that? Annwyl? Because they are Claimed by others."

The toe-tapping began again, but Dagmar was having a hard time with that smile. She couldn't quite hide it. "Not those bitches, dear niece. The four-legged ones."

"Ahh."

They both laughed and Izzy hugged her aunt. "Don't worry. I'll take him to my house. I'll probably stay there anyway while I'm home."

"You're getting me soaked," Dagmar complained, playfully pushing Izzy away. "I can't be coldly calculating when I'm covered in lake water."

"Never fear, dear aunt. You're coldly calculating no matter what you do."

"You're staying at your house?" Dagmar asked, never one to let something slip by her.

"I like my house. Gwenvael had it built for me."

"He did. But you only stay there when you're meeting with some man—"

"Dagmar!"

"—or you're avoiding another fight with your mother. But usually it takes a little time for you two to get into a good, frothy battle of wills, and I haven't heard anything about you sleeping with anyone at the moment—"

"Wait. How do you know when I'm sleep—"

"—so that leaves a third option, which I'm going to assume is you're avoiding dear, sweet Éibhear."

"Dear, sweet *who?*"

Éibhear stepped out of the tub and grabbed a giant cloth to dry himself off.

Home only a few hours and already two fights with his brothers and a tit grab with Izzy. Although the tit grab had been an accident. Not that his brothers wanted to hear that. They just wanted to believe he was the kind of bastard who would run around grabbing a woman's breast without compunction.

Of course, if it had been anyone else, he would have immediately released that breast, but his hand *had been* comfortable. So what was a dragon to do? Besides, Izzy hadn't seemed to mind too much and it was her breast after all.

But leave it to his kin to turn something so innocent into the worst offense ever known to dragon or god.

Bastards.

Éibhear pulled on a pair of black leggings. Clothes that he'd left behind a decade ago and, to his annoyance, his brothers were right. He'd grown since he last stayed in this room. His hips were still narrow, but his thighs barely fit into the material and he wouldn't discuss how the bottom of the leggings did not reach to his ankles. They barely covered his calves.

"I need to get new clothes," he decided, reaching for the things he'd just taken off to have his bath. He loathed putting them back on since they were covered in travel dirt, but at least they didn't make him look foolish. His kin made him look foolish enough, no need to assist them further with that. But before he could get his hands on the calfskin leggings, there was a knock at his door.

"What?"

The door opened and the wounded male he'd seen earlier in the Great Hall walked in. Éibhear wouldn't say he recognized the tall boy as someone he knew, but he recognized those black eyes.

The boy looked him over. Smirked. "Uncle Éibhear?"

"Talan."

"Yeah." He walked in, closing the door behind him. "Aunt Dagmar said you may need these." The boy handed him a stack of clothes. "And I see by those leggings . . . she was right."

Éibhear chuckled, shrugged. "I seem to have outgrown the clothes I left behind."

"Clearly."

While Éibhear changed into the clothes—and thank the gods, they actually fit—the boy lifted the fur cape Éibhear had lying across the bed.

"What is this made of?"

"Buffalo. They're all over the Ice Lands, used for their meat and hides. There's little the Ice Landers don't make good use of."

"What's it like there?"

"Cold. Very, very cold."

"Did you hate it there?"

"No." And realizing that surprised Éibhear. "I wouldn't like to set up a cave there. Or live there in my later years." He moved his shoulder around and cringed when he added, "Our scales tend to freeze together. I can't express to you how unpleasant that can be. Especially when you're about to go into a fight."

Finally dressed in clothes that fit and weren't made of rough animal hide, Éibhear sighed. He'd forgotten what it was like to put his human form in nicer clothes; to sleep in an actual bed, to eat food he hadn't beaten into submission himself.

"So you're the infamous Éibhear the Contemptible," the boy said.

Éibhear faced his nephew. "I am?"

"That's not your name?"

"That's my name, didn't know I was infamous."

The boy studied him, arms crossed over his chest. For someone so young, he was amazingly confident.

"Would you train with me?" Talan asked.

"If you'd like."

"I watched you kick the shit out of my uncles and father. That's what I'd like to learn."

"That was just brotherly—"

"Abuse?"

"Some might say. But I prefer good-natured—"

"Brawling? Battery? Assault? Destruction?"

Éibhear shrugged. "Depends who you talk to."

"So no one knows why I'm here?" Izzy asked while she dried off her body.

"You weren't summoned by any of us, that I know of," Dagmar said, "but I am glad you're here."

"Why?"

"I have concerns."

Uh-oh. Dagmar didn't mention "concerns" unless she was terribly worried.

"Concerns about what?"

Dagmar sighed, looked off. "Oh, where to begin . . ."

Uh-oh.

They invaded quietly, like the Mì-runach. Slipping into his room while he talked to the boy. First, there was Talan's twin, Talwyn. A beauty that one, but dangerous. Unbelievably dangerous. Like her mother. But in those green eyes there was none of the love combined with insanity that Éibhear had always seen in Annwyl's. What kind of leaders would these twins make? Both seemed surprisingly cold, but curious. Like jungle cats that toy with the wounded deer found lying by a tree. They poke with their paws, bite down with their fangs. They test, taste, and wonder . . . is it worth tormenting anymore? Or is it already dead?

But then he met his youngest niece, Rhianwen. She was now called Rhi by everyone and just sixteen winters. She was, in a word, beautiful. Stunning. And he could see why his brothers were so protective of her. Not only because of her beauty—beauty could be found anywhere. It was that wonderful, bright smile; that inherent innocence; and that intense goodness. Her warmth. While her cousins sized Éibhear up like a very large bug they'd found under their beds, Rhi came to him, arms opened wide, tears in her eyes.

"I'm so glad to see you again after all these years, Uncle Éibhear." She hugged him tight, arms around his waist, head resting against his chest. "You've been greatly missed." She sniffed and leaned her head back to look up at him. "Although no one but my mother and aunts will ever admit that to you."

He kissed her forehead and hugged her back. "Don't worry. I already know that."

"He'll train us," Talan told his sister.

"Good. Something new to learn."

"Later," Rhi chastised. "At least let him get comfortable before you come at him with your stupid requests."

"Fine."

"Whatever."

Then the twins were gone, quickly, quietly. It was a little more than frightening.

"Don't let them worry you," Rhi said, although he hadn't

spoken a word. "They're not nearly as horrible as everyone thinks they are . . . but they are annoying."

"Good to know."

She stepped back, took his hands into hers. "I've heard you're a bit of a reader."

"More than a bit."

Rhi grinned. "So am I! Although I love to draw as well. I bet we're just alike, you and I!"

Uh . . . all right.

Dagmar blew out a breath, smoothed down the front of her unadorned dress. She no longer wore a kerchief over her long hair as she had when she'd first arrived, even though it was custom among the Northland women. Instead she wore her hair in a simple, single braid that reached down her back— something, Izzy was sure, Gwenvael delighted in unbraiding every night. But other than that, she looked no different from the Northlander who'd first arrived with Gwenvael all those years ago. She still wore her simple gray gowns, with fur boots in the winter and leather boots in the summer. And her spectacles. Gods, who could forget those spectacles that Gwenvael spoke of as if they were breathing human beings? As always, they were perched primly on her nose, while those sparkling gray eyes watched Izzy. Calculating. Dagmar always calculated.

"I'm . . . concerned."

"About Lord Pombray's son?"

"Oh, gods no." She rolled her eyes. "That boy and your sister are the least of my worries."

Izzy dropped to the ground and pulled on socks and her boots. "So it's the twins then."

"It's Talwyn. She's become . . . close. To the Kyvich. Especially Commander Ásta."

Izzy shrugged, tugging her boots on and wondering if she should get another pair now that she was home for a bit.

"Well, she's young. And Ásta is an attractive woman." She stood and stomped her feet to get the boots perfectly fitted. "I'm sure it's nothing to be worried about. Some women are just more comfortable with other women. It doesn't mean she can't breed with a male when she's ready to have a child and then she and the other woman can raise the child togeth—"

"No, no." Dagmar eyed Izzy. "That is *not* what I meant, Iseabail."

"Oh." Izzy shrugged. "Then what's your concern? They were her protectors. Of course Talwyn's close to them, just as I was close to my protectors." When Dagmar only stared at her, Izzy said, "You think they want something more?"

"She's a powerful girl. Her fighting skills . . . and I've been told she has untapped Magick about her. Not at the same level as Rhi does, of course, at least she hasn't shown it in front of any of us. But that Magick is something the Kyvich would be drawn to." True. The Kyvich were warrior witches who pulled their number mostly from outsiders. But . . . "They only take children, Dagmar. That's what I was told."

"And that's true." Dagmar adjusted her spectacles. "In the Northlands there are stories of the Kyvich coming in from the Ice Lands and snatching female newborn babes from their mothers' arms. But, like most, power is what draws them."

"And Talwyn has power."

"Much of it."

"And my sister?"

"She is a Nolwenn witch by blood. The Kyvich barely speak to her."

"And Talan is male."

Dagmar smirked. "Very."

"I see. Like uncle, like nephew?"

"He hasn't quite racked up the same body count with

women as Gwenvael the Handsome, but he's clearly working on it."

Izzy picked up her bag, shoving her dirty clothes and weapons into it. Then she hooked her arm with Dagmar's and the pair headed back to the castle.

"Do you want me to talk to Talwyn?"

"I don't know. To be blunt, Izzy, whether Talwyn stays here or goes off and becomes a Kyvich means very little to me. I love her, but I have no illusions about my niece."

"But . . . ?"

"It's Annwyl."

Of course it was Annwyl. A brilliant warrior, a benevolent queen, but get on the wrong side of her and she'd been known to decimate entire battalions with nothing more than her sword and rage.

"You're worried about what she'll do."

"We don't want the Kyvich seeing us as enemies. That I do know. I've been trying to read up on all their past dealings with other monarchs to ensure we don't cross any lines we're unaware of, but it's not like there's much out there about the Kyvich. They mostly keep to themselves."

"Well, let me see what I can find out. Knowing Talwyn, she's simply using them to learn new fighting skills."

Dagmar sighed. "I truly hope that's all it is."

Éibhear lifted his niece so she could reach the book high on a shelf.

"Got it?"

"Yes!"

Smiling, he lowered Rhi.

"Here." She handed the book to him. "I think you'll like this."

"Did Annwyl like it?"

"Of course not. There was no war, death, spies, or

dry historic details about war, death, or spies. Just romance."

"Perfect." He leaned down and kissed her on the cheek. But before he could stand again, she wrapped her arms around his neck and hugged him tight.

"I'm glad you're home, Uncle Éibhear. It's been so very long."

"I know. But I'll be back more, I think." He hugged her, making sure not to squeeze her too tightly. She was such a little thing and he worried that he'd break her. "Are you all right, Rhi?"

She sighed. Heavily. One of those sighs he remembered her making when she was still just a babe. At an age when one should never have those kind of deep, meaningful sighs. But, unlike his whiner brothers, she didn't sigh simply because she was annoyed at Éibhear's breathing or because the horse for their dinner had run away. When Rhi sighed, it was usually for a very good reason.

She released him and stepped back, head down. "I'll need your help with Mum and Izzy."

"Your mum, I can definitely help with. Izzy . . ."

Her gaze snapped up and locked with his. That beautiful, earnest face. Éibhear couldn't imagine what he'd do to the male who broke the heart that went with that face.

"You don't understand, Uncle Éibhear. You do have a great effect on Izzy."

"Rhi, I haven't seen your sister in years. She says she's forgiven me . . . but I'm not sure I believe her. I think she hates me."

"She's never hated you. That's the problem."

Surprised by her words, Éibhear said, "Well . . . I'll, uh, keep that in mind. But this isn't about that Pombray boy is it? Because your mother and Izzy will be the least of your worries—"

"No, no." She waved that away. "It's something else."

"Perhaps you should tell me what it is so I can devise a plan to handle the two most stubborn women in the world."

Rhi sighed again. "I will, but later." She started to walk away, stopped, and added, "But don't leave." Walked a few more steps, stopped. "I mean, don't leave for a really long time. Like a month or so." A few more steps, another stop. "I mean, if it's terribly important, of course you should go. I'll completely understand. But I'd appreciate if you could hang around, at least somewhere in the vicinity. . . ." Rhi stopped. "Now I'm getting on my own nerves."

Chuckling, Éibhear walked up to his niece and held out his hand. "I know what will get your mind off such great worries, little niece."

Rhi's smile grew, her nose crinkling as her small hand slipped into his. "Book shopping?" she asked hopefully.

"Book shopping."

Izzy gawked at the table. "Really?" she asked the dragon next to her.

He shrugged massive shoulders. "It got a little out of hand."

"A *little*?"

He winced, gazing at the books that had been delivered by three carriages. "Well, you like to read, don't you?" And she heard the begging in his voice.

"Not really." She patted his shoulder. "Have fun putting them all away in the library."

"You're not going to help?"

She headed toward the big doors. "I'd rather set myself on fire."

"I can manage that well enough," he muttered.

Izzy stopped, looked at him over her shoulder. "What was that?"

He sighed. "Nothing."

"That's what I thought."

That's when Izzy noticed the boy. He stood in the corner, probably hiding there, hoping Éibhear wouldn't notice him. She could understand that. When he was focusing on something, Éibhear had a brutal frown. Made him look like the mass-murdering bastard she'd heard him called over the last few years.

"Why don't you help him with all those books . . . uh . . . ?"

Eyes wide, the boy stuttered out, "Fred . . . Frederik. Reinholdt."

"Dagmar's nephew." Although it was somewhat easy to tell that just from the look of the boy. Pale, like he'd never seen the suns, and tall, like most of the Northland men. Not bad looking but a bit fearful to be around this brutish lot. "Can you read?"

"A bit." He glanced away. "It's a bit of a struggle."

"No matter. You learn to read by doing and gods know, Éibhear needs the help." She took the boy by his shoulder and led him to the table. "This has to be cleaned up by dinnertime."

Éibhear blew out a breath. "Damn. Dinner."

Laughing, Izzy left.

Éibhear glared at the cute ass walking out of the Great Hall, then refocused on the boy. "Frederik?"

"Yes, sir."

"Nice to meet you. Name's Éibhear."

He frowned up at him. "You're very . . . tall."

"So are you . . . for a human boy."

"You're really a dragon?"

"I am."

"And the lady?"

"Lady?"

"Who just left."

Éibhear laughed. "I wouldn't call Izzy a lady. Might get you punched. That's General Iseabail, Daughter of Talaith."

"You have women generals? She goes into combat? And you let her?"

"What you'll learn, lad, is that you don't *let* the females of the Southlands do a damn thing. You simply get out of their way or pray they don't run you down." He motioned to the books. "Let's just get these to the library. We'll organize them later."

By the time Iseabail walked down the Great Hall stairs, Morfyd was coming around the corner. She wore the white robes of a healing cleric, her bag of herbs and spell paraphernalia over her shoulder.

"Morfyd!" Izzy waved and Morfyd rushed over, the pair hugging each other tight.

"Izzy! I heard you were back. I'm so glad to see you." Morfyd stepped away, looked her over. "You're too thin."

"Am I?" She glanced down at herself, frowned. "Really?"

"To my eyes. Where are you off to?"

"To my house. I'm exhausted."

"You're not coming to dinner tonight?"

"No, but Uncle Fearghus said there might be something in a day or two, and that I'll be attending." She grinned. "There will be dancing."

"Of course. Now, I'm glad you're here. Your sister has plans to spend time with Lord Pombray's son."

"Isn't Brastias escorting them?"

"He is, but I'll need you to manage your father. He's already burned the poor boy and . . . Iseabail! Stop laughing!"

"You know how Daddy is. Remember Lord Crom? All he did was put his hand on my lower back and the next thing I knew he was flying over the tops of the trees and Daddy was dropping him from his talons. . . ." She thought a moment and asked, "How is he anyway?"

"Dead. It wasn't the fall that killed him. Or even the landing. It was Briec following up the whole thing with enough flame to wipe out a village." She patted Izzy's arm. "We didn't tell you that part at the time. It would have just upset you."

Appalled, Izzy demanded, "But he barely touched me!"

"And you were barely sixteen. It was completely inappropriate and Briec had warned him off. Twice. But he kept staring. The touching was the final straw. Now Lord Pombray's son is your sister's age, but that won't matter much to your father."

Izzy folded her arms over her chest. "What else have you lot hidden from me over the years?"

"Oh, lots of things. But it was always for the best."

Before Izzy could argue that point, Morfyd asked, "So what brings you here? I thought we'd see you closer to the fall harvests."

"I have no idea."

"You have no idea why you're here?" Morfyd frowned. "So you just . . . wandered away from battle?"

"You know how my mind wanders. . . ."

"Izzy."

Izzy chuckled and replied, "Ragnar sent Éibhear to retrieve me, but Éibhear doesn't know why. My mother doesn't know why. No one seems to know why. But here I am."

"And that doesn't concern you?"

"Keita has always said I'm too pretty to be concerned with anything."

"Gods!" Morfyd exclaimed. "If you start taking advice from that small-brained idiot—"

"I'm joking. Of course I'm concerned. But it's not like I was summoned to a pit in one of the hells. At worst, I'm home for whatever problem may come up." She patted her aunt's shoulder. "Don't worry. With me and Brannie here, I'm sure everything will be just fine."

She stepped around Morfyd and headed toward the kennels.

"Good. And Izzy?"

Izzy stopped and faced her aunt.

"Have you heard from Rhydderch Hael?"

Taking a breath, Izzy outright lied. "No."

Her aunt studied her. "You let me know if you do."

"Of course," Izzy stated, again heading toward the kennels.

She had no idea why she'd just lied to Morfyd, but her gut had told her that, at least for the moment, it was the best idea all around.

Chapter 13

Éibhear, as was his way, got lost in the books. Instead of merely piling them in the corner of the library and going to take a nap before evening meal, he ended up attempting not only to organize the new books he'd brought to the library but the ones that had been there before Annwyl's father's time.

To be honest, he'd thought Dagmar's nephew would have wandered away by now—he seemed a constantly dazed boy—but, like Éibhear, he seemed comfortable in the library, quickly and easily taking orders on where to place books or what shelves to clean off so they could start again.

It was a nice, quiet time such as Éibhear realized he hadn't enjoyed in quite a while. As one of the Mì-runach, spending more than a few hours reading, once or twice a week, was frowned upon. "Who has time for books when there's drinking and whoring and killing to do?" Old Angor would demand before slapping some book Annwyl or Talaith had sent to Éibhear from Éibhear's hands and shoving him toward the closest pub.

Not that Éibhear minded drinking and whoring and killing. He didn't. But he'd always felt that reading and book buying fit easily into that list as well.

Frederik handed over another book to Éibhear. "I wish I could read better."

"Spend time in here and you'll be able to. Reading is learned by doing. It's a skill almost all can have to some extent as long as they practice." He leaned in and added low, "Besides, it's a wonderful escape from your family when necessary." He shrugged and stood tall, looking at the spine of the book. "Unless, of course, they track you down and—"

"My dear sweet son!"

Éibhear bit back a sigh and slowly faced the front of the library. He smiled. "Hello, Mum."

Izzy had just stirred the simmering stew once again when she heard the knock.

Grinning, she dropped the ladle on the table and charged across the small room. She snatched the door open and grinned.

Brannie held up two bottles of Bercelak's ale, her smile wide. But it was what was behind Brannie—or, in this case, *who*—that had Izzy pushing past her friend and straight into the arms of the dragon standing there.

"Celyn!"

Big arms tightened around her waist, lifting Izzy from the ground and holding her tight. "My little Izzy."

"Pack it in, you two," Brannie said, walking into the house. "There's stew and bread and ale. . . . We can save the hugging for later."

Éibhear hugged his mother, smiling when she whispered in his ear, "Oh, how I've missed you, my son."

"I've missed you too, Mum. So much."

"Did you miss me too, *boy*?" Éibhear could hear the sneer

in that voice, his own lip starting to curl in annoyance as he spotted his father in the doorway.

His mother quickly pushed him back and asked, "And who is this young lad?"

Father and son snarled at each other until his mother shoved Éibhear's shoulder. "Introduce us, son."

"This is Frederik Reinholdt. Lady Dagmar's nephew."

"Ohhh, well aren't you a strapping lad!" his mother exclaimed. She motioned Frederik closer. "I'm Queen Rhiannon, but you can call me Queen Rhiannon."

Gazing at Rhiannon, his mouth slightly open, Frederik took the hand Rhiannon offered and bowed low from the waist. "My . . . my lady."

Rhiannon's smile was wide as she leaned in and said, "Aren't you just adorable! I could just eat you right up!"

"*Mum!*"

"Well, I don't mean literally!"

Izzy took the stew off the fire and placed it in the middle of the table, while Brannie put bowls and spoons out and Celyn poured the ale. It was an old routine that they'd started a few years back.

Hard to believe, though, considering all that had happened.

Although Izzy knew many didn't believe her, she'd never planned for things to end up as they had among her, Éibhear, and Celyn. She'd been young and she'd been . . . curious. There had been a few among her fellow soldiers who'd offered to satisfy that curiosity for her. Some politely and some with an outright, "I'll fuck ya proper," which did nothing but cause Izzy to reach for the closest weapon or simply throw a punch. But it was Celyn who'd kept her interest merely by being sweet, funny, and confident. He didn't offer anything because he didn't need to. And, one night, alone in the woods, they took the next logical—at least to her—step.

But it had never occurred to Izzy that things would turn out so badly. Then again, she'd never thought Éibhear would find out. And if he did find out, she hadn't thought he'd really ever care. And although the sixteen-year-old Izzy, who'd fallen hard for the dragon from the first time she'd seen him and his blue hair, had wanted to believe that he'd cared about her, that he'd been jealous, the more jaded, realistic nineteen-year-old she'd been at the time knew better. Knew it was more about ego and competing with his cousin than it was about Izzy.

Thankfully, though, that was a long time ago and much had changed. At least for Izzy it had.

"So have you seen my cousin?" Celyn asked, after he'd finished his stew, pushing his now empty bowl away and leaning back in his chair, long legs stretched out, hand around a cup of ale.

"He escorted us home."

"And how did that go?"

Izzy tried to drag her fingers through the tangled, dirty mess of Macsen's fur. It wasn't that she didn't groom him. She actually groomed him often, but by the time she was done combing through the back end, the front end was already a tangled, dirty mess again. But since the dog didn't seem to mind . . .

"Why do you ask?"

"Because I'm pathetically curious."

Izzy laughed. "At least you're honest."

"As one of the chosen Dragon Queen Personal Guard, I am bound in blood to be honest." He glanced off and added, "Unless the queen tells me to lie . . . which she has."

"Shocking," Brannie muttered, reaching for the bottle of ale to refill her cup.

"Ahhh, the jealousy of a sibling. So bitter about my assignment, dear Brannie?"

"No. Just tired of hearing Mum go on and on about it."

"Oh, little sister, you shouldn't be so sensitive. You know Mum just loves me more than she loves you—ow! That's my shin, human female!"

"I know!" Izzy snapped, sorry she'd gone barefoot for the evening because Celyn's shins were like granite.

"You may not realize this, brother, but Izzy is loyal to *me*. So don't make me unleash her on you."

"And now you're making fun of me," Izzy complained.

"No. It's a serious threat," Celyn admitted. "Used by many in the family. Especially Briec. He loves threatening those who annoy him—"

"Which is everyone," Brannie stated while grabbing the last loaf of bread and tearing it into three pieces.

"—with his beautiful eldest daughter who will rip the scales from your back and tear the still-beating heart from your chest before spitting on your corpse."

Izzy put her hand to her chest, her voice trembling as she fought tears. "That is the *sweetest* thing I've ever heard."

"He adores both his girls."

"I needed to hear that." She took the chunk of bread from Brannie. "I've been feeling a little . . . bad today."

"Bad?" Celyn's teasing expression changed to one of concern. "About what?"

"Éibhear told me that the family has been keeping him away because they didn't want him around when I was. And Daddy and Fearghus say that's mostly true. But they also said that Granddad forced Éibhear to join the Mì-runach and for the last ten years he's been stuck in the Ice Lands. No one should be stuck in the Ice Lands. No one."

Celyn and Brannie stared at her for a long moment, looked at each other, then back at her, both saying together, "*No*."

"No? What do you mean no?"

"No one tells the Mì-runach anything," Celyn explained. "Except for the queen. She tells them what she wants and the Mì-runach make it happen."

"Make it happen? How?"

Celyn shrugged. "Any way they want to. The Mì-runach end up in the Mì-runach because they won't follow orders. At least not any orders that come from anyone but the queen."

"If they can't follow orders then why—"

"No. I said they *won't* follow orders, not that they can't."

"That's even worse then."

"As warriors, they're often too good to not be used."

"That was our grandfather," Brannie added. "He was a mighty warrior but the worst among the rank and file. Before our grandmother—"

"He loved fucking and eating and drinking. And he loved a good battle. But he hated taking orders."

"Hated generals and commanders."

"Hated being up in the morning."

"Especially after a good night of fucking and drinking."

Izzy, laughing, asked, "So he joined the Mì-runach?"

"One doesn't join the Mì-runach."

"Not willingly," Brannie noted.

"So they're forced," Izzy surmised, again feeling bad about Éibhear's situation.

"More like given little option," Celyn replied. "It's usually a choice between the Mì-runach or the salt mines."

"Many take the salt mines."

"But if you survive the first two years of training . . . you become Mì-runach."

"Survive the training?"

"Which is hard enough, but when you're full Mì-runach, you still go into battle without armor—"

"—without colors."

"—without anyone really leading."

Shocked, hands pressed to her cheeks, Izzy asked, "Do they at least have weapons?"

"Sometimes, I guess." Celyn shook his head. "I'll be honest, Iz. It's not something I'd do."

"But . . ." And Izzy couldn't help but cringe in disbelief. "*Éibhear*?"

"After what happened to Austell the Red . . ." The young Dragonwarrior recruit had been killed during the final battle of the war against the Iron dragons. It was something that Izzy had heard Éibhear had taken very badly, for some reason blaming himself, but no one would ever tell Izzy exactly why. After a while she'd stopped asking because she had the feeling she didn't really want to know why Éibhear would blame himself.

"Well," Celyn finally went on, "my cousin was never quite the same."

"He was impossible to train. Refused to listen."

"Fought everyone. Éibhear was just angry."

"So Grandfather sent him to the Mì-runach?" Izzy said, motioning for the bottle of ale from Brannie.

"I wasn't surprised that Uncle Bercelak would send him," Celyn noted. "But I was surprised the queen let him go."

"Because it was Éibhear?"

"Because no dragon prince has ever been in the Mì-runach in any of its forms."

"Its forms?"

Brannie shrugged. "The Mì-runach have been around nearly as long as dragon armies have. But they didn't have an official name until Grandfather Ailean joined. Before that they were just, 'Those crazy bastards that'll kill for a pint and a whore.'"

"Lovely."

Celyn laughed. "They're a bit more organized now, but they're still those crazy bastards. And I have to say that from what I've heard, Éibhear fits in perfectly."

"The rumor is that the entire Ice Land sighed in relief when Éibhear the Contemptible finally left their territories."

Izzy, deciding she didn't want to drink anymore, pushed her

half-filled mug away. "So then you don't think the Mì-runach were forced to keep him away—"

"The Mì-runach kept him in the Ice Lands because that's where they were needed these last few years. And I'm sure with his reputation and his skills in battle, no one in the Mì-runach would have been fine with Éibhear just flittin' off to a family feast or for your sister's birthday celebrations."

"When you're Mì-runach, they *are* your family. Only your mate matters more." Brannie thought a moment. "If any of them actually ever have one."

"So, his brothers ordering the Mì-runach to keep him in the Ice Lands for the last ten years . . . ?"

"It never happened."

Izzy dropped back into her chair. "Then why the hells would they let him believe that they did?"

Celyn reached over and patted her hand. "Because your father and uncles are cruel bastards, luv. How could you not have figured that out by now?"

Izzy snatched her hand back. "Oh, shut up."

Queen Rhiannon sat down beside her youngest offspring on the hill that overlooked the castle of Garbhán Isle and the surrounding grounds. The last time she'd sat here with her son, he'd been making the very nasty transition from child to adult. Now, as she looked up at the profile of that face, she saw what that change had cost him. There were no longer any soft lines there. No longer any perfect, smooth human skin. Instead, his jaw was strong and she could see that it had been broken at least once. His cheekbones were now sharp, and he had scars on his neck and face, which meant steel blades had cut past hard scales to the flesh underneath.

When she'd sent tasks to the Mì-runach, she'd had to struggle not to think of her son possibly being part of the team they'd send in to accomplish them. The thought of him running, screaming, into enemy territory, wearing no armor, and destroying all in his way until he reached his goal was something that often kept her up at nights. Not only what might physically happen to him, but what could change him. What could turn him into a dragon she'd rather not speak to, or hear from, or ever admit was her offspring.

In other words, would being a Mì-runach make him into a bastard?

Of course it had been hard to tell at evening meal. What with her mate and elder male offspring picking on him so. Éibhear hadn't said much. Just kept eating, until he'd finally gotten up and walked out. Then she'd been forced to hear all the arguing between her sons and their mates. Honestly, did that ever *end*? But at least those human females did what they could to protect Éibhear.

Rhiannon readied her speech. The speech she'd given more than once over the years to Éibhear and, when they were much younger, to her older sons. The one that included things like:

"I'm sure your father didn't mean that."

"Of course your father loves you."

"No. He didn't try to sell your egg to the highest human bidder."

"And of course, he never tried to kill you while you slept!"

She readied that speech, but before she could recite it as she'd been doing for the last few centuries, her son said, "Izzy didn't come to dinner."

Rhiannon blinked, closed her mouth. "No. Morfyd said she was tired and wanted to sleep."

"But she's not in her room."

"She has a house now."

Her son finally looked at her, those bright silver eyes curious . . . as always. Especially when it came to Iseabail.

"A house? Izzy has a house?"

"Gwenvael had it built for her. It's just outside of town."

Rhiannon leaned in a bit and said low, "I think she was feeling a little crowded here."

"Talaith?"

"The twins. They're appallingly nosey." When her son only stared at her, she added, "Not like me!"

He grunted and looked back out over the land. "I bought a castle."

"Whatever for?"

"I like sleeping in a bed."

"You can have beds in caves."

"I have a cave, too. But I wanted a castle."

She shook her head. "Just like your grandfather. I couldn't believe when your father kidnapped me and took me to Ailean's *castle* rather than a cave. Imagine! An entire dragon family *forced* to live in a castle."

"Must you always point out you were kidnapped by our father?"

"I was."

"Dad says you were tossed on his doorstep like so much royal trash. And you were haughty about it, too."

"I was not haughty. I'm just better than him. Once he understood that, we were fine."

And then, there it was. The thing she'd been missing for so long now. Éibhear the Blue smiled.

"I missed you, Mum."

"I missed you, too." She rested her head against his arm, marveling at the size of the muscle under her ear. "And I'm glad you're home. At least for a little while."

"Yeah. Me, too."

After her friends left, Izzy cleaned off the table, gave Macsen a break outside, and washed up. She was about to slip into bed when a knock on the door had her throwing a nightdress over her naked body and grabbing her sword. She cracked the door open a bit, but she immediately lowered her weapon.

"Yes?"

"I had a bad dream."

Izzy opened the door but blocked the way so her sister couldn't walk in. "You had a bad dream?"

"Yes."

"So you walked all the way over from the castle, in a nightdress and robe, so that you can sleep in my bed?"

"Yes."

"The stuffed bear is a nice touch."

"Thank you."

"And you came here alone?"

"No, no. The twins are with me."

Izzy leaned out and looked around. "The twins are where?"

"In the trees."

"Why . . ." Izzy glanced up, trying to understand this. "Why are they in the trees?"

"To sleep."

"They don't want to come in?"

"They like to sleep in trees. I, however, do not." Rhi tightened her arms around her body. "Getting colder . . ."

"You just expect me to kick Macsen out?"

"Macsen adores me!" Rhi pushed her way through. "You're so mean!"

Laughing, Izzy stepped out and said to the trees, while hoping not to disturb her nearby neighbors, "You can sleep on my floor."

"No thank you," came back to her. She shrugged and went inside, closing the door behind her but leaving it unlatched. She knew if the twins didn't come inside, they would stay in the trees all night, ensuring Rhi's safety.

Izzy walked into her bedroom to find her sister wrestling with Macsen on the bed, the dog trying to get the stuffed bear she'd brought along with her.

"Give it, you vile beast!"

"If you two aren't going to play nice . . ."

"You two?"

Macsen tore the bear from Rhi's hands, leaped off the bed, and began to prance around the room. Almost like a small horse.

"Now you're just being mean, Macsen!"

"That's it." Izzy held her hand out. "Toy. Now."

Macsen stopped, stared at her. "*Now.*"

He spit the toy at her feet and Izzy swiped it up, putting it on a shelf that, in theory, he shouldn't be able to reach.

"On the bed," she ordered. And to her sister, "Under the covers. No crowding."

Giggling, Rhi dived under the sheets. Knowing her sister was so happy to see her really did mean a lot to Izzy. As a general, there were days her men loved the sight of her, and other days when they absolutely dreaded it. But no matter the day, Rhi was always excited. Izzy got in the bed behind her sister.

"Your feet are freezing!" Rhi complained.

"Then you should have stayed in your own bed, whiner."

As soon as Izzy relaxed, Rhi was there, her arms wrapping around her sister's waist, her head against Izzy's shoulder.

"You were missed at dinner," Rhi said into the dark.

"I know. I'm sorry I didn't come." Izzy hugged her sister a little tighter. "I just . . . couldn't face it. I knew you'd understand."

"Oh, I did! I wish I could miss dinner more often." She was quiet for a moment, then added, "Uncle Éibhear looked particularly disappointed."

"Rhianwen—"

"Uh-oh. Full name used."

"Exactly. So hear me well, sister. There is nothing and will be nothing to discuss when it comes to *your* Uncle Éibhear. Do you understand?"

"I do."

"We can't mention him at all?" a male voice said from the dark and Izzy quickly realized that the twins were now in her room, on her bed. Stretched out across the bottom of it.

"I thought you two were going to sleep in the trees."

"It was less comfortable than we thought it would be," Talwyn said around a yawn.

"So we came in," Talan added.

"And where's the dog?"

"Between me and Talwyn."

Rolling her eyes, Izzy snapped at Macsen, "Good protection there, you dozy bastard."

"Ssssh," Talwyn whispered. "He's asleep."

Deciding there was no point in fighting this, she closed her eyes and tried to go to sleep.

She knew the attempt would be a waste of time, however, when the giggling started, followed by the complaining about the giggling, and then the snoring. By the gods, the snoring!

Chapter 14

"You look like battered shit." Light brown eyes glared up at him and Éibhear quickly held up his hands. "Just an observation."

"Well, you can take your observation and shove it up your big, fat—"

"Happy morn, Uncle Éibhear!" Rhi nearly shouted while jumping between him and Izzy.

"Hello, little niece." He leaned down and kissed her cheek. "You look beautiful this fine morning."

"'You look beautiful this fine morning,'" Izzy sneered under her breath while Rhi showed off her dress.

"I think it's the dress. Auntie Keita says the color brings out my eyes."

Abruptly, Izzy stood tall and looked quite awake. "Keita's here?"

"Aye. She arrived earlier this morning."

"Good. Now maybe I can find out who the bloody hells summoned me here."

"Are you still wondering about that?" Éibhear asked.

Izzy's jaw tensed. "As a matter of fact, I am. And stop talking to me."

"But you're so friendly."

Rhi pinched his arm and whispered, "Stop it."

"But she makes it so easy."

She sighed in disgust, and then looked behind Éibhear. "Morning, Frederik."

"Uh . . . morning . . ." The boy frowned and they watched him stand there . . . frowning.

Finally, fed up, Rhi reminded him, "Rhianwen."

"Right. Right." He nodded. "Rhianwen. I just have to remember . . ." Then he flicked his hand in her general area, and Éibhear decided it was probably best not to ask what that meant.

Instead, he focused on the training ring nearby. In the ring was Talwyn and one of the Kyvich witches. A woman with black tattoos on her face and arms, and, if Éibhear was seeing correctly, several fingers missing from both hands. It looked as if those fingers had been hacked off.

Talwyn hefted a huge sword, but her right shoulder was too low. The Kyvich saw that as well and rammed her maimed hand against it. A hit that would have broken the shoulder of a strong human male.

"Straighten your shoulders, idiot! I've told you before!"

Talwyn readjusted her shoulders. The Kyvich walked around her, punched her in the back of her thigh. "Strengthen that leg or I'll bleed you again."

Without even looking away from Talwyn and her trainer, Éibhear reached out and caught hold of Izzy's arm, yanking her back before she could clear the fence.

"Leave it," he ordered her.

"That's my cousin she's slapping around," Izzy snarled, trying to yank her arm away.

"You're exhausted, you haven't eaten, and you're still mad at me, even though you lied and said you weren't. You'll just take it out on that poor, deformed witch."

"She's not deformed. She lost those parts of herself in battle. And I am *not* still mad at you. Just let it go already."

"Rhi, you're an excellent judge of liars. Has your sister forgiven me or is she just mollycoddling me while planning to beat up some helpless witch trying to assist my young niece?"

Rhi looked back and forth between them and said, "Why don't I get you both some bread. You must be fairly starving! Be right back." Then she was off toward the castle, moving more quickly than Éibhear had thought she'd be able in that long dress."Release me," Izzy ordered, not bothering to try to pull her arm away.

"Not unless you promise to play nice with the mortal enemies of your mother's witch sisters."

Izzy reached for the gold dagger she had tucked into her sword belt and, laughing, Éibhear released her. She didn't pull the weapon, but she also didn't try to go over that fence again. Instead, they stood next to each other and watched.

"She's good," Éibhear finally admitted, after watching his niece for nearly half an hour.

"She's been good since birth. But she wants to be the best."

"And her brother?"

"He just wants to be good. His father seems to think fucking is all he aspires to"—*like his Uncle Gwenvael*, remained unspoken—"but I don't think he's remotely as straightforward as he likes to pretend. Kind of like your sister—"

"Good morn to my beloved family!"

"Keita," Izzy and Éibhear said together, and then laughed.

Izzy faced Keita.

"Oh, my sweet girl," Keita said, embracing Izzy. "Don't you just look beautiful?" She stepped back, gripping Izzy's hands, and looked her over. "Just, *just* beautiful."

Nodding, Izzy asked, "What do you want, Keita?"

"Nothing! Nothing at all." She pulled Izzy close, slinging

one arm around her shoulders. "I'm just so glad to see you. It's been ages!"

"It was ten months ago. You wanted something then, too."

"Aren't you going to greet me, sister?" Éibhear asked from behind them.

"I'm still not talking to you."

"Still? When did you start? The *not* talking, I mean, because usually I can't get you to shut up."

Snarling, Keita pulled her arm from Izzy's shoulders and spun around, pointing an accusing finger at her brother. "I have nothing to say to you. In fact, I'm sure I'll have nothing to say to you for the next several centuries!"

"And yet words keep spilling from your lips . . ."

Knowing well how ridiculous and pointless this could get, Izzy moved between the siblings and asked, "Keita, can you tell me who sent for me? Éibhear didn't seem to know."

"Well, I didn't tell Éibhear to do anything. I told him *not* to come get you. That was for me and Ragnar. So that way we could have spent some time with you, talked, and simply enjoyed—"

"Keita," Izzy cut in. "Who sent for me?"

"I did, which is why *I* was planning to come for you."

Izzy shook her head. "Why would you send for me? What's wrong?"

"Oh, nothing's wrong. Nothing at all." Again Keita put her arm around Izzy's shoulders, pulling her in close. "I'd just like you to meet someone I think you'll find really . . . interesting."

Izzy yanked away from the dragoness. "Are you telling me you summoned me from a gods-damn *war* so that I could meet some male?"

"Not just any male. A royal human!"

Afraid she'd smack her own beloved aunt in the mouth, Izzy started to walk away, but Keita yanked her back with a

G. A. Aiken

surprising amount of strength for a dragoness known for her physical weakness.

"Now, now. I know what you're thinking."

"You really don't. Or you'd get your hands off me."

"You're thinking that I'm talking about just some random, useless male that could barely give you an orgasm, much less beautiful jewels." Izzy tried to walk away once more, but again she was yanked back. "But I'm talking about a male with much more potential than that. And he likes your type."

Izzy was about to make another attempt at escape, but she stopped and looked at Keita. "My type?"

"Uh-huh. Your type."

Not sure what she could mean, Izzy tried to guess. "You mean . . . my coloring?" With so few people from the Desert Lands venturing into Dark Plains, Izzy and her mum were often considered "exotic" by some males, based on their skin color alone.

"No. I mean more your . . . build."

"My build?"

"She probably means those sturdy shoulders," Éibhear tossed in.

"Why are you speaking when I'm no longer talking to you?" Keita snapped.

"You keep saying that," he shot back, "but then you keep talking to me."

"I guess I'm unclear," Izzy cut in, desperate, "what you want from me."

"It sounds like she's trying to whore you out."

Keita swung on her brother, her small fist hitting him in the chest. And Izzy cringed from the sound of cracking bones and watched Keita grip her hand and stomp her feet. "Damn you, Éibhear!"

"Why are you yelling at me? I'm not the one trying to whore out our niece."

"I am not trying to whore out anyone! You overbearing bastard!"

"Now you're calling me names? Where did our love go, Keita?"

"Oh, shut up!"

"I think I'm going to get first meal," Izzy said.

"You're not going anywhere, Iseabail. Not until we're done talking."

Izzy looked at her aunt. "Trust me, Keita. We're done."

Dagmar sat at the table, going over what would be needed for security during the upcoming harvest festival. Bercelak had already promised her several troops' worth of his Dragonwarriors and all she needed now were the numbers from the human troops. Many more royals would be coming in and she wanted to ensure their protection. It would not do to have any of them assassinated while under the queen's protection.

"Dagmar."

"Oh, good. Brastias. Do you have those numbers I asked for?"

Morfyd's mate and Annwyl's commander general walked up to her. "I do. I just got them."

He handed over the parchment and Dagmar quickly examined the numbers of troops that could be spared, her mind immediately organizing.

"This will work well. Thank you."

"Of course." Brastias turned away from her but then suddenly faced her again. "And before I forget, I can assume you're done with those barracks? I'll need them for the commanders who will be coming in with their troops."

Dagmar looked up at the commander general. "What barracks?"

"The one you had your nephews in."

"I'll need to find out from them when they're planning to leave before I can say with any certainty—"

"But they've already left."

"What? What do you mean they've left?"

"They left last night some time. The gate guards told me."

Confused, Dagmar slowly got to her feet. "They left without a word? Are you sure they didn't just go hunting?"

"The guard asked because of Annwyl's hunting restrictions until after the feast. They said they were going back to the Northlands—and to tell you 'bye.'"

Talaith, who'd just walked over to the table with a bowl of hot porridge, stared at the pair. "Really? But I saw Frederik earlier. He was with Éibhear. Would they have left their cousin?"

Dagmar closed her eyes, her hands curling into fists, the parchment she still held crumpled into a ball. "Those *bastards!* They were planning this!"

She couldn't believe she'd been so stupid. That she hadn't seen this coming. That she'd wake up one morning and her nephews would be gone—but Frederik would remain. It was a family practice that the Reinholdts had become well known for. Bringing useless male family members for a little "visit" and then leaving without them. Dagmar knew all the signs. Knew that's what was coming. But she'd been in the Southlands for so long, dealing with much more rational beings than her own brothers, that she'd ignored all those signs. And now she was stuck with that . . . oh!

"Calm down," Talaith soothed.

Pressing her balled fists against her eyes—and her sudden headache—Dagmar snarled, "I will not calm down! I should have known they would do this. I should have known! They left that illiterate boy here with me and what the battle-fuck am *I* supposed to do with him?"

Brastias cleared his throat and Dagmar dropped her fists, not in the mood to hear any soothing words from him or

Talaith. But she found grey eyes much like her own gazing at her from the Great Hall entrance. Frederik standing there with Keita, Izzy, and Éibhear, the entire room now silent, even the servants aghast.

Yet before Dagmar could say a word, Keita folded her arms over her chest, looked up at Éibhear, and smugly said, "You can't tell me this is not worse than me whoring out Izzy."

Talaith blinked. "Wait . . . you did *what?*"

Yawning, Ragnar walked out of the room he shared with Keita and headed toward the Great Hall. As he neared the stairs, he saw Rhianwen sitting at the banister, her long legs poking through the free space between the wood bars and hanging over the side. Her hands were wrapped around the bars and she peeked through to watch something in the Great Hall below.

Ragnar sat down next to her and without looking at him, she smiled and said, "Hello, Uncle Ragnar."

"Hello, my dearest Rhi. What drama did I miss while I took a bath?"

"One second it was all quiet and I was just sitting here thinking." She glanced at him, smiled. "I sit and think a lot."

"I know. I like that about you."

"Then Uncle Brastias came in and told Auntie Dagmar that her nephews had left in the middle of the night and left Frederik behind."

Ragnar winced. Such a Northlander thing to do and the only sign of weakness that any Northland male—of any species—was willing to show. Although they didn't believe in killing the weaker ones of their Horde, they weren't above "visiting" a relative with the weaker member and then leaving them.

"Poor Frederik," Rhi sighed. "I'd feel horrible if my kin just *left* me."

"It's not the kindest thing, Rhi, but trust me when I say, it was in Frederik's best interest. My own father did it to me when I was barely ten winters old. He left me with Meinhard's father for what he said would be a few days. . . . I didn't see him again until I was nearly ninety. And you know what? Best thing that ever happened to me. And I'm guessing Frederik being here . . . best thing that ever happened to him, too."

"Perhaps, but Auntie Dagmar was not happy." She dropped her voice to a whisper, although he didn't know why she bothered, with all the screaming coming from below. "She yelled something about the illiterate boy and Frederik was standing there!"

"Oooh. That's not good."

"I don't think she meant it as it sounded, but you could tell it probably bothered him."

"Probably."

"But before anyone could apologize to him, Keita said something about whoring Izzy out and it was all downhill from there."

Ragnar nodded, looked off.

"It's all right to laugh," Rhi said. So he did.

"I love that female!"

Rhi joined him. "I know."

"What would possess her?"

"She seemed to think it wasn't as bad as what Auntie Dagmar said. Mum didn't agree. They've been at it ever since. Izzy's been trying to calm everyone down. . . . It's not working."

"Should I go and help?"

"I wouldn't." She reached over and picked up a small tray. "One of the servants brought me cheese and bread. Here. Have some. I find it makes the viewing even better."

"I agree." He chose a slice of cheese and a slice of bread to put it on. "Now all this drama aside, how are you doing?"

Rhi sighed and turned her head to look at him, resting her

temple against the wood bar. "Not as well as I'd like, Uncle Ragnar. I think . . . it's time."

"I think you're right."

"They'll never agree."

"But your sister's here now. Maybe she can help."

"Perhaps." Violet eyes lowered. "But I'm afraid."

"I know, Rhi."

"At some point . . . I much fear I'm going to end up killing someone."

Yes, Ragnar thought. *You probably will.*

While Izzy struggled to calm down her mother and Keita, Éibhear turned around and escorted Frederik outside to the stairs. He crouched in front of the boy.

"I need you to do me a favor."

"It's all right," the boy said. "I knew they were planning this. At least I guessed it. I just feel bad for Aunt Dagmar."

"Don't. She's got a lot on her mind. I doubt any of this has to do with you at all. But I do need you to check on something for me. My three friends, I haven't seen them since last night. Can you go into town and find them for me?"

He nodded and Éibhear gave him a leather bag with some gold coins.

"What's this for?"

"Just in case. Trust me. Ask for Aidan. He usually talks for all of them."

"I'll take care of it."

"Thank you."

Éibhear watched the boy walk down the stairs. Nothing worse than finding out your own kin don't want you. He didn't blame Dagmar as much as those ridiculous brothers and nephews of hers.

Standing tall, Éibhear headed back into the Great Hall, meeting Izzy at the doorway.

"Can't stand it anymore?" he asked.

"They're not letting me get a word in. I'm going to see if I can find Brannie."

"Then dress shopping? So you can woo Keita's friend?"

Her lip curled, eyes narrowing. He was glad to see her look of disgust. He didn't want to think about her even considering involving herself in whatever Keita was up to.

Without another word, she walked out, and Briec and Fearghus walked in. They stood on either side of Éibhear.

"What are they arguing about now?" Briec asked.

And Éibhear could have just said, "Oh . . . nothing to worry about." He could have.

He didn't.

"Keita wants to whore out your eldest daughter."

Confused, Briec frowned, but Keita heard Éibhear and spun around, stomping her tiny, bare foot.

"Éibhear! Stop saying that! I'm not trying to whore her out!"

"Then what the hells are you trying to do?" Briec demanded, knowing their sister well enough to suspect that if she was bothering to defend herself, there was a chance she was doing *exactly* what she was trying to say that she wasn't doing.

And now that Briec had taken over arguing with Keita, Talaith stepped out. She stopped by Éibhear's side. "Where did Izzy go?"

"She said to find Brannie."

"All right. Thanks."

She started to walk off, but Éibhear took a quick step back, leaning down to get a good look at her face. "Everything all right, Talaith? This thing with Keita—"

Talaith quickly dismissed that with a wave and an eye roll. "Don't worry," she said, reaching up and patting his shoulder. "I'm fine." She pulled her hand away, then reached up and patted his shoulder again. Then his entire arm. "Gods, Éibhear."

"What?" he asked, looking down at his arm.

But she didn't answer, just walked off in search of her daughter.

Izzy heard her name called and stopped, turning. Her mother ran up to her.

"Do you have some time to talk?" Talaith asked.

"About Keita? Really?"

"Not Keita. I'm letting your father deal with that." She stepped closer, glanced around, and lowered her voice. "It's about Rhi."

"My house? I'll make us some tea."

Her mother nodded. "Sounds perfect."

Arm in arm, mother and daughter walked to Izzy's house. And although they chatted amiably, Izzy knew her mother well enough to know that something was bothering her. Something that had nothing to do with Keita's latest outrageous political maneuver.

Once at the house, Izzy sat her mother down at the table and pulled out some cake that she'd bought for the dinner she'd had with Celyn and Brannie the evening before. She cut several pieces and put them on a plate before her mother. Then she went about making the tea.

By the time Izzy poured the tea and sat down at the table cattycorner from her mother, it was easy to see how distressed she was. Taking her mother's hands in her own, Izzy said, "Mum . . . what is it?"

"I'm so glad you're home. I need your help."

"Tell me. What do you need?"

"I'll need your help with your father. You're so good with him."

"Anything, Mum. Just tell me."

"Your sister . . ."

"What about her?" Izzy pushed.

"Her skills as a witch . . . they're . . ." Talaith licked her lips, took a breath. "I want to send her to her grandmother for training. Proper training."

Izzy winced. "Grandmum, eh?" She shrugged. "That won't be easy. But I'm sure I can come up with something to get Dad to agree. Although it'll be hard for Rhi on Devenallt Mountain, being unable to fly . . . wait. Can she fly?"

Talaith shook her head. "No, no. Not your grandmum. Your grandmother." Talaith licked her lips again and admitted, "*My* mother."

Izzy stared at her mother for a long moment. Then, when she truly understood what she was saying, Izzy flung her mother's hands away and roared, "*Have you lost your fucking mind?*"

"That is enough!" Dagmar snarled, stepping between Briec and Keita and swinging her arms in an attempt to stop the ridiculous slap fight between siblings.

"Your lady is very brave," Éibhear stated to Gwenvael before taking a bite out of the fruit he held.

"She is. I've seen her face down some of the worst tyrants with absolutely no fear."

"You mean Dad?"

"He was one." Gwenvael glanced at him. "Did you start all this?"

"I'd really say that Keita started it, but I did escalate the argument to the free-for-all you see before you."

"Nicely handled, little brother. I'm usually the only one who creates this level of discord."

"I'd found that creating discord, as you call it, among the Ice Landers, made them much easier to kill because they were so distracted. I have to admit . . . I've used that to my advantage."

Gwenvael put his hand to his heart. "Are you saying that *I* helped you become a better killer?"

"You have, brother. You have."

"I'm surprisingly proud of that."

Dagmar faced Keita. "I thought I was to handle Lord Madock."

"You were taking too long and once I discovered his taste for women with muscular thighs bigger than his entire body, I thought of Izzy."

"Wait," Briec said. "Are you saying you want Lord Madock dead?"

"You're just getting that?"

"And you expected Izzy to kill him? A man she doesn't even know?"

"All Izzy does every day is kill," Keita snapped back. "She kills and she orders others to kill. So why are we acting like she's some weak little child I'm trying to marry off?"

"Why didn't you just ask her that then?" Dagmar wanted to know. "To take care of Madock? Rather than this pretending you want her to meet and entertain a man more than twice her senior?"

Keita shrugged. "Celyn was twice her senior and no one seemed to have a problem."

Gwenvael sucked his tongue against his teeth.

"What's wrong?" Éibhear asked him.

"I'm sad Talaith wasn't here for that one. It would have led to a lovely fistfight."

"A fight Keita would have lost."

"Gods, yes. She's so busy protecting her face, Talaith just hits her with repeated body shots until she passes out."

Izzy leaned back in her chair and gazed at her mother, her mouth slightly open. "How you can even consider—"

"Izzy, I understand your concerns but—"

"My concerns?" Izzy rubbed her forehead, tried to be calm. "Mum, that bitch abandoned you. She tossed you out, left you defenseless, all because you'd fallen in love with my birth father and gotten pregnant with me. How could you ever forgive her for what she did to you? What she allowed to happen? It was because she abandoned you when you needed her most that Arzhela was able to get to you. To ruin your life for sixteen years."

"I never said I would forgive her, Izzy. I remember everything. The horrible things she said and did when I told her that I was in love with your father. That I was pregnant with you. How she purposely waited until I was hours away from labor before she told me to get out because I'd betrayed my sisters. And just before I left, news came that your father . . ." Talaith cleared her throat, took a breath. "That your father had been killed in battle, yet she still threw me out of the temple. So understand that I have no intention of forgiving Haldane, Daughter of Elisa for a gods-damn thing. But we have to be realistic about your sister."

"What can your mother teach her that Rhiannon can't? That Morfyd can't? They're both white Dragonwitches and—"

"Right," she cut in. "They're both white dragons. Dragons, Iseabail. Not humans. And Rhi's half human."

It was something they never really talked about except as a way to explain how difficult Rhi and the twins could be at any given moment. Because it had never mattered before. Not to Izzy and not to the rest of the family. So why was it important now?

"I know she's half human, Mum. What does that have to do with anything?"

"It has everything to do with it when it comes to Magick, when it comes to power. And Rhiannon's ability to control her Magick, to rein it in, was born into her. The control of human Magick, however, needs to be taught."

"And you can't do that?"

"Not for your sister. I've tried, Iseabail. Gods, have I tried. But her power . . ." Talaith fell back in her chair, her eyes locked on a spot across the room. "Her power has grown, only now it fluctuates with her moods. It wasn't too bad when she was a child but when she came into her first blood . . ." Talaith shook her head. "She set Gwenvael on fire."

Izzy's back snapped straight. "She did *what*?"

"I know. He's a dragon, but he was on fire. It was a good thing he is a dragon because he recovered after a few days. Even so, there was a lot of whining for all the females to take care of him, which was actually more annoying than anything else that happened."

"Mum."

Her mother looked at her. "Hhhm?"

"She set him on fire?"

"You know Gwenvael. He started it."

"But if it hadn't been Gwenvael . . ."

"Exactly, Izzy. And that was when Rhi was barely fourteen winters. She's been working with me, Morfyd, Rhiannon, Ragnar, a few powerful dragon Elders . . . and although she tries hard, so very hard . . . once her anger or, even worse, her fear and panic come into play"—Talaith wrapped her hands around the mug and gazed down at it—"the damage continues to get worse."

"What about Talan and Talwyn?"

"They protect her, just like always. That has never changed, I doubt it ever will. They're equally powerful, but in different ways." She looked at Izzy, smiled. "Just like you."

"Powerful? Me?" Izzy shrugged. "Anyone can be powerful, Mum, with three legions at your back."

"Don't underestimate yourself, Iseabail. What you lack in Magick, you more than make up for in physical power and skill. Besides, dismissing anyone who lacks Magicks is something your grandmother would do. I'm sure you don't want to make that same mistake."

"What do you want me to say, Mum? About this?"

"Help me with your father. He listens to you."

"I don't know." She hated that woman for what she'd done to Talaith. Hated her.

"Izzy—"

"Let me think on it a bit, eh?"

"All right." Her mother pushed her chair back and stood, leaving her tea and the cake untouched. "But not too long, luv. Your sister tossed the twins around like rag dolls yesterday . . . and she was only *mildly* annoyed then. I fear what she may do when she's good and pissed off. . . ."

Chapter 15

Brannie sat beside Celyn on the Garbhán Isle battlements, their legs hanging over the edge, their arms resting on the railing. And together they watched their father, the great Bram the Merciful, stop in the middle of the oversized courtyard. One second he was walking and the next, he was digging through that bag of his. Whenever he traveled more than a hundred feet from his home door, their father had that bag or he went back for it. But he seemed to spend more time going through it, or complaining about what wasn't in it, than doing anything else.

Even now, a good two hours' flight from his home, and what was he doing? Going through his damn bag!

Brother and sister looked at each other, then back at their father. Although Brannie—and Celyn for that matter—had very little in common with their father, she did adore him. Unlike most of the males among her kin, he was the kindest dragon she knew. And although all his hatchlings had followed the way of the Cadwaladrs rather than the way of Bram the Merciful, he never showed disappointment or envy of dragons who had offspring more comfortable in libraries or royal chambers than in battlefields.

Even better, he made their mother very happy. Still, after

several centuries together. Unlike her Uncle Bercelak and Queen Rhiannon, however, Brannie's parents kept their private lives, well . . . private. Occasionally she saw her mother on her father's lap when they were human or their tails intertwined when they were dragon, but if their father ever chained up their mother, Brannie could say with great relief . . . she'd never walked in on that.

Shame her royal cousins could not say the same thing.

"What do you think he's looking for?" Brannie asked.

"His sanity?"

She laughed and leaned over the railing. "Daddy," she called out and her father stopped searching in his bag, but he didn't move at all.

"Daddy," she called again. And now her father looked around him, appearing a tad panicked. She looked at Celyn, but he could only shrug.

"Daddy! Look up!"

He did, but when he saw his youngest daughter and son, he let out a breath, his hand against his chest. "Gods, Branwen the Black! You scared me to death! I thought you were calling me from the Great Beyond."

Brannie frowned. "Beyond what?"

Now her brother laughed and her father shook his head. "Brannie, my love, how I've missed you."

She grinned. "I've missed you, too. But why are you here?"

"To talk to the queens. But"—and the bag digging began again—"I can't find all the paperwork. Gods, I hate when this happens. I hate not having everything I need when I must see Queen Rhiannon."

She didn't ask why he didn't worry about Queen Annwyl the same way. It wasn't because he feared her less—he didn't—but because Annwyl didn't make it her business in life to torment poor Bram. It wasn't vicious. In fact, it was Rhiannon's way of showing how much she liked their father. Too bad Bram just saw it as pure torment.

"Do you want us to go get it for you?" Brannie asked. She didn't like her father to travel as much as he used to. He was getting older, although it was hard to see since he was still so very handsome, and she worried about him. Especially since he traveled mostly on his own. Only on Queen's orders would he allow for a protective guard. "We can be there and back by tomorrow, before your meeting."

But a bony elbow rammed into her side.

"Ow!" she complained.

"I have plans tonight," he whispered.

"Oh, by the gods," she sighed. "Please don't tell me you're starting up again with Izzy."

"No, I'm not starting up again with Izzy. And are you going to keep throwing that in my face any time I say I have plans?"

"Maybe!"

Disgusted, although she didn't really know why, Brannie turned from her brother to finish talking to her father, but he was gone.

"Where'd he go?"

"Wandered off that way." Celyn motioned toward the Great Hall doors.

"I don't want him traveling so much, Celyn. He's not getting any younger."

"Neither are you, but we aren't holding that against you."

Fed up, Brannie caught her brother by his black hair, lifted him up while she stood and then hauled him over the railing, throwing him to the ground below.

"*You vicious cow!*" he screamed up at her.

She started to scream back at him, but something out of the corner of her eye caught her attention and she walked across the battlement to the other side. There she saw Izzy walking along with that ugly dog of hers. Brannie had been around Izzy for many years now. They'd been through battles and nights of too much drink and other nights of too much kin, and she knew when something was bothering her friend.

Worried it was Éibhear, she went down the battlement stairs, walked past her still-yelling brother, and out one of the side doors. She tracked down Izzy heading away from the castle and deep into the woods.

"Iz!"

Izzy stopped and turned, watching Brannie run up to her. She forced a smile. "Hi, there."

Brannie halted in her tracks, glared. "Do you expect me to believe *that* smile?"

Realizing it was futile, Izzy let the smile go and her shoulders slump.

"What's wrong?"

Izzy threw her arms out and announced to the trees, "Everything!"

Nodding, Brannie suggested, "Would you like a stage to make this speech?"

Izzy pursed her lips to stop from chuckling. "Bitch."

Brannie slung her arm around Izzy's shoulders. "I know, I know. It's a flaw. Now tell me what's wrong."

Izzy did. She told her of her surprisingly short but incredibly painful conversation with her mother. While she talked, they walked, until they ended up at one of their favorite spots. A quiet lake surrounded by trees and boulders. It was too small for dragons in their true form, so it was mostly used in the evening by dragons with human mates. And during the day . . . by Izzy and Brannie.

Dropping onto a boulder, Izzy stared out over the calm lake. "I don't trust that woman."

"Your mum?"

"No. That bitch who bred her."

"I can't say that I blame you. Do you think your mother's really going to send Rhi to her?"

"I do. But that's madness. What if she turns her against us? Giving that evil bitch someone as powerful as my sister seems a foolish move."

"But keeping your sister here with no way to control her power seems more foolish. At least if she destroys everything around her, she'll be safely in the south and far from us."

Izzy gawked at her cousin, and Brannie added, "Not that I don't care about the Desert Land people. I'm just saying it won't be *our* problem."

Looking back at the lake, Izzy wondered what would be the best decision. Trusting her mother was making the best decision about a woman who'd tossed her out while pregnant and barely sixteen?

"What do you need, Iz?"

Yeah, that was Brannie's way. If she didn't have an answer, then she wanted to know what she could do for you to help you get through whatever your problem was. An important trait in an ally during battle. An invaluable trait to have in a friend.

"I need time to think. This isn't some battle I'm going into. This is my sister's life. But trying to find time to think with this family . . . the twins will want me in the training ring, Rhi will want to talk dresses—although Keita's here, so she may help with that—and my mother will keep staring at me, waiting for me to talk to her about it."

"I've got the perfect thing," Bran said excitedly. "Go to me da's place."

"Why?"

"He's here to meet with Annwyl and Rhiannon tomorrow. The place is empty except for his assistant. And that one's quiet as a mouse. You'll just need to bring back one of Da's all important papers."

Izzy finally smiled. "I love your father. He's so nice."

"Isn't he?"

"And yet none of his children—"

"Yes," Brannie cut in. "We know. We know."

Disgusted, Éibhear walked on, his hand around Frederik's small shoulders.

"We don't know why you're mad," Aidan argued from behind them. "It's not like we haven't done this before."

"But to involve the boy—"

"We didn't involve the boy. You did. You sent him."

"To drag you lot off the floor of a pub. Not get you from the jail."

"Still don't see how that's our fault," Cas complained.

"And he didn't have enough money for all three of us."

Éibhear stopped walking, faced the dragons behind him. "What do you mean he didn't have enough?" he asked Uther, who'd made the statement.

"He didn't."

"Then how did he get all three of you . . ." Éibhear briefly closed his eyes. "Please tell me you didn't"—and he covered the boy's ears with his hands, although it was more like he wrapped his hands around the boy's entire head because the area was so small—"kill the jailer!"

"Of course we didn't. Wait." Uther thought a moment. "Could we have? I thought that wasn't okay here."

"If you didn't kill the jailer, how did you get out?"

"The boy convinced him," Cas admitted.

"And he was good, too." Aidan smiled at the boy. "Could talk his way out of anything, I think."

Now impressed, Éibhear patted the boy on the back, the slight youth stumbling a bit. "Excellent job."

"Thank you, sir."

The boy walked on and that's when Aidan added, "Didn't

have to pay a gold farthing." The boy stopped walking. "Got us out for nothing."

Before Éibhear could *not* ask where the money he'd given Frederik was—he didn't really care—the boy faced him, light grey eyes wide as he said sadly, "I just wanted to help you, my lord. You and your friends. It's so hard," he added sadly, his eyes now downcast, "to find out you're not wanted. But maybe I can make myself useful here. Perhaps."

Then, with a sad sigh, he turned and walked off.

"Oh," Éibhear reasoned, "he'll do well here."

"Gods, that was brilliant," Aidan laughed. "I couldn't have done better myself."

"Isn't that your Iseabail?"

"She's not my any—" Éibhear cut himself off, watching as Izzy slipped out of the forest from farther down the well-traveled road and joined the mass of people walking toward the nearby town. "Where's she off to then?"

"Crazy thought . . . into town?"

Éibhear glared at Aidan before refocusing on Izzy. "With her horse and that damn, disgusting dog? And dressed for travel?"

"There's Branwen." Aidan pointed at Éibhear's cousin, who was on the road back to Garbhán Isle. "I'm sure if you ask her nicely she might—"

"Oy! Branwen!"

Aidan sighed. "That doesn't sound nice, idiot."

Éibhear caught up to his cousin.

"What?" she snapped.

"Where's Izzy off to?"

"No idea," she lied. And he knew she was lying. So he handled it like he used to when they were still hatchlings. He grabbed his cousin by her legs and flipped her upside down, shaking her.

"You going to answer me now?"

"Piss off!"

"Still not nice," Aidan complained.

"Quiet," he snapped at his friend. "Tell me where she's going," he ordered his cousin.

"I'll tell you nothing, bastard! Now let me up!"

"I'll let you up when you tell me what I want to know."

"Do you know who I am?" Brannie demanded. "I'm a captain of the Dragon Queen's army! You'll do as I say, Mì-runach scum, or face my—"

Éibhear slammed his cousin into the ground head first, holding on to her leg so he could yank her up again. "What was that?" he asked . . . nicely.

Aidan sighed, shook his head. "Branwen, dear, you had to know that was not the best way to come at a Mì-runach . . . I mean, *really.*"

She was on the road for about an hour when Macsen suddenly stopped in his tracks, his gaze moving up, his long tail sticking out straight, hackles up.

Izzy quickly dismounted Dai and pulled her sword.

It was a mistake made by many warriors who'd never fought with or against dragons before. But staying mounted on your horse when fighting dragons—the idea being the warrior could ride away quickly if necessary—was a foolish thing because for a dragon, catching horses was like catching chickens for a fox. They did it for a meal or sometimes just a treat. So when facing dragons she didn't know, she always dismounted and pulled her weapon—and waited.

The air around her stirred, trees beginning to sway, and she knew large wings were flapping her way.

Izzy lowered her body, readying herself to strike.

Claws dropped to the ground and blue wings and hair temporarily blinded her as she heard Éibhear bellow, "It's me! It's me! Don't do anything!"

When Izzy was able to finally see again, she saw that

Éibhear had one claw over his eyes, his head turned. She almost laughed, realizing he was expecting her to strike. Although that was a good expectation.

She re-sheathed her sword. "What are you doing here, Éibhear?"

Spreading his talons, he peeked at her through the clear space.

Izzy held her hands up so he could see she'd put her sword away. *The big baby!*

Relaxing, he dropped his claws and faced her. "Thought I'd come along. Keep you company."

"I don't need company. In fact, what I need is some time to myself."

"Why?"

"Because."

"Because why?"

"Because I said so." Izzy quickly held up her hands again to stop what could easily become a childish spat. "I'm merely going to your Uncle Bram's house to pick up some papers that he left behind. I'll be back in the morning."

"Oh. All right then."

With a nod, Izzy re-mounted her horse and settled into the saddle. Éibhear stepped back, allowing her to pass. But she held the reins and looked up at him. "You're going to follow mc anyway, aren't you?"

"Yes."

He said it so simply, it made her feel kind of stupid. Like she should just understand that he'd be following her to Bram's whether she wanted him to or not.

"Why?" she decided to ask, rather than yell.

"There's some dangerous roads between here and Uncle Bram's."

"There's dangerous roads everywhere. I've never needed you to follow me around before, so why would I need you now?"

"You've had an army at your back before. Now it's just you. I'd rather not take the risk."

"You'd rather not take the risk? *You?*"

"Aye."

"*You'd* rather not take the risk with *my* life?"

"Aye."

"You're an idiot."

"Well, you and my brothers agree on something."

Tired and worried about more important matters, Izzy said, "Do as ya like, Éibhear. You always do." Then, with a touch of her knees, her horse moved forward. Macsen eventually followed but only after barking at Éibhear until they went around the bend in the road.

Éibhear landed about a half-mile from his uncle's home. A small castle near the Bolver Fields. He shifted to human and changed into his clothes, walking the last bit to the castle.

By the time he walked through the open gate, Izzy was dismounting her horse. He expected her to snarl at him again for coming along, but she didn't. Instead she looked around and asked, "Uncle Bram always leave that gate open?"

"He used to until Ghleanna became his mate. Nothing drove her crazier than to find the gate open. Is that how you found it?"

She nodded and, taking the reins of her horse, walked toward the main building.

"What's his assistant's name again?" he asked.

"Robert."

"You check inside, I'll check the other buildings."

Éibhear searched the grounds and even went outside the gates and looked around for about two miles, but he found nothing. When he returned, Izzy had put up her horse in the unused stables and was now sitting on the big table in the middle of the hall. The table was only used for dining when

Ghleanna and Éibhear's cousins were in attendance. Otherwise, the table was covered in books and papers. And now Izzy's butt.

"Nothing," Éibhear said when he walked in. "You?"

"Empty." She glanced around. "I guess Robert could have gone into town. Perhaps he'll be back later."

Standing next to her, Éibhear folded his arms over his chest. "Unless he had work to do. Depending on how much responsibility Uncle Bram gives his assistants, Robert could be gone for days. Do you know what Bram needs?"

"Yes, and a general idea of where it should be. Still . . ."

"You sound extremely disappointed," he noted. "Were you and Robert . . . friendly?"

"I'm friendly with lots of people, Éibhear. But if you're asking if we were fucking, then no—"

"I was not asking—"

"But he does make a wonderful leg of lamb and I am really hungry."

"I can make you leg of lamb."

"Thank you, but I prefer my meats cooked rather than burned to an unidentifiable crisp."

"That's Morfyd. She always overcooks the food. I, however, am a wonderful cook. I cooked for your mother. Didn't she tell you? And by the gods of piss and blood, *what is that horrible smell?*"

"Oh, yes," she sighed, not bothering to look at him. "The porridge story. Haven't heard that in six . . . months. And that horrible smell is my dog. He's under the table."

"Can't we put him outside?"

"No, *we* cannot."

"Then can I—"

"Leave my dog alone. He's not bothering you."

"He's bothering my senses. Between that smell and that slobbering sound he's making."

"He has allergies, it makes him drool."

"And this is who you sleep with?"

"He sleeps on his back so there's much less drool." Then she added, "Although he does tend to wake up in the middle of the night choking."

Shuddering, Éibhear stepped away from the table. "I don't want to discuss this anymore. I'll find something to feed us and you find what Uncle Bram needs." He headed off to the kitchens. "Are we leaving tonight?" he asked as he walked.

"I have no idea what you're doing, but I'm staying the night. I need time to think . . . preferably by myself."

Éibhear stopped and faced her. "Will you be less caustic if I get a little food in you?"

"I might be," she snapped. "As I said, I'm hungry and I have *a lot on my mind!*"

"Now we've got bellowing," he muttered, again heading toward the kitchens. "Lovely."

Annwyl sat at the desk she rarely used, one foot on the edge of the desk, her gaze focused on the stained-glass window. When the knock on the door came, she ignored it. But, as she'd learned over the years, there were few who lived at Garbhán Isle with her who let one ignored knock deter them. Yet she also knew that whoever was on the other side of that door was human, for dragons rarely knocked at all, and if they did knock, they rarely waited for her answer.

By the third knock, Talaith's voice said from the other side, "Come on, you bitchy sow. I know you're in there."

Laughing a little, and also a little relieved to be pulled from her darker-by-the-day thoughts, Annwyl called, "In."

Talaith entered, closing the door behind her. "You all right?"

"Do I have to be?"

"You should at least try. For the children."

Then they laughed because some days it seemed like the last thing their children needed was them.

Talaith sat down in a chair on the other side of the desk, her hands resting on the wood. She wore her usual ensemble of black cotton leggings, black knee-high boots, and a loose cotton shirt. This time in a bright blue. Her long hair was loosely tied with a leather strap at her nape, the curly tendrils reaching down her back, and she wore no jewelry except for a lone silver necklace that she kept under her clothes and close to her heart. She was a woman with simple tastes and yet the most beautiful Annwyl had known.

She tried not to hate Talaith for that.

"How did it go with Izzy?" Annwyl asked.

"Surprisingly awful. Who knew she hated my mother so much? She's never even met her."

"Do you really not know how protective Izzy is of you?"

"I don't need protection."

"It doesn't matter. Not to Izzy. As far as she's concerned, your mother is a demon incarnate and deserves to burn for eternity for what she did to you."

"Well"—Talaith shrugged—"she's right, but that's not the point."

Izzy would have to say that going through Bram the Merciful's desk was quite fascinating. The dragon seemed to have some connection to *everyone*. He had correspondence from the hills and valleys to the west that went far past the territorial lines of the Sovereigns. He also had ongoing correspondence with the people of the east, who lived far across the dangerous seas. He'd also been in communication with warlords from the Northlands and Ice Lands, attempting to broker peace between different tribes and hordes. There were other documents that she assumed were from dragons. She couldn't read them since they were written in the old language of the dragons, but based on the size of the documents . . . yeah, probably dragons.

"Find what you need?" Éibhear asked her from the doorway.

"I think so." She held up a document. "Does this look right?"

He took the parchment from her and studied it. "Based on what you told me, it does. But Annwyl will never agree to this."

"If anyone can talk her into it, it's Bram." Izzy dropped back into the chair. "But you're probably right. She hates the Western Horsemen and their horse gods." The nomadic tribes in the west had been the bane of Annwyl's existence for many years. They were mostly slavers, raiding weak, poorly defended towns and kidnapping children and the weaker men and women to sell to the Sovereigns. Annwyl hated slavery of any kind, which made her an enemy of the Horsemen. A much hated enemy.

"They tried to kill the twins and Rhi when we were all away at war against the Iron dragons and Sovereigns," Éibhear reminded her.

"True. And all those involved were wiped from this world by Annwyl's sword and rage when she returned to Garbhán Isle."

"I believe your axe was involved also."

"Well, I was her squire. I couldn't leave her to fight alone."

"When do you ever?" He handed the parchment back to her. "Food's ready."

"Yeah, all right." She looked at the other papers she'd set aside. "I think I'll bring these as well." She scooped them up and put them into her travel bag. "Just in case."

Izzy followed Éibhear back to the hall, but she stopped and closed her eyes. "Gods . . . that smells wonderful."

"I had to go with boar. There was no lamb."

"I'm so hungry I don't care."

"No wine either. I looked everywhere."

"Oh, I know where that is. He hides it."

"Hides it? From who?"

When she stared at him, mouth open, he nodded. "Right, right. His own offspring."

Izzy went to the closet buried deep in Bram's library where he kept cases of wine and ale and pulled what looked the most interesting. When she returned, the food was on the table and a fire was going in the nearby pit. Éibhear had also put out plates and utensils, their chairs cattycorner from each other.

"Will this do?" she asked, figuring the royal would have a better understanding of wine and ale than she.

Éibhear took the two bottles from her and blew the dust off them. Then his eyes grew wide when he looked at the seal. "Gods, Izzy. This is my grandfather's."

"Ailean?"

"We can't take these. It's probably all Bram has."

"You mean except for all those cases he has in the library closet?"

"He has *cases* of my grandfather's ale?"

"Aye."

"That stingy bastard. It never occurred to him to share?"

Izzy took the bottles back and placed them on the table. "Apparently not with you."

"This isn't to be wasted on the meal," he said, moving the bottles away from the plates and moving a carafe of water closer.

"If it's not for the meal, then what's it for?"

Éibhear grinned. "Dessert."

"Have you talked to Talwyn?"

Talaith watched her friend. Annwyl had been so quiet lately. Not like her. It wasn't so much that she was a boisterous monarch. She wasn't. But she wasn't so quiet either. So removed. It was like she was waiting for the other boot to drop.

And maybe she was right to be feeling that way. Although

Talaith had her own concerns with her child, the Kyvich weren't one of them. As mortal enemies of her Nolwenn sisters since the beginning of time—at least that's what she'd been told from birth—the Kyvich tolerated the presence of her daughter but didn't engage her.

Although the last couple of years, the leader of the Kyvich squad would sometimes watch Rhi. Not as she watched Talwyn, with pure calculation. Instead, Talaith saw concern on the commander's hard face. Which worsened as Rhi's power became more and more obvious.

Ásta saw Rhi as a threat, of that Talaith was sure. Another reason why Talaith was beginning to think that sending her young daughter to the south might be the best answer for all.

"Talk to her about what?"

"About her relationship with that Kyvich bitch?"

"What is there to discuss? Ásta and the others are her protectors. Of course she'll feel close to them. They were here when I wasn't."

"Don't," Talaith said, pointing a finger. "Don't you *dare* go down that winding road, my friend. Sacrifices were made those years by us all—and for damn good reasons. So I won't hear you put yourself down or elevate those cunts because of what you had to do to protect your children. Do I make myself clear?"

"Yes, yes, you do," the Southland Queen said quickly, her lips twitching as she tried not to smile.

"Good, good. Now if you want, when Izzy gets back we can talk to them both together."

"Gets back from where?"

"She went to Bram's home to get some documents he forgot. That dragon would forget his head if it wasn't attached."

"She went to . . ." Annwyl snorted a little, looked off.

"What?"

The queen rubbed her nose, shook her head. "Nothing."

"What?" Talaith pushed, her butt wiggling in her chair. "Tell me!"

"I, uh, asked that boy, Dagmar's nephew, if Éibhear was coming to evening meal tonight and he said he was going to Bram's castle for some reason. He didn't know why. I just assumed Bram forgot something again."

"Does . . . Izzy know that?"

"Doubt it."

Talaith stared at her friend until they both began laughing, so hard and loud that Talaith began to cough and Annwyl cry. It was so bad, Briec walked in, watched them for a few moments, then walked out again, slamming the door behind him.

Chapter 16

Izzy pushed her empty plate away and, realizing she couldn't avoid it anymore, lifted her gaze to the dragon sitting quietly to her left.

"All right, fine," she finally admitted. "It was amazing."

Éibhear patted her hand. "I know that hurt to admit."

Swatting at him, Izzy pushed her chair back, stood, and turned so that she could sit on the table, her legs hanging over.

"Do you have something against chairs?"

"They're confining."

"So's the army."

"That's a confinement I've never minded." She pulled one leg up, tucking the heel against her inside thigh, her body turned enough to look at Éibhear. "Truly, though, that was delicious."

His smile full of pride, Éibhear nodded. "Thank you. I'm glad you enjoyed it. Now, maybe you can tell me what the battle-fuck is going on."

Éibhear watched Izzy's defenses immediately come up. Like giant brick walls. "Going on about what?"

"I'll admit, I've not been part of the day-to-day of my kin in quite some time. But I know when something is going on, Izzy. That, I'm afraid, has not changed. And something *is* going on. And I think you know it."

"Is that why you followed me here? Because you think you can bully me into telling you that which my father and uncles will not?"

"I would never try to bully you to do anything. I would, however, try to cajole and lure. Perhaps lull . . ." He thought a moment. "Is that wrong?"

She stared at him, but did not answer.

"I promise," he went on, feeling a sense of hope from the small smile he saw, "the last thing I'm trying to do is bully you or anyone else. But I want to know what's going on. It's clearly upsetting you and worrying my brothers. My brothers don't worry about anything. They're soulless bastards. I love them," he added, "but they're soulless bastards."

"They are not soulless bastards and you know it."

"Tell me what's wrong."

"Why?"

"Because this is my kin and no matter what my brothers think, I do care about what happens to them."

Izzy's anger eased away, but her defenses were still up. Still ready. "Why would they think you don't care?"

"I don't know," he said, shrugging. "It just seems the decision to make me part of the Mì-runach has disappointed them."

"Who told you that lie?" When he frowned, she added, "Anytime they talk about you and your barbarian friends—"

"They're not barbarians."

"—all I hear is awe mixed with a bit of fear and a good dose of concern."

"Concern?"

"For your safety. For your life." She leaned in a bit, hands clasped in front of her. "Is it true you go into battle without armor . . . without weapons?"

Éibhear leaned back. "What?"

"Naked? Just your claws?"

"Wait, wait, wait." Éibhear rubbed his face. "We're warriors, Izzy. Not insane." Gods, what had his brothers been telling her? "We wear light armor and, depending on what our assignment is, sometimes no armor. But we're always armed. More armed than anyone else I know."

"And do you drink the blood of your enemies? And wear their heads as totems?"

"No! What did my brothers tell you?"

"Actually, that last bit was Celyn."

Éibhear rolled his eyes. "Figures."

"It's not true?"

"The Mì-runach have come a long way over the centuries."

"Which means . . . what?"

"We don't drink the blood of our enemies or wear their heads as totems . . . anymore. And I've *never* done any of that."

Her eyes narrowed as she studied him. "Do you smear the blood of your enemies on you?"

"Sometimes," he snapped, frustrated, "but I don't want to get into it. I can't get into it. There are some sacred rites we still perform that are none of your business. Or the business of my brothers."

"Hhhm." She thought a moment. "Fair enough."

"Look, Izzy, we're what you would call a . . . strike unit. We come in, usually under the cover of darkness, and kill either someone specific or as many enemy soldiers as we can. As you can imagine, full dragon armor or human armor for that fact, would not be in our best interest. So we protect our most important bits, arm ourselves to the fangs, and do what we do best."

"That's a good job for you then," she said after a moment of quiet.

"Why do you say that?"

"Because you're a chameleon. You can move around without being detected in the dark or during the day, yeah? But all that armor makes quite a bit of noise, which would defeat the purpose of being able to blend into your surroundings."

Shocked, Éibhear stuttered, "Wait . . . what are you . . . I don't know what you . . ."

She waved his attempted lie away. "I know, Éibhear. I've always known."

"How could you know? Who told you?"

"No one told me. I can see you."

"Wait." Éibhear took a breath, confused. "What do you mean, you can see me?"

"I can see you. I've always been able to see you." She chuckled. "The first time, I thought you were mad. You were creeping around, stepping around everyone. You looked absolutely insane. But then I realized it wasn't that the others were ignoring you. . . . They couldn't see you. But I could. Don't worry, though," she added. "I've never told anyone. About you or Gwenvael."

"Gwen—Gwenvael's a . . ."

"Oh, shit. You didn't know?"

"Does he know you know?"

"No. And please don't tell him I know."

"Why?"

"It'll just embarrass Dagmar."

"Why would it embarrass . . . ohhh." He didn't bother to hide his disgust. "He does things to her when no one can see him, doesn't he?"

"They've got a whole thing going. You don't want to know."

"I really don't."

"But," she said, suddenly smiling, "he does love her. It's so sweet!"

"Ech."

"Ech? Is that even a word?"

"It's not. But I think it encapsulates my disgust quite nicely." He pointed at the still unopened bottles of ale. "Dessert?"

"Is this the next step in your grand plan to get me to talk? Getting me drunk?"

"It's worked before with other humans."

"Éibhear," she said, taking the mug from him. "I drank Aunt Ghleanna under the table." She held up two fingers. "Twice."

"Oh." Éibhear put the bottle down, sighed. "Uncle Addolgar?"

She shook her head. "Can't keep up with me. Still hasn't forgiven me since I wrote 'I love humans' on his forehead after he passed out once."

Éibhear laughed, a sound Izzy hadn't heard in ages. "I don't blame him!"

She laughed with him. "It was Ghleanna's fault. She told me to! Gods, I was functional, but I don't know how many bottles of your father's ale we went through that night."

"My father's ale? You can drink my father's ale?"

"I love your father's ale. Clears me lungs of smoke after we've burned an army fort down."

"You've become quite a woman."

"Are you being sarcastic?"

"Not at all. Even *I* can't drink my father's ale. While it clears your lungs out, it just burns mine." He shook his head, stared at her a moment. "You really can see me? And Gwenvael?"

"Aye." She gestured to her shoulder and the brand burned

into her arm from a bastard god so many years ago. "I just assumed it was something from Rhydderch Hael."

Éibhear poured himself a mug of ale. "What else do you think you got from him?"

"Don't know. I used to think my strength, but Mum figures that was from the Magicks not used when I was born."

"I don't understand."

"When a Nolwenn is about to have a girl, she performs spells and sacrifices to direct the Magicks she'll be born with."

"Direct them where?"

"I don't know. Maybe to her soul or whatever. Anyway, my mother was unable to do this with me at the time and it seems any Magicks I might have had dissipated and instead became bound up in my muscles, my strength. I guess it makes sense . . . but it doesn't explain Annwyl, and she's as strong as me."

"Nothing explains Annwyl." He placed the bottle on the table. "But I'm sure her strength comes from her anger. There's no god or Magicks that can fight that."

"Very true." She held up her mug. "To kin."

Éibhear nodded, touched his mug to hers. "To kin."

They each drank deep. When Izzy lowered her mug, she wiped the back of her mouth with her hand. "Not bad. Very smooth." She glanced at Éibhear. "What do you think?"

He didn't speak, just shook his head.

"You all right?"

Another head shake.

Izzy reached across the table and touched his hand. "What is it?"

"I think I've gone blind," he finally gasped and coughed.

Laughing now, Izzy took the mug from Éibhear and poured the rest of the ale into her own. "Yeah. Right. *You* were going to get me drunk enough to tell you *anything*."

Chapter 17

They sat on his Uncle Bram's table, one of the bottles of ale polished off. But Éibhear was unwilling to open the second. He liked his lungs to be functional . . . to breathe. He was sure if he drank another drop of that ale, breathing would be the last thing they'd ever do.

Yet he was willing to drink as much as he had because, at the very least, it relaxed things a bit between him and Izzy. She wasn't drunk. Not even close. But she was like the Izzy he remembered. The Izzy he hadn't embarrassed in front of their family. The Izzy he hadn't walked away from that last night on the hill outside Garbhán Isle. Instead, she was the Izzy who liked to steal his weapons—weapons very few humans could lift much less abscond with and then "train" with—and argue with him over ridiculous things and play with his hair.

It gave him hope that, even now, when she thought he wasn't looking, she'd stare at his hair. He liked to imagine her fingers itching to run through it.

Laughing, she held up a dagger he'd taken off a Spike a couple of years back. How she'd got it from his leg holster, he had no idea. He'd never seen her move.

"It's gold."

"Mostly. Steel makes up the blade."

"But they use so much."

"They have tons of it. Under all that ice and snow is tons of gold."

She handed the weapon back to him. "Did you find a lot?"

"Of gold? Aye. We all did. Anytime we had a break, we'd start digging around a cave or breaking the ice on a river. I was able to afford my own castle not far from my grandfather's territory. I always liked it there."

"You own a castle?"

"I own a town. It's nice. People are friendly. Has an amazing library."

She snorted. "You and your precious books." She glanced around. "Uncle Bram's place must be heaven to you."

"Too messy. I don't know how he finds anything." He looked at the disorganized stacks of books piled on the floors, studying the titles. "Besides . . . read most of these."

"Why?"

Exasperated, Éibhear demanded, "Who questions reading?"

"I guess I do. Just don't know why you bother."

"Because I like it. Did no one teach you to read?"

"I know how to read, you big bastard. I just read important things."

"Battle histories?"

"Those are quite helpful." Izzy inched closer. "Did you miss being here? In the Southlands? Among your kin?"

"I guess." Then Éibhear admitted, "Well, not at first. At first I was too angry to miss anything or anyone."

"Because of what happened to Austell?"

"That was part of it."

"It's hard losing comrades, Éibhear. Of course," she added, leaning in a bit closer, "everyone tells you that, but it means nothing until you've actually been through it."

"I'm guessing you have."

"More than I care to think about. It never gets any easier, does it?"

Éibhear shook his head. "No. It doesn't. I did try not to get close to anyone ever again. Made the whole dramatic commitment to myself and everything."

Izzy laughed and Éibhear joined her.

"Doesn't seem to have worked, though, if your three friends are any indication."

"There's truth to that. Aidan and I traveled to the Ice Lands together. We met Cas and Uther during a pit fight."

"Pit fight? Is that popular in the Ice Lands?"

"Don't know. It was a Mì-runach pit fight."

"You lot have pit fights? Between you? Whatever for?"

"Sort out issues."

"Issues?"

"Gambling debts, arguments—"

"Women?"

Éibhear lifted his gaze to Izzy's. "Occasionally," he replied slowly. "But mostly gambling debts."

"Do you have any regrets?" she asked.

Frowning, he asked, "About pit fights?"

"*No.*" She took the mug he held in his hand. "No more ale for you."

"I'd already decided on that."

"I mean do you have any regrets in general?"

"I'm a little young for regrets, don't you think? I'm not even a hundred and fifty yet."

"All right."

"Why? Do you?"

"Just one."

"And what's that?"

"That I never got a chance to kiss you."

Éibhear studied her for a moment and took the cup out of her hand. "And no more ale for you, I'm afraid."

Izzy laughed. "I'm not drunk, Éibhear."

"I didn't say you were. Just don't want this to get . . . uncomfortable. And, by the gods of death and pain, *what is that smell?*"

Sighing, Izzy leaned over a bit and snapped her fingers. "Oy. You. Out."

Macsen whined, but Izzy didn't want to hear it. "Out," she pushed. "Now. Go for a walk or go kill something."

Her dog dragged his long body out from under the table and headed out. But he stopped long enough to snap at Éibhear, his fangs near the dragon's face.

"I hate that dog," he muttered once Macsen was out the door. "I really hate that dog."

"He's loyal and I love him. There'll always be room in my bunk for him."

Éibhear shuddered. "I had no idea you wanted to live your life alone."

Izzy chuckled, propped her elbow on her knee and her chin on her raised fist. "So did I make you feel uncomfortable with my answer to your question?"

"No. Should I feel uncomfortable?"

"I don't think so. But haven't I always made you feel uncomfortable?"

"No, you haven't."

"You are such a liar. And a bad one."

"Over the years I've become a very good liar."

"As good as Gwenvael?"

"No one's as good as Gwenvael. Except maybe Dagmar."

Izzy sat up straight and lowered her arm. "Well, I'm sorry."

"For what?"

"For making you feel uncomfortable . . . again. It's just something I do, it seems. Although it only seems to come out with you."

"You didn't and have never made me feel uncomfortable."

"Good." She turned and uncrossed her legs, hanging them over the table's edge. "I'm off to bed. We'll need to get an early start." She slid off the table. "If we don't get there before midday, Bram will start pacing. Ghleanna hates when he paces."

She glanced back at him, smiled. "Night."

When he didn't say anything, Izzy walked toward the stairs that would take her to the second floor and the room she used whenever she came to visit with Brannie. She didn't worry about Macsen. He'd find something to kill, eat, and cover himself with blood; run through a nearby stream to get some of the blood off; and finally return to her a few hours before dawn so that he could snuggle up to the back of her knees and snore until it was time to head out again.

Honestly, that dog was the most reliable thing in her life besides Brannie, her squire, and her horse.

Izzy reached the stairs, but before she had her foot on the first step, Éibhear said from behind her, "I lied."

"About what?" she asked around a yawn.

"You did make me uncomfortable."

She snorted a little. "I know."

"Because I've always wanted to kiss you."

Izzy's hand landed on the banister, her fingers gripping the worn wood. "Oh?"

"The problem is, I grew tired of feeling uncomfortable a long time ago."

Slowly, Izzy faced the dragon. He was standing now, watching her from under all that damn blue hair. Gods! That hair! It would be the death of her. And unlike some humans, the dragons never seemed to lose their hair. It might grey, like her grandfather Bercelak's, but his was still long and thick and shiny and mostly black.

Bastards. Every last one of those damn dragons . . . bastards.

Well . . . was she just going to stand there and stare at him? What was he supposed to make of all that staring? Especially when she kept frowning at him like that. Or maybe it was a glare. Hard to tell really.

"Are you saying you want to kiss me *now*?" she asked, and he had no idea what to make of that tone.

So Éibhear shrugged. "Figured why not?"

Her head tilted to the side. "Figured why not?"

"Yeah."

And that's when a book flew at him, slamming into his forehead. The power of it had him stumbling back against the table and he placed his hand where the book had met flesh and bone. He glanced down at the book and asked, "You threw *The Ancient Philosophies of Seòras* at me? Do you have any idea how old this book is? And why the hell are you throwing books at me anyway? What did I do?"

"You exist! I think you exist just to torment me."

"You started this, Iseabail."

"I started nothing. I asked you a simple question and you went all Éibhear the Terrified on me. As usual." She stalked toward him. "And that's when I decided, 'Fine. I'm done with this.' And in typical Éibhear fashion, *that's* when you decide, 'Eh. I might as well kiss her. Couldn't 'urt.'"

"First off, that's not how I sound." Gods! She made him sound like a bloody halfwit. "And second—"

"I don't want to hear it."

"What?"

"I don't want to hear it. That's all you bloody do. Talk!"

Seething now because he had no idea what he'd done,

Éibhear growled out between clenched teeth, "You, of all beings in this universe, have the nerve of accusing *me* of talking too much?"

"At least I have something to say."

"No, you don't! You babble. Constantly! Until my bloody ears bleed!"

That's when she swung on him. But this time, he was kind of expecting that move, so he caught her arm and flipped her back on the table. She kicked him in the jaw, and gods! The woman's legs were damn powerful. If he were truly human, his head would have been separated from his neck from that blow.

Éibhear stepped back, black smoke swirling from his nostrils, a low growl rolling past his lips as he gripped his jaw and popped it back into place. By the time he was done, Izzy had placed her hands behind her and flipped her body backward so that she landed on the other side of the table.

"Running?" he couldn't help but taunt. "The great general of Queen Annwyl's armies?"

"You should know by now, Éibhear the Ridiculous, I don't run."

Then a wooden chair came flying at his head. Éibhear leaned back and the chair careened past him and into the far wall, breaking into pieces on contact.

"You'll have to explain that bloody chair to Bram," he told her.

"I'll tell him it was your fault. He'll believe *me*." She grinned. "They all do."

Their gazes locked and they watched each other, for how long, Éibhear didn't know. But then he saw her eyes briefly stray to where they'd placed their weapons while they ate. At the same moment, they were both running, heading for those piles of weapons. Izzy was fast, her long legs getting her to the pile quickly. But he was fast, too, leaping over the table and slamming into her just as she reached out for an axe. His axe!

Éibhear lifted her off her feet and swung her around. He had her arms pinned, but her legs were free and the damn woman kicked like a psychotic mule. She brought her head back, ramming it into his chin, almost dislodging his jaw again.

Fed up, Éibhear spun Izzy around and slammed her into the wall, pinning her there with his body.

Panting, the pair stared at each other until Izzy asked, "Ready to kiss me now?"

The dragon's silver eyes narrowed on her. "I see how you've come so far in the human armies, Iseabail. Because you're completely insane."

She laughed, her tongue reaching out and swiping up blood that leaked from her split lip. "I may have heard that accusation before, but I refuse to accept or acknowledge it. Now kiss me . . . or get the battle-fuck off me, Éibhear the Blue."

His gaze lowered to her mouth and she saw his brain turning while he, as always, agonized over his decision. She imagined he couldn't be like this in battle or even with other women. She just didn't know why he insisted on being so obsessively concerned for her.

"Waiting," she pushed, the one word no more than a snarl.

That's when he released her, Izzy's drop to the floor a little unsettling since he hadn't even lifted her up all the way to eye level.

"And you can keep waiting," he shot back seconds before he turned away from her and headed toward the stairs.

Smirking, Izzy watched him.

"Éibhear?"

Fed up, Éibhear spun around to face the unhinged female that he was trapped in this bloody castle with for the night.

"What is—" he just managed to get out before a piece of the broken chair rammed into his leg bone. The pain of it shocked him and he automatically dropped to one knee. Then Izzy was there, her strong hand gripping him by his jaw.

"Let's just get this over with, shall we?" she said.

Then she kissed him.

Not a silly, girlish kiss or even an angry, biting kiss. But a demanding, passionate kiss that tore the breath from his lungs and did to him exactly what he'd always feared. Tore any control or rational thought he'd believed himself to possess completely away from him.

Damn her!

She pulled away first, stepping back, a triumphant smile on her face. "There. That wasn't so hard now, was it?"

Her tone was unbelievably condescending and superior, which only made him want her even more. Why? Because he was pathetic! He didn't deserve to be a dragon. The mightiest of higher beings!

The pompous brat stepped away from him, tossing aside the piece of chair she'd used to temporarily incapacitate him.

"Night!" She gave him a little wave that made him hate her a bit and that's when something in Éibhear snapped. Like the last piece of rope he was hanging on to.

Éibhear stood to his full height and reached out, catching hold of Izzy by her chain-mail shirt and swinging her around until she was in front of him.

"Really?" he asked.

As usual with this insane female, Iseabail the Dangerous showed no fear, no concern, nothing but humor at his expense.

"Really?" she shot back, her arms extending from her body. "Really . . . what are *you* going to do? The great, pious, beloved Éibhear the Blue. What are *you* going to do?"

Éibhear's grip on her shirt tightened, the little metal rings that made up the protective garment digging into his fingers. And he realized in that moment that he'd have to show Izzy the Dangerous that the "great, pious, beloved Éibhear the Blue" had been dead and gone for a very long time. . . .

Chapter 18

Izzy would be the first to admit that over the years, it was this sort of thing that often got her into the worst sort of trouble. Well . . . her and Brannie. Poor thing. That dragoness had pulled Izzy out of more scrapes that Izzy's mouth had gotten them into than either would ever care to admit. But Brannie wasn't here right now and Izzy wasn't exactly in a situation she didn't want to be in.

More fool her.

What exactly was wrong with her anyway? Was she still harboring the desires of her sixteen-year-old self? The same girl who had gone from having only three soldiers protecting her as they lived their lives on the road to having an entire family to call her own, including a mother, father, uncles, aunts, cousins, grandparents . . . and Éibhear. Handsome, chivalrous, impatient, terse Éibhear.

Well, with her he'd been impatient and terse. With everyone else, he was the wonderful, sweet, adorable Éibhear. The blue dragon everyone loved. But Izzy would be the first to admit, she'd seamlessly moved from loving him to hating him. He'd driven her absolutely insane for years. Hot one second, cold the next.

Of course, at the moment . . . she seemed to have him decidedly hot.

Using his grip on her shirt, he pulled her closer, his gaze locked on her mouth. To be honest, Izzy expected him to do what he always did to her any time they got too close to anything that even hinted at sex. But Izzy wouldn't pull away first. She wouldn't let him off the hook. If he was going to walk away, he could walk away. She wouldn't help him by—

Yanking her up until she was on her toes, Éibhear leaned down and took her mouth with his. Her thoughts tumbled away as his hands released her shirt and moved to her shoulders, shoving her back against the wall, his lips still against hers.

Sure, Izzy could have fought him off. He was a tough challenger, but so was she. But the truth was, Izzy didn't want to fight him off. All these years, all her long days on patrol thinking about him and what he might be up to and those long nights in her bunk dreaming about him, this was what she'd always wanted.

Well, this and one other thing . . .

And deciding not to wait any longer for that, Izzy did what she'd dreamed of since the very moment she met Éibhear the Blue all those years ago.

She dug her hands into his blue hair and held on.

Gods, his hair. Not his hair!

All these years he'd never willingly let Izzy near his hair because . . . well, because he was afraid of *this*. Of what was happening right here.

When his mother, or Talaith, stroked his hair, he felt a great sense of comfort and, very often, quite sleepy. But from the first time Iseabail had dug her hands into his mane and demanded he take her flying, his feelings were far from comfortable or sleepy.

And he blamed the damn woman who, at the moment, had her fingers gripping his hair.

His hair!

Éibhear tried to pull her hands away, but Izzy only tightened her grip and kissed him harder. Her tongue slid inside his mouth and Éibhear used his body to pin her against the wall.

There were many things he should be doing. Either pushing her away or seducing her. He did neither. Like some out of control hatchling, he reached for her leggings, gripping them and pushing them down her hips.

He'd have been appalled by his lack of finesse, too, if Izzy hadn't already beaten him to it, his leggings nearly around his knees.

By the time he got hers down to her knees, she'd already gotten off her boots. Seconds later she'd managed to get out of her leggings completely. One indescribably long leg wrapped around his waist—flexible!—and the other around his calf.

Then, with no thought or even a modicum of self-control, he lifted her just a bit and drove home with one brutal thrust, burying himself inside Izzy and making his cock the happiest thing on the planet!

Izzy barely managed to bite back a scream of pure pleasure and instead buried her mouth against the flesh between Éibhear's neck and shoulder. She bit down hard and held on, her arms wrapped around his shoulders, while she tried to stop herself from saying or doing something—anything!—that might destroy whatever self-respect she'd built up for herself over the years.

Because, gods of thunder and suffering, this sudden, rather rude, entertainingly brutal fuck was turning out to be the best one she'd ever had. Without foreplay, without a kind word said between them, without a gods-damn bed!

But Izzy didn't care. She didn't care about anything at the moment. Especially once Éibhear started moving, his thrusts hard and merciless, his thick cock buried deep inside her.

She tightened her arms around him and unwrapped her leg from his calf so she could raise it and open herself more to him. She *felt* him growl against her neck where he'd buried his face. He braced his legs farther apart and his strokes became stronger, harder, his cock powering inside her.

Izzy began to shake, her grip on him becoming even tighter. So tight, she was grateful he wasn't human. Grateful she wouldn't have to revive him from strangulation or take him to a healer for broken bones.

The trembling began in her toes and raced up her legs and spine, spreading out through her body until an orgasm like she'd never felt before exploded from her, her screams lost against Éibhear's neck.

When her entire body clenched around him and she screamed into his neck, Éibhear's knees almost buckled and his eyes rolled to the back of his head.

Then he came. Hard. Harder than he ever had before. So hard, he almost blasted the wall behind them with flame, and he had to fight hard to control the urge, not wanting to burn Izzy while in the throes of passion. That just seemed rude.

When he got the feeling back in his legs, Éibhear realized he had his leggings down around his ankles and his still-hard cock inside a half-naked and panting Iseabail.

A situation many might consider . . . awkward.

Chapter 19

Éibhear started to place her down on the table but seemed to reconsider that and pulled a large cloth from his travel bag, put it on the table, then carefully placed her naked ass on his uncle's furniture. Once he had her there, he slowly backed up—and out—until he could sit down beside her.

And that's what they did. They sat there, staring off at the wall across from them. In silence, they went on like that until Izzy couldn't stand it anymore.

"Well . . . we got that out of our system."

"Aye. That we did."

"And now we can move forward."

"Right."

"Great." Without looking at him, she reached over and patted his shoulder. "Glad we took care of that."

From the corner of her eye, she could see him nod, but he still didn't say anything. She was grateful. The last thing she needed at the moment was talk. Real talk anyway. She didn't want to analyze what had just happened between them. She didn't want to look for anything deeper and she definitely didn't want to start talking regrets. Instead, she wanted the glow from that orgasm to last as long as it could and that meant no deep conversation with Éibhear and his deep thoughts.

Deciding escape was her best plan at the moment—as a general, she always knew when to retreat—Izzy slid off the table. "I'm off then. Dinner was great."

She crouched down—she was not about to bend over—and picked up the rest of her clothes and walked toward those damn stairs again. The stairs she couldn't quite manage to actually get up. Even now!

"You know . . ."

Izzy stopped at the sound of Éibhear's voice, her eyes closing in frustration, her hand gripping the banister. Her escape . . . so close! "Aye?" And she tried hard to keep the dread out of her voice.

"Look, I'm thinking—"

Oh, no. Please don't think.

"—since we're not going back tonight—"

Gods, please. I don't want to spend all night talking about this one gods-damn fuck.

"—maybe we should really be sure—"

I always get trapped with the emotional ones. And this time it's all my fault!

"—we've really gotten it out of our system."

See? I knew he would do . . . wait. What?

Izzy faced him. "What?"

Don't look down. Don't look down.

Éibhear knew if he started staring at her pussy, his eyes would stay locked and then his mouth would be right there. So it was best to stare at her face. Although the look of astonishment she had at the moment made it hard not to laugh.

"What do you mean," she pushed, "see if we've gotten it out of our system?"

He shrugged, trying to look as casual as possible. The worst thing he could do with Iseabail was show her how desperate he felt at the moment. And gods, he was desperate. Desperate to be back inside her. The need was crawling up his spine and beginning to eat at his brain.

His poor beleaguered brain that was working hard at the moment to focus on her face.

"Well, once is usually a good idea. Yet sometimes one starts wondering if perhaps there should have been more and then it becomes this obsession again, but by then it's just too awkward."

"And you want to—"

"Since we have all night . . ." Éibhear shrugged and slid off the table. He kicked off his boots and leggings—thankfully before he'd tripped over them and made a complete fool of himself—and walked over to Izzy. "It makes sense, don't you think? A few more times. Just to be sure, of course."

She eyed him and he didn't know what to make of that look. So he kept his mouth shut. He was glad of it, too, when she asked, "Will we have to talk?"

"Not if you don't want to."

"And it's just to get this out of our system, yeah? Nothing else?"

"Nothing else."

All right, that last bit might have been a huge lie, but he could see that Izzy could go either way at the moment. She could wrap her legs around his head or make a run for it.

"Couldn't hurt," he suggested, keeping his voice as casual as he could manage even while his cock pointed at the bloody ceiling.

When she gazed off, her mouth one tight line—she was clearly debating with herself—Éibhear decided to help her out. He slipped one arm around her waist and with his free hand took the clothes from her, tossing them onto his travel bag.

"It's not like we have anything better to do tonight."

Her smile was small but there. Even better, when he pulled off her shirt, her nipples were hard and she'd begun to pant.

Izzy swallowed and asked, "Just to get this out of our system. We won't have to discuss this tomorrow or anything, will we?"

For Éibhear, there was nothing to discuss.

"No. We won't have to discuss it tomorrow."

"Yeah, well . . . all right . . . uh . . ." Éibhear leaned down and sucked Izzy's nipple into his mouth. "Gods," he heard her sigh out as her fingers slid into his hair again and held on.

Fearghus looked up from his book and watched his mate pace back and forth in front of him. He'd brought them to his cave tonight because he could tell she'd needed some time away from life at Garbhán Isle. Dark Plains was their refuge and, if he was to be honest, the refuge for those at Garbhán Isle when their human queen became . . . tense.

And Annwyl had been getting tenser and tenser every day for quite a few months now. Not that he blamed her. He knew what had her worried and he was equally as worried, but he was also realistic.

There were just some things they could do nothing about.

"You're going to wear a hole in that rock floor."

She stopped and faced him. "Why aren't you worried? Why don't you care? This seems to be *your* precious daughter they're targeting."

"They're not targeting—"

"What would you call it? Seducing?"

Fearghus sighed and set his book aside. He lowered his head so that it rested on the inside of his claw while he tapped the talons of the other.

"Why are you looking at me like that?" she demanded, hands on her hips.

"I'm waiting for you to have your explosion of rage, so that when you're done, I can talk to you like a rational dragon. I gave up long ago trying to talk over your screaming, my love."

She folded her arms under her chest. "They're trying to steal our daughter from us, Fearghus."

"You know as well as I that no one can make Talwyn do anything she doesn't want to do. That includes the Kyvich."

"They're trying to lure her away from the safety of her people. Away from her brother and cousin."

"Away from you, you mean?"

"I'm the only one who can protect her!" Annwyl bellowed, pointing at herself. "There's no one else who can protect her like I can!"

"You mean besides Talwyn herself?"

"I *knew* you'd throw that in my face."

"You were the one who taught her to protect herself. You also taught the boy."

"Can't you call him by his name?"

"He irritated me today."

"He irritates you every day."

"Do you expect me to argue that point?"

"You know, our son really does—"

"Does? Does what?"

"Tolerate you more than others."

"Thank you. I find that comforting when I wake up from an afternoon nap and find him hovering over me like an angel of death."

"You're being paranoid. But let's be honest."

"Oh, please let's."

"Talan is my son and Talwyn is *your* daughter."

"Which means?"

"That you should be the one to talk to her."

"I have."

Annwyl stepped closer. "And?"

"She didn't tell me anything she hasn't already told you. But I know her, Annwyl. There's something going on."

"I knew it!"

"But there's nothing to be done. She's stubborn and contrary and determined . . . just like her mum. So I wouldn't bother arguing with her."

"I am *not* contrary."

His eyes crossed and he rolled onto his back. "Of course you're not."

"I heard sarcasm in that statement."

"Perhaps." He motioned to her. "Come here, luv."

Annwyl walked closer until she reached his open claw. She climbed onto that, then up his arm and onto his chest until she could stretch out stomach down, her head right under his snout. As always, she showed no fear of his dragonform.

"You know," he reasoned, "instead of sitting around, worrying about things that may or may not be happening, why don't you go do something that you might enjoy?"

She planted her hands against his chest and lifted herself up enough that she could look him in the eye. Then she grinned.

"I meant something relaxing with the children."

"Oh." She lowered herself back down.

"What I plan to do to you tonight will only be relaxing after we're done."

"Good to know." Annwyl laughed and stroked her hands across his scales, something that Fearghus had always adored. "All right, so what should I do with the children? As it is, they're never around."

"Plan something for tomorrow, so they don't have time to come up with an excuse, and start with Rhi. She always ropes in the other two. And bring that pale boy who's been lurking around."

"His name's Frederik, and from what I hear he'll be staying for a while."

"Perfect. Take them for a picnic or something."

"Will you come?"

"I'm off to Devenallt Mountain tomorrow with Gwenvael and Briec to meet with Bercelak."

"Anything wrong?"

"No, not at all. Just time to look at Mum's armies and see if we should be doing anything different. At least that's the plan. What it really ends up being is Dad and Briec arguing, me sighing a lot, and Gwenvael pissing Dad off so much that at some point he has to duck a tail to the eye. To be honest, I'd rather be on a picnic with the pale boy."

Annwyl rested her chin on her raised fist. "No Éibhear?"

"No Éibhear what?"

"He's not coming to this meeting?"

"Why should he? He's not in Mum's army. He's a Mì-runach."

"I really don't know what that means, although you all say it with that mix of disgust and horror in your voices."

"It means he's a violent bastard that can't be trusted around the army. So, no. He won't be there."

"Personally, I think you're all too hard on him. You're still treating him like a baby. He's a grown dragon now, Fearghus. Quite matured."

"Yeah," Fearghus snorted, not really seeing it. "Right. Quite matured."

Izzy reached out blindly, her hand pressing against the stone wall of the room she always slept in any time she'd come to visit her Uncle Bram with Brannie. But to be honest, at this moment, she really had no idea where she was, why she was here, or even what her name was. At this moment, all she knew was that it was a stone wall her hand was pressing against and the biggest, most talented cock she'd ever had inside her was making her come. Again.

Her toes curled, and her hard breaths turned into a short

scream, her body tightening around the male currently on top of her, kissing her, fucking her.

She hadn't known it would be like this. She'd *dreamed* it would be like this, but she'd never thought it actually would be. Too many times, Izzy, Brannie, and often Brannie's sisters talked about the potential some male had one day and the sad disappointment he turned out to be the next. Sometimes, one of them might be pleasantly surprised or damn happy. But this?

Gods, this . . .

Izzy tore her mouth away from Éibhear's because she couldn't breathe, that orgasm still ripping through her system. But pulling away was a mistake because Éibhear took the opportunity to nip the side of her neck. Something that she secretly adored. And, gods, once he'd discovered that, if she didn't find other uses for his mouth, he drove her insane with the gods-damn nipping.

Whimpering, her body shaking, Izzy felt Éibhear bite down on a spot right beneath her ear and somehow, some way, the bastard got another orgasm out of her when the last one hadn't quite finished.

As Izzy screamed out again, she was so glad that when this was all over, they wouldn't be talking about it. They wouldn't be analyzing it. Because if she thought about any of this too much, she'd end up back where she started at sixteen. Head over boots for a big blue bastard with gorgeous blue hair who couldn't make up his bloody mind about what he wanted.

Izzy cried out again, her amazing legs tightening around his waist. Éibhear's eyes crossed at the grip her legs had on him. He'd never known a female, human or dragoness, who had legs as strong as Izzy. Legs that held him so tight he was positive he saw stars.

He reached over and caught hold of the hand Izzy had

pressed to the wall and pinned it against the bed. She whimpered when he did that. Gods, he loved when she whimpered. Just the sound of it made his toes curl.

Between the whimpering, the panting, the incredibly strong thighs, and the way her pussy gripped his cock like the tightest fist he'd ever felt, Éibhear could say, with all honesty, that this was the biggest mistake he'd ever made.

He knew that now because he realized he'd been right all those years ago about Izzy. He might have been young, but he'd never been stupid, and he'd known from the beginning that she was trouble. Trouble wrapped up in long legs and a bright smile. Of course, it was even worse now because he felt no guilt. None. The longer he stayed inside her—and he had every intention of staying inside her all night—the less he cared about anyone or anything except what was happening between them at this moment.

So what if his brother thought of Izzy as his daughter? So what if all of Éibhear's kin considered her a niece, a cousin, a grandchild? So what if she was the most feared general in all the territories? So what if she had feet as big as Annwyl's? Who cared? He didn't. Not anymore.

Éibhear pulled his mouth away from her neck and Izzy leaned up, pressed her forehead against his chin, then brought her mouth up and bit his jaw. At the same time, she tightened her pussy so that he came hard, his entire body pinning her to the bed as he continued to fuck her until he was dry.

He clung to her for a bit before he finally rolled off. Both of them covered in sweat and panting, they lay there for a good ten minutes until Izzy finally admitted, "You know . . . *still* not out of my system."

"Good," Éibhear said as he rolled back on top of her, pushed his still hard cock inside her, and gasped out, "Because it sure as battle-fuck ain't out of mine."

Chapter 20

"Wake up."

Éibhear turned over and snuggled back into the covers. He wasn't ready to face the day yet and he definitely wasn't ready to face the wrath of Izzy. He had a feeling it was coming. After their amazing night together, he was prepared for her not to be able to face the morning. But she wouldn't put him off. Not forever.

"Get up," Izzy pushed. "We have company."

Éibhear rolled to his back. Izzy stood by the open stained-glass window. She was freshly bathed and dressed, her wet hair combed off her face. She must have gone to the lake behind the castle.

"Who?"

She shook her head. "No idea. But they're armed. A small squad. Don't see any colors, though." She glanced at him. "They look like a protection unit."

"They could be here for Bram." He pushed the fur covering off and got up, walking naked over to the window to stand beside Izzy. She smelled wonderful. He wanted to kiss her good morning but decided against it. He wasn't really in the mood to be pushed away at the moment.

"Do you recognize them?" Izzy asked.

"No." He leaned in, sniffed the air. He smelled flame and power. "They're dragons."

"You sure?"

"I am."

"But no one you recognize?" He shook his head and Izzy looked back at the small group of riders on horses, long brown capes and fur hoods covering their faces and bodies.

Izzy slid her foot under her sheathed sword, which was lying on the floor, and flipped it up into her hand. "I'll take the ground, you take the air."

He nodded. "I'll meet you outside then."

Izzy slipped out the side door of Bram's castle. The previous evening, Éibhear had closed and barred the front door that led to the hall, and if she opened it, she'd give away her presence.

As Izzy eased out into the brisk morning air, she heard a soft "moof" behind her and looked to see Macsen crawling up to her feet. Her dog had amazing instincts. Like a wolf, he knew when to keep to the shadows and when to attack. It helped when she was involved in night raids.

Body tense, he waited by her side, waiting for her signal. Izzy motioned with her hand, indicating he should stay by her side and low. With that order given, she crept forward, listening for anything that would tell her someone was coming from behind. She reached the end of the building and peeked around the corner. Now that she was a bit closer, she could see that these riders were trying their best to look like a small traveling party. The clothes under their capes were plain, not too expensive but not too poor. Yet she still saw that nearly all of them had weapons. A lot of weapons. And the way some of the riders moved . . . definitely soldiers.

At the front, two riders—leaders by their demeanor— looked around and one of them finally gestured to the others.

Dismounting their horses, three other riders started to set off, but one of the leaders held up a gloved hand—a female, Izzy guessed from the slightly smaller frame under the hooded cloak—and stopped the men. Even though Izzy couldn't see the female's face, she could tell that she was studying the front of the building. Izzy took a small step and saw that Éibhear was . . . well . . . he was *standing* on the front of the building in his dragonform. She'd seen him do that sort of thing before but it still fascinated her. Considering their size, dragons didn't seem to have too many issues with gravity.

But what concerned Izzy at the moment was that the female seemed to be able to see him. Or, at the very least, sense him. Yet Izzy had seen Morfyd, a powerful white Dragonwitch, look right past her baby brother, unaware she was practically walking on his head.

Éibhear moved the slightest bit and the head under the cloak jerked. Perhaps she heard him. Perhaps she didn't. Izzy didn't know. She heard the female take in a breath, a sure sign she was about to unleash her flame. Something that didn't worry Izzy. Although fire dragons could use their flame against their own kind to shove or batter, the flames themselves could do no damage. Southland dragons were made of fire and their scales were an added protection.

But before the female unleashed her flame, the hood of her cloak slipped back and Izzy immediately recognized her. Recognized her and knew what that particular female's flame could do to one blue dragon who had absolutely no idea of what was about to hit him.

He felt confident the dragoness couldn't see him, but she did sense him. Could be she was a witch of some kind. His mother and sister Morfyd belonged to one of the most powerful breeds of Dragonwitches, but there were others at different levels of power. Still, it really didn't worry him. Instead he just waited to see what she'd do, and when he heard her take in a deep breath, he became even less concerned. Because of his size, some dragon's flame wasn't even going to knock him off the building, much less harm him. Yet as the dragoness leaned forward in her saddle, the hood of her cloak dropping back to reveal a very pretty human face, Izzy's scream from the far side of the building shocked them all.

"Agrippina! *No!*"

The She-dragon's head snapped around and the flame she was going to unleash on Éibhear was instead directed at Izzy. The flame was so powerful, Éibhear reared back and the stones that made up that part of Bram's castle broke apart and melted. She made stones *melt*.

Éibhear had never seen anything like it, but he didn't have time to analyze any of that because Izzy had been standing there two seconds before.

Pushing off from the building, Éibhear unfurled his wings and raced around the damaged building.

"Izzy!" he bellowed. "Izzy! Answer me!"

"I'm here!" She stood, appearing from behind a large boulder. He'd forgotten how fast Izzy could move, but he was grateful for it.

He landed beside her, the land shaking.

"Are you all right?"

Tears streamed down her face and she shook her head. "Macsen."

The dog? She was sobbing over that dog.

She pointed to the smoldering remains of melted stone and seared wood beams. "He was standing over there," she said around sobs. "I thought he was right beside me."

Éibhear discreetly sniffed the air and, aye. He smelled burnt dog fur. Best not to say that, though.

"I'm sorry, Izzy. I know he meant a lot to you, but we have other things to worry about—"

"Macsen!"

Éibhear blinked and watched Izzy push past him and over to a pile of still burning debris. And dragging himself out from under that debris came Izzy's dog. With his dirty, matted fur burning in some spots, the big beast stumbled away from the debris and toward Izzy. But he suddenly stopped, dropped, and rolled around in the dirt for a bit. When Izzy reached him, the fire on his body was out and with a good shake, all that dirt went flying, making Izzy laugh. Then she dropped to her knees and hugged that disgusting, bizarre beast.

"You poor thing! Are you all right?"

"Izzy!" Éibhear snapped. "We have much bigger concerns than your gods-damn devil dog!"

"Iseabail?" another voice asked and Éibhear saw one of the riders standing at what was left of the corner of the building. It was a voice Éibhear didn't recognize.

The rider pulled the hood of his cloak back, long, dark silver hair spilling out, and . . . an eye patch. The dragon wore an eye patch.

Izzy looked up from that slobbering beast who didn't seem to be hurt at all after being on fire and crushed under all that debris, and her smile was so wide and bright that Éibhear just assumed it was because she was happy her dog was safe. But then she released the dog and charged over to the one-eyed dragon, launching herself into his arms.

"Gaius!" she crowed. And that's when Éibhear knew that this was Gaius Lucius Domitus—the Rebel King of the Quintilian Provinces. An Iron dragon descended from the enemies of the Southland dragons and the bastard who liked to send books with strange notes to Izzy. A dragon Iseabail the Dangerous was currently hugging.

Bugger.

"What are you doing here?" Izzy asked as she stepped back. It had been years since Izzy saw Gaius last, but that had never mattered. Their friendship had been forged in the blood-filled ending of the Quintilian Overlord Thracius. Since that time, Gaius had worked to take full rule over the Quintilian Provinces, but Thracius's daughter and a son or two still lived and still caused problems. Great problems. And there were many who felt any of Thracius's offspring were the rightful heirs to the throne. If that meant getting rid of Gaius, they'd be more than happy to make that happen.

Which told Izzy that whatever was going on was important because Gaius didn't usually leave the Provinces for any length of time. He could rarely afford to.

"I was hoping to get an audience with Queen Annwyl and Queen Rhiannon, if possible, and I knew Lord Bram could help us with that. We sent word to his assistant, Robert, yesterday. He met us in town last night and we discussed our concerns with him first. He led us back here today to stay until Bram's return, but when he saw the gate closed—which he was sure he'd left open—we had him wait down the road while we checked everything out." He smiled. "I must admit, I'm glad it was just you. It's not like I have one of my legions at the ready."

Izzy gave a short shake of her head. "I don't understand, Gaius. Why didn't you send an emissary rather than coming yourself?"

"Oh . . . we did. But we sent him directly to Garbhán Isle and apparently Annwyl felt he was lying about who he was and, uh . . ."

Izzy held up her hand, not needing to hear anymore. "You weren't close to your emissary, were you?"

"No. Varro"—the King's human general and friend—"was wise enough to send a messenger no one really liked. So when that head came back to us . . . we chalked it up to a lesson learned."

Izzy cringed and nodded. "Understood." She patted his shoulder. "Actually, this works out well. Uncle Bram is with

Annwyl and Rhiannon now. I can escort you to Garbhán Isle myself."

"I'd really appreciate it. Losing my eye was one thing, losing my whole head . . . that would be more problematic."

Laughing, Izzy gave Gaius another quick hug. "Let me get my things together and then we can head out."

"That sounds fine but, uh . . ." His words drifted off and his gaze focused behind her.

"Someone you know?" Gaius asked.

Izzy looked over her shoulder and she saw that Éibhear had shifted to human and now stood behind her. Naked.

Yes. Very subtle.

"This is . . . my uncle"—and the glower she got for that was priceless—"Queen Rhiannon's youngest son."

"Oh, yes," Gaius said, his entire body becoming tense under that cape. "Éibhear the Contemptible."

"Éibhear, this is Gaius Lucius Domitus, the Rebel King."

Éibhear grunted. He *grunted*. Even Fearghus, a known grunter, didn't grunt at fellow royalty.

Gaius's one eye narrowed. "I'm going back to my sister," he said, his expression wary as he watched Éibhear closely. "We'll meet you out front, Izzy."

"Aye."

She waited until he cleared the corner before facing Éibhear and demanding, "Is that how you were taught to greet a fellow royal? Even my father is better at it than you. And my gods, that is saying something."

"I'm your uncle?"

Oh. So that's what was bothering him. Izzy could have done a lot of things at this moment to assuage Éibhear's annoyance. A lot of things.

She didn't do any of them.

Instead she said, "Well . . . you are my uncle." She brushed a bit of nonexistent dirt off his bare shoulder. "And I was your ward until years later when you finally had your vile, dirty uncle way with me."

"Izzy."

"I guess I should just be grateful punishments weren't necessary. Dirty, dirty punishments involving chains, whips, and a nurse maid."

"*Izzy.*"

She tapped his cheek with the tips of his fingers. "Don't worry, Uncle Éibhear. I won't tell. Last night will just be our dirty little secret."

"That's not what I'm —"

"We have to go. Whatever's going on, Annwyl will want to know about it right away." She turned to leave, but a big arm slipped around her waist and spun her back around. Éibhear pulled her into his body, holding her there while he stared down into her face.

"Do you really think I'll just let you walk away from what happened last night?" he asked, not sounding angry . . . just challenged.

"Do you really think you can stop me?" Izzy grinned. "Are you really up to trying?"

At the same time, they both looked down. Because their bodies were so close, neither could see the erection currently pressed between them, but Izzy could easily feel it. He was hard as a steel spear, sooooo . . .

"Well, guess that answers that." She pulled away from him. "Come on, Macsen," she called out and her dog loped to her side. Part of his fur was crispy from the flame, but he still seemed to be doing well. Although she did have to pull out a piece of still-sizzling, melted stone from his mouth. Gods, the beast chewed on anything!

* * *

Éibhear watched Izzy walk away with that ridiculous dog that he wasn't really convinced *was* actually a dog.

She'd dismissed him. He knew all the signs. After years among the Northland dragons and a lifetime among his kin, Éibhear knew when he'd just been dismissed like a pesky gnat flying around her nose.

Honestly, he'd been treated like that so often, he normally didn't worry about it unless someone got on his nerves. But Izzy wasn't getting on his nerves. She was pissing him off. Still!

And she'd finally have to learn that was always a mistake.

Chapter 21

Annwyl watched Dagmar's young nephew lean over the picnic basket to look inside. She tried not to frown too much—she'd been told her frown could be terrifying—but she didn't like anyone's nose that close to the food they'd all be partaking in.

Placing her hands on his shoulders to gently pull him away, she jumped when the boy nearly came out of his skin.

"Sorry," she quickly said. "Didn't mean to scare you."

"No . . . um . . ."

"Would you like to come with us?" she offered. Annwyl felt so bad for the boy, remembering her own youth, when tormenting her had seemingly been her idiot brother's only pastime. She could tell that this boy's own kin probably hadn't been much better, probably just with a bit less outright hatred.

"It's just a picnic with the twins, Rhi, Dagmar, Talaith, and Fearghus's Uncle Bram. We talk books. Well . . . *some of us* talk books. Talwyn glowers."

The boy looked down at his feet. "I don't read much. It's a bit of a struggle."

Dagmar had muttered something about the boy not being too bright, but not everyone was a reader. Talwyn certainly wasn't, but Annwyl would hardly call her conniving, plotting daughter thick. And Dagmar could be a bit of a snob when it came to intelligence. The barbarian wasn't above using *anyone,* no matter their intelligence level, but she only accepted those she deemed "smart *enough*" into her inner circle.

But Frederik was just a boy. A boy who didn't fit in anywhere by the looks of him, and that was something Annwyl completely understood. Gods, she'd had to involve herself with a completely different species before she found those who considered her tolerable to be around.

"I'm here! I'm here!" Rhi skipped down the stairs in a lovely midnight-blue dress with a fur cape draping her small shoulders. The leather bag her father had had made for her nearly ten years ago was over her shoulder and most likely filled with parchment for sketching, drawing quills, and inks. She brought little else when she traveled any distance from the castle.

"It's such a lovely day out!" she happily chirped. "And just before winter. I hope there's cheese!"

Annwyl fought not to laugh. "Aye. There's cheese. I know how you love your cheese."

"Is Daddy coming?"

"Your father, Fearghus, Gwenvael, they're all off at Devenallt Mountain with your grandfather."

"Ahh, important doings amongst the males."

"That's doubtful."

"And Auntie Keita? Uncle Ragnar?"

"Off to Keita's cave for the day."

Rhi smiled at Frederik. "Are you coming, Lord Reinholdt?" And only Rhi would call a fourteen-year-old boy lord anything.

The boy frowned, deeply, but didn't answer. Rhi scratched the back of her neck. "Well . . . hmmhm."

Annwyl was about to ask the boy what he was doing, but

a voice right behind her barking, "Mum," startled the holy crap out of her.

"Talan!" she snapped, facing her son. "Stop sneaking up on me."

"I didn't." He dropped into a chair and immediately grabbed one of the baskets and began to dig through it. The boy was a bottomless pit of hunger. No matter how much he ate, he never seemed to be filled.

Annwyl snatched the basket back. "Where's your sister?"

"She's not coming."

"What do you mean she's not coming?"

He lifted his hands and shrugged. "She's not coming."

Irritated, Annwyl demanded, "Why not?"

"I don't know." He reached into another basket and pulled out a loaf of bread. "She was out in the training area. I said, 'Oy! Let's go!'"

"And what did she say?"

"Nothing. One of those Kyvich told me"—and Annwyl's son lowered his already low voice even lower—"'My lady won't be attending.'"

Feeling her anger begin to build, Annwyl asked, "And which Kyvich said that?"

Talan shrugged. "Don't know. One of them burly ones."

"They're all a bit burly," Rhi whispered, probably feeling horrible for even suggesting such a thing.

"I don't mind that," Talan went on. "Just not sure about all that shit on their faces."

"That shit," Rhi snapped, "is part of a sacred ritual that—"

"Blah, blah, blah, don't care. Can we just go already, Mum?"

"Not without your sister."

"Mum, leave it. If she wants to play sword fighter with the burly witches, let her. It's not like she contributes to the bloody conversation."

"That's not the point!" Annwyl roared. "I'm queen!"

Talan sighed, his head resting against the chair back. "And we're off . . ."

"I am queen here and I rule. *I* rule here! Not the gods-damn Kyvich. Not your sister. Me!"

"*Mum.*"

"No! I said she was going to the fucking picnic and she's going to the fucking picnic! *And I dare one of those cunts to try and stop me!*"

Talan watched his mother storm out the door, her muscles taut; her fingers already twitching to grab one of the two swords that were strapped to her back and went with her everywhere—yes, even on a picnic with family.

Even as he debated exerting the energy necessary to get up and go after her, a rather large foot, considering the size of the girl attached to it, rammed into his leg.

"Ow!"

"That was horribly handled, Talan!" Rhi accused.

"What did I do?"

"How could you tell your mother that?"

"I thought I handled it pretty well. I didn't tell her that I saw 'Fuck that bitch queen' in the Kyvich's eyes, did I? *That* I kept to myself. I thought you'd be proud."

"Oh!" Rhi threw her art bag onto the table, lifted the skirt of her dress, and ran after his mother.

At that point, Talan noticed the new boy. "Hey, there, Freddy."

"It's Frederik."

"Yeah, whatever. You'd best get Auntie Dagmar."

"Why?"

"Because chances are high my mum is about to cut off someone's head."

"Literally?"

"Oh, yeah," Talan laughed. "Mum doesn't like you or you piss her off . . . she's cutting off your head."

The boy stepped back, his mouth open in horror. "But . . . she doesn't . . ." He cleared his throat. "She doesn't seem like she'd do that."

"Well, she wouldn't do that to you, if that's what you're worried about, because you're family . . . and a little too young. But mostly because you're family."

"Uh-huh."

"So you're safe." Then he added for good measure, "Just don't betray us. Family or not, Mum will take your head if you betray us. She's big on loyalty."

"I wasn't planning to—"

"Just figured I'd clarify." Talan ripped off some of the bread from the loaf and stuffed it into his mouth. Once done chewing, he realized the boy was still standing there, staring at him. "What are you? Fourteen winters?"

"Fifteen in two more moons."

"Yeah, well . . . still too young to drink. Let me know when you can. We'll go to the pub. Get some women. You like women?"

"Uh?"

Talan sat up, ignoring the way the boy quickly stepped back. He motioned him away. "Go on, Freddy," he said, his sister's snarled *Get out here. Now!* ripping through his head. "Go get Dagmar."

Rhi tried to stop her aunt. Tried to hold her back. But there was no holding back Annwyl the Bloody when she was on a tear. When she was angry. And with every step she took toward the training ring, her anger grew . . . and grew.

"Please, Auntie Annwyl, let me talk to Talwyn. *Please*."

But it wasn't Talwyn that Annwyl wanted. No. Rhi's aunt would rather blame the witches than her daughter. The tension between the Southland queen and the Ice Land witches had been growing steadily, day by day, since Talwyn was a child.

And talking was really not what Annwyl was about. She left talking to Auntie Morfyd and Dagmar. Annwyl was a queen of action—brutal, violent, deadly action—and Rhi doubted that would ever change.

It definitely wouldn't change in the next five seconds.

Annwyl stalked up to the training ring, went through the open gate and over to the three witches busy talking to Talwyn. Something that they could have done at any time, so Rhi wasn't clear why this casual-looking conversation couldn't have waited until after their picnic. Something she was sure her aunt had already noted.

Talwyn! Her cousin looked up, green eyes narrowing, when Rhi screeched in her head.

What's going on? Talwyn demanded.

What do you think?

Bloody balls.

Well, don't just stand there! Rhi snapped in her cousin's head. *Do something.*

But when Talwyn averted her eyes, Rhi knew that her cousin wouldn't be doing anything to stop this. Nothing!

Rhi began to panic, but she was also angry. Angry that her cousin was letting this happen without lifting a finger. And Rhi's panic and anger together were not a good thing. And realizing that made her panic even more.

Auntie Annwyl walked up to them; her body looked relaxed even though Rhi knew it was not. She could see the rage and fear coming off her aunt in big gushing waves.

"Can we help you, m'lady?" one of the witches asked. Her name was Odda. She smiled a lot, but Rhi avoided her because that smile was a lie. She tried to hide it, but she was mean and didn't like being here. She especially didn't like Auntie Annwyl.

"No," Annwyl said. She motioned to Talwyn. "Let's go."

Odda gave that smile. "I'm so sorry, m'lady, but Commander Ásta has asked us to work with Talwyn today. So she'll have to miss your little picnic, I'm afraid."

"Are you under some impression I'm asking your permission? For anything? On my territory?" She motioned again to Talwyn. "Move. Now."

Talwyn took a step, but Odda held up a finger and to Rhi's shock, her cousin stopped. Instantly, without question. When had she started doing that? Following orders? From anyone? She never followed orders. Even sane, logical ones. Not ever!

"Perhaps another time, my lady. But today . . . I do have my orders."

It all happened so fast, Rhi didn't see anything until blood splattered across the front of her pretty dress. That's when she saw the blood-soaked dagger in Annwyl's hand and the brutal slash across the left side of Odda's face. It traveled from just beside her eye, across her cheek, and out the corner of her mouth. Blood poured down her jaw and onto her shoulder and chest.

The witch's blue eyes darkened and her fingers curled into fists as Annwyl stepped in close and said, "I know your lot can fix that, so in a day or two it'll be nothing but a faint memory. But get between me and mine again— and the next cut will be something you can't fix. Understand me?"

The pair had their gazes locked, but Rhi watched as more Kyvich suddenly appeared. They knew when their sister witches had been harmed or were in danger, and they protected their own, the way Annwyl protected hers. So Rhi's body began to shake when she saw those Kyvich come from the stables, from the blacksmith, from their quarters.

An arm went around her and Rhi looked up at Talan.

"Aye, my lady," Odda answered Annwyl. "I understand."

Then the witch backhanded Annwyl, sending her flying across the ring and into—and *through*—the wood fencing.

They were moving down the road toward Garbhán Isle at a good clip when Izzy saw her mother not far ahead.

"Mum!"

Talaith turned and waved. "Hello!"

Izzy rode her horse to her mother's side. "Hello, Mum."

Her mother stepped closer, placed her hand on her booted foot. "Feel better?" she asked low.

"Uh . . ."

She knew what her mother was talking about and to be honest, she hadn't thought about it much once the fuck festival began between her and Éibhear. But she wasn't about to say *that* to her mum. Not now. Not ever.

"We should talk more," Izzy said instead. "I still have many concerns."

"I know. I know. So do I. Perfect timing, though. I was heading back to the castle. We're having a picnic." Talaith glanced back. "Oh. You brought company."

"Aye. Gaius Domitus."

"The Rebel King? He's here?"

"With his sister. He came to see Uncle Bram. He wants an audience with Annwyl and Rhiannon."

"Gods. This can't be good." Talaith held her hand out to her daughter. "I'll ride with you. I'm sure Annwyl's at the—"

Talaith's words stopped abruptly and her gaze focused on the other side of Izzy's horse. Izzy looked over at the forest but didn't see anything.

"Mum?"

Talaith blinked, then caught hold of Izzy's arm. "Your sister," was all she said. All she needed to say.

Izzy hauled her mum onto her horse and looked at Gaius over her shoulder. "Wait here. Someone will be back for you."

"All right."

"Macsen. Stay. Protect!"

"Izzy," Éibhear asked from above her, the power of his wings making the forest trees sway. "What is it?"

"Just follow," her mother ordered and Izzy spurred her horse toward home.

Talan tried to stop his cousin, but she'd always been stronger than she looked and she easily pulled away from him, stepping between an advancing witch and his unconscious mother.

"Please," Rhi begged as she quickly cut in front of the witch. She brought up her arm, most likely to ward the witch off, but this was a Kyvich and as far as the Kyvich were concerned, Little Rhi was no more than a Nolwenn witch. Their most hated enemies.

Rhi hadn't even touched the witch, but the Kyvich grabbed his cousin's arm and twisted. He and his sister locked gazes across the ring, but neither moved to intercede, to step in. But Talan was much kinder than his sister and offered the following advice, "I wouldn't do that if I were you, Odda."

Not surprisingly, the witch ignored him. She'd never liked him. None of them really had. They were only interested in his sister. To the Kyvich, she was the true power. But their narrow vision would be their enemy when it came to the three of them.

Like at this moment. This very moment.

* * *

Talaith dismounted her daughter's horse, Izzy right behind her. She slapped the horse's rump and sent him running toward the stables.

With one quick look at the training ring, Talaith could easily see what was going on. Yet she knew as she stepped closer, it was already too late. She was too late. She grabbed her eldest daughter's arm before she could run in there and do what she always did when it came to her sister. Protect her.

"Mum?" Izzy asked.

With no time, Talaith yelled out, "Éibhear! Take her!"

"Mum!"

"Take her!"

A blue tail with a sharpened steel-like tip came down and wrapped around her daughter's waist, yanking Izzy up. Talaith charged a few feet over and landed in the dirt in front of a nearly unconscious Annwyl, her hands coming up, a powerful chant on her lips, a mere second before everything around them exploded.

Dagmar was rushing toward the Great Hall doors, Frederik by her side. She saw Morfyd running down the stairs and she motioned to her.

"You'd best come along, Morfyd. We may need you to—"

Morfyd's arms went around Dagmar and Frederik and she yanked them both back, a spitted-out chant slamming the heavy wood doors shut. They hit the floor in a heap as the ground beneath them suddenly shook.

Dagmar quickly covered her head as weapons and tapestries that had been tacked to the walls began to crash around them, the long dining table they ate at nearly every day moving several feet while the chairs turned over.

And just as quickly as it started . . . it stopped.

Dagmar lifted her head, glad to see that her spectacles had survived this new . . . issue.

"What the battle-fuck was that?" she demanded.

Morfyd helped Frederik sit up, taking a moment to look him over for any damage before saying, "Rhi."

One second Izzy was being dragged away from her mother and plopped onto Éibhear's back and the next he was bellowing, "*Down!*"

She took hold of his hair and ducked between his shoulder blades. Seconds later they were flipping and spinning out of control, heading up and up until Izzy briefly wondered if she could reach out and touch the clouds.

It seemed to take forever for Éibhear to get control again, but it was probably not even a minute. When he finally got himself righted and was able to hover, Izzy raised her head and demanded, "What the hells is going on?"

"I don't know." He shook his head. "I really don't know."

Izzy leaned over the tiniest bit so that she could look around Éibhear. That's when she realized how far away they were from actual ground. In fact, as many times as Izzy had ridden on the back of a dragon, she'd never been this high before.

"Rhi," she said softly.

"What?"

"Rhi did this."

"That's impossible," Éibhear argued, his head turning enough to look at her. "She's just a little—"

They stared at each other for a very long moment until Izzy ordered, "Get me down there *now*."

Éibhear spun around. "Hold on." Then he sped back to the earth below.

Éibhear wanted to know what the mighty hells was going on, too, but his curiosity would have to wait. His main concern was getting his little niece to safety.

He'd known from her birth that Rhi was powerful. Magicks flowed through her like water through a river. Even he could see it, and the world of Magicks was not where his skills lay. But he hadn't realized until now exactly how powerful the girl truly was, and why his kin were so concerned.

Although it wasn't her lack of control that had them worried—it was the fact that others would want that power for themselves or to destroy it. Which made his little niece very vulnerable, unlike her cousins who had never been vulnerable a day in their lives.

As Éibhear neared the ground, he felt Izzy stand up on his back.

"Take Rhi out of here!" she yelled over the rushing winds. "Find my house! I'll meet you!"

"And what are you going to—*Izzy!*"

But it was too late. The crazed female charged over his head and dived off his snout like she was diving off a cliff into the ocean. He tried to grab her, but she flipped past him, and landed on Brannie, who'd come up under him. She grabbed hold of Brannie's mane and held on until Brannie dropped a bit lower; then she let go.

Letting out a sigh—and suddenly understanding why Talaith worried about her eldest daughter all the time—Éibhear dived down. He saw Rhi just standing there. He knew even if he screamed at her to run, she'd continue to stand there. Unable to move. Unable to function.

Izzy landed in front of Rhi, her body in a crouch, her sword out. After a breath, she stood tall, her mother moving in beside her.

Knowing Izzy and Talaith could take care of themselves, he did what he'd just done to Izzy. Using his tail, he snatched his niece up and yanked her out of what was about to become a very dangerous situation.

He knew it was about to become dangerous because Annwyl the Bloody had just picked herself up off the ground, while Morfyd the White and The Northland Beast were coming out of the Great Hall and heading to the training ring.

Aye . . . dangerous indeed.

Chapter 22

Izzy stood by her mother, her head lowered, gaze locked on the three witches who stood across from them. Unlike the others near the training ring, the witches weren't on the ground, trying to pick themselves up. Instead, they were standing tall, the witch named Odda had her hand raised, and Izzy sensed she'd surrounded herself and her comrades with some kind of protective wall. Talaith probably had done the same thing for the twins and Annwyl, the queen currently getting to her feet while Talan went to his sister's side.

"Your daughter's strength has grown, Nolwenn," Odda said to Talaith, her fingers closing. She tightened her hand into a fist, her knuckles cracking. "She seems to have outgrown you, this place."

"Mind your own, Kyvich," Talaith shot back. "Or my daughter will be the least of your worries."

"Really?" Odda asked, suddenly moving forward. "And what will you do, Nolwenn, when she's unable to restrain her power and she kills someone you care about? Or destroys your little utopian kingdom here?" The witch stopped a few feet away from Talaith. "You know what has to be done. Just do it already."

Izzy quickly cut between her mother and Odda, her sword out and ready, her body tense.

"Stay away from my sister."

"Or what, General?" Odda asked, her smile smug. "What can *you* do to a Kyv—"

The witch's words were cut off and Izzy stumbled back into her mother as a white claw slammed into the ground, smashing the witch into the earth.

Izzy looked up at the dragoness standing over her. Her grandmother smiled. "What did I miss? I sensed I was missing something!"

Rhiannon looked down at her claws. "Did I step in something? I feel like I stepped in something."

Izzy covered her mouth with her free hand, desperately trying to stop the laughter and failing miserably at it.

Behind Rhiannon, Commander Ásta walked toward the training ring, the rest of the Kyvich falling in behind her. Rhiannon saw them and looked back at Izzy.

"My dearest Iseabail, do be a dear and check on your sister for us."

"Yes, ma'am." Izzy turned to her mother, winked. "Let me know when it's safe to come back," she said low; then she went off in search of Éibhear and her sister.

Rhiannon had been in a valley not far from Garbhán Isle, indulging in some grazing cattle, when she'd felt her granddaughter's panic and anger, felt her Magicks growing beyond her slim body. She'd raced here, afraid of what she'd find. Afraid of what her granddaughter might have done. But looking around, Rhiannon saw that once again, they'd all gotten off easy. But how much longer would they?

Shaking her head and making a most annoying "tsking" sound, the Kyvich commander walked around the fence, her gaze on Rhiannon.

"This is a bit of a mess, isn't it?"

"Started by your people," Rhiannon replied.

"Of course. And I do apologize." She motioned to the two witches that had been with the one currently splattered across the bottom of Rhiannon's claw, and dismissed them. Rhiannon knew she had landed on her, but she didn't like that particular witch anyway. Hadn't from the beginning.

"I think, Commander Ásta," and that came from Dagmar on the other side of the fence beside Morfyd, "the time has come for us to reexamine our agreement. The twins are now eighteen and you aren't protecting Rhianwen."

"Very true, but—"

"So I think it's time to end this," Dagmar stated calmly. Her hands were folded primly in front of her, her steel-grey eyes focused on the commander. As always, Dagmar Reinholdt showed no fear, no doubt, no anger. She wasted no words and was unbelievably polite, but none of them were fooled. None of them ever would be. "You need not run out of here this very moment, of course. It's been so many years, I'm sure you have ties, connections, you'll need to address. But I think for all concerned . . ."

"Of course, Lady Dagmar. I understand. Perhaps we can talk before we move on."

"Absolutely. We owe you and the Kyvich a great debt. We'll not forget."

"Nor will we."

The commander walked off, her witches following, heading toward the nearby forests.

When they were gone, Dagmar looked at Rhiannon's claw and then up at Rhiannon herself. "Very subtle, my liege."

"Oh, my dearest girl, I'm a dragon. I'm *never* subtle. Have you learned *nothing* from my son?"

* * *

Izzy first tracked down Brastias and asked him to get Gaius and Agrippina and to keep them safe. Especially now. Annwyl would be even more . . . well, on edge, after this little event. So Izzy didn't want her queen killing anyone by accident. Izzy also sent one of the squires to track down Bram so that he could meet Gaius and find out what had him so concerned now, after all these years, that he'd risk coming to Annwyl's territory without warning.

Once she'd taken care of all that, she ran back to her house. She walked inside and found a human and dressed Éibhear making tea, and her sister sitting on her bed—staring.

To be honest, Izzy had expected tears. Sobbing. That's what her sister usually did after this sort of thing. She sobbed. Hysterically. Sobbed until she practically passed out from exhaustion. But not this time. This time she simply sat and stared.

When Izzy came through the door, Éibhear looked at her over his shoulder and frowned, gave a short head shake.

She went and sat beside Rhi, patted her sister's knee. "Everyone's fine. You haven't hurt anyone." Odda, of course, didn't count because their grandmother had killed her.

"Uh-huh."

"So you don't need to worry."

"Okay."

"What is it, Rhi? Just say it."

"There's nothing to say."

"It's me, Rhi. I know you. There's something you want to say so just—"

"*I'm going to kill everyone!*"

Startled at the yelling and the statement, Izzy pulled her hand back from her sister. "What?"

"Don't you see?" Rhi stood, began pacing. "That's where I'm headed. I'm going to end up killing everyone I love or, even worse, betraying them."

"Why would you think such a thing?"

"Because I'm a font of pure, unbridled evil! How can you not see that?"

Izzy stood. "Who told you that?"

Rhi huffed at that. "No one has to tell me anything," she said defensively, which made Izzy think that someone *had* said something to her. "I just know. I feel it inside me, waiting to be unleashed by my uncontrollable rage!"

Izzy glanced over at Éibhear, but all he could do was shrug. He was as confused as she was.

"What does Mum say? Dad? Gram?"

"Nothing. No one ever says anything to me. I'm sure it's because they've resigned themselves to their fate and they're merely waiting for death to come to them all."

Izzy rubbed her eyes with her fists, then asked again, "*What?*"

Talaith carefully placed a piece of ice on the bridge of Annwyl's nose where the swelling was the worst.

"How does that feel?"

Annwyl shrugged at her question and Talaith crouched next to Annwyl's chair, placing her hand on her friend's arm. "Don't worry. We'll figure this all out."

Her friend looked at her, one eye black and a bruise on her cheek. "Do you really believe that?"

"No. But I'm trying to be hopeful."

Through the Great Hall gates, Briec, Fearghus, and Gwenvael stalked in. They'd been off at Devenallt Mountain with their father when everything had gotten out of hand, but Talaith had called for Briec as soon as things had settled. She knew better than to not inform him about a problem involving just one of his "perfect, perfect daughters," let alone both.

Briec stopped in front of Talaith and Annwyl. Sighing in

exasperation, he swung his arms from his body, forcing both Fearghus and Gwenvael to stop in their tracks and lean back before they were hit with his big forearms.

"I leave you females alone for five minutes," he accused, "and my perfect, perfect daughters end up in danger—*again!*"

"It wasn't our fault," Annwyl argued, the chunk of ice melting into a little pebble against her face.

"Then whose fault is it?"

Annwyl looked at Talaith and together they pointed across the room and said, "Dagmar."

Startled, the Northlander glared over at them. "Did you treacherous females just throw me under the carriage?"

"Head first," Annwyl mumbled while reaching for more ice to put on her nose.

"Why don't we sit down and discuss this?" Éibhear offered.

"What's there to discuss?" Rhi demanded, flinging her arms in the air. "I'm doomed! We're all doomed! What's there to talk about?"

"Well, to start . . . do you want biscuits with the tea I put out?"

Rhi sniffed, nodded. "Biscuits would be nice."

"Excellent."

"Wait, wait." Izzy gawked at them. "Biscuits? Tea? What are you two talking about?"

Éibhear and Rhi smiled at each other before Éibhear explained, "We can't sit around discussing pure evil without tea and biscuits, Iz. It's just not done."

Fearghus crouched in front of Annwyl and took the chunk of ice she had pressed to her skin. He sighed when he saw her damaged face. "Your head certainly takes more abuse than the rest of you."

"They're all jealous of my astounding beauty. So that's what they try to destroy."

Smiling, just glad she was okay, Fearghus leaned in and kissed his mate's cheek. "Are you sure you're all right?" he asked her low, while Briec and Talaith argued on the other side of the table and Gwenvael and Dagmar quietly plotted in the far corner of the room.

"I'm fine. Feel a bit foolish, though. I learned long ago never go straight for a Kyvich. I should have snuck up on the twat."

"I thought you were just going on a picnic," he reminded his mate.

Annwyl looked off and instead of replying to his statement, she said, "She admires them, you know. Wants to be them."

"Who? Talwyn? *Our* Talwyn? Annwyl, I honestly don't think Talwyn admires or wants to be like anyone. Our daughter is uniquely horrifying. . . . That's why I love her."

"Then what—"

"It's knowledge our girl craves, Annwyl. She uses the Kyvich as she uses everyone else she thinks can teach her something."

"They want her for one of their own, Fearghus. And they're not going to let me stand in their way."

"They'll never have her, luv. Not really. Not like they think they will. Talwyn's soul belongs only to her. I thought you knew that."

"But I can't even have a bloody picnic with my own children because of these twats!"

"You didn't think we'd hold on to Talwyn and Talan forever, did you?"

"Why not? Lots of royals' kids live with their parents until someone dies."

Fearghus chuckled. "Someone dies because someone poisons all those in the way of their inheritance. But for dragons—and our offspring are half dragon—living with parents for any length of time is simply not an option."

"Why?"

"Because they irritate the living shit out of us and it's the only way to ensure we don't kill them while they sleep."

"Oh." Annwyl shrugged. "Well, when you put it that way . . ."

"Annwyl?"

Annwyl leaned forward a bit to see who spoke to her. It was Brastias . . . and he wasn't alone. Behind him were two dragons in capes. Fearghus recognized the smell of flame if not the scent of the dragons themselves.

"Someone here to see you."

The tallest of the pair stepped forward and pulled back the hood of his cloak. "Hello, Annwyl."

Just one look at the steel-colored hair that fell forward had Fearghus standing, but, after a second, he recognized the face. He especially recognized the black eye patch. The Rebel King of the Quintilian Provinces.

Considering Annwyl had traveled and fought at the side of King Gaius Domitus long before Fearghus had, he'd expected her to remember the dragon. Then again, perhaps he should have known better. . . .

"Yeah?" Annwyl asked.

The Iron blinked, glanced at Fearghus. "It's me. Gaius."

Annwyl frowned. "Gaius who?"

"From the west?" he tried.

"The west of where?"

At this point, Gwenvael was laughing hysterically, Briec

could only shake his head, and Dagmar was rushing across the room to properly greet a powerful monarch.

Pretense gone, the king folded his arms over his chest and snapped, "Good gods, woman! Did that wolf you kept talking about lick the sense from your thick head?"

"Look—" Annwyl began but Gwenvael cut her off.

"Wait. I'm sorry. What was that about a wolf? And what was it licking?"

Annwyl swiped her hand through the air. "It isn't what you think, Gwenvael."

"I can think many things, so you really do need to clarify."

"The god who helped me was a wolf, and he liked to lick my forehead." Annwyl shrugged. "It helped me focus."

"Wolf god?" Talaith asked. "The god who helped you was Nannulf?"

Annwyl sighed. "I guess." She focused on the Iron. "So you're Gaius, right? Yes. Now I remember. The Rebel King and all that."

"Right. The Rebel King. You rescued my sister, Agrippina," Gaius said with a sweeping gesture to the female standing behind him, "fought by my side in battle and together our armies destroyed Overlord Thracius. *That* Rebel King."

"Yeah, yeah. I remember." She studied him for a long moment before asking, "Were you always missing that eye?"

"Annwyl!" Dagmar barked, her small body now standing in front of the Iron as if trying to protect him.

"It's a fair question! I mean, did I take it myself? Because that could be awkward!"

"No," the Iron replied. "You didn't take my eye. I'm not sure why you'd think you had."

"I had a lot going on then," Annwyl admitted. "I was killing and dismembering people all over the place. Your eye could have definitely been a casualty." She smiled. "Glad to know it wasn't me, though."

Dagmar faced the Iron, quickly bowed her head. "King Gaius, I'm sorry about the confusion. I'm Dagmar Reinholdt, Vassal of Garbhán Isle and Battle Lord—"

"And my piece of ass!" Gwenvael announced from the other end of the table while he dropped into one of the chairs. "So keep your grubby Sovereign claws off her."

"—and," Dagmar continued desperately, "I'd like to welcome you and your companions to Garbhán Isle. If you don't mind staying human, there are rooms here, but we do have some lovely caves—"

"Rooms are fine," the Iron cut in, his glower still on Annwyl. "But we really came here to meet with Bram the Merciful."

"Izzy," Brastias cut in, "said she'd make sure to have him sent here."

"Excellent. Thank you, Brastias. While you're waiting, my lord," Dagmar offered, "why not take a few minutes to freshen up after your long journey in one of the available guest rooms? We can have some food sent up or you can eat down here—and *who let this disgusting animal in the house?*"

Izzy's dog immediately sat, slobber-filled tongue hanging out of his mouth as he gazed up at her.

"Izzy left him to watch out for our visitors while she handled some other . . . things," Brastias explained.

"Well . . . he smells. So could you please put him outside . . . or in a pit somewhere. Perhaps a shallow grave."

"Not sure Izzy will like that last one, but I'll see what I can do." Brastias grabbed a piece of bread from the table and swiped it by the dog's nose. "Come on, boy."

Since the dog would and did eat anything, he immediately followed.

Dagmar let out a breath and again focused her attention on the royals. "Now . . . where was I?"

"You were welcoming us to Garbhán Isle."

"Oh. Right."

* * *

Éibhear escorted them to the table, got them seated, then proceeded to pour them tea. When he was done with that, he put out a plate of sweet biscuits and sat down at the table. He smiled at them. "Now isn't this better?"

"Much," Rhi said, sipping her tea. "Thank you, Uncle Éibhear."

"You're welcome."

Izzy slammed her elbows on the table and buried her face in her hands.

"What's wrong?" Éibhear asked.

"This," she said, dropping her hands and looking over Éibhear and her sister. "This is what's wrong with our family."

"Our love of tea?"

"*No.*" She closed her eyes and took a breath. "The fact that we don't address anything directly."

"I didn't say we couldn't address anything. I just think we should do it over tea."

"It's soothing," Rhi added.

The two smiled at each other again and Izzy decided that was it.

Pushing back her chair, she stood. "Get up. Let's go."

Éibhear's eyes narrowed. "Go where?"

Bram the Merciful decided to meet with King Gaius and his sister up in their room. After what he'd heard from the Cadwaladrs about the latest event between the Southland queens and the Kyvich witches, he knew that energy levels would be high. With high energy levels came ridiculous arguments, violent outbursts, and fistfights. Always with the fistfights. It still amazed him that although the Cadwaladrs were the low-born battle dogs of the Southland dragons, it was the ones who were heirs to the Dragon Queen's throne who were the most violent and unpredictable.

He didn't need any of that sort of thing around the current ruler of at least part of the Quintilian Provinces.

Since the war against Overlord Thracius had ended, Gaius Domitus and his twin sister, Princess Agrippina, had taken over rule, but those who once ruled with Overlord Thracius, especially one of his sons, refused to bow down to the Rebel King. So the Provinces had become divided and a constant civil war had been going on since. Bram knew well the reputation of Thracius's son and he knew that Queen Rhiannon could not afford for the Rebel King to lose. Any offspring of Thracius's was a danger to the safety of the Southland dragons, something Bram was not about to forget or dismiss.

"What is it you need from us, King Gaius?"

"Gaius, please." The young dragon dropped into a chair, long legs stretched out in front of him. He looked exhausted, probably having come to the conclusion that obtaining rule was one thing, keeping it something else altogether. "I don't really have the luxury of niceties at the moment." He glanced at his sister, motioned to the bed. "Sit down, Aggie, before you drop."

The dragoness glanced at Bram before asking her brother, "Are you really sure we're safe here? That crazy woman didn't even remember us. And we've never met the Dragon Queen, so she and her offspring have no reason to feel the need to—"

"You're safe here, my lady," Bram promised. "On my honor and my name, you, your brother, and the soldiers you've brought with you will be kept safe and protected as long as you're in Garbhán Isle."

"Yes, but . . ." She sat down on the bed, her body turned toward Bram. "The human queen. Can she be trusted?"

"Aggie—"

"She didn't even remember your name, Gaius."

"Annwyl doesn't care," Bram admitted.

Lady Agrippina blinked. "Pardon?"

"She doesn't care. About you. About your brother. About your problems in the west. She doesn't care."

"Then why are we here? And how are we safe?"

"Oh, you couldn't be safer."

The twins frowned at the same time and Bram explained, "What I mean is Annwyl does not care about politics. Who's in charge and where, means nothing to her. But if you're a threat, she'll destroy you. If you're an ally, she'll protect you with her life."

"Even though she doesn't seem to remember us?" the king asked.

"Annwyl remembers bloodshed. And fights. And betrayal. So, you really don't want her to remember you when she's not seeing you every day."

"Oh," Lady Agrippina said, the sarcasm heavy, "well, that makes me feel better."

"You're under the protection of both queens, no one will touch you. Now tell me what you need."

The two Iron dragons looked at each other and some unspoken communication passed between them. Then the king said, "Is there a way you can get me or our representatives into the Desert Lands?"

"Not without many months, possibly years, of treaty negotiations. The current treaty we have with the Sand dragons took me a decade and even then . . . the signing was not a simple thing. May I ask why you'd need to go into the Desert Lands?"

Again, the twins looked at each other. After a moment, Agrippina admitted, "Our spies tell us that our cousin Vateria is now in the Desert Lands."

"Is Vateria still considered a threat?"

"Oh, yes. She has every intention of getting the Provinces

back under her family's banner and she'll do anything necessary to make that happen."

"You're worried about the Sand dragons striking against your troops?"

The king nodded. "We are. Any relationship we'd hoped to have with the Sand dragons was destroyed by our uncle during the early years of his reign."

"Aye. I remember. He kidnapped and killed one of the old king's daughters. The late King Abasi."

"Exactly." The king looked at his sister. "Perhaps I can get in there. Undetected."

"I wouldn't suggest that, my lord," Bram said in his most soothing I-want-Rhiannon-*not*-to-kill-everyone-in-the-cavern voice. "The Sand dragons are not to be trifled with."

"I'm not going there for the Sand dragons. I'm going there for my little traitor of a cousin."

"I understand but—"

"You understand nothing. She . . . tortured my sister. For months." The king glanced at her, but she was staring out the window. "For that alone—"

"Tell me, my lord, is this about protecting your people and your reign or getting even with the dragoness who abused the sister you love?"

"Does it matter?"

She'd blocked him, so it took some time for Talan to track down his sister. He should have known to look in the trees. Since she could walk, she'd spent most of her days in the trees. It had always driven their nanny, Ebba, insane. She was a centaur and climbing trees, no matter her form, was not one of her favorite activities.

Ebba. He missed her. Although she planned to come back, she'd gone home for three months because her father was unwell. A shame really. She'd always had a way with Talwyn and, most importantly, kept the Kyvich leader at bay.

But all that was meaningless now, wasn't it? Because his sister had made up her mind. And, like the two suns in the sky, that was something that would never be changed.

Talan grabbed hold of the lowest branch and pulled himself up into the old tree. He climbed until he reached the branch his sister sat on. He dropped down next to her, letting out a relaxed sigh once he was comfortable.

"So were you going to let Odda kill our mother or just let her wound her grievously instead?"

"Mum's not exactly a weak flower."

"Mum's not a witch either. Like a pit dog, she'll fight anyone, but that doesn't mean she should. And it's not like she and Odda got along in the first place."

"It wasn't that bad."

"Mum kept calling Odda The Twat."

"She calls everyone she doesn't like The Twat. Especially men."

Talan studied his sister. "So you're really going to do this?"

"I have to."

"Oh? Has someone put a crossbow to your head?"

"You may be against this, but I'm sure Mum will get over it."

"It's not Mum I'm worried about. It's Rhi. We both felt the power of what she was unleashing at the training ring. If we hadn't been there—"

"I know."

"And yet you think it's a good idea to leave her? Now?"

"So I have to stay while you go?"

Talan looked away from his sister's steady gaze. And that's when she snapped, "Gods . . . you idiot."

"It's for the best I stay."

"It is *not* for the best. They've sent for you. I've done the research, brother. That is not common."

"Are you not going to miss us at all?"

Talwyn slumped a little. "This isn't about that and you know it."

"All I know is that we're strongest when we're together."

"And all I know is that the only thing we've been doing the last five years is coasting. Our skills haven't grown."

"Our skills or our power?"

"Both."

"What is it, sister? Do you hope to be both Dragon Queen *and* Southland Queen?"

"No. I hope to keep this bloodline alive and thriving for the next few millenniums. And if you think the three of us can do that sitting here while Mum and Dad take care of us, you're an idiot."

"Oy. You two."

They both leaned over and looked down. Izzy stood under the tree. Behind her stood Éibhear and Rhi. "Come on."

"Where?" Talan asked.

"To see the family. Time to talk this out."

Talwyn grunted. Never a good sign. "I have nothing to say to my mother."

"I don't care. Get your ass down here."

Lips pursed, Talwyn looked off. Talan knew that meant his sister had dismissed Izzy and that she had no intention of going anywhere. But Izzy was a top general in Annwyl's army and she was used to very large men following all her orders without question. So for Talwyn to think her cousin would tolerate this for even one second . . .

Really, she should never have taken her eyes off Izzy.

Without a word, Izzy walked around Éibhear and grabbed the axe he had strapped to his back. She hefted it, spun, and threw it. Talan quickly raised his arms and grabbed onto the tree limb just above him, but Talwyn was still looking off, so she didn't realize the axe had hit the tree limb they were on until she was falling.

She hit the ground hard, ass first.

Hands on her hips, Izzy asked, "Ready now, cousin?"

Talan released his grip on the limb and dropped to the ground. He landed on his feet and smiled at Izzy. "We're ready." He took hold of his sister's arm and yanked her to her feet, ignoring her snarl of pain because of her now-sore ass. "More than ready," he insisted. "Bring on the kin!"

Chapter 23

Dagmar was busy slapping Gwenvael's hand off her thigh for a fifth time when Izzy walked through the Great Hall doors with Éibhear, the twins, and Rhi behind her.

"Oh, good. You're all here," Izzy said.

"Everything all right?" Dagmar asked.

"No. Rhi believes herself to be pure evil and Talwyn is under the impression she doesn't have to follow orders anymore."

"Oh," Annwyl announced to the room as well as her daughter, "you can take orders from the bloody Kyvich but not a general in my army?"

"She's my cousin."

"*And a general in my army!*"

"*And I'm a princess!*" Talwyn yelled back.

"*Not if I rip that title from your hide!*"

"All of you," Talaith bellowed, "shut up!"

Mother and daughter stopped yelling, but they were clearly not happy about it as arms were crossed over chests and feet began to tap impatiently against the floor.

Talaith leaned forward, studied her youngest daughter. "You think you're evil?"

"Pure evil," Izzy clarified, which got her a rather vicious

glare from Rhi. An expression Dagmar had never thought the young, perpetually smiling or sobbing girl was capable of.

"Why would you think you're evil?"

"It's a feeling I have."

"No. Someone told her."

Rhi glowered at her sister. "I never said that."

"You didn't have to," Izzy shot back. "I know you."

"Well, who told her that?" Talaith demanded.

And, as one, they all turned and looked at Gwenvael.

He blinked, sat up straight. "I would *never* say such a thing to my dear sweet niece!"

"You said it to me," Talwyn snapped.

"That's because you're not my dear sweet niece. You're the rude little cow who threw a knife at my head."

"I wasn't aiming for you. I was aiming for Mum."

"She's right," Annwyl admitted. "I just ducked behind you." She shrugged. "Sorry."

"It wasn't Uncle Gwenvael."

"Then who?" Talaith pushed. "And you might as well tell me now because I'll just badger you until you do. Ask Izzy."

"She really will," Izzy said on a sigh.

Rhi looked down at her feet and finally whispered, "It was our great grandmother."

"*My* mother said that to you?" Bercelak asked. "Because she's been gone from this world for some time, luv."

"No." Rhi cleared her throat. "Adienna."

Rhiannon got to her feet so fast that her chair scraped the floor and slammed into the wall. "You spoke to my mother? *My* mother?" She looked at Bercelak. "I did kill her, didn't I? I know she tried to use you to murder me first, Bercelak, but then I clearly remember the life draining from her body while I snapped her neck with that chain and my bare hands. I didn't dream that, did I?"

Dagmar leaned over and whispered to Gwenvael, "Have I mentioned that I adore your kin?"

"More than your own?"

"Do you really have to ask me that?"

Briec walked up to his youngest daughter and placed his hand against her cheek. "You've seen your ancestors. You've been to the other side."

"Why?" Talaith asked. "Were you called?"

"No." Rhi nervously combed her hair behind her ears. "I just thought it would be nice to meet them. They're kin."

Using the tips of his fingers, Briec lifted his daughter's chin until he could look into her eyes. Eyes like his own. "You traveled to the lands of the dead?"

She nodded.

"Where did you learn to travel to the other side?"

Rhi shrugged. "I just knew."

The same answer his daughter had been giving him for more than a decade now. One not given to avoid answering the question but instead proving that her power far exceeded most of theirs. Even his mother, as far as Briec knew, had never traveled to the land of the dead. It was rumored Annwyl had been there, but she'd been dead at the time, so it made sense.

"Adienna," Rhiannon asked, stepping closer. "And she was with your Great Grandfather Ailean and Great Grandmother Shalin?"

"No. She wasn't there. With them."

"By the gods, Rhi," Talaith gasped, her hands covering her mouth.

"You've been to the hells," Briec guessed. "You've been to the hells and you met with my grandmother."

"Not for long."

Rhiannon stood beside him now. "Long enough for her to tell you that you, your power is evil."

Briec still held her chin so Rhi lowered her eyes. "She said I was just like her. That I'd be taking her place one day.

Everything I've read about her says she was a treacherous and purely evil female, so if I'm just like her . . ."

Rhiannon pushed Briec aside and caught hold of his daughter's chin, gripped it tight. "If you were just like her, my darling girl, I would have killed you at birth. With the same claws that killed her. Trust me when I say you are nothing like her. Nothing. Instead she does to you what she once did to me. She . . . she . . . well, excuse the term, my darling granddaughter, but that bitch fucks with your head. And you believe her."

"She seemed nice."

Éibhear, who'd been silent for most of this, finally said, "Rhi, luv, she was in hell."

"She said it was a misunderstanding."

Rhiannon finally laughed as she wrapped her arms around Rhi and held her close. "Trust me . . . there was no misunderstanding with that bitch. She's where she belongs. And you need to stop thinking the best of everyone. Majority of them don't deserve it."

"Then what is it?" Rhi asked, pulling back a bit so she could look her grandmother in the eyes. "Why can't I control my power?"

"From what I can tell, your power is like the most beautiful and worst of nature itself. You're the tsunami, you're the hurricane. Your power can destroy, but it can also create something new."

"So then I'll never be able to control it, and I'll continue to put those I love at risk."

"Except Mum says she's got a *brilliant* idea about that."

Surprised by Izzy's sarcastic tone, Briec looked to his mate. Her eyes were wide as she stared at their eldest daughter. "*Izzy.*"

"Let's get it out there, Mum. Now. All of it. I mean it's your idea, might as well stand behind it."

"What idea?" Briec cut in.

"Tell them, Mum."

Talaith blew out a breath, closed her eyes. "I thought per-haps . . . we could send Rhi to the Nolwenns for training. Send her to my mother."

Briec faced Talaith, gazed at her until he finally admitted, "I'd had the same thought."

"Daddy!"

Her father held his hands up at Izzy's words. "Before you get upset—"

"Too late! How could you think about sending my sister to that treacherous bitch?"

"Because I think we've run out of options."

Izzy shook her head. "She threw my mother into the street like trash. She was sixteen and alone and with child."

Rhi stepped away from their grandmother and walked over to Izzy. "But if she hadn't done that," she said softly, "I wouldn't be here."

Izzy rolled her eyes. "Oh, shut up."

"Well, thank you very much, you mean cow!"

"Like you thought that line of bullshit would work on *me*."

"Both of you stop it." Talaith stepped between them. "This isn't a decision for either of you. Your father and I will make this decision."

"But—"

"So suck up the pain!" her mother yelled at Izzy.

Growling, Izzy stalked over to the doors and stared out into the courtyard, arms crossed over her chest.

The hall fell silent and stayed that way until a throat-clear from the stairs had everyone turning. Uncle Bram stood there.

"Sorry to interrupt."

"So what do the Irons want, peacemaker?" Bercelak demanded of his sister's mate.

"Revenge."

Annwyl threw her hands up. "What did I do now?"

It took Great Uncle Bram a few minutes, but he finally convinced Auntie Annwyl that the Rebel King and his sister weren't looking for revenge against her but instead against Vateria. And while he did that, Rhi sat with her cousins in three chairs pushed up against the wall and watched her mother and sister. They weren't speaking. Mum was sitting by Daddy and seething. Izzy standing in the Great Hall doorway, staring out into the courtyard . . . and seething.

Although rare these days, it was never good when Mum and Izzy couldn't agree on something. This, however, was even worse because this was about Rhi. It wasn't that she had any great desire to leave her family, but to be honest, if she was going to destroy all around her with a misplaced spell, she'd rather do it to the witch who'd deserted her mum than Rhi's own family. But trying to explain anything to either her mum or Izzy, when they were both this angry, would be a waste of Rhi's breath. So she sat and listened to all the high-level politics. Talan was asleep in his chair and Talwyn was busy sharpening her sword, but Rhi was fascinated!

"How dangerous is she?" Grandmum asked Uncle Bram. "Really?"

"In my opinion . . . very."

"He's right," Auntie Annwyl agreed. "I only saw her from the fighting pit, but I remember that I really wanted to kill her. A lot."

Grandmum sat down across from Uncle Bram. "What does this Rebel King want from me?"

"Well, they were hoping that I could help them or their representatives get permission to enter the Desert Lands."

Grandmum laughed. "Not with King Heru now in charge!"

"That's what I told them. It would be a long, arduous process and I'm sure by then, Vateria would only move on."

"So what's the next option?"

"We send in our own to track Vateria down."

"And why would we do that?"

"There are many reasons."

"Name one that would actually make me care. Because at the moment this seems more like an internal family issue than a political one. And I don't involve myself in other dragons' family issues."

"I understand, my queen, and normally I'd agree with you. But it's believed that Vateria is working to secure an ally that will help her family regain their dead father's throne. With what I've been hearing lately about unrest in the Desert Lands, the citizens might be eager for such a move, depending on what she can promise."

"I understand that, Bram. And she could be sucking the cocks of every Sand Eater soldier in the hopes of getting her own army. But until she actually puts that army into play for her own benefit, I have no intention of striking her down simply because she doesn't know how to treat her cousin properly."

There was a long silence after Grandmum's words and she looked around the Great Hall at everyone staring at her and demanded, "What? What are you all looking at?"

"That was just so"—Auntie Morfyd shrugged—"*rational* of you."

"Aye." Uncle Fearghus rested his arms against the table and studied his mother. "I thought at the very least you'd send in Keita to poison her."

Auntie Morfyd grinned. "I thought that, too!"

Aghast, Grandmum snapped, "I'm not a monster!"

"Heh."

Everyone looked down the length of the table. Auntie Annwyl covered her mouth. "Oh, did I say that out loud?"

Grandmum's eyes narrowed while her children quietly laughed. "I'm not saying Vateria's not a problem. I'd just prefer we had something a little more concrete on her than she tortures her cousin." Although to Rhi that alone seemed more than enough.

"We'll send someone south," Uncle Gwenvael suggested. "Get more information and find out if Vateria's truly a threat or if she's just fucking one of the Sand Eaters for entertainment."

Grandmum nodded. "I like that idea. Who will we send?"

Izzy, who was still staring out into the courtyard, her arms folded under her chest, looked at Grandmum over her shoulder. "I'll go."

While everyone else took a moment to be stunned, Mum jumped to her feet. "Like hells you will!"

"I'm going, Mum."

"This has nothing to do with Vateria, Izzy. This is all about my mother."

Izzy shrugged. "Two vile bitches, one stone."

"I forbid it."

"I don't report to you, my lady." And Rhi winced at that one. "And before Annwyl tries to stay on your good side—"

"I haven't said a word!" Auntie Annwyl complained.

"—keep in mind that none of *you* can actually blend in while in the south. But I can."

"I don't care what bloody Annwyl says about a bloody thing!" Mum roared. "*You will not do this!*"

"Wait." Daddy gripped Mum's wrist and pulled her over to him and onto his lap. "Everyone just wait." He looked Izzy over for a moment. "I'll ask you straight out, Iseabail, Daughter of Talaith and Briec. . . . Are you planning to kill your grandmother?"

"I'd like to," Izzy immediately shot back. "But no. I want

to look her in the eye. I want to find out for myself whether my sister can be trusted with her."

"And if you think she can be?"

Izzy rubbed her nose with the palm of her hand, scratched her cheek, then spit out, "Then I'll bring her here to meet with Rhi." Her sister looked over and Rhi felt her heart stop in her chest. "You can make your decision then, Rhi, about what you want to do next."

Rhi jumped up and sprinted across the room and into her sister's arms. "Thank you, Izzy! Thank you!"

Izzy tightly hugged her back. "You're welcome. But," she felt the need to add, "if I don't like the evil cow—"

"I know. I know." Rhi bounced on her toes while continuing to hug her sister. "Still! You're trying!"

"You can't go alone, Iseabail," Uncle Bram warned her. "Although your many weapons and dressing as a warrior will work to your benefit as long as you remove your colors, women don't usually travel alone in the south. They either travel with family members or other women."

"I'll ask Brannie."

"She hates the desert heat, I'm afraid."

"I'll get her drunk first, and she'll go far enough with me that by the time she sobers up, it'll be too much trouble to head back."

"Ah, yes," Uncle Bram sighed. "A father does love hearing that about his daughter."

Once the decision was made that Izzy would be going and, of course, somehow tricking poor Brannie to go along, she disappeared with Bram to get a quick lesson in Desert Land etiquette; Talaith stormed off, most likely to rant about her firstborn, Briec following her with an eye roll and a sigh; and everyone else went their own way until dinner time. All except Talan, who was still asleep in a chair, snoring.

Éibhear decided to leave the boy where he was and headed outside. He saw Frederik sitting on the stairs, looking quite bored, and decided to give him a task.

"Think you can find my friends again?"

He quickly got to his feet but almost fell off the steps doing so. "Yes, sir. I saw them heading into town earlier today."

"Good. Go get them for me, would you? Tell them I need to see them now. So they need to put down whatever ale or whore they may currently have in their hands."

With a grin, the first Éibhear could remember seeing from the boy, Frederik nodded. "I will, sir." Then he charged off. Almost ran into a horse merely standing in the road, minding its own business but . . . well . . . whatever.

"You've been awfully quiet."

Éibhear looked down at his mother. "I have. Sorry. Lots of things going on."

"I get worried when things are too quiet, so I don't mind a little activity." His mother slipped her arm through his and together they walked down the steps. "So . . . you going with Izzy when she heads south?"

"Do you really have to ask me that?"

Rhiannon's head tipped back as she laughed. "No, I guess I don't." She patted his arm with her free hand. "But I hope you know what you're getting yourself into. Izzy's a true warrior, with a warrior's soul. If she thinks for a minute that you're just trying to protect her—"

"Don't worry. I have all sorts of excuses that even she will have to agree with. They're all very logical and sane . . . unlike her."

They stopped in the middle of the courtyard and Rhiannon faced him. "Be careful in the south, my son. They do things differently there."

"After the Ice Lands, Mum, I can handle anything."

"True. But you didn't have Iseabail the Dangerous's adorable little ass distracting you while you were in the Ice Lands."

"Mum."

"What? I'm not blind. Just remember. She may not be blood, but your brother sees her as his daughter. So you can't just fuck this one and toss her away like you and your brothers have been doing since you each stumbled out of your eggs. You can't treat this one like a whore. She's family!"

"*Mum.*"

"What?"

Chapter 24

Izzy was up and dressed before the two suns had risen. She'd slept in her old room in the castle, her sister curled up next to her. Before she walked out the door, Rhi stopped her and hugged her tight.

"Please be careful."

"I will be. I promise." She kissed both her sister's cheeks and gave her another hug. "I shouldn't be long. Don't fight with Daddy."

"Okay."

Izzy opened the bedroom door and Rhi added, "And bring me something."

"Bring you something? Like what?"

"Something pretty. But local. But nothing with big bows, small bows are fine. Color-wise, silver and pink are good. Or very dark reds. No bright reds. And Mum won't let me wear black yet, but she is okay with blues and—where are you going? Well, I like green, too! Dark green! And good luck, Izzy! I love you!"

Izzy made it down the stairs, where her father was waiting. He smiled at her. "Silver and pink are her favorite colors, though."

"I've decided. She's not allowed to spend any more time alone with Keita. Pink?" she sneered. "Really?"

Chuckling, Briec leaned down and kissed her on the cheek. "Please. For the sake of *my* sanity, be careful. Your mother will be absolutely intolerable if any harm comes to you. And, I will definitely miss someone who irritates me so little."

Izzy hugged her father. "I promise to keep myself safe just so you won't have to hear any complaints from anyone."

"That's my girl."

Izzy stepped away from her father and pulled her travel bag over her shoulders. "I love you, Daddy."

"I love you."

She smiled and headed toward the Great Hall doors.

"And Izzy—" She stopped, faced him. "When you meet your grandmother, think about Rhi. Not your mum. Not you. This is about your sister, don't forget that."

"I'll remember. I promise not to kill the old bitch unless I have to."

Briec quickly looked away, cleared his throat. She knew he wanted to laugh, but he was trying to be stern. She guessed she wasn't helping him.

"Thank you for that."

Izzy walked to the doors and pulled one open. "Tell Mum I'll talk to her when I get back."

She didn't wait to hear her father's response, instead heading down the stairs and across the courtyard to the stables.

"Morning, General," one of the stable hands said as he walked out, stopping to hold the door open for her.

"Morning, Richard."

Izzy walked inside but stopped short when she saw her mother standing by Dai's stall. Dai had his head over the stall gate and Talaith petted him from his forelock down to his muzzle.

"You're spoiling him," Izzy said as she stood on the other side of the horse.

"Can't help it. He's beautiful."

"And loyal."

Talaith smirked. "Yes. Loyalty."

"Don't worry, Mum. I have no intention of killing the old bitch. I still think this is an insane idea, but if there's a chance she can help . . ."

"Do you think that's why I'm worried about you going? It's not. While I'm sure my mother will be more than happy to help your sister, she'll have no use for you, Izzy. And those she doesn't have use for—"

Izzy took her mother's hand, held it to her chest. "Leave her to me. I promise to be careful. Very careful."

"And what about traveling through the Desert Lands? It's a vast region, Izzy."

"I have maps and—"

"No worries," Izzy heard from another stall, and she dropped her mother's hand and spun around to see Éibhear standing by the horse he'd rode into Garbhán Isle just a few days before. "Oh. Sorry to startle you. Just cleaning out the muck from this one's hooves." He patted the horse's rump. "Isn't that right, girl?"

Taking the horse's reins, he led her out of the stall. "As I was saying, Aidan lived quite a few years in the Desert Lands with an uncle. So he'll be leading us once we cross Southland borders."

"Oh." Talaith looked back and forth between Izzy and Éibhear. "I didn't know you'd be going with Izzy on this trip."

"Mum wants us to handle the Iron dragoness if she turns out to be a true problem. It's not the first time the Mì-runach have taken on this type of excursion. Besides, it'll be nice to see where you come from, Talaith."

"Right." Her mother's eyes narrowed the tiniest bit, but she didn't question Éibhear, which seemed strange since one of Briec's biggest complaints about his mate was that she asked too many damn questions.

"Well," Talaith said, going on her toes as Éibhear came down a bit so she could kiss his cheek. "Both of you be careful. And I hope you'll be back in time for the harvest festival." She kissed Izzy's cheek. "Good luck, luv."

"Thanks, Mum."

Talaith stepped back, looked both over again, then said, "Yeah, well . . all right then." And off she went, cutting around Éibhear and his horse to head out the door.

Once her mother was gone, Izzy faced Éibhear and stared at him.

He smiled. "Well, you ready then?"

Aidan yawned and wished, again, that he was back in bed where he belonged. Honestly, the things he was sometimes forced to do for friends . . . which was probably why he didn't have a lot of them.

He glanced over at Uther, watched the dragon in human form stick his nose against his horse's neck.

"You can't eat it, Uther."

"I know."

"Then stop smelling it."

"It's not my fault he smells yummy."

"We'll find you something to eat once we get on the road."

"Why are we doing this again?" Caswyn asked. Instead of sniffing his horse, he merely laid his crossed arms over its back and his head on his crossed arms. A few times Aidan was sure he'd heard snoring. Then again, Caswyn was one of the few dragons he knew who could sleep while standing up . . . and with his eyes open. Aye. It was off-putting.

"Because Éibhear's a desperate idiot," Aidan replied to his comrade's question.

"That's what I thought."

The gorgeous Lady Talaith walked out of the stables. And, gods, she was *gorgeous*. If her mate wasn't a clearly unstable monarch whose brothers were even more unstable, Aidan would at least display his wingspan. He'd always found there was something about gold dragons in the early-morning suns with their wings unfurled that could entice any female. But he'd heard enough from Éibhear and his own kin—when he was still forced to talk to them—about the insanity of the Gwalchmai fab Gwyar and Cadwaladr bloodlines to know that there were some females simply not worth the risk.

Although if there was one who might possibly be risk-worthy . . .

As she walked by them, Aidan saw a mother's concern on that beautiful face and felt the need to assure her. "We'll take very good care of your daughter, my Lady Talaith."

She stopped, looked at each one of the Mì-runach, smirked, and said to Aidan, "When my daughter is being a general, her legion's well-being is of utmost concern to her. However, when she's doing things without her legion, she'll take risks that most would consider highly dangerous. Hence the name, Izzy the Dangerous, that she'd received long before I'd met her. So I say this as someone who is sure that all of you have someone who cares for you the way I care for my daughter—whatever you do, don't let her get you killed. Because something does tell me . . . she's really going to try with you lot. She's going to try very hard."

They watched the royal walk off.

"What was that about?" Aidan asked his comrades. His stupid comrades.

"Don't know," Uther sighed. "But I do like that dagger she's got holstered to her leg."

"Aye," Caswyn agreed. "Very sexy. I think it's her thighs."

"Could anyone," Aidan asked, "be as stupid as you two?"

"Before you get upset—" Éibhear began, but Izzy cut him off with a slight wave of her hand.

"No, no. I'm not upset."

Éibhear forced himself not to shield his head with his hands. He just knew she was going to throw something at his head. "You're not?"

"No. It'll be good to have Aidan along with us if he truly knows his way around the Desert Lands."

"He does. Even knows where to find the Nolwenns."

"And the Mì-runach as protection? Could a general ask for more?"

"I guess not."

"Then that's fine. Let's get going."

She turned and he took a quick step back, but she merely grabbed the reins of her horse and his and headed out of the stables.

Beginning to panic, Éibhear looked around, expecting to see an arrow flying at his head or an assassin with a poisoned knife hiding in a corner. But there was nothing.

Shaking his head, muttering to himself about being foolish, he followed after Izzy. He'd just stepped outside the stables when a smelly, drooling, snarling mass of dirty, disgusting fur collided with his head, knocking him to the ground.

Izzy watched her dog express exactly what she was feeling without her having to do anything. Say anything. Dagmar had to give orders to her perfectly bred dogs. But that wasn't necessary with Macsen.

Éibhear grabbed hold of both sides of Macsen's neck, holding him tight, but the dog kept snapping, kept trying to rip his face off.

"Call him off!" Éibhear yelled. "Or I'm setting the bastard on fire!"

Izzy gave a short whistle and Macsen pulled back. Éibhear released him and the dog jumped off his chest and walked around him, snapping at his head once more before going to Izzy's side and sitting at her feet.

"See?" Izzy said, pointing at the dog. "That's loyalty. Loyalty and he listens to me. I find that invaluable."

Éibhear got to his big feet, brushing dirt off his leggings and fur cape. "He's a *dog*, Izzy."

"Yes. Just a dog. And yet he still manages to be better than you."

She mounted Dai, patting his big neck once she was seated. "I won't try to stop you from coming with me, Éibhear. But if you get in my way, I'll crush you and the Mìrunach scum with you. Clear?"

She didn't wait for him to answer, simply turned her horse around and, with Macsen running by Dai's side, she went off to the pub where Celyn had taken Brannie for a little late-night drink.

Éibhear went out of his way not to look at his comrades, focusing on Izzy riding away from them. Besides, he didn't need to see his fellow dragons' faces to know exactly what they were thinking.

"You fucked her, didn't you?" Aidan demanded.

Éibhear shrugged, still not looking at them. "Maybe."

"Do you know how I can tell? Because she *hates* you."

"It's not hate. It's confusion. I've overwhelmed her with my—"

"Stupidity?" Aidan shook his head. "When your brothers find out—"

"Let's deal with one nightmare scenario at a time, shall we?" Éibhear snapped.

"Are we really going to do this?" Aidan asked him. "Because from what I can tell she hates you; her mother just gave us dire warnings; and you had what I can only term as a pathetic, love-sick look on your face *even* while she was threatening you and all of us."

"Was that what I was looking at?" Uther pulled back his top lip in disgust. "I find that disturbing."

Fed up and unwilling to talk about any of this, Éibhear strode to his horse. "Mount up, Mì-runach. We ride!"

Chapter 25

Brannie opened her eyes and briefly wondered when she'd gotten on her horse. And why she'd gotten on her horse. And why she seemed to be riding somewhere on her horse.

She blinked, trying to clear her vision. She was so tired and a little sick, the motion of her horse not exactly helping with that.

When her vision was a little more clear, Brannie looked around. Izzy was riding ahead of her, Éibhear behind. Both seemed to be pouting.

Surrounding Brannie were the other Mì-runach.

"Where are we going?" she asked.

"To the Desert Lands," Aidan said, sounding annoyingly chipper this early morning. And loud. Why was he yelling?

"Why are we going to the Desert Lands?"

"To face witches and possibly kill a treacherous Iron dragoness, unless this is all an elaborate trap and they kill us first, of course."

Brannie let out a long sigh. "I kind of knew I'd regret drinking with my brothers last night—I just had no idea how much."

* * *

First meal was a mostly silent affair, with everyone concerned about . . . well, about everything.

Even Dagmar, who tried not to worry about little things since Talaith and Morfyd were so good at that, was concerned. Concerned that Annwyl would be plunging them into a war with the Kyvich. Although now that she thought about it . . . that wasn't really a little thing, was it?

Rhi charged down the stairs, dressed in a pretty gown, a fur cape around her shoulders and her bag with all her art supplies over her shoulder.

"Good morn, all!" She reached around her mother, taking a loaf of bread. She tore off a piece, shoved it in her mouth, and cheered, "I'm off to draw!"

"Stay near the castle grounds," Briec ordered. "And away from the Kyvich."

"I will, Daddy." She kissed him on the forehead and walked out.

Waiting a few extra seconds, Dagmar nodded at one of the female guards and she followed Rhi out.

Unbeknownst to Rhi, Dagmar always had the girl followed once she was outside the castle gates. She'd tried to do the same with the twins, but the guards kept losing sight of them. Although it took some time for Dagmar to find out about that because the guards had always been afraid to tell her. So, instead, they'd finally told Annwyl and she told Dagmar. She tried not to think too much about the fact that the guards had been less worried about telling Annwyl the Bloody they'd lost track of *her* children than of telling Dagmar.

While the guard went out the door, Frederik was coming in. Only one of the double doors was open and Dagmar watched the poor boy try to move around the well-armed and well-armored woman. It was kind of like an awkward dance.

Letting out an annoyed sigh, the guard moved back and allowed Frederik through. He came in quickly, heading for the stairs.

"Have you eaten, Frederik?" Annwyl asked him, causing the boy to stumble over his own feet. But at least he managed not to fall on his face.

"Uh . . ."

"That sounds like a no." She pointed to the table. "Food. You need to eat."

He walked over to the table, then walked into it, stepped back, then sat down in a chair across from Dagmar.

"Good morn, Frederik."

He nodded, but didn't look at her. "Auntie Dagmar."

Talaith got up from the table and proceeded to get him a bowl of hot porridge and some bread while Annwyl widened her eyes at Dagmar and motioned to Frederik with her head. Dagmar didn't like to be ordered by anyone to apologize, but Annwyl was queen and since she didn't stop nodding at the boy, Dagmar could only guess that the monarch was serious.

Letting out a little sigh, Dagmar began, "Frederik, about yesterday . . . about what I said—"

"Good morn, my wonderful family!" Keita announced as she walked into the Great Hall with Ragnar. "How is everyone this beautiful morning?"

"Why are you in such a good mood?" Briec's eyes narrowed. "Who did you kill?"

Laughing, Ragnar walked around Keita and sat at the table, reaching for one of the platters of meat.

"How dare you?" Keita snapped at her brother. "To suggest that *I*—"

"Oh, aye," Annwyl laughed. "Someone's dead somewhere."

Keita walked over to Frederik and placed her hands over his ears. The poor thing, he was beginning to look completely traumatized.

"Must you say such horrible things around the boy?"

Gwenvael chuckled. "I very much doubt the boy cares." He focused on Frederik and yelled, "*Do you, Frederik?*"

Dagmar glared at her mate. "Why, by all reason, are you yelling?"

He shrugged. "I have no idea."

"Leave the boy alone." Keita moved her hands from his head and leaned down, yelling at the boy, "*Are you enjoying your time here, Frederik? Is there anything we can do for you?*"

Dagmar slammed her hands on the table. "Why are you both yell—"

"That reminds me," Ragnar cut in, his calm, reasonable voice snapping her back.

"Reminds you about what?"

He reached into his bag and pulled out a book and a small wood box. He walked around to Frederik, moved his porridge out of the way, and put an open book on the table in front of him. "Can you read that?"

"*Ragnar?*"

He held his hand up at Dagmar, silencing her.

"I can," Frederik said low. "Just not very well."

"Right." Ragnar crouched down next to him and pulled a pair of spectacles out of the box he held. Taking his time, he placed them on Frederik, adjusting them behind the boy's ears and around his nose. "Now look again."

The boy shrugged, his gaze moving to the book in front of him. He stared. Blinked. Leaned in a bit. Blinked.

"I . . . I don't understand."

"It seems you have the opposite of what your Aunt Dagmar has. She has trouble seeing far distances. You have trouble seeing close up. That's why you struggle with reading. It probably gave you headaches when you tried to read? Your eyes felt tired?"

"Sometimes."

"Did you teach yourself not to squint?"

Frederik looked over the glasses at Dagmar. "I used to squint. My father said it made me look weak. So . . . I stopped."

Dagmar, shocked, focused on Ragnar. "How did you know?"

He shrugged. "It was a guess. And the more Keita and Gwenvael talked to the boy, the louder they became. Before Frederik arrived, they only seemed to do that with you."

"But"—Keita covered the boy's ears again, and whispered—"he still seems clumsy and awkward. You don't want to convince him that these pieces of glass will cure all his problems."

"You have a point." Ragnar reached across the table, grabbing a piece of fruit from a bowl. He tossed it to Talaith. "Lady Talaith. If you please."

Talaith shrugged and pitched the fruit at Frederik's head. Dagmar cringed, afraid it would hit him directly in the face. But he caught the fruit in his hand. Without even looking.

"Oh." Keita stepped back. "I see."

"So do I." Dagmar pushed her chair back and stood.

"Where are you going?" Gwenvael asked her.

"To write my father." She walked toward the hallway that would lead to the small office she kept inside the castle, her two dogs slipping out from under the table and following her. "This level of deception and lies must be addressed immediately."

"Aunt Dagmar—"

She stopped, faced the boy, raising a single finger. "No, Frederik. There's nothing more to discuss."

Frederik lowered his gaze. "I understand."

Gwenvael rested his chin on his raised fist, smirked at Dagmar. "What *are* you going to do with him, my love?"

"What do you think?" Dagmar demanded. "Keep him! I'd never send a plotting little liar like this back to the dullards of my family. Oh, no. I will keep you, boy, and I will train you, and I will use you to the fullest extent of your twisted capabilities." She clapped her hands together. "I'm so damn excited!"

She spun around and again headed to her office, but she heard Gwenvael say to the boy, "Welcome to the family, Frederik."

* * *

They stopped for a brief meal break in the woods not far from the road they were traveling. Izzy sat down next to Brannie, offering her some dried beef and bread.

"Are you still not talking to me?" Izzy asked.

"I'm hungover. But you can't just keep kidnapping me anytime you want to do something ridiculously dangerous."

"But if I ask you when you're sober, we spend hours arguing before you just finally agree. This cuts down on the arguing."

Her cousin glowered at her. "You are a plotting little cow and some days I loathe you."

Izzy put her arm around her cousin's shoulders and kissed her cheek. "But most days you love me because there's nowhere else you can get this level and diversity of combat training."

"Yes, I just need to survive long enough to enjoy the benefits."

"Don't worry. You'll be general before you know it."

"Unlike you, that has not been my lifelong goal. I do have a question, though, cousin."

"Hhhm?"

"Macsen seems to have taken a sudden and rather brutal dislike to Éibhear."

"He never liked Éibhear."

"But he seems to dislike him even more now." She jerked her head toward the other end of the clearing and Izzy watched the big blue idiot trying to get her dog to release the dragon's tight ass, which was currently caught between Macsen's jaws.

"Perhaps he simply finds Éibhear irritating and confusing."

"Macsen finds Éibhear irritating and confusing? Macsen? The dog?"

Taking one more bite of her bread, Izzy stood and walked over to pry her dog off Éibhear.

* * *

Brannie watched Izzy try to call off that dog of hers. Although if Brannie were to be honest, she'd have to admit that Izzy was not trying very hard. Not as hard as she would if this was one of her soldiers.

Aidan sat down where Izzy had been sitting.

"What?" Brannie asked him.

"My, we are awfully snarly. I think I saw fang."

"What do you want, Mì-runach?"

"Just sitting here, being entertained by our friends."

"Éibhear isn't my friend. He's kin. A blood relation."

"Which means what exactly?"

"To a Cadwaladr, it means that if I have good cause, I could beat the scales off his back and get away with it."

"Ah, yes. More confirmation I never want to meet the rest of your family. Although you're so welcoming . . ."

Brannie went back to eating her bread and meat until Uther sat on the other side of her. She had to admit, being surrounded by Mì-runach was unsettling. Her mother had raised her with two beliefs about the Mì-runach: they were invaluable in battle, but you should never turn your back on one.

"But what about granddad?" Brannie had asked, holding on to her mother's tail while the dragoness had walked through a forest near their home. "He was Mì-runach."

"And the worst of the lot, my girl. The worst of the lot. Especially to his offspring. We never turned our backs on your grandfather. Addolgar did once . . . he still has that scar where his head got split open."

So Brannie assumed if her own grandfather couldn't have been trusted, then obviously three strange Mì-runach she didn't even know could definitely *not* be trusted. Yet Brannie still felt the need to ask them a question.

"Perhaps it's the leftover ale still rolling around my head, but . . ." She motioned to a bickering Izzy and Éibhear while the dog kept barking and trying to re-attach itself to Éibhear's ass. "Has something changed between those two?"

The Mì-runach looked at each other and then over at the arguing Izzy and Éibhear. Izzy's dog was in her arms now but still attempting to lunge at Éibhear's face.

Together, the males stated, "Not at all."

After a few more hours of travel, they stopped in a town pub for a meal and to discuss the remainder of their trip.

Izzy had been sure that Éibhear had made up all that centaur shit about Aidan knowing his way around the Desert Lands in order to convince her mother he and his friends were necessary. But it turned out Aidan had spent years in the Desert Lands and remembered well his way there and around.

He pulled out a map and spread it out on the table, pushing the empty bowls and plates out of the way so they could all look.

"I know of at least seventeen ways we can sneak into the Desert Lands unseen, including taking the pass through—"

"Wait," Izzy cut in. "Why do we need to sneak into the Desert Lands? Both Annwyl and Rhiannon have an alliance with the Desert Land rulers."

Aidan looked down at the map and back up at her. "I thought this was a kill assignment. Isn't this a kill assignment?" he asked Éibhear.

She saw Brannie quickly turn her head away when Izzy snarled, "*No*. This isn't a kill assignment."

"But that's what we do," Aidan insisted. "We kill. We sneak in and kill. Are you unclear on what the Mì-runach do?"

"I didn't invite you people!" Izzy looked at Éibhear. "Fix this. Fix this right now."

He held his hands up and said to Aidan, "We're not there to kill anyone."

"Then why are we going?"

"*I'm* going to see my grandmother," Izzy said.

"We just left your grandmother."

"Another grandmother!"

"*Well, how many do you have?*"

"That's it!" Éibhear ordered them all. "That's it."

Éibhear stopped a moment to glare at the people in the pub who'd started to stare at them. When everyone looked away, he focused back on the group.

"We've got two things to do when we get to the Desert Lands. See if we can find Vateria Flominia and if we do, learn whether she's causing problems. Then I'll report that back to my mother. The other task is to escort General Iseabail to the Nolwenn territories to meet with her grandmother and—"

"Did you make an appointment?" Aidan asked Izzy.

Izzy looked around. "Did who make an appointment?"

"You."

"Make an appointment with my grandmother? Why would I do that?"

"Powerful rulers wait months to meet with the Nolwenns."

"I'm her granddaughter."

Uther said around the chicken leg he was currently sucking marrow from, "Thought she kicked your mum on the street."

Izzy was nearly across the table, her hands around the big bastard's throat before another big bastard scooped her up and took her out of the pub.

"I don't know how this is going to work if you can't control your temper."

Izzy pulled herself away from his arms, which he didn't really want her to do, but he knew better than to grab her back.

"Why are they here?" she demanded, facing him. "For that matter, why are *you* here?"

"We both know why I'm here."

"Why? For more fucking? Will you finally get your chance to brag to Celyn when we get back? Laugh about it at the pub? Or have another reason to blame me for your gods-damn misery? To again point the finger at the whore who came between cousins?"

Éibhear answered the only way he could think of at the moment, "Are you *still* going on about that?"

Izzy's hands curled into fists and she took an angry step forward. But then, just as suddenly, she took a quick step back, looked around, and finally—wonderfully—laughed.

"You rude bastard."

Éibhear joined her, the two of them standing in some alley in some town neither knew much about, laughing.

"Sorry. I couldn't resist."

She waved the apology away. "It's a little matter."

"You're worried about meeting her, aren't you?"

"I want to do what's best for my sister. But this is about her future and if I get it wrong . . ."

"That's why I'll be with you through all this. Your sister but *my* niece. I'm not about to let her train under someone not worthy of the challenge. And if we can also find out whether Vateria is in the Desert Lands for my mother, that's even better. We'll accomplish more in a few weeks than most of my kin accomplish in a few thousand years."

"You know, I've seen Vateria, I know what she did to her cousin. Why Grandmum isn't just getting rid of her is beyond me."

"The last thing we need is for other dragon kingdoms to think we're here to kill on order."

"So she sends in the Mì-runach? That seems like a good plan to you?"

"The Mì-runach have done reconnaissance. We're good at it."

"I can see that. All four of you just . . . blend."

"You'll see." He turned back toward the pub door. "And, while we're at it, if we can manage to get in a little more of that fucking you were talking about—that works for me as well."

"Oh, that was subtle," she complained, following behind him.

"I'm known for my subtlety. That was the other option for my name. Éibhear the Contemptible or Éibhear the Subtle."

"Did you have other name options?"

"Aye. There was Éibhear the Despicable. Éibhear the Rude. And Éibhear the Murdering Rat Bastard Who Should Burn in the Farthest Reaches of Hell." He stopped just in the doorway, looked down at Izzy. "I think that was my favorite."

Chuckling, she pushed past him. "Of course it was."

Chapter 26

For three days they rode far south. It wasn't an easy trip. Not remotely leisurely, all of them exhausted and cranky by the time they bedded down for the night—except for that damn dog that never seemed to get tired—and each league they passed led to warmer and warmer weather. It might be fall in Dark Plains, but it felt like summertime the closer they got to the territorial lines between the Southlands and the deserts.

But just when Éibhear didn't think he could stand going another mile, Brannie rode up beside him. He reined in his horse, as did she, and she pointed off to the right. "Do you know what's over there?" Brannie asked.

"No."

"Salt mines."

Éibhear shrugged. "Do you need some salt?"

She let out that annoyed sigh—it was a sound she'd been making a lot on this trip—and said, "No. But the Queen's troops are there. That means fresh meat, ale, perhaps a bed or a nice cave. Just for a night."

He really did like the sound of that.

"What's going on?" Izzy asked when she reached his side.

"The salt mines are near here. We can get fresh food and drink and a nice place to sleep with my mum's troops."

Izzy gazed at him a moment; then she looked at the rest of their travel party, who now waited expectantly, before she focused on him again.

"You do know I'm human, don't you?"

He was surprised by her question. "I'm aware."

"And you want me to be the lone human with an entire troop of dragons? And aren't the salt mines a sort of prison for your kind?"

"I'm sure the salt mines have whores," Caswyn added while looking around what was becoming more and more barren territory the farther they traveled.

Éibhear gawked at him, eyes wide, wondering what the hell the dragon had been thinking.

When Caswyn looked back at them all—and realized they were all staring at him—he clarified, "Not that you're a whore. Just that dragons usually have whores around and they're usually human. So you should feel quite comfortable."

When everyone's mouth opened a little wider, Caswyn sighed and said, "What I mean is—"

"Please stop talking," Brannie desperately cut in. "For the love of all the gods in all the worlds, please stop talking!"

"I was just trying to put her at ease."

"They'll have ale?" Izzy asked Éibhear.

"*Lots* of ale."

She walked her horse around him. "Thank the gods for something," she muttered, and spurred her horse off the road and toward the salt mines.

After stabling their horses in town not far from the salt mines—yes, for the horses' own safety—the traveling party arrived at the main mountain that overlooked the entire border-line between the Southlands and the Desert Lands.

Izzy rode Brannie to the entrance but dismounted once they'd landed. Without waiting for the others, she headed toward the caverns.

"Izzy," Éibhear called out. "Wait."

But Izzy wouldn't wait. If she didn't want to become an immediate target of some pushy dragon, she needed to show no fear from the beginning. And entering while riding on Brannie's back, or with Éibhear at her side, only ensured that none of the troops would take her seriously.

Izzy walked into the large cavern. It was, she'd admit, a bit overwhelming to be amongst all these dragons who weren't kin or friend. She'd never felt like a tiny woman before . . . until now.

Standing in the middle of the cavern, Izzy kept her hand on the sword at her side. After a few moments, one of the dragons lifted his head and sniffed the air. He looked around the cavern until his gaze moved down to her.

"Who are you?" he asked.

"Iseabail the Dangerous," she said loudly so that everyone would hear. "General of Annwyl the Bloody's Eighth, Fourteenth, and Twenty-sixth Legions."

The dragon studied her for several long moments before he finally nodded and said, "Nice to meet ya, lass. Let us know if you need anything."

"Thank you," she replied, feeling a little disappointed. She'd expected more of a reaction. A little something. Did humans just wander into their caverns all the time?

"Izzy?"

She looked up, forced a smile. "Fal. Hello."

Brannie and Celyn's older brother, Fal. Although Izzy considered him family like all Cadwaladrs, she didn't always like him very much.

"What are you doing here?" He grinned. "Had to see me, eh?"

And that was why Izzy didn't like him very much. Ever

since he'd found out Izzy and Celyn had been together, he'd been on a quest to get between her legs. It wasn't that he wasn't attractive. He was. But he was also a bit of an annoying prat, too. Not a charming prat like Gwenvael. Just annoying.

"I'm on a trip with—"

"Brannie?" Fal asked, his gaze behind Izzy. He smiled, but it quickly faded and the busy activity around Izzy abruptly stopped. She turned, afraid of what she'd find . . . but it was just Brannie, Éibhear, Aidan, Uther, and Caswyn.

Yawning, Brannie stomped up beside Fal and Izzy.

"Fal." She nodded at her brother. "You got fat."

Izzy gasped. "Brannie!"

"He is. Dragons can get fat, you know, Iz. The Cadwaladrs just choose not to." She cut her brother a hard look. "Or should I say *most* of the Cadwaladrs choose not to."

Fal gripped his sister's forearm. "I need to talk to you."

"What? You need some diet tips—hey!"

Izzy watched Fal drag his sister off; then she noticed that everyone was staring at Éibhear and the others. A few leaned over to nearby comrades and whispered, rather loudly, "Mìrunach." But there was a tone of disgust and fear. A tone she didn't much appreciate.

They were all still part of the same army, still there to protect the Dragon Queen and her subjects. So the Mì-runach did it a little differently? What did that matter?

"Oy!" Izzy yelled out, as she did with her own troops. "Don't you lot have work to get done? Now?"

"And who the hells are you?" some upstart demanded.

"I am Iseabail the Dangerous," she called up to the rude bastard. "Daughter of Talaith and Briec the Mighty. General to Annwyl the Bloody's Eighth, Fourteenth, and Twenty-sixth Legions." She threw down the horn-handled dagger her father had had made for her many years ago. "And killer of the dragon whose horn that used to be, Olgeir the Wastrel." She crossed her arms over her chest. "Who are *you*?"

* * *

Aidan leaned in and whispered low into Éibhear's ear, "I'd initially found her large shoulders a tad off-putting. But I must say that at this moment . . . completely understand the attraction."

Éibhear didn't answer him, but instead watched the troops go back to their work. Izzy swiped up her dagger, tucked it back into the holster attached to her sword belt, and marched over to Éibhear's side. She motioned him down with a wave of her hand. He lowered himself a bit. "Aye?"

"Why does everyone hate you? Other than the obvious reasons, of course."

Smart-ass. "Because we're Mì-runach."

"You'd think they'd appreciate what you do for your queen."

"You'd think."

She looked so annoyed by how the others had treated him and his comrades. Whether she realized she was upset for him, Éibhear didn't know, but he was enjoying it. Enjoying her. He wouldn't mention that, though. He knew it would only piss her off.

"I'm not discussing it!" Brannie roared as she came stomping around a corner, her idiot brother Fal following behind her.

"You can't just bring bloody Mì-runach here, Branwen! Not without permission of—"

Brannie spun around and faced her brother, her sharpened tail pointing in his face, dangerously close to his eye. "The Mì-runach are part of this army, you idiot. They need no one's permission to go anywhere on Her Majesty's territory. And Éibhear is your cousin. He's *kin*. A Cadwaladr by blood. Never forget that, Fal the *Tepid*."

Éibhear leaned down a bit more and whispered, "That name will stick."

"Aye. I'm afraid you may be right." Izzy cringed a bit,

but added, "Tragic really, but from what I understand . . . deserved."

"You two going to start braiding each other's hair next?" Uther grumbled. And, when they all turned to look at him: "I'm hungry!"

"We'd best get him fed," Aidan warned. "You know how he gets."

Éibhear glanced around. "There's got to be something to eat around here until we can get a proper meal." He pointed across the cavern. "There. Cow's legs."

Izzy looked over. "Good gods, those are cow's legs. They just have cow's legs lying around? Like treats?"

"What would you expect a dragon to eat?" Éibhear asked her. "Chicken legs?"

"I guess you have a point, but . . ."

Uther now stood in front of them with a cow's leg, using his fangs to rip meat off the bone. His eyes rolled to the back of his head and he sighed loudly. "That's good."

Izzy gazed up at Éibhear. "Eww."

Izzy put her hand to her mouth to hide her laugh and keep food from flying out. When it was decided that the Mì-runach were staying—dealing with Izzy was one thing for these dragons, but dealing with Captain Branwen the Awful was definitely another—a small feast was thrown together in one of the caverns with a long dining table, plates, and utensils. And, in honor of Iseabail, everyone came as human. At least they said it was in honor of Iseabail. Izzy really thought it was more about getting a chance to hang around the human prostitutes in their less intimidating forms.

"Stop, Brannie," Izzy got out around the food she still hadn't swallowed.

"Look at him. All puffed up. I can't believe that's my brother."

They both looked over at Fal. The brown dragon was keeping human prostitutes enthralled with tales of wartime heroism that managed to leave out how many times Brannie and Celyn had been forced to save his rather useless ass.

"What's really tragic is he's not even smart enough to help Daddy with all his peacemaking, politics, and book . . . stuff. He's bloody stupid!"

"Would you stop?" Izzy begged, her voice barely a whisper, her attempts to stop her laughter getting weaker by the second.

"And look at 'em," she coaxed Izzy, gesturing to the women. "Look at 'em all. 'Ohhh, Fal,'" she mimicked in a high-pitched voice. "'You're so handsome and brave.'"

Izzy pushed her nearly empty plate away. It was rare for her not to finish a meal but what could she do? Brannie would have her choke to death!

"But," Izzy whispered, "they *are* prostitutes, yes?"

"Oh, yes."

"Then is romance really required?"

"It is when you're cheap."

"Ahhh. I see."

Brannie leaned in closer, her voice dropping even more. "Now you see why me mum sent him here. He's hopeless."

"But he seems quite happy."

"Because there's no safer or more boring an assignment then the salt mines."

"It's a very important job, though, Bran. Guarding salt." Izzy cringed, unable to imagine spending her life guarding a seasoning for meat. "Look, as long as he's happy . . ."

"As long as there's fresh pussy and ale within flying distance, my brother will always be happy." Brannie sneered in disgust, dismissed it all with a wave of her hand, and asked, "So, you getting nervous about meeting your grandmum?"

"First off, that woman is *not* my grandmum. Rhiannon is my grandmum. That other bitch is just the body that carried my mum."

"You're not one for forgiving, are you, Iz?"

"I forgive. When you're not an outright cunt to me mum." She looked intently at her cousin. "Family's all, Brannie. Family's all."

Brannie started laughing hysterically. "I still can't believe you used that one on him!"

"All right," Aidan admitted. "I like her. I like Izzy."

A fist slammed into his face, snapping his head to the side.

Aidan cracked his neck, moved his jaw around to make sure he still could, then looked back at his friend. "I mean, I like her as a fellow being and I like her for you. I didn't mean I like her so let me get her into a corner so I can fuck her blind."

"Oh." Éibhear gave a small shrug. "Sorry then."

"No, no. I like getting punched in the face for no bloody reason."

"It's a habit. What can I say?"

"Thought you only did that with family."

"'Thought you only did that with family,'" Éibhear imitated-sneered back at him.

Aidan looked around the table, remembered why he'd never fit in with the regular army in the first place. Gods, what a miserable life to lead. "On the way back, let's stay in a town when we need a break. Or even a bloody barn."

"Aye." Éibhear sat up, his elbows on the table, his hands rubbing his tired face. "We should have stayed where we left the horses. We'd have had to stay human, but at least we'd have a bed and I wouldn't have to deal with—"

"Cousin? Oy. Cousin!"

Éibhear let out a long breath. "What, Fal?"

His cousin leaned in, his arm around one of the prostitutes, and whispered, "So did you get her yet?"

The Mì-runach, who sat on the other side of Éibhear and could hear Fal, stopped eating. They might have stopped breathing.

"Don't know what you mean," Éibhear tried, really hoping his cousin would let this go. Although Fal believed himself as charming as Gwenvael the Handsome, he didn't realize he lacked the one thing Éibhear's brother had in abundance: intelligence. For it was intelligence that was the thin line between endearing rapscallion and idiot bastard.

"Izzy," the idiot bastard pushed. "You finally get her or has my brother still got you beat there?"

Éibhear clenched his jaw, the back of his neck began to itch, and his hands curled into fists, but he said nothing.

"Have you even tried, cousin?" He leaned in closer and Éibhear realized Fal was well into his cups. "From what I've heard over the years, it's really not that hard to get in there."

Still, Éibhear said nothing. Not yet.

He focused across the table, his gaze on Izzy. She was chatting and laughing with Brannie, oblivious to what was going on.

"Look," the idiot pushed, "if you don't want her for yourself, you should give her to your Mì-runach friends there. Or maybe when you're done with her. That's what you do for friends. Not that you have friends anymore. Not since you got poor Austell killed. But I'm sure you know what I mean. They'll appreciate the gesture."

Aidan pushed his plate away, fell back in his chair. Caswyn had his face buried in his hands, and Uther was hunched over the table, his entire body tensing so hard that it seemed he was shaking. He wasn't. He was tense. Tense was never good when dealing with the Mì-runach.

Brannie glanced over at him. She kept up her conversation

with Izzy, but she was a Cadwaladr, too. If there was one thing every Cadwaladr learned to do at an early age, it was to be painfully aware of when their kin was doing something incredibly stupid. Brannie studied Éibhear's face before turning back to Izzy. She laughed at something her friend said and then watched Izzy get up from her chair, thank the commander of the outpost, and excuse herself from the table. She walked off and Brannie watched her until she'd left the cavern.

Then Brannie's smile faded and she relaxed back in her chair, her gaze moving back to Éibhear's.

With a nod, Éibhear grabbed the back of Fal's head and rammed it against the table, again and again, and then a few more times for good measure. When he was done with that, Éibhear stood up, grabbed his cousin by the back of the neck, lifted him up and flipped him over.

Fal slammed into the table, a loud hiss of air leaving his lungs. He shifted back to his dragon form and so did Éibhear.

That's when the officers got to their collective feet and quickly shifted to their dragon forms, ready to fight for their idiot comrade. But the Mì-runach were ready to fight for Éibhear and four Mì-runach against a large contingent of officers and their troops was . . . well . . . not really fair to the officers and their troops.

Brannie got to her feet, removed her clothes so as not to rip them, and shifted to her dragon form. She held her front forearms away from her body.

"Well?" she roared, abruptly facing the salt mines commander. "*Come on then!*"

Izzy wandered away from the cavern. She didn't know what was going on and she probably didn't want to know. But she'd known Brannie for so long, they'd been through so much together, that Izzy knew something about the She-dragon's brother was upsetting her. So Izzy had left and found her way to one of the exits. The Dragon Queen's troops had been industrious over the years and they'd built a lovely little balcony directly into the mountainside.

She'd admit, she didn't just walk out there. She tested it a bit to make sure it was sturdy. The dragons could fly away if it wasn't. All Izzy could do was go to her death with great dignity. Since she had no plans of doing that anytime soon, she tested the balcony until she felt certain it was safe enough.

Resting her arm on the balcony's edge and her chin on her fist, Izzy looked out over what should have been her homeland. She should have been born and raised in these sand-covered lands.

Gods, how much different would her life had been? Would she still be Izzy? The Izzy she was now? Or would she be a true Nolwenn, practicing the most powerful of Magicks and deigning to meet with royals who needed her help? She really didn't know. Did the place make the person? The people one surrounded oneself with? Or was a person born, not made? Perhaps it was a combination of things. She didn't know, and she left those kinds of philosophical debates to those who read more than one book every two years.

She still had to admit, it was hard. To love the family you had but still wish to have known your father. She'd asked her mother questions about him over the years, but to this day, thoughts of him still cut Talaith and Izzy didn't like to be the one to upset her. It wasn't like Talaith had had a happy life after leaving her home with the Nolwenns. It had been hard and painful, filled with worry for the daughter she'd never had a chance to get to know and desperation to get that daughter back. Izzy's life had been a little lonely, a little sad but nothing like her mother's. So she kept questions about her true father to a minimum, assuming she'd get her chance to meet him in the afterlife.

"He would have liked you, from what I can tell."

Izzy closed her eyes. The last being she wanted to deal with at the moment was Rhydderch Hael.

"And what would I have to give to bring him back? Just my soul?"

"I'd never ask that of you. My mate has use for warriors' souls, but I don't. Besides, I couldn't bring your father back if I wanted to. He's not mine to return."

She looked over at the god. He stood next to her as human, his gaze fixed across the Desert Lands. She wondered what he saw that Izzy could not.

"What do you want from me, dragon god?"

"Your love?"

"No, seriously. What do you want?"

Rhydderch Hael laughed. "I've missed our talks, Izzy."

"So have I," she admitted. "But I no longer trust you."

"That's probably a good idea. You have your concerns and I have mine. Of course, mine involve entire universes and yours just a small part of one."

"Is this what you want from me?" she asked. "To come into the Desert Lands, meet with the Nolwenns, and what? Kill my grandmother? Has she crossed you somehow?"

His smile was . . . warm. Like an indulgent father. He reached out and caressed her cheek. "My dear, sweet Izzy. I assure you I'd never waste your blood debt to me or your considerable talents on your human grandmother."

"I don't understand."

"You're young, Iseabail. You may lack the powers of the Nolwenns but not their longevity. I'll have use of you . . . in time."

"And you're keeping me alive to do what?"

"*Keeping* you alive? Me?" He laughed again. "Do you really believe that?"

"I'm still alive," she insisted.

"Your sheer will has ensured that. Well, your sheer will

and that high bit of insanity. Honestly, though, Izzy. It's been your skill that's kept you alive. You've grown into a mighty warrior without my help."

Confused, Izzy asked, "If you didn't want me for my blood debt, why did you bring me here?"

He sighed, sounding a bit exasperated. "Something neither you nor your mother can grasp—I don't bring anyone anywhere. Dragon gods don't do that. We don't order mortals to do our bidding because dragons will go out of their way not to do it. So, instead, we . . . manipulate. We bargain. We blackmail." He stood behind her now, his arms braced on either side of her, trapping her between his human form and the balcony wall. She felt intense heat coming from him, like standing over a volcano. It didn't burn her, though. It didn't harm her. But it was powerful.

"And, sometimes, little Izzy," he said against her ear, "we entice. I knew Briec the Mighty would be enticed by your mother and I needed her someplace safe. His holding on to her, though, that was his decision, not mine. Personally, I couldn't have cared less if he kept her or not. But over the eons, to get what I want, I've found that dragons are more easily enticed than threatened or bullied. Entice them and they'll go anywhere I need them to."

"You bastard." Izzy closed her eyes, rage pouring down her like rainwater. "This has nothing to do with me."

"In some ways you're right. It has nothing to do with you. Then again, it has *everything* to do with you. But don't hate me for being who I am, little Izzy. For I am a god." He leaned in and kissed her cheek. "Do me a favor, though, would you? Watch your flank."

"My . . ." Izzy spun around. Rhydderch Hael was gone, but in his place was something else. A dragon. Similar in form to the ones she'd known all her life but . . . different in two ways. The moon overhead told her his color was red, but the red had a bright bronze overlay that sparkled in the light in a way her own dragon kin's scales did not. And his scales . . . they weren't scales as she'd known them all her life. Because these scales had no separation between them. Instead they were like a hard shell perfectly formed over his entire body, with only room for the wings, limbs, and eyes. The dragon's hair was long but had warrior braids throughout and the color had that same bronze overlay. He was, in Izzy's estimation, the most beautiful thing she'd ever seen. His coloring made him look like a jewel glittering in the moonlight.

But he was no Southland dragon, of that she was sure. She also had no idea where he'd come from, which was why she slowly brought her hand down and wrapped it around the metal stick she kept on her sword belt. A metal stick given to her years ago by master blacksmith Sulien.

"Praying to your gods, human?" the dragon asked.

"I pray to no god. Not anymore."

"But choosing the right god will set you free." He lowered his long neck until they were eye to eye, lifted one talon, and brought it to his snout. "Ssssssh, human," he said on a whisper. "Let's make this quick so no one has to get hurt."

Izzy nodded and replied, "We can at least make it quick." Then she brought Sulien's weapon around and thought about what she needed at the moment. That's all it took. A thought and the weapon extended in length and the flat tip turned to a spike. She took firm hold of the steel in both hands and rammed it forward, forcing it into the dragon's eye and straight into his brain.

Izzy yanked out the weapon, the dragon roaring in pain, his claws covering the hole where his eye used to be. He'd be dead soon, so Izzy turned away from him and leaned over the balcony edge. That's when she saw more dragons climbing up the side of the mountain. They did this, she guessed, because the flaps of their wings would signal their approach to any dragon within a league.

So if silence was what they wanted . . . it would not be what Izzy would give them.

Stepping back and lifting her weapon, the wonderful thing growing longer and wider with another thought, she opened her mouth and yelled out, "*Éibhear!*"

Éibhear had Fal pinned to the floor with his back claw and was about to start stabbing at his cousin with the tip of his tail when he heard Izzy call out his name. If she'd called anyone else, he'd have continued fighting. But Izzy would never call his name unless . . .

He unfurled his wings and lifted himself up above the fray going on in the cavern. "*Mì-runach!*" he bellowed out. "*With me!*"

Izzy wasn't about to try to kill a swarm of dragons she knew very little about and had never faced in battle, and who outsized her. So, instead, she ran. Sometimes even the greatest warriors in the world needed to run—and she wasn't the greatest warrior in the world.

Izzy ran, hoping she was heading toward Éibhear and the others, but she wasn't sure. Even worse, she knew now that these attackers were after her. She knew it when she heard one call out, "She went down here! Go! Go!"

Wings scraped against tunnel walls, claws slapped against rock as the foreigners searched for her.

She had no idea what they wanted, but she wasn't about to worry about it now. She just wanted to get someplace safe and—

A claw reached out from a dark cavern, Izzy seeing it too late to avoid it. It wrapped around her and yanked her into the darkness. She brought her weapon up, to strike at least once, but before any of that happened, the foreigner blew out a small breath. She felt something like sand hit her in the face and Izzy breathed it in before she could stop herself. Instantly her body went limp, her ability to fight or scream or anything else, for that matter, gone.

"Sleep, little human. Sleep," the dragon soothed.

Since she was fairly certain she had no choice, that's what Izzy did.

Éibhear blocked an axe to the face, slammed the weapon to the ground, and rammed his body into his attacker, shoving him into the wall. Éibhear thrust his sword into the attacker's mouth and twisted. Once the body stopped moving, Éibhear pulled his sword out and turned toward all the fighting.

"Sand dragons. Breaking the alliance with my mother?" He shook his head. "No. That doesn't seem right."

Aidan, with a sword in each claw, impaled two enemy dragons running toward them. He ripped out his weapons, the dragons' insides spilling onto the floor, and faced Éibhear. "Then what the fuck are they doing?"

"I don't know." He looked around. "And where the fuck is Izzy?"

Aidan shrugged, cut another Sand Eater in half. "Caswyn! Uther! You see Izzy?"

"No," Caswyn called back from across the tunnel. "And we've been looking."

"Éibhear!" Brannie came around the corner. "I found this." She held up a metal stick.

"What's that?"

"A weapon Uncle Sulien gave Izzy. She'd never leave it behind."

"Then where is she?" Aidan asked.

"I don't know. But there was no blood, no bones. If she was eaten, she'd never go down easy."

"Oy!" Caswyn called out. "Hear that?"

Éibhear tried to listen around all the sounds of battle. At first, he didn't know what Caswyn was talking about, but then he heard it. Barking.

Éibhear pushed past the battling dragons and ran out to one of the ledges. He leaned out and saw that stupid dog running straight into the desert. He'd refused to stay back in the town with the horses, unwilling to be too far from Izzy's side. So they'd left him in a small cavern at ground level for his safety. Éibhear had forgotten all about him.

"Go," Aidan ordered, pushing Éibhear's travel bag at him. "Go. Get her. We'll deal with this here, and come for you two later."

"We don't even know if she's been taken."

"That dog wouldn't go anywhere without her. If we found him sobbing in a corner, I'd say she was dead. But he's running after her. And if anyone can track her down, it's that mangy mutt. Now go."

Éibhear took his travel bag, slinging it across his shoulders.

"Take this as well." Aidan shoved the map of the Desert Lands at him. "For our queen, for our honor."

Éibhear repeated the favorite Mì-runach saying, "For our queen, for our honor." Then over the side he went, letting the wind lift his wings and his ears lead him to where that damn dog was tearing through the desert in search of his mistress.

Chapter 27

They were well into their meal when Gwenvael heard screams from outside. He looked up from his lamb and asked, "Did anyone know Mum was coming here tonight?"

Everyone was shaking their heads when Rhiannon stormed into the Great Hall . . . naked. Although Gwenvael was just grateful that she wasn't trying to come inside while still in her dragonform. That always led to repairs and Annwyl complaining incessantly about the cost of good stone masons.

"Problems!" she yelled as she walked in. "Problems!"

Morfyd gasped at the sight of their naked mother and jumped up from the table. One of the servants tossed a fur cape to her before she'd even made it across the room and she immediately wrapped it around their mother's shoulders at the same time their father rushed into the Great Hall. At least he had on leggings and was busy trying to pull on his boots.

"I wish you wouldn't run from me like that," he snarled at Rhiannon.

"We don't have time for all these human issues about their naked bodies! We have problems!"

"It's probably that idiot boy's fault!" Bercelak lashed back.

Young Frederik's head snapped up, his attention finally

pulled away from the book he'd been reading all through dinner. Now that he had his reading spectacles and didn't have to pretend he was as stupid as the rest of the males in his family, the boy always seemed to have a book in his hands.

Gwenvael leaned over and whispered to him, "He doesn't mean you. You're fine."

"Oh. Good. Thanks." Then back to his book Frederik went.

"What's going on?" Briec demanded while still sounding amazingly bored. It was definitely a skill Gwenvael's brother had. One none of Briec's siblings had ever been able to master.

"We've been attacked! And betrayed!" Rhiannon announced.

Annwyl instantly stood, her hand on her sword, and Fearghus quickly ordered her to "sit down. Now."

Grumbling, the human queen did just that. Fearghus had definitely gotten faster over the years at stopping his mate before the killing could commence. Something they all appreciated about Fearghus.

"Who's attacking us?" Keita asked, needing this information so she could plot which poison would work best.

"Those bloody Sand Eaters have attacked *my* salt mines."

"King Heru?" Fearghus asked. "He sent his troops to attack the salt mines? Is he in desperate need of salt?"

"No, he does not—" Rhiannon cut herself off. "He's not attacking the salt mines, idiot. He's attacking us!"

"Us as in all of us?" Briec asked. "Or us as in the royal you?"

"Bercelak!" Rhiannon bellowed.

Their father quickly took over, stepping in front of their mother and saying, "All we know is that the salt mines were attacked just a little while ago by a battalion of Sand Eaters."

"Sent by King Heru?" Fearghus pushed.

"We don't know."

"Have we lost ground?" Briec asked.

"No."

Fearghus and Briec glanced at each other and Gwenvael.

Frowning, Fearghus asked, "You're saying that the troops we have on the Southland border repelled a full-on assault by Sand Eaters? *Those* troops did that?"

Because they'd had peace on that border for so long and the weather was so miserable, usually only the worst of their troops went to the salt mines. And, if they were attacked, it was assumed that those dragons would just give the rest of them enough time to gather resources and prepare to repel any efforts to push farther into their territory. Honestly, they were nothing more than disposable guard dogs.

Bercelak looked back at Rhiannon and she shrugged. "Tell them."

Nodding, Bercelak said to them, "There were Mì-runach at the salt mines."

Briec shook his head, confused. "Why were Mì-runach in—'"

"By the gods," Talaith gasped. She shot to her feet. "Izzy!"

"She's safe," Bercelak quickly assured her. "Rhiannon talked to Brannie and she says Izzy is fine. Éibhear's keeping her safe."

"Éibhear's with Izzy?" Briec turned accusing eyes on his mate. "And you knew, didn't you?"

"Of course I knew. I guess I just don't see what your problem with it could possibly be."

"Don't see the problem? How can you say that?"

"They're not blood related, Briec. Unless, of course, it's the fact that *my* daughter is not of royal blood that bothers you."

"What?"

"Just admit it. That's what this is really about. You don't think my daughter's good enough for your royal brother."

"Actually," Gwenvael clarified since Briec had become so angry his human face was almost as purple as Ragnar's hair, "we don't think that idiot is good enough for our little Izzy."

"*Little* Izzy?" Dagmar asked.

"Relatively speaking, of course."

"You lot are so mean to poor Éibhear." Annwyl glared at the males. "No wonder he hasn't been home in ten winters."

"He's Mì-runach," Fearghus explained.

Sounding frustrated, Annwyl snapped, "I still have *no idea* what that means."

"It means we don't want our little Izzy getting mixed up with Éibhear the Contemptible!"

"He's your brother!"

"Not by choice!"

Bercelak slammed his meaty fists onto the table. "What does any of *that* have to do with our current problem?" their father demanded.

"Nothing," Gwenvael replied. "But it's tons more interesting than some boring Sand Eaters."

"I should have smashed your egg when I had the chance," Bercelak shot back at Gwenvael.

"Father!" Gwenvael gasped, his hands to his heart. "That's so hurtful. Don't you love me at all?"

"No!"

"Excuse me!" Rhiannon snarled, pushing past her mate and staring down at her children. "Don't any of you," she demanded, "care about my poor sweet baby boy and the danger he's in?"

"No," every adult male in the room replied.

By following that damn dog, Éibhear was able to eventually catch up to the Sand Eater who'd taken Izzy. The dragon held her in one claw while careening low over the land. Éibhear had no idea what the bastard had done to her, but to say he was pissed off was really an understatement. He picked up speed, closing the distance, but just as he was near enough that he could swoop down and snatch Izzy from the Sand Eater's claw, the dragon suddenly dived first. He dropped to the ground, Izzy cradled close to his body. Then, before Éibhear could reach him, the Sand Eater's wings came up and around, slamming closed with Izzy inside.

Éibhear blinked, surprised. He'd never seen that before. The Sand Eater went from dragon to tortoise in seconds, but Éibhear had no idea why. Then, as he hovered there, confused, he heard it. The sound roaring toward him. He looked up and watched the wall of sand bearing down. He raised his gaze and realized that if he moved quickly, he could go far enough up and wait the sandstorm out.

He lifted his snout, ready to shoot up, but he heard barking and again focused on the ground.

That dog. That damn dog. He was barking at the Sand Eater's protective shell. Barking and scratching and trying to chew a hole in it so he could get to Izzy.

Éibhear knew he should let that damn dog be carried away by the storm. Carried away and never seen again. No more drool or smell or gas.

And yet . . . and yet, Éibhear couldn't stand the thought of Izzy's broken heart. She loved that damn dog and he couldn't just fly away and leave the big idiot to fend for himself against nature.

So, while calling himself stupid the entire time, Éibhear dove toward the ground and that damn dog. He'd just scooped the beast up in his claw, his wings unfurling to take them both back out, when that wall of sand rammed into him and tossed him—while still holding that damn dog—around like a rag doll.

Izzy was wondering where she was when the storm suddenly came. It sounded awful, but she was quite comfortable and dry and . . . and not alone.

Izzy opened her eyes, one hand reaching out in front of her.

"Your poor human eyes," a voice from the darkness said. "Let me help you with that." She heard what sounded like rock scraping against rock, saw a flicker, and then light. A small torch and a brown dragon with vibrant green eyes gazing down at her. He had that same bronze overlay to his color, sparkling even more in the dim light.

"There," he said. "That must be better."

Izzy looked around. "Where are we?"

"You're safe."

"Safe from what?"

"Sandstorm. They happen out here all the time." He rested his massive dragon head in the middle of his claw. "Gods, you're beautiful for a human."

"At least you didn't say delicious."

He laughed. "No. You're safe with me."

"Safe with the dragon who kidnapped me?"

"Rescued. There is a difference."

Izzy shook her head. As her mother always liked to say, *Dragons and their bloody centaur-shit semantics.*

"Such a huge difference, too, between rescued and kidnapped."

"You're safe, are you not?"

"I don't know you, and you definitely don't know me. I don't even know why you felt the need to 'rescue' me."

"I was sent to fetch you. To keep you safe from those nasty traitors."

"Traitors?"

"To the great King Heru. He rules over these beautiful lands with an even and steady claw. But like your Southland queens, he does not brook traitors to his dominion."

"But why would he send anyone for me? How did he even know I was here?"

"Our magi are powerful. They see much. Especially when the human granddaughter of Rhiannon the White is heading toward territorial lines."

Izzy sat up, resting her back against . . . well, against

this dragon's shell. "What does being the granddaughter of Rhiannon have to do with anything?"

"You don't know?"

"I know I'm a general in Annwyl the Bloody's army. My grandmother hasn't had to babysit me in quite some time."

The dragon chuckled. "The Dragon Queen often seems as if she lets her offspring run wild and free, uncaring if they return to her alive or dead. But we, the other dragon kingdoms, understand quite well what her offspring do not."

"And what's that?"

"That the bitch is cruel and unforgiving. And if you really want to piss her off, allow one of her offspring to be harmed. So although you are merely a granddaughter and not blood, as you are clearly a child of this land, the other kingdoms are well aware of her affection for you."

"That's quite sweet, but if it's true, what about her son?"

"Which one?"

"The one who traveled with me. Did your powerful magi not tell you about him?"

"Oh. The youngest male," he sneered. "Yes. They were well aware."

"And?"

"And what? He's a Mì-runach. Not only would King Heru never let such a despicable beast into his court, we assume Éibhear the Contemptible can take care of himself. With that in mind, the only instruction I received was to retrieve you." He smiled, bright white fangs gleaming in the dark space. "And I am so happy that I have."

"You won't be for long, though," she softly told him.

"And why is that?"

"Because I know my family."

"What does that—aaaaaahhhhh!"

Izzy ducked her head, watching as the Sand dragon and his shell-like wings were flung away from her.

"Comfortable?" Éibhear demanded, glaring down at her through all that sand in his hair.

"You're blaming me? I was kidnapped!"

"Aye. You clearly look terrified!"

He couldn't believe this! He'd come all this way, saved that damn dog, and what did he find Lady Love-A-Dragon doing? Flirting! With a Sand Eater! Oh, the hypocrisy!

Izzy got to her feet and proceeded to wipe sand off her tight ass. "Éibhear—"

"Stay here," he ordered her. "First I kill him and then we'll discuss this."

"Discuss this? Discuss what?"

Annoyed she was playing this game with him, Éibhear faced the Sand Eater and got a sword handle to the snout for his trouble.

"Dammit!"

Izzy laughed, hands on her hips.

"Where's the loyalty?" Éibhear demanded.

"I don't have any for such a whiny baby! And speaking of which . . . where's me dog?"

"Again with that bloody mongrel? You didn't even ask about me!"

"Well you're standing here, aren't you? You're alive. Breathing, apparently. Whereas I don't see my wonderful, loyal, non-whiny dog!"

"Ungrateful female!"

Izzy frowned and Éibhear immediately calmed down.

"What's wrong?" he asked.

She suddenly looked down at the ground.

"Izzy?"

A dragon's claw came up through the sand and wrapped around Izzy's legs. With one pull, she was dragged down, disappearing under the sand.

"Izzy!" Éibhear charged over to where she'd been standing. Her dog stood on the other side, accusing Éibhear with his eyes.

"It's not my fault!" Éibhear argued. "It's not!"

That damn dog didn't seem to believe him and Éibhear wasn't sure he did either.

Snarling, he faced the Sand Eater who'd taken Izzy. He stalked over to him, ready to wring the truth out of the dragon, but with a little wave, the bastard suddenly disappeared under the sand, too.

Éibhear roared. Even if he had to dig up the entire desert, he wouldn't stop until—

That damn dog barked and ran past Éibhear. Following him, Éibhear watched Macsen head straight to a sand dune. As soon as he got to it, he began to dig. Éibhear walked around once, curled his claw into a fist and rammed it into the dune. Instead of finding more sand, he found nothing. An open space.

Using his tail, Éibhear picked up Macsen and held him tight before he pushed his way inside the dune and dove head-first into blackness.

Desert Land Sand dragons, or Sand Eaters, as they were called among other dragon breeds, were unique among their kind. Not because their natural weapon was, actually, sand. But because of their scales. Or, really, scale. Unlike most dragon breeds, Sand dragons didn't have multiple scales covering their vulnerable flesh. Not really surprising when one realized they spent most of their life in a sand-covered land. One of the most brutal tortures endured by other dragons was to have their scales lifted and something sharp and painful placed beneath. So to be around sand all day, every day, would make life miserable for the Sand dragons if they had to keep ripping open their own scales to clean sand out from under them. Instead, their bodies had one smooth scale—like a shell. A shell that could split to create wings or encircle the dragon to protect him or her during a sandstorm.

It was all quite fascinating and intriguing, but it was also why three of the Mì-runach—the mightiest and most feared of the Dragon Queen's warriors—were currently huddled together like frightened hatchlings. Because what else could they do?

Branwen the Awful stepped out of the cavern, her body covered in blood, and tossed the empty shell to the floor. The shell she'd systematically ripped off the back of one of the few Sand Eaters they'd bothered to capture rather than kill.

"He told me nothing," she said.

Of course he hadn't. The bastard had been too busy screaming.

Aidan glanced at his friends, but both Caswyn and Uther shook their heads. Aidan, however, was made of stronger stuff than that. He cleared his throat and asked, "Anything else that could help us? The queen will want to know—"

"I know. I know." She snapped her talons. "Oh! There was something. I totally forgot with all that damn screaming." She went back into the cavern. As one, the three mighty dragons leaned over and peeked inside, terrified at what they might witness but unable to help themselves.

They shouldn't have looked.

Branwen slammed her claw into the back of the Sand Eater trying to crawl across the floor. Like any dragon without his shell, this one looked strange, all that blood unable to hide the fact that at the moment he was no better than a weak, defenseless human.

"Give us your claw," she ordered.

"Kill me," the Sand Eater begged. "Kill. Me."

"Stop whining." She pulled her claw from his back and

stomped on his forearm. She raised her axe and brought it down, smoothly hacking off his front claw. Picking that up, she came back out of the cavern.

Without even saying a word, all three of them backed up. She didn't seem to notice. Aidan had heard over the years that General Iseabail and Captain Branwen had spent more time than was good for them with the human queen, Annwyl, but it wasn't until this moment that he realized the truth to that.

She held up the claw, the palm toward them.

"What is that?" Caswyn asked.

"Tattoo. A rune of some kind."

"A rune?"

"Runes mean Magick," Aidan explained. "And Magick means gods."

Branwen nodded. "Exactly. We need to get this back to the queen."

"You'll take it?"

"No need. Rhiannon allows me to communicate directly with her like I do with me mum. And once we finish here, I'm going after Izzy. I don't know what's going on but . . ." Her words faded off and Aidan would at least admit to himself that he was afraid to ask her what she was thinking. He didn't want to know what she was thinking. Ever.

"I understand," he said quickly before his comrades could argue the point. "We'll go with you."

Branwen shrugged, headed back into the cavern. "Whatever."

Once she disappeared inside, Uther grabbed Aidan around the throat.

"Have you lost your mind?"

"I'm not going anywhere with her," Caswyn said in a desperate whisper.

"We're Mì-runach," Aidan choked out.

"That doesn't mean we're stupid."

"No." Aidan knocked Uther's claw off. "But we are loyal

to each other. And we're not about to leave Éibhear alone with Izzy *and* her."

"She's his cousin. I'm sure he'll be safe."

"Loyalty," Aidan reminded them. "Until death. Remember the commitment we made to the goddess of war and death, Eirianwen?"

"Weren't we drunk at the time?"

"That's not the point!"

A Sand Eater's head bounced out of the cavern and across the tunnel floor.

"Sorry," Branwen called out. "Lost me grip!"

"But that big blue bastard will owe us for this," Aidan vowed. "He'll owe us big."

Chapter 28

Coughing and shaking her head, Izzy tried to get all the damn sand off her.

"Sorry about that."

Izzy dragged her fingers through her hair, still trying to get all the sand out. "Where the hells am I?"

"Safe."

"Would you *stop* saying that. It's bloody annoying!" She lifted her head and was finally able to open her eyes.

Izzy gasped. "It's beautiful."

The dragon who'd taken her smiled. "I'm glad you like it." He moved around the cavern of the underground cave. "Our ancestors built this place eons ago and it still holds strong."

Standing in its center, Izzy could see that the cavern went on for miles, with tunnels and chambers shooting off from that.

What she really loved, though, was how open and wide it all was, with light coming not from the few torches attached to the walls here and there, but from the giant colored crystals scattered about.

The dragon seemed to notice that her gaze was focused on the crystals and he explained, "Leagues beneath is a lava river that feeds into the volcanic mountains in your Southlands.

The light from that lava comes up through these crystals and illuminates these caverns."

"It really is beautiful."

"This is the true land of your people, Iseabail. It's not surprising you're drawn to what we have here."

Another dragon came around Izzy and over to the one who'd taken her. "We should go," he said low.

"Of course. Please," he said to Izzy, "this way."

She followed after the dragons for several minutes until they turned down a tunnel. They traveled a few more minutes until the tunnel stopped at a huge chasm. The other dragon wrapped his tail around her waist and plopped her on his back.

"Hey!"

He didn't answer, simply took flight over that chasm and kept flying until they reached a well-populated area filled with Sand dragons. Izzy stared with her mouth open. She saw the same colors of dragons that she saw among her own kin, but again, the Sand dragons had that bronze overlay. To her eyes, they all seemed to sparkle, laughter and conversation adding to the moment.

Izzy knew she was dazzled, but she couldn't help herself. They were all so beautiful.

As the two dragons moved through the crowd, the others grew silent and openly stared at Izzy. She realized that this was a throne room. They were taking her to meet with their king.

A small dais jutted from the rock wall and that's where the dragon carrying Izzy stopped. Her kidnapper, however, kept walking until he'd stepped onto that dais and faced the court of dragons. That's when everyone around Izzy kneeled, heads bowed. It was something even Rhiannon didn't bother getting her subjects to do, the Southland dragons notoriously difficult about basic court etiquette. But these Sand dragons all kneeled without question . . . to Izzy's kidnapper.

Chewing her lip, she looked up, shrugged. *Sorry*, she mouthed at him. When he winked back, Izzy felt a little relief

knowing she hadn't brought down her grandmother's alliance
with a few snotty words. But that feeling of relief was all too
brief when she heard war cries from outside the chamber.

The guards immediately pulled their weapons, but the king
held up his claw. "It's all right. Allow him entry."

"My lord?"

"Do as I instruct."

Izzy tapped the shoulder of the dragon she rode. "You may
want to put me down now."

"You sure you'll be all right?"

"Safer than you, I'm afraid." The dragon lowered himself
to the ground and Izzy easily slid off. Good thing, too, because Éibhear came in just then, two axes out, sand still covering his hair, looking quite homicidal. She definitely found
it sexy.

Gods, I'm pathetic.

"Éibhear," she called up to him, worried he'd start killing
all these frightened royals. "I'm fine."

"We leave now," he ordered, silver eyes watching everyone.

"Don't you want to know, Fire Breather, why I felt the
need to take Princess Iseabail?"

Izzy smirked. "*Princess* Izzy. I like the sound of that."

"When I called you princess, you nearly bit my head off,"
Éibhear needlessly reminded her.

"Didn't much like your tone when you said it, now did I?"

"It's always something with you, isn't it?"

"What's that supposed to mean, you big bas—Macsen!"
Izzy crouched down and opened her arms, Macsen diving
into them, covering her with disgusting slobber and messy
fur. She loved it.

"Of course," Éibhear complained, "you go for that damn
dog first."

Eyes narrowing, Izzy accused, "You're jealous."

"Of a *dog*?"

"Of *my* dog. My loyal, dependable—"

"—never speaks so it can't tell you when you're being an idiot—"

"—dog!"

Izzy looked around and stood. "Where did everybody go?"

The cavern had cleared out, leaving Izzy, Éibhear, Macsen, and the Dragon King of the Desert Lands.

Izzy faced the desert royal. He stared at them, his forearms folded over his chest, one talon tapping.

"Sorry about that," Izzy said.

"Why are you apologizing?" Éibhear demanded. "He kidnapped you."

"He rescued me. There's apparently a difference."

King Heru VII of the Desert Lands watched Princess Iseabail and the youngest son of the Dragon Queen bicker. That seemed to be all they did. Bicker. Once he'd realized that they wouldn't stop soon, he'd ordered his court cleared. The last thing he needed was for his people to know exactly how ridiculous the Southland royal family truly was. He understood the value of having Rhiannon the White as an ally but there were still many who questioned the decision made centuries ago by his father to align themselves with the Fire Breathers. And that concern had only grown when it was discovered that the Southlanders had joined forces with the Lightning dragons out of the Northlands. Barbarians. Rhiannon had aligned her people with barbarians.

"Are you two done?" he asked Iseabail and her—quote, unquote—uncle.

The royal brat eyed him. "Who the hell are you?"

"This is King Heru," Iseabail introduced them, eyes widening in warning at the Blue.

"Centaur shit."

"Éibhear!"

"Why would the king of the Desert Lands kidnap you?"

"What does *that* mean?"

The Fire Breather frowned. "What do you *think* it means?"

"You know exactly what I think it means. And I think you *know* that what I think it means is exactly what you're meaning."

"That made absolutely no sense."

"Shut up."

"But—"

"Just shut up."

Heru put his claws to his head. "Suns above. Are you two like this all the time?"

The couple gazed at him and asked together, "What do you mean?"

Rhi looked up from her sketch to see her grandmother standing a few feet away. "Hello, Gran."

"Hello, my dearest love. Do you have some time to talk?"

"Of course." She put aside her sketch.

"Should I shift?" her grandmother asked.

"No need." Rhi gazed up at her. "I love seeing you like this. You're beautiful."

Her grandmother stretched out, white wings extending from her back until they could lay flat, her tail reaching up and pulling fruits down from a nearby tree.

"I had to look for you, Rhi. You weren't at dinner with your kin, nor in your room, nor outside the grounds."

"Sorry. I just wasn't in the mood to go to dinner tonight. I needed some time alone. That's why I came here."

Grandmum looked around. "Did you create this yourself?"

"Aye."

"Do you bring your cousins here?"

"No."

"Smart girl. You know, it took me centuries to be able to

create my own sacred space out of thin air, Rhi. When did you start?"

"When I was six."

"Well, let's never discuss that again." Her grandmother placed a book open in front of her. "Do you recognize this rune?"

"I do."

"Do you know the god it belongs to?"

"I do."

"Have you talked to him?"

Rhi nodded. "Aye."

"Often?"

"No, no. Just once." She leaned in and whispered, "I didn't really like him."

"Did you make him go away?"

"No. That was Talwyn. She *really* didn't like him. I think the fact that he not only didn't have eyes but no eye holes, really bothered her. She charged him with her sword. She was eight."

Grandmum put her talons to her temples and closed her eyes.

"You all right, Grandmum?"

"Just a bit of a headache."

"Oh." Rhi adjusted the sky so that it wasn't so vibrantly blue and instead was a soft and soothing pink. "Is that better?"

Grandmum opened her eyes and blinked up at the sky. "Did you just do that?"

"Uh-huh."

"You know, love, you don't seem to have a problem controlling all this. Yet you can't seem to control other aspects of your power. I find that surprising."

"I can control this because I'm not upset. Or angry. And I haven't seen Talwyn and Talan all day, so I haven't had to get in the middle of one of their fights." She made her hands into fists. "I hate when they fight," she growled out.

"They're not fighting," her grandmum soothed. "It's just us."

Rhi let out a breath and unclenched her hands. "Exactly."

"Um . . . Rhi?"

"Yes?"

"Did Chramn—"

"Don't say his name."

"Does it have power?"

"No, it's just ugly sounding."

"Right. Okay. Well . . . that particular god's rune. Do you know why anyone would tattoo it into their flesh?"

"Only those in his cult."

"He has a cult?"

"When he came to me, I don't think he did."

"But he does now?"

"I sensed he was planning one."

"*Planning* a cult?"

"Uh-huh."

"And you know this because—"

"I remember him saying he wanted me as his chosen one and there would be thousands, perhaps millions worshipping my existence."

"You're his chosen one?"

"No. He wanted me *to be* his chosen one. I don't think I was anything to him."

"And you turned down the worship of millions?"

"Grandmum," Rhi said, exasperated, "if you think Daddy's bad now about calling me and Iz his perfect, perfect daughters . . . imagine if I had the worship of millions? Millions! And you know what would happen then? Uncle Fearghus and Uncle Gwenvael would have to kill him because Daddy wouldn't stop going on about it. And with Uncle Éibhear rarely being here, he wouldn't be able to stop them. Honestly, I did it for the best of the family.

"Besides," she said in a whisper and pointing at her face, "he had no eye holes. I try not to judge, Grandmum, and people are tragically born with all sorts of problems every day. But he's a god! Are you telling me he couldn't get that fixed?" Rhi pressed her hand to her face, chewed on her lip a bit. "I'm a horrible person, aren't I?"

Grandmum pressed her snout to the side of Rhi's face. "I don't know if I've ever told you this, Rhianwen, but you are truly worthy to be my granddaughter."

"Aww, thanks, Grandmum." Izzy reached up and hugged her grandmother's snout. "I love you, too."

"Now," Grandmum said, pulling away, "we've got some work to do. You up for it?"

"Of course. What do you need?"

Grandmum looked around again at the space Rhi had made herself when she was six and tired of the twins' constant bickering. After a moment, she smiled at Rhi, and said, "I think this will do."

Chapter 29

They were escorted down a long tunnel to a chamber. It wasn't as large as some of the other chambers Éibhear had seen in this underground cave, but it was comfortable enough, with a bed, table, chairs, and a fire pit and freshly slaughtered cow piled right outside the entrance.

"We'll come fetch you when it's time for dinner," the guard said.

"Are you expecting us to stay?" Éibhear demanded.

Because he had no intention of staying. No desire to. He wanted to get Izzy out of here and someplace safe. But the king had insisted they take this chamber and now it seemed he was insisting—through his guards—that they had to have dinner with him. And since everyone around here followed his bloody orders, Éibhear actually had little say in the matter.

"You and his lordship will be dining as human. Princess Iseabail, clothes will be sent to you."

"Thank you."

"And we suggest you keep the dog in this chamber. It will be protected here, but through the rest of our lordship's kingdom, it'll just look like a running snack."

"Understood."

The guard nodded at Izzy. "Princess." Glared at Éibhear and growled, "Prince."

Once they were gone, Izzy said, "You do seem to make friends wherever you go."

"Don't blame me for this."

"It's not my fault either!"

"I never said it was!"

"*Then why are we yelling?*"

"*I really don't know!*" Éibhear blew out a breath. "That was fun."

"Sorry." Izzy walked over to the bed and sat on it. "This shouldn't have happened."

"But it did, and we'll handle it. We always do."

"You don't understand, Éibhear. You shouldn't be here."

Éibhear shifted to human and walked all the way into the chamber. Izzy glanced at him, then quickly looked away. "Put on some leggings."

"Does my manliness overwhelm your delicate lady sensibilities?"

"You do know I'm still armed?"

"All right. All right." He dug into his travel bag and pulled out a pair of leather leggings. He pulled them on, and sat on the bed beside Izzy.

"Do you really not want me here?" he asked.

"No, I don't want you here."

Ow. Well, no one could say that Izzy wasn't direct.

"Izzy, you don't have to worry. I have no plans to . . . prolong our relationship any further."

Izzy looked at him. "What are you talking about?"

"I don't want you to worry that I only followed you in the hopes of getting you into my bed again."

"You don't have a bed. Uther says you only have a bedroll."

"I mean my proverbial bed."

"Oh." She stared at him a moment longer, then asked, "What does us fucking have to do with anything?"

"Isn't that why you don't want me here?"

"No."

Éibhear took a moment to rub his eyes and breathe. When in battle, Izzy had the most amazing focus. But before and after battle . . . well, it couldn't be helped. He had to work with what he had.

"Then what does it matter if I'm here or not?"

"I have no idea."

Éibhear began to work on his temples with the tips of his fingers because that's where his headache was settling. "And yet you don't want me here?"

"Right."

"Because . . . ?"

"Because Rhydderch Hael wants you here."

Éibhear lowered his hands. "Rhydderch Hael? You haven't mentioned him in ages."

"We stopped speaking after the birth of the twins. But he showed up again right after you arrived to fetch me back to Garbhán Isle. Then I saw him again just before the first Sand dragon attacked me at the salt mines. He's used me to get you where he needs you, and that just pisses me off."

"Me? What does he want with me? You're the one with the blood debt to him."

"I know, but apparently he doesn't want to waste my talents." She smirked. "Seems you're not as talented as I am because he's throwing you right into the pit. I just wish I knew what that pit was."

Éibhear shrugged. "Guess we'll find out soon enough."

"You don't seem worried."

"Should I be?"

"When a god makes you take a blood oath to him while

he's wearing your mother's body like a suit of armor, I'd have to say this is a god you *should* be worried about."

"You do have a point."

"You should head back."

"Are you coming?"

"You know I can't. I have to see that Nolwenn bitch."

"Then I guess I won't be going back."

"Éibhear—"

"We're not arguing about it, Izzy, so you might as well let it go."

"But if something happens to you now, it'll be my fault."

"What makes you think that?"

She started to say something but stopped herself, shook her head. "No reason."

"You're a bad liar. Keita would have sold that to me much better." He studied her a moment. "Perhaps you should tell me what the god said to you, Izzy."

"I'd prefer not to."

"I'm sure you would, but we both know I can wear you down. So why delay the inevitable?"

"I don't see why it—"

"Just tell me!"

She scratched her nose and muttered, "He seems to believe you'll follow me wherever I go."

"No," Éibhear immediately replied.

"Exactly. I told him he was—"

"Not everywhere."

"Wait. What?"

"I wouldn't follow you *every*where. Unless you needed me to. Do you need me to?"

"I don't need you to—" She bit her bottom lip, closed her eyes. After a few seconds, she said, "I don't need you to follow me anywhere. And I don't like gods using our kin to get what they want."

"What does he want?"

Izzy shrugged. "I have no idea. I just know that he wanted you in the Desert Lands—and here you are."

Izzy didn't know what bothered her more. The fact that Éibhear seemed completely unfazed by all this. Or the fact that he said he'd follow her anywhere . . . if she "needed" him to. What did that even mean?

"I wouldn't worry about it," Éibhear finally said.

"You wouldn't?"

"What's the point of worrying? It won't change anything."

"I can't live like that," Izzy admitted.

"Why not?"

"Because if you don't worry about the possible worst-case scenario, then it'll happen."

"That is incredibly ridiculous."

"That is *not* ridiculous. What am I supposed to do? Wait to see what happens? Just let horrible things rain down on me and my men?"

"I didn't say you shouldn't plan for possible worst-case scenarios, Izzy. I said you shouldn't *worry* about them. All worry does is cause you to panic and, I might add, make your voice a little bit shrill."

"My voice does not get shrill."

"It does. Sometimes you sound just like your mother when you get like that."

Izzy gasped, outraged. "That is an unfair thing to say to me."

"Well—"

"I am *not* like my mother. Not when it comes to that. I don't sit around obsessing all day about all the little things that can go wrong."

"Right. You just worry about the big things that can go wrong."

She tapped her foot.

"I wouldn't let that bother you, though," he went on. "You're as cute as your mum when you do it."

"Oh. Am I? I see you still have a thing for my mother. Too bad Daddy got to her first."

"That's all right. I can always settle for you."

Izzy froze, her hands curling into fists, the back of her neck getting tight. "Settle for me? You can *settle* for me?"

"You're better than nothing."

And that's when she swung on him.

Laughing, Éibhear caught hold of Izzy's waist and pulled her onto his lap, knees on either side of his hips. Once he had her there, he quickly grabbed her wrists to stop the onslaught of her fists. She had a right hook that clearly one of his brothers had taught her and she used it to devastating effect.

"I'm sorry," he said quickly. "I'm sorry."

"I don't want to hear it. You are such a bastard."

He pinned her arms behind her back and held her like that until she looked at him. "I'm sorry. I was only joking."

"If you'd rather have had my mother, just admit it."

"Your mother is beautiful, but she likes to argue a bit too much for my taste."

Izzy's eyebrow went up. "As opposed to us?"

"We don't argue."

"Uh . . . okay."

Éibhear leaned in and rubbed his nose against her jaw.

"What are you doing?"

"Nuzzling. Animals do it in the wild."

"See a lot of that in the Ice Lands, did you?"

"Nothing else to do but watch animals nuzzle. You know, when we weren't eating them."

Shaking her head, Izzy tried to slip off Éibhear's lap, but he wasn't in the mood to let her go. Although he wouldn't mind if she kept wiggling her ass around like that. It felt wonderful.

"Are you going to release me?"

"No. You might start hitting me again. And your tiny little fists hurt my sensitive human skin."

"You're pathetic," she laughed.

"So my brothers keep saying." He kissed her jaw, moved down her neck.

"Éibhear, we can't."

"Why not?"

"We're going to have to go to dinner soon."

"Not for a bit. We've got time." And even if they didn't, he'd make time.

"I have to change."

"Oh. Well . . . let me help you with that."

Éibhear released Izzy's wrists but only so he could grab hold of her chain-mail shirt and pull it up over her head. He tossed it on the bed behind him and moved in for the bindings she wrapped around her breasts. He got that off in short order, then wrapped his arms around her waist. He pulled her in closer, loving how her tits felt pressed against his chest.

"Now kiss me, Izzy."

"This isn't what we should be doing. I thought we weren't going to let this get complicated."

"Izzy . . . I'm Mì-runach."

"Which means . . . what? Exactly?"

"That when I told you I wasn't going to let this get complicated I was merely lying to get what I want. That's what we do. That's what we're trained to do."

"You were trained to lie? You mean like your sister?"

"No. Keita lies for queen and country, but the Mì-runach lie for ale and pussy."

"You lot need training for *that*?"

"It's definitely a skill."

"Oh, well, when you put it like that . . ."

"Just kiss me, Iz." He nipped her chin. "Before I go mad from the waiting."

"All right. But just a small kiss. Just a little one. And then we have to get dressed for dinner."

"Just a small one. I promise."

Izzy began to lean in, but she suddenly stopped, eyes narrowing on him. "Are you lying again?"

"Mì-runach. Pussy. All we're missing is the ale."

"Ale, eh? Well . . ." She shrugged. "As long as I get something out of it."

"When it comes to obtaining ale, the Mì-runach *never* lie."

Izzy smiled and pressed her mouth to his. Their tongues met and Izzy wrapped her arms around his neck. He held her tighter, his hands tracing the lines of her scars while his cock grew uncomfortably hard in his leggings.

Gods, he had to be inside her. He had to be inside her now. He couldn't wait even a second longer.

"What are you two doing?"

Éibhear and Izzy froze at the same moment, Izzy's eyes opening wide to look at him even though their mouths stayed fused together. He knew that she wanted to believe they hadn't heard anything. But Éibhear knew better. Knew that they *had* heard what they didn't want to believe they'd heard.

"I don't believe you two," that angry voice went on. "I've been worried sick and *this* is what you've been up to?"

Izzy pulled back, her hands immediately covering her chest.

"I have to say I don't expect much from the boy, Iseabail. But I thought you learned your lesson after Celyn."

Éibhear looked around. They were surrounded. Surrounded by beautiful trees and soft green grass and happily whistling birds. Things that he could not only see and hear but feel. Like the extremely large boulder he and Izzy now sat on.

"Mum—" he began.

"I don't want to hear it, Éibhear. From either of you! And Izzy," she went on, "to do this in front of your sister."

Eyes getting impossibly wider, Izzy looked over her shoulder and Rhi waved at her from beside his mother.

"What the hells is going on?" Éibhear demanded, helping Izzy as she scrambled behind him to hide from his mother's imperious glare and Rhi's happily curious expression. Tragically, Izzy's shirt had been left behind in that Desert Land chamber, so all she could do was use Éibhear's bare chest as a shield. "Why is my niece even here?"

"Do you think it's easy to bring those without any Magickal skills into a sacred space? Even for someone of *my* amazing skills? Well," she went on before Éibhear could bother trying to answer that question, "it's not. And I needed Rhi's help. But little did I know what I would be exposing the poor girl to."

"Mum."

"I mean I expect little from you. . . . You're a male. I'm just glad you can think of and speak full and complete sentences."

"*Mum.*"

"But Iseabail, Daughter of Talaith and Briec, what are *you* thinking?"

"*Me?* Why are you putting all this on my shoulders?"

"Because you of all people should know how stupid anything with a penis is! And yet here you are, involving yourself with *my* son. As if *that's* acceptable!"

Izzy gasped. "Why wouldn't it be acceptable? We're not blood related."

"Exactly! So you were not born a royal. You were merely a commoner who has been very lucky. And if you think you'll trap one of my useless sons with that common pussy, you're tragically mistaken!"

"*Mum!*"

"Oh, shut up! Now here. I came to give you this." She threw down a piece of parchment. A rune drawn on it.

"When you don't have your tongue down Izzy the Dangerous's throat, feel free to keep a look out for that rune. You'll most likely find it on those who've already tried to kill you once. And in case you were worried about your cousin Brannie and your three friends, which clearly you were not—*they're fine!*"

"Mum—"

"Och! You stupid, stupid boy!" She turned away but then spun back again, her dragon tail almost taking off poor Rhi's head. Thankfully the girl was quick and managed to duck in time. "And when you two get back, this whole . . . *thing* better be done with!"

"Don't you dare try to order me to—dammit!"

One second he was in some lovely grove with a pretty pink sky and the next he was back here, in this stupid chamber. Damn that female!

"Princess Iseabail?" one of the guards asked from the entrance while he eyed them both. "Is everything all right?"

"Uh . . . yes. Yes. Everything is fine." Éibhear didn't have to look to know that Izzy was busy grabbing her shirt and pulling it on, using Éibhear to block the guard's view.

"We sent you clothes, but no one could find you."

"Uh . . . right. Went exploring. Sorry about that."

"Dinner is about to take place. Should I ask King Heru if you could have more—"

"Time? No. No need." She scrambled off the bed, smoothing the shirt down her unbound breasts. "Let's just go and get our meal. I'm starving."

"Of course." The guard nodded. "Right this way."

He walked out and Izzy went to follow, but Éibhear grabbed her hand and pulled her back. "Don't even *think* of losing your mind over this."

"Too late!"

"I don't care what my mother says or your mother or the mother of all the gods. We do what we want, Izzy. And if that means fucking like bunnies, then that is exactly what we'll do."

"Can we discuss this later?" She snatched her hand back. "Much later?"

Izzy walked out, although he could tell she'd rather be running. Running all the way back to her legions and more killing. Anything rather than face the situation that was right in front of her. Not that he blamed her, but still. She had to know that no matter what happened between them the family wouldn't take this well. She just needed to deal with it.

Back safely in the grove not more than a league from Garbhán Isle, Rhi looked up at her grandmother, who would escort Rhi back to the house now that they were done with their task. But still, something bothered Rhi. . . .

"Why did you say that to Izzy and Uncle Éibhear?"

"I had to, it's nothing to worry about."

"But I don't understand, Gram. I thought you didn't mind them being together."

"Oh . . . my darling girl. When you're a mother you'll understand this better, but if you think for a minute that my blessing their union and telling them that it should have happened years ago would bond those two together for a lifetime, you are a very optimistic girl. Instead, it would only make them go out of their way to do the exact opposite. It's what children do to their parents."

"I don't." She scrunched up her nose. "But Talwyn and Talan do."

"Exactly. No, no. This was ugly but necessary. Either I forbid the relationship now or I risk another three or four decades of those two fighting what everyone else can so clearly see."

"You practically called Izzy a whore, though."

"There's no practically there, but I had to make it convincing. But don't worry. Once I know that idiot and my granddaughter have stopped all this foolishness, I'll apologize to her."

"What about Uncle Éibhear?"

"He's male, darling. It's best to keep things simple and unadorned for the males. You'll learn that, too, as you get older. Now"—she leaned in a bit—"would you like to go flying with Grandmum before we take you home, so you can watch her toss cows around for no other reason than her own amusement?"

"Sounds unnecessarily cruel."

"Exactly!" Rhiannon used her tail to place her granddaughter on her back. "See? Already you're learning what it means to be part of this family."

Chapter 30

"Are you not hungry, Princess? Is the food not to your liking?"

Izzy looked up from the food she'd been toying with for the last forty minutes. As Éibhear had feared, Izzy seemed to be taking his mother's words hard. Then again, not really surprising. Not only did Izzy adore his mother, she respected her. So what Rhiannon had said bothered Izzy more than if it had come from one of the Cadwaladr aunts who'd mostly ignored her over the years.

"No," she said. "Everything's fine."

"Then what troubles you?"

Izzy glanced at the other three dragons who'd come to dinner in the king's privy chamber: Lord Amsi, a duke from the outer regions of the Desert Lands; Bani, the king's personal healer and friend; and Kafele, the king's head magi.

"Nothing," Izzy finally said.

"Now, now, Princess Iseabail. I want you to feel you can be honest with me. And these"—he gestured to the three other dragons—"are my closest confidants. Anything you say to me, you can say to them with no fear that it will spread beyond my chamber."

"I understand, but—"

"No, Princess. Feel free to express yourself here. You are among friends."

An eyebrow peaked. "Really?"

Uh-oh. "Izzy—" Éibhear warned.

"Fine," Izzy went on, ignoring him. "You want me to express myself? Then that's what I'll do."

"Izzy—"

"It's all right, Prince Éibhear. I'm eager to hear Iseabail's thoughts."

At that point, all Éibhear could do was roll his eyes and sit back in his chair.

"Go on, Iseabail," Heru said congenially. "Tell me your—"

"What the battle-fuck do you want with us?"

The duke sat up straight, his glower dark and dangerous. "Perhaps you forget your place, Southland human."

"Keep your mouth shut," Izzy warned, voice low. "Or I'll split your spine.

"Now"—Izzy focused back on Heru—"I'm in no mood to fuck around about this anymore. You came, you got me . . . why? And don't give me any centaur shit about feeling benevolent, or just in a mood, or gods-damn premonitions. All I care about at this point is what *you* want from *me*."

Although Heru looked amused, the duke was definitely not and he seemed unable to keep out of all this.

"Look, *human*," the duke sneered, "you may think you're safe with your barbarian Mì-runach sitting at this table, but I can assure you—"

"I don't need Éibhear's help to kill you. I've killed dragons greater and stronger than you can even begin to dream of being. So hold your tongue or I'll make it part of my wall decoration, along with the horns of Olgeir the Wastrel and the spine of Overlord Thracius!"

Éibhear studied Izzy a moment and asked, "You're the one who took Thracius's spine?"

"I was the one who split it."

"But I was the one who finished him."

"Only because I'd destroyed his ability to fly away!"

"Excuse me," Heru cut in. "As fascinating as it is to hear the violent lifestyle of the Fire Breathers and their human kin, I'm sure Iseabail would prefer to hear the truth of the matter."

"Aye. I would."

"It began a few months back. The conversions."

"Conversions?"

"To the Cult of Chramnesind."

Izzy and Éibhear looked at each other, back at Heru, and said together, "The Cult of *Who*?"

"The Cult of Chramnesind is a blood cult. We don't know where they came from or why they're here, but it's not just those from the Desert Lands who have joined their ranks."

"You say blood cult," Izzy noted, "so you mean sacrifices."

"Many young ones. Human and otherwise. The true zealots, the priests of this cult, are blinded, their eyes usually removed completely during some kind of ritual."

"They willingly allow their eyes to be removed?"

"In honor of their god."

"Chramnesind," Éibhear said.

"Yes."

"Is he a dragon god? I've never heard of him."

"No. He's among the human pantheon of gods."

Izzy glanced at Éibhear. "No offense, King Heru, but you're saying that *dragons* are joining a human cult?"

"I am."

Izzy didn't understand. From what she'd always heard, not only from her kin but from Rhydderch Hael himself, dragon gods could barely get dragons to do their bidding. How, then, could a human god get dragons to join a cult that insisted on self-mutilation and the killing of young ones? Even the most barbaric of dragon tribes didn't believe in the harming of youngsters.

"Why?" Éibhear asked. "What could possibly be the benefit of joining a cult like this?"

"That I don't know. My soldiers have captured exactly two of their loyalists this past year. They both ended their own lives before we were able to question them."

Éibhear leaned back in his chair. "They killed themselves? *Dragons* took their own lives?"

"What?" Izzy asked.

"Dragons don't kill themselves," Éibhear explained.

"Why not?"

"We're too arrogant," he said simply. "Why would we destroy perfection?"

"You're serious, aren't you?"

"Yes," every dragon at the table replied.

"And that's the power we're dealing with," Heru went on.

"If Chramnesind is a human god," Izzy asked Heru, "what is the point of having dragons worshipping him?"

"Other than maybe having them as part of the cult's growing army, I really don't know."

"But perhaps, Princess Iseabail," the king's head magi, Kafele, finally offered, "you could find out for us."

Izzy blinked. "Find out for you? Do you mean ask my grandmother and Aunt Morfyd?"

"No. I mean ask Rhydderch Hael yourself. You are his chosen champion, are you not?"

Izzy stared at the magi for several seconds before she slowly moved her gaze to the king. "Is that what this is about? Is that why you took me?"

"We had to do something. It's believed this cult has infiltrated our ranks."

"Is that why you came for Izzy yourself?" Éibhear asked. "Because there was no one else you could trust?"

"They went there for Iseabail. They knew she was there. I had to move quickly and without concern that there'd be a betrayal."

"Were they coming to take me . . . or kill me?"

"I don't know, but it doesn't really matter, does it?"

"You're right. It doesn't." Izzy pushed her chair back and stood. "Thank you for your help. Of course, my grandmother will hear about all you've done for me."

The king stood as well. "Of course, you'll stay for a bit."

"I can't. I have to get to the city of Sefu."

"Then let me provide you and Prince Éibhear with an escort."

"I need no escort, King Heru. But I truly do appreciate all you've done." She stepped away from the table. "And if I discover any further information, I will get it to you."

"Thank you. And just a word of caution. The suns burn much hotter here in my beautiful land than in your Dark Plains. You may want to travel at night; there are small caves throughout the territory where you can sleep during the day. If that's not possible, sleep under Prince Éibhear's wings for protection."

With a nod, Izzy headed out of the chamber and back to where she'd left her travel bag and Macsen.

Éibhear caught up to her, his stride matching hers. "Are you sure about this?" he asked.

"We have to keep moving. We have to get this settled."

Éibhear didn't reply until they arrived back in their chamber. Then, once there, he caught hold of her arm and walked her back until she was against the wall.

"What is it, Izzy?" he asked, keeping his voice low. "I know you, Izzy. A cult is after you. Normally, you'd be heading toward them, not away."

And Éibhear was right. She would be. Annwyl had always taught Izzy to face her battles head-on unless there was a tactical advantage not to. Yet this particular decision wasn't about Izzy. Not at all.

"When Rhi was young, she told me she had lots of friends. She talked to them all the time. Sometimes Talan and Talwyn didn't mind about her friends, but sometimes her cousins chased those friends off."

"They were gods."

"When I asked her to describe her friends, she told me some were bright like the sun, blinding her. Others were made of earth and shit, but they were ever so nice."

Éibhear chuckled at that.

"My sister and young cousins talk to gods. Now, a god that none of us has ever heard of and has nothing to do with dragons, suddenly starts a cult."

"A cult that's trying to stop you from getting across the desert plains to the Nolwenns."

"My mum was right. Rhi needs to learn how to control her power. She can't be used if she has control of it."

"And saying no to Heru's escort?"

"I don't trust him. Do you?"

"Not particularly. But I assumed that was mostly because I didn't like the way he looked at you."

"You don't like the way any male looks at me. Because you're a very good unc—"

Éibhear's hand went over her mouth, cutting off her words.

"We go alone," he said. "First we get to the Nolwenns and then we take it from there. Yes?"

Izzy pulled his hand away. "No. I'm going alone."

Éibhear laughed. Rather loudly, too. It was rude!

"What is so funny?" Izzy demanded.

"That you think for even a bloody second I'd let you travel into the Desert Lands on your own."

"I'm not asking your permission, Éibhear."

"Nor am I asking yours."

Izzy pushed away from him. "I knew you'd act this way. Don't you see? With all that's going on, I can't afford to spend time watching out for you."

Slowly Éibhear turned from the wall and faced her. "Excuse me?"

"Éibhear, you haven't spent that much time with gods. *I* have."

"And?"

"And I know how they think. Rhydderch Hael may have interest in you, but he doesn't care about you. He won't protect you."

"*And?*"

"Which means I'll have to do it instead."

"Because I can't protect myself?"

When Izzy took a moment to think about that, it was Éibhear's turn to push past her, storming over to his travel bag.

"I'm not trying to hurt your feelings, Éibhear. I just know what the gods can do and now it doesn't seem like we're dealing with one god but two. And getting between two gods—"

"Shut up." He opened his bag and quickly checked it to see what he'd need for his travels.

"Excuse me?"

"I said shut up." They'd need water and some dried beef before they were on their way. Something he was sure the Sand Eaters would provide if he asked.

"What are you telling me to shut up for?"

"Because you're pissing me off."

"And how did I do that? Because I bother to care enough to protect you?"

"No, Izzy. Because you're being a snobby bitch."

"What?"

"Were my words not clear?" He stood, leaned down a bit so he could look her straight in the eyes. "I said you're being a snobby bitch."

"You son of a—"

"Yes, only the great Izzy knows about the gods."

"Éibhear!"

"Only the great Izzy knows how to fight against evil and battle zealots!"

"I never said—"

"Only the great Izzy knows how to kill enemy dragons and manage my brothers."

"I did not say—"

"Only the great Izzy—"

"Stop calling me that!"

"—knows how to be the best warrior in the universe! Anyone else is just someone she has to protect like her little sister or the squirrels around Garbhán Isle."

"I only protected the squirrels because Daddy kept setting them aflame while laughing!"

"What you, great Izzy, my brothers, and father fail to realize isn't that I don't need anyone's protection. Or that I don't want anyone's protection. What you all fail to realize is that I've had to learn to protect myself because I was the only one I could rely on."

"What are you talking about? You have two thousand first cousins alone to watch your back."

"It is *not* two thousand. At least not the first cousins."

"What about a mother who would destroy the world to protect you?"

"My mother would destroy the world for *any* reason."

"One sister who's been known to poison anyone who hurt your feelings."

"She hasn't done that in years. Not since I turned seventy winters."

"Another sister who made one of your warrior uncles cry when he *suggested* that you were getting chubby."

"Those were hurtful words. I didn't eat for *hours* after he said that to me."

"Brothers who have always had your back in combat. And a father who loved you enough to teach you to kill without compunction or care."

"And your point?"

"My point is that you've been protected all your life. I don't hold it against you. You grew up with a family that loved you and cared for you and ensured your safety while I, when barely born, was ruthlessly ripped from my mother's arms and held captive until taken by three rough-and-ready soldiers and forced to travel from town to town, city to city, until I could be reunited with my mother years and years later—all that is not something I'd ever hold against you."

"Yes. I see you not holding it against me. And by the way, you've mastered your mother's guilting skills brilliantly."

"I am not trying to guilt—"

"Guilt!"

"I'm done with this conversation."

"Good." Éibhear pulled his travel bag over his shoulders. "Let's go then."

"Éibhear, you're not listening to me."

"I often don't, but it's nothing personal." He shrugged. "So . . . you ready to go?"

Izzy looked around the room. What she was looking for, he didn't know. "All right," she said, grabbing her own travel bag. "Let's go!"

Éibhear's eyes narrowed. She'd given up way too easily for Izzy, but she was already walking out of the chamber, so he had to follow.

They asked for and received extra food and water for their travels and a more accurate map of the lands. Once back topside, Éibhear said, "We'll only have a few hours of travel before the suns come up, but that's better than nothing."

"Okay."

Éibhear stripped off his clothes and shifted to his natural

form. Once he shook out his wings, he lowered his body down and said, "Get on."

Instead of coming to him, though, Izzy just stood there, staring. And staring. Until Éibhear knew exactly what she was trying to tell him without saying a word.

Éibhear shook his head, adamant. "No."

"Then we should begin walking now."

"That will take forever."

"I won't leave him. He was there when we needed him."

"I'm not a horse, Izzy."

"I know. I would never have asked Dai to carry Macsen."

Gods, she was horrible. Just downright horrible. But some days she couldn't help herself.

The dragon turned his head away. "I'll not do it. I'll not bring that dog anywhere."

"All right." Izzy picked up her travel bag, slinging it over her shoulder. "Come on, Macsen." She started to walk. "We'll meet you at Sefu in a few weeks or so, Éibhear."

"You'll never last out here if you can't find a cave to stay in during the day. The suns will burn the skin from your back."

"My people are from here."

"They also travel by horse."

"I'm sure I have some natural defense. But you can go."

"You know I won't leave you, Izzy."

"Then you won't leave us."

"You can't seriously expect me to bring that bloody dog."

"I'll not leave him, Éibhear. I'll not leave my Macsen."

"Your Mac—" He gritted his fangs together. "Fine."

Izzy stopped. "Fine what?"

"I'll bring . . . that."

She faced him. "You promise not to throw him off your back when we're in flight?"

"Off my back?"

"Well, you're not bringing him in your claw."

"Izzy—"

"We're walking." She started off again.

"All right! All right!" She heard him sigh. It did really take all the strength she'd built up over the years to stop herself from rolling on the ground with laughter. "I'll take him."

"And you promise not to throw him off your back?"

"I promise."

"Or just leave him anywhere because that will really—"

"I'll guard the little bastard with my life. Now can we just go? Please?"

"All right." She headed back toward him, gesturing to her dog. "Take a break, Macsen."

The dog took off and began to circle around Éibhear. While he did, Izzy grabbed hold of Éibhear's hair and pulled herself onto his back. Once she was settled, she noticed that Macsen had slowed down until he was right by Éibhear's back leg, his own leg lifted. She didn't think the dragon had noticed until his long neck suddenly stretched down, his snout pushing into Macsen's. "Piss on my leg and that'll be the last thing you ever do with that penis."

Slowly, Macsen lowered his leg, walked a few feet away, and pissed in the sand. When he was done, he came back and, with a mighty sigh, Éibhear used his tail to place the dog on his back right in front of Izzy.

With her hands holding onto Macsen's hips, she got him to lie down. "We're ready."

Éibhear's wings unfurled, but before he took off he said, "If you tell anyone about this—"

"Not a word. To anyone. Promise."

"And does *he* promise?"

Izzy blinked. "You want the *dog* to promise?"

"You say he's a dog. I don't know what he is."

"He's a dog!"

"Promise!"

Because she knew Éibhear wouldn't let this go, she tapped Macsen on his right side so that he barked. Once. It was something she'd taught him long ago for amusement. Who knew it would actually come in handy at some point?

"Thank you," Éibhear muttered.

"You just thanked a dog."

"So you say!" he accused.

Deciding this wasn't the time to attempt to rationalize with a dragon, Izzy kept silent—for once—petted her dog, and enjoyed flying.

Chapter 31

Just before the two suns rose, Éibhear caught sight of a cave. It was half out and half buried in the sand near a dune. It seemed like the perfect place, especially since he didn't know if they'd find another one before the suns were high in the sky.

He landed right outside the cave, lowering his body so Izzy could slip off and take that stupid dog with her.

"Wait here," he told her. "I'll check out the cave, make sure it's safe."

She didn't reply and he didn't wait for her to. She'd been completely uncommunicative since they'd left Heru's court and Éibhear doubted that would change in the span of a few hours.

He made his way into the cave, worried it was as small as it seemed from the outside. But, thankfully, it was more of an underground cave and moving down a bit, he found some roomy caverns that would be perfect to sleep the day in. He was about to set off to explore a little more when he realized that Izzy was behind him, holding a lit torch.

"I thought I told you to wait."

Izzy gave a light, carefree laugh. "I simply adore how you

think I'd take your orders at any time or for any reason in this known universe. That just amuses me so much. Such a sense of humor you've gotten."

"You couldn't have simply said, 'I don't take orders from you.'"

"I *could* have."

Sighing, Éibhear headed off in one direction and Izzy the other with her sword out. After about fifteen minutes, they met up back in the cavern.

"All clear," she said, dropping her travel pack and stretching out her shoulders. "Not even a rat."

"If dragons use these to rest in, vermin of any kind would be foolish to stay here. For some of us, rats are like little warm treats."

"For some, but not for you?"

He couldn't help but pull back his lips over his fangs. "No. There are some things I simply will *not* eat."

Izzy got out her bedroll, spread it out on the ground, and sat down. She dug into her travel bag and took out some dried beef and her canteen of water.

Éibhear shifted to human and followed her example by pulling out his bedroll and spreading it out. By the time he sat down on it, he got a view of Izzy sharing her food with that damn dog.

"You're giving him your dried beef?"

"I made sure to bring enough for him. Don't worry. He's my dog, I'll take care of him."

"We should have left him behind."

"Oh, yes, I should leave my precious dog alone with strange dragons who still eat dog. Brilliant plan." She looked up, frowned. "Why am I staring at your penis?"

"Because it mesmerizes you?"

"Can't you put on leggings?"

"I *could*." Then he smiled, which just seemed to piss her off more.

Her lip curled a bit, but she went back to feeding that damn dog rather than yelling at him.

Éibhear took out some of his own food and ate while he watched Izzy. She pretended to ignore him, but he didn't buy it. Not anymore.

"How long have you had him?" he finally asked her about that damn dog.

"Three years now."

"Do you ever bathe him?"

"Whenever I bathe in a lake or river, he bathes. He loves the water."

"And yet he never seems very clean."

"He loves the water, but he also loves mud, blood, shit, cow urine—"

"Wait. Specifically cow urine?"

"Don't ask me why. It's just a thing he has."

"And you really don't think he's been spit up from the underworld?"

"No, I do not."

"Because I've never seen this breed of dog before."

"That's meaningless. The world is filled with things neither of us have seen. Besides"—she lifted the dog's head—"how can you look in these eyes and think anything about my Macsen is evil?"

"Because his one good eye is red?"

"What?" She lifted his head more so she could look at the dog without moving. "Oh. That. That's just the reflection of the light from the torch."

"If you need to believe that to get through the night."

"I can't believe you're afraid of a little dog."

"He's not little and I'm not afraid. I just find him vile. Like rats. I find them vile too."

"But rats aren't loyal and they carry disease."

"You have no way of knowing if that dog carries disease or not."

She let out a frustrated sigh. "Leave my dog alone."

"All right. But when he steals your soul in the middle of the night and tosses it into the lowest pits of one of the hells, don't come crying to me."

Izzy, disgusted that anyone could not love the beast slobbering on her leg, pulled a Desert Land map from her travel bag and looked it over.

"So where are you going to sleep?" she heard Éibhear ask her.

"Sleep?" She looked up from the map. "Right here."

"Is there room?"

Frowning, Izzy looked down at her bedroll and immediately sighed. Macsen was on his back, four legs relaxed and spread open, his snores filling the cave chamber. It wasn't pretty, but it proved one thing. The dog had come to trust Éibhear because he never exposed his belly to anyone he didn't trust.

"He'll make room for me," she muttered, returning to her map.

"I'm sure there's truth to that. I know I'd make room for you."

Izzy lifted her gaze to lock on the dragon sitting across from her. He sat cross-legged, elbows resting on his big thighs, shiny blue hair falling into his face, bright silver eyes watching her close.

"You can't be serious," she said.

"About?"

"We've been arguing for the last two days."

"So?"

"And you still want me in your bed?"

"I want you anyway I can get you."

Izzy didn't even have to look to know that he was hard and ready. Perhaps, she reasoned to herself, any pussy sitting across from him would do, but she didn't know.

"You do understand we can't keep this up, don't you?"

"I can keep it up for hours so—"

"No, no." Gods, this dragon! "I mean whatever is going on between us—we can't keep this up."

"You don't know what's going on between us? Should I draw a diagram?"

"I don't need a diagram, Éibhear. I'm just saying that . . . it's just that . . ." Izzy let out a frustrated breath. "What I mean is . . ."

"What's the matter, Izzy? Is my fine human form distracting you?"

Yes! "No!"

"No need to get snappy. It was just a question."

"I'm simply trying to explain that—"

"Why don't we forget about explaining anything right now."

"You may have a point," she sighed out, rubbing her face with her hands.

"Instead you can get naked and come sit on my cock and we can save explanations for another day."

Izzy's hands covered her face and she moved a couple of fingers so that she could stare at the dragon with one eye.

"I think I miss the days," she mumbled around her hands, "when I used to get you flustered just by grabbing your tail."

"You still get me flustered by grabbing my tail, but that, too, can be a discussion for another day."

Izzy dropped her hands to her lap and gawked at him. "Do you really want me that badly, Éibhear the Blue?"

"I want you more than my next breath. And yes, it does

matter who's sitting across from me. Since I'm guessing that's what you were wondering."

Bastard. He did know her well, didn't he? After all these years. After all they'd been through. Maybe he knew her better than most.

"Izzy," he said low before making his eyebrows dance.

Izzy covered her mouth, but the laughter slipped through her fingers.

"Well," she finally said while getting to her knees. "You were nice enough to carry my dog. Guess I could make the sacrifice."

"The sacrifice? Yes, it's always very nice to know that being with me is something you're *lowering* yourself to do."

With her chain-mail shirt now resting on the snout of the snoring dog—and no, getting hit in the face with a shirt made of metal didn't manage to wake up the idiot—and her bindings removed and tossed aside, Izzy now stretched across the small divide between them. Her hands were braced on either side of his hips and her mouth wonderfully close to his.

Éibhear brought his hands up, framed her face. Izzy had grown so beautiful. The battle scars across her nose, cheek, and jaw only enhancing that beauty somehow.

"You going to kiss me?" she asked. "Or just keep staring?"

"I don't really know yet." He stroked his hands down her face, her neck. "I like being able to look at you without worrying that I'll be battered into a blood-covered mess by three bastards who, after all these years, still violently abuse me."

Izzy smirked. "Funny, it looked like Daddy and the others got the worst of it."

"They started it. I was merely defending myself."

"You're such a lying piece of—"

"Now, now. Let's not get vicious." He tugged her a bit closer, brushed his lips against hers. "At least not yet."

Izzy slipped into his lap, her legs on either side of him, her arms resting on his shoulders. Éibhear kissed her while his hands slid down her throat and across her chest. He cupped her breasts; his thumbs brushed her nipples. Izzy groaned, her eyes closing.

This wasn't fair. The dragon had barely touched her and again she was melting in his hands, falling apart under his fingers. She should be toying with him, using him, making his life a living hell just for her cold amusement. Yet she seemed unable to do any of these things. Instead she dug her fingers into his hair, pulled him closer.

Those big hands slid lower until they wrapped around Izzy's waist. Then Éibhear leaned forward, pushing Izzy back, his mouth kissing her mouth, jaw, and throat. When she was bent back as far as she could go, one of Éibhear's hands released her waist and, seconds later, Izzy felt a finger pushed inside her, followed by another. She groaned louder, her body shuddering.

Éibhear wrapped his lips around her nipple, tugging and teasing it with his tongue.

Izzy's body went hot, then broke out in a sweat. Her hands gripped Éibhear's shoulders.

Gods, she felt delirious. Crazed. She couldn't think straight and felt like she had no control over her body.

He moved to her other nipple, his teeth grazing the tip before he sucked it hard into his mouth and played with it using his tongue. And the whole time the two fingers he had inside her kept stroking in and out, his thumb occasionally brushing her clit. Not enough to make her come, but just enough to drive her insane.

Izzy tried to close her legs, hoping to keep Éibhear's hand

right where it was, thinking maybe she could ride it until she came, but he stayed between her thighs, keeping them apart with his body.

Unable to take any more, she shook her head, tried to pull away. Just to get a few seconds to breathe, to calm down so that she could manage all this. But the hand on her waist moved up her back until his hand cupped her shoulder and held her in place, keeping her captive.

Izzy whimpered, desperate. She didn't know what to do. She was confused, overwhelmed. It wasn't supposed to be like this. It wasn't supposed to be this intense, this out of control. No matter what she may have daydreamed when she was sixteen and had no idea what sex was really about, as a rational adult, Izzy knew sex with *anyone* shouldn't be like this. Nothing should. It was too much, too good, too everything.

She pushed at Éibhear's shoulders and he finally loosened his grip. Relief and disappointment warred inside her as she started to drag herself away. But Éibhear took hold of her thighs, lifted them to his shoulders. Before Izzy could say a word, his head was between her legs and his tongue inside her pussy.

Izzy grabbed the back of Éibhear's head with every intention of pushing him away.

Yes. That was her intention. Definitely. Absolutely.

Too bad intentions meant nothing when faced with the most perfect tongue.

Izzy twisted and turned, no longer trying to get away, but simply unable to fight her body's response any longer.

That perfect tongue moved up, finally settling on her clit, massaging it with the tip until he wrapped his lips around it and began tugging. By the second tug, she was sobbing. By the third, she was screaming, her back arching, her thighs tightening around Éibhear's head until she was sure she must be killing him. Not that she cared. Not at the moment when nothing could distract Izzy from the orgasm violently ripping through her, tearing her apart from the inside out until she could do nothing but lie on the ground and whimper.

Éibhear finally pulled away, his hands stroking her sweat-soaked body while he stretched out next to her. He pushed her hair off her face, gave her a soft smile. "You all right?"

"I hate you," she whispered. "I've always hated you."

"Lying won't make this any easier, Iseabail."

"Shut up."

He laughed and wrapped his arms around her, pulling her into his body. She felt his hard cock pressing against her leg, but he seemed more than willing to wait for her.

Of course that only made Izzy hate him more.

Éibhear knew now why she was mad at him.

Well, at first he didn't. At first he was completely confused. Until, about twenty minutes later, when she'd climbed on top of him and straddled his waist, sliding his cock inside her. Then, with those light brown eyes he'd dreamed of more than a thousand times over the years gazing down at him, she rode him. Her hips rocking against him, the muscles inside her pussy squeezing and releasing his cock, until he thought he might go blind. Even worse, Izzy took her time, her hands stroking his chest, his shoulders. But it was her moans, the wetness of her pussy, the way her thighs gripped him so very tight that told him what he needed to know.

So, yes, he understood why she was mad at him. Because he felt the same way. Éibhear knew she could ask anything of him and he'd move the suns to make it happen. Knew he'd do anything to keep a smile on her face, to keep her safe.

Pissed off at himself, he gripped her waist and rolled over, pinning her beneath his body. She gazed up at him and he got the feeling she knew what he was doing. Trying to maintain control of an uncontrollable situation. But she didn't make fun of him or tease him, simply leaned up until she could kiss him, her arms around his neck.

No. He'd never have control of this situation, no matter how hard he might try. It was just impossible. So Éibhear didn't bother fighting it anymore. What would be the point? Instead, he took her arms from around his neck, pinned them above her head, and fucked Izzy with everything he had inside him, knowing full well that Izzy was the one female who could handle it.

With her body stretched out, stomach down, Izzy rested her head on her crossed arms and enjoyed the feeling of Éibhear's hand stroking her legs and back.

"Where did you get this scar from?" he asked, the tips of his fingers moving over the lines of the raised flesh along her back.

"Not sure."

"Izzy, it's at least eighteen inches long and dangerously close to your spine. How could you not be sure?"

"Do you know how many battles I've been in? How many times a healer has worked on me? Sometimes they leave scars, sometimes they don't. Besides"—she planted her elbow and propped her chin in her palm—"I used to hate sitting around, listening to older warriors talk about all their scars. Comparing them. Bragging. What's the purpose? All that matters to me is that I'm still here with all me important bits."

Éibhear chuckled. "Now you sound like Ghleanna."

"She taught me much. So did Addolgar."

"My father's siblings gave us all battlefield lessons. Although I think Aunt Ghleanna stopped talking to me some time ago."

"Why?"

"Apparently she had greater hopes for me than the Mìrunach."

"If the queen thinks the Mì-runach serve a purpose, it's not for Ghleanna to question. Besides, from what I've seen so far, there's no shame in what you lot do."

"Planning to start your own Mì-runach among your legions?"

"Of course not. We don't need a gang of crazed warriors charging into battle with nothing more than their rage and a couple of swords."

"And why's that?"

"Because we have Annwyl. She *is* our Mì-runach, we need no other."

Laughing out loud, Éibhear rolled to his back, Izzy joining him. And the pair continued to laugh and talk and fuck until the suns went down and they could start their journey again.

Chapter 32

For three nights they traveled and slept during the day. The third night when they couldn't find a cave, Éibhear used his wings to cover Izzy and that stupid dog.

Although he was grateful for his protective scales, he was even happier that he had his fur cape in his travel bag. He didn't mind the heat much and it cut down on the sand that was getting into the crevices between his scales. Before they took flight each night, Izzy would have to help him clean out any areas that might affect his flying and he just willed himself to ignore the itching in the other places.

Most Southland dragons who came to the Desert Lands—and there were many who loved it here—didn't travel this way. Usually, they brought protective tents to set up each day. But the tents their group had originally brought with them were back with their stabled horses near the salt mines. Éibhear had no idea how much he'd wish he still had them.

Still, it could be worse. He had his cape, the heat wasn't destroying his will to live, and he had Izzy. Her constant chatter during the flights made the long nights bearable. She did spend less time talking to him and more time talking to that ridiculous dog, but at least it seemed to keep the damn thing calm. The dog mostly slept during flights and barked warnings during the day when they were sleeping. Of course most of those warnings were about the big scavenger birds that were all over these lands. But once they realized that the dragon carcass lying under the hot desert suns wasn't dead, they quickly flew off. It was still nice, though, to know the dog had some purpose other than to amuse Izzy with his constant drooling.

Waking up just as the suns set, Éibhear lifted his wings carefully off a still-sleeping Izzy before he sat up and stretched.

He pulled the map out and looked it over. Finally, they were nearing civilization. They were nearing Sefu.

Yawning, Izzy turned over, her arms stretching wide. Her eyes fluttered open and she smiled up at him. She always smiled up at him when she first awoke, and each time she did, the power of it hit him right in the gut. But just as quickly, she frowned, as if remembering she normally didn't have a good attitude when she first woke up.

"Hello."

She grunted at him, and sat up.

"Did you sleep well?"

"Well enough." She reached into her travel bag and took out a canteen. She drank from it while that idiot dog ran off to relieve itself.

"Izzy, if you don't mind another long night of flying, I'm thinking we should—"

The dog snarled and Izzy held up her hand, cutting off Éibhear's words. Even stranger, the dog walked backward toward them, teeth bared, hackles up. This was not the same reaction they'd been getting whenever some hungry bird got too close. This was something else.

Since he knew Izzy understood the dog better than he did, Éibhear looked at her.

"Shift to human," she said low.

"Turn your face away," he ordered to protect her fom the flames that would come from his shifting. Once done, he grabbed his travel bag and pulled out a pair of leggings, cotton shirt, and boots.

Éibhear had barely pulled his boots on when Izzy stood, her gaze focused straight ahead. By the time he also got to his feet, he could see the riders. They wore light armor and their horses were leaner than the Southland horses. And they were coming right for them.

Izzy stepped in front of him. "Watch out for Macsen."

Did she really believe that he'd protect that dog before her? Actually, she probably knew that he wouldn't, which was why she specifically told him to.

The riders at the front reined their horses in, stopping dead in front of them. The others circled around back. Although where they thought Izzy and Éibhear would escape to, out here, in the middle of nowhere, Éibhear didn't know.

One of the lead riders barked something at them, but neither Izzy nor Éibhear understood him, so he tried again, this time speaking in the common language of these lands.

"Who are you? Speak!"

"Name's Iseabail. This is my travel partner, Éibhear."

"What province do you come from? Who are your people?"

"I'm not from hcre."

The soldiers looked her over. "You're not?" the leader asked.

"No."

"Why are you here?"

"We're heading to Sefu. I need to meet with the Nolwenns."

"You?" The men laughed.

"Well, that's where we're going so if you'd just—"

"You're very well armed," another soldier noted.

"Just for safety."

"And him?" the leader asked, motioning to Éibhear.

"My protection. A slow-witted mute, but he's good at destroying things with his head."

Rude cow!

The leader looked them over again, and Éibhear immediately knew that the man didn't like what he saw. Probably a good decision, too, since they *were* lying.

"We'll escort you to Sefu."

"That's not necessary."

"It is for us."

"In other words, we have no choice."

The leader smirked. "Not really."

Izzy looked over the bars on the cell door she was currently locked behind. "That went well."

She heard snoring and knew it was her dog. Bastard could sleep through anything. She faced Éibhear. "Don't you think?"

He pointed at his mouth, shook his head.

Izzy rolled her eyes. "You take everything so bloody personally. I was only joking."

"Ha," he said. "Ha. Ha."

"It was the slow-witted part, wasn't it?"

"What do you think?"

"They're very paranoid," Izzy noted, looking back at the bars. "You are frightening to look at, but it seems a little unreasonable that your terrifying demeanor alone should get us thrown into a cell."

"Did you notice when we got here? The city gates had to be opened for them. I'd always heard Sefu was an open city, with visitors able to come and go as they please."

"They're preparing for war?"

"I don't know. Maybe. Or maybe it's all that civil unrest among the humans the salt mine commanders kept talking about."

"I guess it could be a lot of things, but I'm not sure it

matters at the moment. I think there are bigger issues." Izzy
again faced Éibhear and motioned to the wall behind him.
"Well . . . get to work."

Éibhear blinked. "Get to work doing what?"

"Tear the wall down so we can go. I'm this close to finally
meeting that treacherous bitch. I'm tired of waiting."

"They haven't done anything to us, Izzy. At least not yet."

"So?"

"So I'm not going to bring the prison down around their
ears just so you can go confront some old cow."

"Where's your loyalty?"

"Where's your rational military thought?"

"What does that mean?"

"I can get us out of here, but that doesn't mean I can
destroy the entire city. At least not this city. Didn't you look
at the ramparts? They have those catapults that are built like
giant crossbows. Something tells me those are for dragons
that may attack the city. If you think I can handle those all on
my own—"

"Fine, fine."

"If you weren't so obsessed with your grand—"

"I'm not obsessed."

"When the guards come back, just tell them the truth. Tell
them who you are. What you want. They obviously know
you're lying."

"Fine."

"It's just a suggestion—"

"Zazazaza!" Izzy waved her hands in Éibhear's face to
keep him quiet.

"What was that noise you just made?"

"Don't irritate me."

"I'm not trying to irritate you, Izzy. You are just really
tense. You're expecting a fight and you haven't even gotten
one yet. So you're looking at me for one."

"Well . . ." She shrugged. "You're here."

When Éibhear laughed, she felt relief. She *was* tense and she was being a complete bitch to the easiest target. A big blue dragon. Targets really didn't get easier than that. But it was unfair to him. Even after she'd told him what Rhydderch Hael had said to her, he hadn't displayed one moment of anger toward her. Didn't blame her for anything. Or tell her she should have told him about her talk with Rhydderch Hael when she was still with her army. Instead, he'd taken her and her dog—or "damn dog" to use his words—to the Desert Lands.

So to quote Annwyl on more than one occasion during their time together as queen and squire, Izzy knew she needed to "Stop being a twat and remember who's covering your plump ass."

"I'm sorry, Éibhear."

Éibhear blinked, not sure he'd heard correctly. "Huh?"

"I said I'm sorry. You're right. I'm very stressed and I'm taking it out on you. I shouldn't be, and I'm sorry."

Looking around their cell, Éibhear asked again, "Huh?"

"You." Izzy turned away from him and toward the guard standing at the door. "You have visitors."

Soldiers came around the corner. Like the ones who'd picked them up in the desert, these soldiers wore light armor, but the female one at the front wearing a helm with a long horse's mane coming from the top seemed to hold a higher rank.

"Names," one of the soldiers ordered.

Any bit of progress Éibhear had made alleviating her stress vanished in the face of those orders. Izzy's arms crossed under her chest and her foot began to tap. Never a good sign when dealing with Izzy.

"I said names," the soldier repeated.

"Heard the first time. Amazing what politeness can get you, though."

The higher-ranking soldier motioned another forward. This one was more polite.

"We need your names."

"I thought this was an open city," Izzy countered. "I don't understand—"

"I'd prefer you just answer my questions. Quickly."

"Izzy," Éibhear pushed. "Just answer him." If things turned ugly, he could easily shift to dragon and kill them all. But these soldiers simply wanted to know who they were.

The female officer's eyes narrowed. "Thought you were mute."

Éibhear sighed. "Do you see what you started?" he asked Izzy, which only made her laugh. "Now you have to tell her."

"Fine. I'm General Iseabail of Queen Annwyl's army."

"Annwyl? Annwyl the Bloody?" The female officer glanced at the others. "Lovely."

Éibhear caught hold of the back of Izzy's shirt before she could reach through the bars and strangle the captain to death. If there was one thing Izzy never tolerated, it was anyone saying anything negative about Annwyl; her aunt was her one true blind spot.

Oblivious to the danger, the polite soldier asked, "And why are you here, General?"

"I want to meet with the Nolwenns."

"So do many others, but your queen should have come on her own."

"I'm not here for my queen. I'm here for myself."

The female officer gave a little snort. "Planning to overthrow your mad queen and hoping the Nolwenns will help you because of the color of your skin?"

Éibhear would always be grateful for the speed of his hands. Because he managed to pull Izzy away from that cell door before she gripped the bars and yanked them right out of the ceiling and floor they'd been imbedded in.

And while she swung wildly and cursed, Éibhear explained, "The queen knows the general is here, but it has nothing to do with Queen Annwyl. The general's people are from here originally."

"And who are her people?" the polite soldier asked.

"She's the daughter of Talaith." Éibhear saw it out of the corner of his eye. The captain's head lifted, tilting to the side.

"Talaith?" the soldier asked.

"Talaith, Daughter of Haldane," Éibhear added.

The officer finally stepped forward, pushing the males out of her way. She was a strong woman. Tall, powerfully built, a multitude of warrior braids and long feathers mixed in with her brown, curly hair. Éibhear had a hard time seeing her face, though, because of the nose guard on her helm.

"Daughter of Haldane?" the officer asked.

Éibhear pushed a struggling Izzy behind him. "You know Haldane?"

The woman shook her head. "No. Not personally. Everyone knows the Nolwenns, though."

"Do you think you can help us get a meeting with them?"

"I really don't know." She kept staring, trying to look around him, but Izzy was still behind him cursing and trying to pry his hand off so she could come out swinging.

Éibhear shook her once to get her to focus.

"What?" Izzy snapped, but hearing her speak without yelling or cursing, Éibhear pulled Izzy back around.

"General Iseabail," Éibhear said, "this is—"

"Captain Layla," the officer introduced herself.

Izzy nodded. "Captain."

The captain stepped closer, looked Izzy over. "With us," she finally said. "Please."

She walked off and one of the guards unlocked the cell door, pulling it open.

Izzy glanced up at Éibhear. "Wherever you go," he muttered.

She nodded and headed out. Éibhear followed, but he glanced back at the dog, which was still snoring away. "Oy! Idiot! Let's go."

The dog's eyes opened, but he only stared at Éibhear without moving. Then Izzy whistled and the dog rolled off the cot to his feet and charged after his mistress.

Disgusted, Éibhear followed them all, wondering where they were going—and what would happen when they got there.

Chapter 33

With soldiers surrounding them, they were walked out of the jail and through the city. Izzy had no idea where she was going, but she truly hoped it was to the Nolwenns. She longed to see that bitch so she could tell her how horrible she was before handing her sister over to her. Izzy still shuddered at that, giving her sister over to the Nolwenns, but what could she do?

After about fifteen minutes of traveling through the city's central market, they turned down a street and stopped in front of a building. The captain looked at her men. "You lot wait out here."

"Captain, you sure?"

She nodded. "Yes." She motioned to Izzy and Éibhear. "You two come with me."

Izzy looked at Macsen. "Wait here," she told him. She didn't try to bring the dog with her because she knew she'd have Éibhear with her inside and Macsen would warn her of any problems that came from the outside.

The dog sat, tongue hanging out, already starting to drool. She stopped long enough to give him some water from her canteen, then went inside behind the captain.

Izzy had barely gotten a few feet when she realized that she was in a home.

"The Nolwenns are here?" she asked.

"I can't get you in to the Nolwenns. They have no interest in seeing me."

"Then what are we doing here?"

The captain didn't answer; she just kept walking through the house. It was a lovely place. Lots of white linen and comfortable furniture. And even though it was hot out on the streets, it was cool inside.

After several minutes, they made it to the back of the home and into an open area with grass and a covering over the top made of more white linen and large, leafy trees. This outside area was filled with women, men, and children. The older women and men, plus the younger children, were dressed in loose-fitting clothing that covered and protected them from the sun. But the older teens and the adults wore the same light armor that the captain wore.

"Mum's home!" one of the children called out and several of them ran over to hug her.

Another strong-looking, older female in armor stepped forward. "Who've you brought with you, Layla?"

The captain took off her helm. "This is General Iseabail from Dark Plains. One of Queen Annwyl's generals."

Suddenly looking very concerned, the older woman demanded, "Why is she here?"

"I thought you should meet properly. General Iseabail, this is my mother, General Maskini. She is commander of the city's army."

Izzy frowned, her gaze moving off.

"What is it?" Éibhear whispered.

"Feel like I've heard that name before."

"And Mum," Captain Layla continued, "this is Iseabail, Daughter of Talaith. Who is Daughter of Haldane."

Everything in that small area seemed to stop, all eyes

focusing on Izzy. Part of her wanted to back up, but as a soldier of the Blood Queen's army, she would never yield. So Izzy stood her ground and asked, "Is my mother your enemy?"

General Maskini walked up to Izzy, stared at her for several long moments, until, finally, she burst into tears.

The general's sobs were so great, she stumbled and Éibhear immediately caught her in his arms. He took her to a chair and lowered her into it.

An elderly woman made her way through the staring people in the backyard. Éibhear noticed that she had the same eyes as many of the others. The same as Izzy's eyes. Talaith had always said that Izzy had her father's eyes. Light brown and intense . . . just like her.

The elderly woman clutched her hands together. "Your name is . . ." She cleared her throat, tried again. "Your name is Iseabail?"

"Aye. My kin call me Izzy."

"Your kin?"

"My family."

"A family of your blood?"

"No. My mother . . ." She struggled for the right word. "She married my father. I was adopted by his family." She pointed at Éibhear. "That's my uncle."

And Éibhear tried not to panic when all those male eyes focused on him with clear hostility. He hadn't even touched Izzy. Hadn't done anything to suggest . . . and yet they knew, didn't they? Males always knew.

"So you never met your birth father?"

"No." Izzy began to wipe her hands on her leggings. One of the signs that she was nervous. Éibhear hadn't seen her do that in ages. Not since her mother had confronted her about Rhydderch Hael and the brand he'd burned into her arm. "My mother said he died before I was born."

"Do you know his name?"

Izzy closed her eyes and repeated what her mother had most likely told her a very long time ago, "Sethos, son of . . . son of . . ." She cleared her throat. "Son of Maskini."

The elderly woman reached out and took Izzy's hands in her own. "And grandson of Zarah. Most beloved grandson, my dearest Iseabail. Most beloved."

Izzy gazed at the woman holding her hands. But suddenly, abruptly, she pulled away. "I'm . . . I'm sorry. I just . . . I just can't."

Shocked, Éibhear watched her as she fled back inside the house.

"Izzy!" He got up to go after her, but Zarah stopped him, her hand resting against his forearm.

"Give her a minute. I know this can't be easy for her."

The woman had absolutely no idea.

Izzy ran through the house, but it was large and long and before she knew it, she had no idea how to get out again. Desperate, she realized that at the very least, she wanted a quiet space to get control of herself.

She went down a hallway but saw two of the soldiers who'd escorted her and Éibhear here.

Unwilling to let *any* soldiers see her like this, Izzy went through the first door she found and quickly closed it, both hands pressing into the wood, her body leaning forward. And that's when the tears came. She tried to stop them, but she simply couldn't. Even worse, she chanted what she'd chanted the first time she was caught in a burning building during a battle and couldn't find her way out, "Mum . . . gods, Mum . . ."

"Don't let her do that to you."

Startled, Izzy spun around, her back against the door. "Sorry, I . . ."

"My daughter is only tough on the ones she thinks have some promise."

Izzy shook her head. "No, I—"

"It's all right. I won't tell her I saw a thing. Take a moment, catch your breath."

The man appeared to be in his sixtieth winter or so, his grey hair cut very short, his arms bulging with muscles. He had a sword in his hand and she realized he was a blacksmith and this was his workshop. She'd managed to step outside again, the house going from out to in and back again like a lovely maze.

Izzy wiped her face with her palms and stepped farther inside. The weapons were beautiful things. Lots of curved swords and gold and steel daggers, many adorned with jewels. Unlike the weapons that were popular in Dark Plains, these appeared ornamental, but Izzy knew weapons and these were as deadly as they were beautiful. They reminded Izzy of the weapons Annwyl wore during family parties and important events, given to her by Fearghus.

"Your work is beautiful," Izzy said.

"Thank you."

She pointed at one of the swords. "May I?"

"If you'd like."

She picked up one of the bigger swords and marveled at the lightness of it. Throwing herself into the safety of what she knew—battle and war and weapons—Izzy walked over to a clear area and lifted the sword. She gave a few practice swings, not sure if she'd like to work with these curved swords. But it was always nice to test out other weapons, to see what different armies used.

When Izzy lowered the sword, the man watched her intently. His pleasant expression replaced by a deep frown.

"I'm sorry." Izzy quickly replaced the weapon, thinking

she must have crossed some kind of cultural divide she hadn't been aware of.

"You're not a trainee, are you?" he asked.

"No, sir. Not anymore."

"You have true skill. And strength." His eyes narrowed a bit. "Where are you from?"

Izzy sighed. "That's a bit complicated."

He put the weapon he'd been sharpening on the floor and stepped away from the table. "Do I know you?" he asked.

She shook her head. "I don't think so."

"Then why do I feel like I do?"

"I have to go."

"Please don't."

Izzy moved toward the door. "I do. Someone is waiting for me. He'll be worried." She got to the door, but a large hand pressed against it. She could remove that hand, but she wasn't sure she could fight anyone at the moment.

"Look at me. Please."

Izzy slowly turned to face the man. She realized she was crying again when tears fell on her chest.

He lifted her chin and looked into her face.

"By the holy suns," he whispered, both hands now framing her face. "How did I not see it as soon as you walked in? How did I not know?"

"I have to go," Izzy begged, the sobs making it hard to get the words out. "I have to."

Big arms went around her, pulled her in close. "But you've come home, my beautiful child. Where are you planning to go when you've come home?"

Chapter 34

Éibhear sat in a chair, all the humans staring at him. He hadn't felt this uncomfortable since he'd been captured by an Ice Land troop and strapped over a pointy stake. His Mi-runach brethren had saved him that day, but he wouldn't be saved today. Unfortunately.

Finally, one of the inquisitive children said, "Why are you so pale? Are you dying?"

"No."

An older child then asked, "Did you know your hair was blue?"

"I am aware."

"Why is your hair blue?"

"Well . . . uh . . ." Gods, where had Izzy gone? How could she just desert him like this? He understood she was over-whelmed, but . . . but he needed her!

One of the women dressed in armor leaned in close. So close he thought she might kiss him. At least she was pretty. "Are you a dragon?"

Éibhear had to work hard not to jump at her question, but he was more than a little surprised.

"Why do you ask?"

"Because we get some here. They pretend to be human."

She leaned in even closer. "Their hair's different from yours. Colored real bright. But they're pale like you."

"Must be the scales."

"Is Iseabail safe around you?" Zarah asked, one of her grandsons helping her into a chair across from Éibhear.

"Safer than even she realizes."

That answer seemed to satisfy everyone because they moved back a little, giving him a bit of space, so that he could finally breathe.

"So, dragon," one of the males asked, "who are your people then? Or do you have people? Do you have lizards?"

"I am not a lizard. Nor can I communicate with them. But I do have people."

"How can you have people when you're not human?"

"Having one's own people is not limited to humans. It's a common term used not only by dragons but by centaurs and Minotaurs and those jackal-headed men that you Desert Landers have running around. So yes, I'm a dragon *and* I have people."

"Then who are they exactly?"

"I'm Éibhear the Contemptible. Youngest born son in the House of Gwalchmai fab Gwyar, fifth in line to the throne of the White Dragon Queen, Scourge of the Northland territories, Most Reviled Enemy Dragon of the Ice Lands, Honored Member of the Mì-runach, and bare-fisted champion of the Mì-runach Yearly Pit Fights three winters in a row."

The entire clan was silent, all of them staring at him until Zarah finally asked, "You're a prince?"

"Aye. Izzy's a princess, too."

"How is she a princess?"

"Talaith is with my brother, Briec the Mighty."

Everyone started talking at once and Éibhear couldn't really understand anyone. But then Zarah snapped, "Quiet!" And they all were.

She leaned forward and asked, "Talaith is with a dragon?"

"Aye."

"How did this happen? Was she handed over in sacrifice?"

"No one really does that anymore in Dark Plains. And no one's forced Talaith to be with Briec. She's with him because she loves him. She wouldn't be with him otherwise. My brother's too irritating for anyone who doesn't love him."

"Talaith loves a dragon?"

"We're very loveable. Most of us."

"And how does your dragon brother feel about Iseabail?"

"He adores her. Briec calls her his perfect, *perfect* daughter."

Another of Zarah's grandson's folded his arms across his chest and asked, "And are you her perfect, *perfect* uncle?"

"Not by blood."

"Did your brother adopt her?"

"Yes."

"Then you're her uncle."

"Yes, but not by blood."

"And that point matters?"

"Trust me," Éibhear insisted. "It matters."

"I should have realized you were my grandchild immediately," Zachariah said as he poured Iseabail a cup of coffee. "You look so much like my boy." *And your mother.*

He placed the cup in front of Iseabail and sat down across from her at his work table.

"I'm sorry I got so upset," she said, her eyes downcast. "I just didn't—"

"You were overwhelmed. It's understandable."

"I should get back to Éibhear."

"No. You should stay here. Drink your coffee. He'll be fine. The family will take care of him."

She picked up the cup and held it in her hands. Zachariah studied her while she studied the cup. Mighty suns, his boy would be proud of her. She was strong, healthy, and beautiful.

But there were questions Zachariah had. Ones he simply couldn't wait to ask, even though he knew he should.

"Iseabail—"

"Izzy. You can call me Izzy."

"Izzy, why . . ." He cleared his throat, tried again. "You may not know the answer to this, but why did your mother not come to us? When your grandmother threw her out? We would have taken her in. I thought she understood that."

"It's very complicated, I'm afraid," Izzy sighed out.

"Complicated?"

"Well, anytime you deal with gods, it gets complicated."

"Gods? Oh, of course, your mother is a Nolwenn."

"I think being a Nolwenn had little to do with it. She just wanted to make sure she had someone strong enough and smart enough to do the task and that turned out to be Talaith."

"Wait. Who is 'she' then?"

"Arzhela."

"The goddess?"

"Right. She needed someone to kill Annwyl and just used me to keep my mother in line while Mum became an assassin."

"Your mother's an assassin? How the hells did that . . ." Zachariah stopped talking, thinking of everything the girl had just told him. "Did you say Ann . . . Annwyl? The Mad Queen of Garbhán Isle?"

"Aye. She hates when people call her that, though, so I wouldn't. Besides, she's not nearly as crazy as everyone accuses her of being. True, she'll cut your head off as soon as look at you, but only if you're an enemy. She'd never do it to family."

"All right."

"Mum tried to kill her, too, and Annwyl forgave her, then took us in. So my aunt is extremely misunderstood."

"Uh-huh."

"I'll be honest, though." She rested her arms on the table,

her hands still around the cup. "I'm quite torn. If Mum had stayed here, I'd just be another Nolwenn, casting spells and making appointments with royals. But because of what happened to Mum, I've seen the world, led legions into battle, and I have a little sister I can't imagine not having in my life. But I feel so guilty when I think like that. It's like being glad all those horrible things happened to Mum and my birth father."

"That's ridiculous, and as a soldier you should know that. Making the best of what you have, of what you've been left with, does not make you anything more than human." Zachariah studied her a moment, then asked, "Is that why you're here, Izzy? To avenge your mother?"

"No. I need Haldane's help for my sister."

"And if Haldane doesn't help you?"

"She'd be foolish not to be of help to me. The last thing she wants is the wrath of my grandmother coming down on her head." When Zachariah frowned, she added, "My adoptive grandmother. Queen Rhiannon."

"Rhiannon? Why do I know that name?"

"She's the Dragon Queen of the Southlands and a powerful Dragonwitch."

Zachariah stared at his son's child. "_That_ Rhiannon is your adoptive grandmother?"

"Well, when Daddy took Mum as his mate, the entire House of Gwalchmai fab Gwyar and the Cadwaladr Clan accepted both of us as their kin."

Sitting up straight, Zachariah said, "Are you telling me your adoptive father is a—"

"Dragon? Aye. Briec the Mighty. Second oldest son of the Dragon Queen, second in line to the throne—"

"I don't give a damn about his titles, girl. Why is your mother trapped with a dragon?"

"I wouldn't say she's trapped. Although she would, especially when Daddy hasn't checked her fruit appropriately."

"Checked her fruit?"

"You don't want to know. But no. She's not trapped. She could leave, but she'd break his heart. He loves her. Loves me and, of course, there's Rhi, which is why I'm here."

"And who's Rhi again?"

"My sister. Their daughter."

Appalled and confused at the same time, "Talaith had a child with that . . . that . . ."

"That dragon. Aye. They had my beautiful sister, Rhianwen. Rhi for short."

"Izzy, how is that even possible?"

"Gods."

"Gods?"

"Aye. That's how Annwyl had her twins with my uncle Fearghus. But, you see," she went on without a breath, "I thought it was Rhydderch Hael again who made it so she could get pregnant by Daddy—Rhydderch Hael is the father god of all dragons—but he said he wouldn't do that for my mum because she wasn't talking to him so he wasn't talking to her. I'm not talking to him either, but with me, he won't shut up."

"The gods talk to you?"

"Only one. Now, my Aunt Dagmar—you might have heard of her as the Northland Beast—"

"I thought that was a man."

"A lot of people make that mistake. Anyway, she talks to gods all the time."

"A religious woman then?"

She laughed. "Dagmar? No. She's a follower of Aoibhell."

"The heretic?"

"I wouldn't call her that unless you have an hour or two to listen to why Aoibhell was not a heretic and why you should care about the distinction, which I'm assuming you really don't want because that can be overwhelming and you seem like a man who has little time for what Daddy calls Dagmar the Beast's Unholy and Nonsensical Ramblings."

Zachariah stared at his son's child for a long time, then finally said, "You are so like your mother."

Izzy's smile was wide and just like her father's. "Awww, that's so sweet. Thank you."

A knock at the door helped Zachariah extract himself from the non-direction this conversation was taking.

"Enter."

At first Zachariah thought a bear that had lost his fur in some sort of tragic accident had wandered into his forge. What other answer could explain the thing with long blue hair that took up his entire doorway?

"What's wrong?" Izzy asked it, and that's when Zachariah realized that the thing she was talking to was the Éibhear she'd spoken of earlier.

"Just checking on you."

"I'm fine."

"Having a nice chat then?"

"Not having an unpleasant chat."

Zachariah heard a horrible, grinding noise, his gaze desperately searching the room in an attempt to find out where it might be coming from.

"Don't look at me that way, Izzy," the giant ordered her. "I'm hungry."

"Go get something to eat then."

"I'm not leaving you."

"I'll be perfectly fine. I don't need your protection."

"I'm not leaving you anyway."

"Because you're my uncle and you love me?"

Zachariah watched the pair, the way the giant's jaw clenched and unclenched. And the way Izzy smiled. Zachariah knew that damn smile. That mischievous, "I'm enjoying tormenting you" smile that his son had managed to perfect when he was still a boy.

Yes, this woman, this powerful general and warrior *was* his granddaughter.

And this giant . . . loved her.

"Izzy—"

"Say because you're my uncle and you love me. It will make my grandfather feel more comfortable with you around his family. He wouldn't want them to be unsafe just because of me."

"I will not say—"

"You will or I'm telling Daddy!"

"Is that what you say to your troops?" the giant shot back. "You'll tell your daddy on them if they don't follow your orders?"

"If it's necessary to get them to do what I want."

Zachariah looked up at the giant. "So you're Izzy's *uncle*?"

"Not by blood."

"And that matters?"

"It matters."

Another grinding sound came from the giant's stomach.

"Like two mountains shifting," Izzy muttered.

"Well, if you fed me!"

"*Should I feed you like a mother bird to a baby chick?*"

"All right." Zachariah stood. "You'll both eat with us." He glared at the giant. "With us, foreigner. *With us.*"

The giant scratched his big head. "As opposed to . . ."

"Dining on my family!"

Mouth open, the giant stepped back. "I would never do such a thing! *I* don't eat humans."

Izzy looked up, all wide-eyed innocence. "Even during battle—ow! What was that pinch for?"

"Nor do I believe in eating humans. Even though my parents did. And my brothers." He shrugged, gazing off. "And Keita." He looked back at them. "Well, they don't do it now," he sneered. "Not since Annwyl became part of the family. And when Talaith joined us, we stopped eating horses." He gazed off again. "I think we're beginning to run out of livestock, though."

Deciding he was done with this bizarre conversation, Zachariah headed toward the door. "Tomorrow we'll take you to the Nolwenn sanctuary. Perhaps using my mother's name can help you get in to meet Haldane. She was the city's commander general for thirty years until she retired. And you'll stay here for the night." Zachariah stopped and glared at the giant. "In separate rooms, *Uncle*."

He looked back at his granddaughter, smiled, and walked out.

Once the old man walked out, Éibhear closed the door and faced Iseabail. "*Would you stop calling me uncle?*" he spit out between clenched teeth.

"But you are my uncle. An uncle who loves his dear, sweet, and much younger niece. What's wrong with that?"

"Have you noticed that everyone in this family of yours is a warrior? Or a soldier? Or a giant-armed blacksmith?"

She clapped her hands together. "I can't *wait* for him to meet Rhona and Uncle Sulien!" she cheered, mentioning two of the family's best blacksmiths. "Imagine the weapons we'll get when they compare ideas."

"You may not have noticed this, but your entire Desert Land family of warriors and soldiers and blacksmiths hate dragons."

"Oh, no, no. I think they're simply frightened of dragons because they don't know them yet or understand them. I just think they hate you specifically, which is a completely different issue." She jumped up. "Gods!"

"What's wrong?"

"I forgot Macsen. I left him outside."

"He's fine. I let him in while I was trying to track you down. I gave him some rocks to eat."

"He doesn't eat rocks. He just chews on them until they break into pieces."

"And that doesn't bother you?"

"Should it?"

"Yes!" Izzy chuckled, but it faded away, and he saw the worry on her face. "What's wrong?"

"I don't know if we should eat with them."

"Other than their hating me, why not?"

She rubbed her hands against her leggings. "What if, after they talk to me, they don't like me? What if they're disappointed?"

"You think these people will be disappointed? In *you*?"

"What do you—"

"They're casually sitting around in their armor. The men *and* the women. The children have toy swords . . . and maces . . . and morning stars. Your great grandmother Zarah is missing three fingers from one hand and has an axe wound in her back. She pointed it out to me with great pride. That's *your* great grandmother. While you are a revered and feared general in Annwyl the Bloody's army. A monarch they seem relatively terrified of. So I really don't think you're going to disappoint your father's family, Izzy. In fact, the way they've all been glaring at me— as if I'm running around wagging my cock at everyone— proves, to *me* at least, that they at the very least feel protective of you if they don't already adore you. Now"—he pushed her toward the door—"can we eat before I'm forced to gnaw my own arm off?"

She pulled the door open. "Can I call you Uncle Éibhear at the dinner table?"

"No, you may not, evil viper."

Chapter 35

Dinner wasn't nearly as unpleasant as Izzy had feared. In fact, she enjoyed herself. She didn't think Éibhear did, but he put up with it, which she truly appreciated.

"Can I ask," Izzy said to her Aunt Layla, who was the one who'd taken her out of the jail, "why were Éibhear and I taken into custody? I understood this to be an open city?"

"It is." Layla shrugged. "Or perhaps was. We've been having problems with cults lately."

"What cult?" Éibhear asked.

"It has no name, but we've been finding sacrifices in the tunnels under the city. Found a few bodies out in the desert, too. Nasty bit of business."

"So I've ordered," Izzy's general grandmother, Maskini, interjected, "that anyone armed but not wearing colors is to be brought in and detained until we can question them." She smiled at Izzy. "You were armed and not wearing any colors." She glanced at Éibhear. "And you were just sort of terrifying."

He shrugged. "Sorry."

"You know"—Izzy looked at everyone around the table—"I'm a little surprised."

"About what?"

"That there are so many female soldiers here. Mum told

me about my father, but she didn't really discuss life here in the Desert Lands except to say that women didn't travel alone."

"No one should travel alone," Layla said before sipping her wine.

"And," Zarah explained, "the women of our lands have been warriors for a few centuries now. But we weren't always. At one time, we followed the rules the human gods set up. Men fought the wars and the women had and raised the children."

"What changed?"

"Long ago an enemy battled with the men of this very city far out in the desert."

"Leaving the city defenseless."

"Exactly. The gates were closed and barricaded, but it was no good. Those gates came down. It was . . . very bad. Some of the women chose to kill themselves and their children. But one woman, who'd already lost three of her children during the siege, was so filled with rage, she rallied the surviving women to fight. They were smart, though. They waited until the soldiers were quite drunk and then they killed them. They killed them all. When the men returned, it was decided that the men would never leave their women defenseless again, but they all knew that wasn't good enough. Because a woman has to know how to protect herself. So the women trained, their daughters were trained, then their granddaughters. And with every generation we've become stronger, more powerful. Now we're a force. Now we're never left defenseless, no matter who is in or out of the city."

Understanding the desire to never feel defenseless again, Izzy nodded and ate more of the oxen that was their dinner. It was good and she found the spices quite interesting.

"Tell us, Izzy," Maskini asked, "how did you become a general of three legions?"

Izzy swallowed the food in her mouth and replied, "Killed a lot."

Éibhear winced at Izzy's answer. Even worse, she didn't seem to notice that everyone had stopped in mid-chew, all of them looking at each other.

"What Izzy means is—"

"What I mean is I killed. A lot. That's what I do. No one sends in Izzy the Dangerous to keep the peace or hold a line. They send me and my troops in to decimate. If they want to keep the peace, they send in General Borden of the Tenth and Thirteenth Legions."

"And this started for you . . . when?" Zarah asked.

"Well." She took another bite of oxen, thought a moment. "I killed my first Northland dragon when I was seventeen. With the help of me mum."

Zachariah blinked. "You killed a dragon with *Talaith*?"

"Uh-huh. Right after that I was assigned to a legion as a private. Then when the war against the Irons and Sovereigns started, I became Annwyl's squire and that's when things became . . ." Izzy looked up at the ceiling, puffed out her cheeks a bit, and finally finished with, "Well . . . yeah. It's been a while."

"All right." Zarah focused on Éibhear. "And what about you, Prince Éibhear?"

Izzy giggled, but he ignored her and said, "You can just call me Éibhear. We don't really use titles. Well . . . my mother does, but that's because she really likes her title."

"I see. And do you serve in your mother's army?"

Éibhear cleared his throat. "Sort of."

"What does 'sort of' mean?" Zachariah demanded.

"I'm Mi-runach."

"What's that?"

"Berserkers," Izzy volunteered.

"We are not berserkers."

"They fight naked," she went on. "Bare handed in the middle of battle."

"We do not." He looked at the family staring at him. "We don't. I promise."

"I have a question," one of the teen boys asked. "How did you find one of our battle dogs?"

"Is that what I'm smelling?" Maskini complained, now peering under the table, where Macsen had been for most of the dinner. "All this time I thought it was the damn dragon."

"Well, I haven't had a chance to bathe in a few days," Éibhear shot back, insulted.

Ignoring that, Izzy asked the boy, "*Your* battle dog?"

"This is a Desert Land battle dog. You'll find them in almost every army in the region."

"Really? I found him near the Western Mountains when my legions were battling one of the horse tribes."

"He was a long way from home then."

"Are you sure he's not really a demon?" Éibhear had to ask.

Izzy threw up her hands, but the boy nodded and asked, "The rock eating?"

"And he chewed up the head of my steel axe." Éibhear looked at Izzy. "By the way, you owe me an axe."

"I told you not to leave your weapons out. The dog can only resist temptation for so long."

"They're excellent battle dogs," Zarah explained. "Absolutely loyal to their masters until their last breath. I had one for years that I adored. Although he smelled and insisted on chewing up diamonds. I could never take him into the jewelry district with me because he'd leap up on the displays and gobble up all the diamonds." She shook her head. "Never liked the rubies, though, which I always found much prettier."

"See?" Izzy asked Éibhear, sounding quite proud. "He's a dog from a mighty line of battle dogs."

"He smells," Éibhear reminded her. "Even after you bathe

him, he smells and he drools and we won't even discuss the gas problem."

"Ahh!" Zarah cheered. "I've got something that will help with the gas."

"But not the smell and drool?"

Zarah grimaced a little at Éibhear's question. "That you'll just have to learn to live with, I'm afraid."

"Yeah, you'll have to learn to live with that, *Uncle* Éibhear," Zachariah grumbled while the other males glared.

Éibhear began to look over at Izzy, but he saw her twist her lips and he knew she was trying not to laugh. And if he looked at her now, they'd both laugh and be unable to stop. So he kept looking straight ahead and praying that this damn dinner would end soon.

"Do you think I'll be able to meet with Haldane tomorrow?"

"We can try," Layla said, walking Izzy down a hall filled with bedrooms. Éibhear had left Izzy alone for a couple of hours with her family. She didn't know where he'd gone. He'd simply slipped out—for such a large man, he did move like a jungle cat—and she hadn't seen him since. But she appreciated it. She appreciated the chance to get to know her birth father's kin. To hear stories about him as a young man and to hear about his love for a young Talaith. Even then her mother had been a beauty and, according to Maskini, a rebel. She'd fought against the Nolwenn restrictions from the very beginning and had been admired for it. When Izzy's father had died in battle and Talaith, pregnant with Izzy, had gone missing, the family had been devastated. Izzy knew it bothered them to hear her call Briec "Dad" or "Daddy," but they also seemed to understand that he'd been the only father she'd really known. And, more importantly, he'd been a good father to her.

He'd protected her and Talaith. They cared more about that than what Izzy chose to call anyone.

"Haldane has never been—"

"Human?"

Layla laughed. "Some might say."

They stopped at the last room at the end of the hallway. "Listen, Izzy, the family was wondering about Macsen—"

"I'm so sorry he ate that chair."

"No, no. That's not really a problem. But we were wondering if you'd mind if we borrow him tomorrow for a bit."

"Borrow him?"

"We have several females at the Imperial Guards Dog Kennels that are currently in heat. Maybe we could drop him off on our way over to the temple. Maybe leave him for the night?"

"You want to have *my* dog alone with a bunch of lusty bitches?"

"I like to occasionally bring in some new blood," Layla said around a little laugh, "and Macsen is an exceptional specimen."

Izzy frowned. "He is?"

"For our battle dogs, yes. In fact, you could probably sell him to a private breeder for an astounding amount of gold."

"Oh, I'd never give him up, but . . ." Izzy frowned again. "Really? You want Macsen?" She shook her head. "Anyway, I think he'd be more than happy to help out the Imperial Guards. . . . He's giving that way."

"Of course he is." She pushed open the bedroom door. "You can sleep here for the night."

"And Éibhear?"

"He's down for the night in a room up the hall." Layla cleared her throat. "Father insisted. Hope you don't mind."

"Not at all."

Izzy stepped into her room, but stumbled to a stop.

"Is something wrong?" Layla asked Izzy, her face etched with concern.

"Uh . . ." She rubbed her nose. "No. It's . . . um . . . lovely."

"Do you need anything?"

"No, no. Not at all. I'm fine. This is great. Thank you."

Layla smiled at her. "Iseabail . . . I can't tell you how glad I am you found your way home." Izzy began to speak, but she cut her off. "I know you can't stay. But maybe you can visit? Spend some time with the family? I look at you and I see my little brother. I don't want to lose that again."

Izzy hugged her newfound aunt. "You won't."

"Good. Good." Layla stepped away from her. "Sleep well, Izzy."

"You, too. I'll see you in the morning."

Layla walked out and Izzy closed the door, turned, and folded her arms over chest.

"Are you insane?" she whispered to the dragon in human form sprawled on her bed.

"Who knew your Desert Land family was tougher to get around than my own? They put me on the other side of the house!"

"Which is where you should be. In your own room."

"I've been sleeping with you for the last few nights. Why would I change that now?"

She walked to the bed. "Because," she explained, still whispering, "I think it would be rude to fuck under their roof when clearly they're not okay with it."

"Who said anything about fucking?"

Frowning, Izzy asked, "You just want to sleep with me?"

"If I hope to sleep well . . ." He patted the bed. "I promise, just sleep."

"Where's Macsen?"

"Under the bed and quite comfortable."

"*Under* the bed?"

"He's not outside, is he?" Éibhear gazed at her with those silver eyes. "Don't make me sleep alone, Izzy."

Gods, how could she resist that? Pathetic weakling that she was. It was the blue hair. It had to be the blue hair. She'd been enamored of it since she'd first met him. And if he lost it all? Well . . . all right. Perhaps she'd still be attracted to him, but she doubted she'd be so weak about where she slept and with whom.

Removing her travel clothes, Izzy slipped on a long cotton shirt that reached her knees and got onto the bed with Éibhear. She turned away from him and he settled in behind her, his arm around her waist, his face buried against the back of her neck.

"You worried about tomorrow?" he asked.

"Probably more than I should be."

"Don't worry. I'll be there every step of the way."

"To protect me from my grandmother or my grandmother from me?"

Soft lips kissed the back of her neck before she heard, "Both."

Annwyl sat up in her bed, a book open on her lap. Fearghus would be coming home late tonight, but that just meant she had a little time to herself to read. Unlike most nights when she ended up happily wrestling with Fearghus.

In fact, she was so looking forward to some time to herself, when she heard that knock on her bedroom door, she sighed and crossed her eyes before she said, "What?"

The door opened and to Annwyl's surprise, her son stuck his head in. "Hello, Mum. Got a minute?"

"Of course. Come in." She put a leather strip in her book to mark her place and put the book aside.

"What are you reading?" he asked.

"A history about wars in the Eastlands."

"Interesting?"

"Very. But you didn't come here about books, my love. What is it?"

Talan closed the door and walked into the room, sitting on the bed by Annwyl's hip. "I have something to show you."

"Then show me."

The boy sighed before pulling a scroll out of the top of his boot and handing it to his mother.

"Someone sending you messages?" Annwyl asked, taking a look at the once-sealed document. Usually Annwyl was informed about any messages that came in for her offspring, but she'd heard nothing about this. Not even from Dagmar.

"Aye."

"Instead of me reading it, just tell me, Talan."

He cleared his throat and Annwyl realized this was the first time she'd ever seen her son look . . . uncomfortable. And, to be honest, knowing he had the ability to feel that emotion was surprisingly soothing to her.

"It's all right, Talan. Go on."

"Promise you won't get mad?"

"No."

Her direct answer made him laugh. "True, I shouldn't ask the impossible."

"I thought you'd have known that by now. So what is it? What's in this scroll you think I should see—without your father here?"

"Far, far to the west, past the Sovereign Provinces, is a brotherhood of monks."

"Monks?"

He shrugged. "Monks."

"And what do the monks want?"

"They've offered me a place to be trained in Magicks involving nature. Powers almost completely pulled from the earth as opposed to the gods."

"You want to join a monastery?"

"Not permanently."

Annwyl had to quickly scratch her head to stop herself from laughing. "Do they know that you don't think of this as a permanent solution?"

"I don't know what they know. I just know what I know. And I know I've learned all I can from Aunt Morfyd, Aunt Talaith, and Grandmum. But I'm not done learning."

Annwyl glanced down at the scroll in her hand. "Can I ask you a question?"

"I know I can't have sex while I'm there."

"That wasn't going to be my question, although your immediate response was quite telling. Best not have that same response around your father. Understand?"

"Yes, ma'am."

"Good. Now my question is this. . . . Are you and your sister leaving because of me?"

It was only a moment, but she saw the look of surprise on her son's face. The fact that Annwyl knew, without anyone telling her, that Talwyn was also getting ready to leave blindsided him. But he quickly concealed his surprise and answered, "I promise, Mum, if we could, Talwyn and I would stay here forever. Just . . . loafing around and getting in fights."

"But you can't because . . ."

"You know why. This isn't the end of it for us. We're not meant to be nobles like Lord Pombray's boy or even our uncles. But what you've been telling us from the beginning is that without knowledge, we can't lead, we can't fight, we can't do anything but hope others protect us. And, Mum . . . we just don't have that luxury anymore."

Annwyl nodded. "My own words thrown back at me . . . and yet they were brilliant words."

Talan grinned. "Just like your son."

Annwyl took his hand. "Are you truly comfortable with your sister going off with the Kyvich?"

"No. Not because I think it will be bad for her. But *I* know she has no intention of staying. And when she's ready to go, that will be a problem."

"For her?"

"For them."

"And this . . . monastery? This is what you want?"

"No. But this is what I need. I will admit, I almost turned it down. Almost walked away. But you always said to trust my instincts and my instincts tell me to do this. Now. Not later. Right now." He kissed the back of her hand. "And because I know you're thinking it, I only *look* like I'm not listening to you. But I hear every word. And thank you. For surviving. For doing what you've done. I know for a fact, no other female in this universe could have been *my* mother."

Fighting tears, Annwyl wrapped her arms around her son's massive and still-growing shoulders and hugged him tight. They stayed like that until the bedroom door opened again and she heard Fearghus's voice.

"Remind me why I bother dealing with that old bastard. And don't say it's just because of blood ties." Fearghus stopped and eyed his mate and son. "What did the boy do now?"

With his head resting on Annwyl's shoulder, Talan replied, "Everything you've only dreamed about."

Annwyl immediately caught Fearghus's grasping hand and snapped, "Fearghus, no!"

"Just one punch to the head! Just one!"

Chapter 36

For a half an hour Izzy sat there and watched her grandmother—and the commander general of the city's protection force—try to negotiate Izzy's entrance into the Nolwenn temple. Her aunts and uncles, a few of her older cousins, and her grandfather stood with her and Éibhear, waiting as well. But as the suns moved overhead, the heat beginning to sear Izzy's brain inside her skull, she began to get more and more annoyed.

She tried not to get annoyed. She tried to focus on other things. Like the beauty of the city. Sefu was a grand city with a major river that connected it to the ocean and several major Desert Land ports. Bustling and well-designed, Sefu boasted one of the largest libraries and a major theater.

Yet even thinking about those things only managed to irritate Izzy more because she wouldn't be able to enjoy them. Not when she had things to do.

Maskini made her way down the long stairs.

"I'm sorry, Izzy," she said when she was close enough so that she didn't have to yell her failure. "They suggested that you come back tomorrow. They're expecting one of their appointments to cancel and they say—Izzy? Where are you going?"

"All of you wait here."

Taking the stairs two at a time, Izzy walked up to the temple doors. She pressed on them, but they were solid marble and bolted from inside.

"Izzy?" She looked over her shoulder at Éibhear. He'd followed her up the stairs and now watched her.

She stepped back and motioned to the doors. "Get them down."

Éibhear glanced around. "You sure about this?"

"You have no idea how sure I am. Now do it."

Éibhear shrugged and took a couple of steps down. He stripped his clothes off and handed them to Izzy. He motioned her farther away with a wave of his hand, and then he shifted, his natural powers even stronger when dragon.

Once in his dragonform, he took in a deep breath and unleashed a stream of flame at the doors. The thick marble buckled, the heat melting part of the door. But still it stood strong. With his flame still shooting straight, Éibhear ran forward and rammed his shoulder into the marble. The doors were torn off their hinges and flew inside, crashing into the walls and ceiling before landing several feet away.

Stepping back, Éibhear gestured to the now open doorway with a tilt of his head. Izzy placed his clothes down and walked up the stairs and into the temple. Éibhear glanced back at Izzy's shocked family, their eyes wide, some with their mouths open. He winked at them and followed Izzy inside.

Izzy entered the Nolwenn temple. It was quite a beautiful place. And big. So big, Éibhear was able to follow her inside without shifting back to human.

Looking around at the marble statues and marble floors, she demanded, "Where's Haldane?"

"So you're Talaith's daughter?" a young witch asked her.

"Haldane," Izzy repeated as she walked up to the young witch.

"She has much to do, I'm afraid, and I don't think she'll be able to find the time to meet with the child of a traitor—"

Izzy cut off the witch's words by laying her out with a right cross to the jaw. The witch dropped to the floor and Izzy stepped over her.

"I want to see my grandmother," she said loudly, her voice echoing amongst all that marble. "And I want to see her now."

As she walked down the long hallway, witches emerged from smaller rooms, looking at her, but saying nothing.

Finally, Izzy reached a huge doorway. She turned inside but after a few feet stopped, blinking several times.

Éibhear came in behind her and she heard his quick intake of breath.

"Gods," she heard him whisper.

Even before Izzy had been reunited with her mother or known what she looked like, Rhydderch Hael would always tell Izzy that she greatly resembled her mother *and* father. She had her mother's face but her father's eyes and smile, he'd say. And, after one night with her birth father's family, Izzy knew the truth of that just from what they all said about her. So she'd expected her grandmother to look quite a bit like Talaith. Yet she never thought she'd look like a mirror copy.

"So," the witch said, "you're the one that my daughter gave up all this for." Dark brown eyes looked Izzy over. "You." And she could hear the disappointment in the witch's voice. "Well . . . your mother never was very smart."

At more than four hundred years old, Haldane, Daughter of Elisa, showed no signs of age except for a few gray hairs at her temples.

It was, to say the least, disconcerting, for Izzy to see her "mother" standing there but know it was not her mother. The last time this had happened, her mother's body had been taken over by Rhydderch Hael so that he could get into another god's realm and kill her. But this witch standing on a dais, looking at Izzy as if she were completely meaningless, was simply not her mother. She wasn't possessed with anything but a cold, calculating mind. A heartless bitch.

And Izzy wanted her dead.

"Oh," the Talaith lookalike announced to the other witches slowly walking into the room. "She's brought a dragon for us. Is he a gift?"

"I need to talk to you, witch."

"After all these years? More than three decades and you come to my door now?"

"It's not for me. It's for my sister."

"Right. The child that should not exist."

"But she does exist."

"And you fear her power."

"I fear nothing about my sister. But I want what's best for her."

"So you'll hand her over to me?"

"I want what's best for her."

The witch chuckled. "If you want me to care at all for this child, you should have brought her with you. You should have let me look in her eyes."

"You can return with me to Garbhán Isle and you can look in her eyes to your heart's content."

"You want me to travel into foreign territory with"—she flicked her hand at Izzy—"*you*?"

"That is my plan."

The witch pursed her lips, shook her head. "No. I don't

think so. However," she added, smiling at Éibhear, "I'll happily accept your gift."

Éibhear looked at Izzy.

"I think," he began, "that you misunderstand my presence here, mistress. I am Éibhear the Contemptible, Son of—"

"I don't care," the witch cut in. "A gift is a gift." That face that looked so much like Talaith's turned cruel when she spit out, "We'll have such wonderful use for your bones."

One of the witches near him swung out her arm and something wrapped around Éibhear's neck, yanking him back. He gripped at it, but he only felt his own scales. Yet he knew something had hold of him, was pulling him away from Izzy.

Another witch stepped forward and she swung her arm out. Something caught hold of his legs and yanked them out from under him. Éibhear ended up on his belly, slowly being dragged off somewhere.

Haldane looked at her granddaughter. "As for you," she sneered and flicked her hand again. Izzy's entire body lifted and flew back as if flung by the gods themselves.

Mum! Éibhear called to his mother. *Mum! Izzy needs you!*

Haldane looked at him. "Call to your mummy all you want, dragon. She'll never hear you. She'll never find what's left of you." She jerked her head toward the back of the big room. "Take him downstairs and get him ready. There's a full moon tonight. I plan to take full advan—"

Haldane's words were cut off as a giant piece of statue flipped across the hall and rammed into the witch's chest, shoving her back and to the floor.

"Haldane!" one of the witches screamed out.

Izzy walked back into the room and she looked . . . very angry. But not only that, there was something else. . . .

Éibhear squinted, looked closer. Something was sparking off Izzy's body. And she was angry enough, he could easily believe it was coming simply from her rage. Yet he didn't think so.

Another witch rushed to stand in front of a groaning Haldane, several others hurrying to their fallen leader's side to help her. The witch raised her hand, pointed her finger. She began to chant words Éibhear didn't understand, had never heard. And power roared up from her body and flew out of her hand, hitting Izzy right in the chest.

Izzy stopped, waved her hands and the energy that had slammed into her was tossed away. It reminded Éibhear of those times the Mì-runach would get drunk and play "war in the snow." They'd toss giant balls of snow at each other and one would simply flick the ice and snow off his body before grabbing more snow and building another ball to retaliate with. That's what Izzy was doing.

This Magick . . . it didn't touch her. It didn't hurt her. Not the way it was supposed to. Not the way it would hurt anyone else.

Instead, the Magick seemed to be doing something else to Izzy. It made her stronger. Éibhear didn't think that strength would last, but it was giving her enough power to move forward. Guards that would give their lives to protect the Nolwenns suddenly appeared, running in from hidden doorways, weapons out and at the ready. They charged Izzy and she unsheathed her sword and axe. With both hands, she tore into those attacking guards. Blood and pieces of those men flew around the hall, splattering all that beautiful marble and the witches who maintained it.

Izzy cut her way through those guards and over to Éibhear. Dropping her weapons, she used her bare hands to reach down and pull off the bonds he'd been unable to see or feel. She released him and he got to his claws.

More guards ran in and Éibhear unleashed flames that burned the flesh from their bones and turned them to ash where they stood.

"*Enough!*" Haldane's voice rang out. Three witches had helped her to her feet, their hands keeping her steady.

She eyed Izzy and finally said, "Your mother."

Izzy stepped in front of Éibhear. "My mother what?"

"She did this. She protected you while you were still in the womb. From us. From other witches. When Magick strikes you, it does nothing but give more strength to those oversized muscles you have." Haldane gave a soft laugh. "My child was always smarter than she pretended to be."

"Because she knew you'd try to destroy me."

"If I could have rung your neck before you took your first breath . . . I would have. And she knew it."

"You could always try now. I'm right here."

"That will be unnecessary," another voice chimed in and all the witches fell to their knees—even Haldane. The older woman walked from behind Éibhear, smiled at him and Izzy. "Hello to you both."

"Who are you?" Izzy demanded.

"The name is Elisa. I'm a Nolwenn Elder." She leaned in and whispered to Izzy—although Éibhear could hear her well enough—"And your great grandmother."

Izzy's eyes grew wide. "You must be a million years old."

"*Izzy.*"

She looked up at Éibhear. "What?"

Izzy could see some of Talaith in this witch's face. Not as much as there was in Haldane's, but she could see the resemblance. In her eyes, her cheekbones.

"Mum never mentioned you."

"She had no reason to. I gave her little thought. I assumed that she, like her mother, like *my* mother, like I, would follow the path of the Nolwenn. What was there for me to do with her until she was older and had some real power?"

"Because she's your blood? Because you are her grand-mother?"

Elisa laughed. "You are truly your mother's child."

"And proud of it."

"I know. I can see it. Feel it even."

She motioned to the witches and guards filling the hall. "All of you . . . out."

"My lady—" one of them began, but dark brown eyes un-faded by age locked on the witch and she immediately closed her mouth and bowed her head.

"Don't make me say it again," Elisa ordered. It took less than a minute for that chamber to clear out.

The witch faced them. "Tea?"

"Ooh," Éibhear said. "I'd love a cuppa."

Izzy spun around, her hands raised, her mouth open, top lip curled.

"What?" Éibhear demanded. "I like tea!"

Chapter 37

Izzy was still nursing her first cup of tea while Éibhear—now in his human form and dressed—and Elisa were well into their second. The witch had also pulled out biscuits and she was pleasant enough, but, at the moment, it meant nothing to Izzy. Nothing. Not after what had just happened between Izzy and her grandmother. That horrid bitch. Izzy had always known that woman wasn't worthy of having even a second of Rhi's precious time. But then Izzy kept going back to the bigger issue of what Rhi did need in her life.

"Your rage comes off you in waves, Iseabail."

Izzy looked up at her great grandmother, Elisa. Based on what she could guess, Elisa was a good six hundred years old, and yet she looked no more than fifty winters or so. Izzy had to admit . . . she liked the idea of going into her sixth- or seven-hundredth winter looking this good.

Other than that, though, she was just pissy about the whole thing.

"I hated that woman before I ever saw her," Izzy said plainly, "and now I hate her even more."

"You're so like your mother. She was honest like you."

"She still is."

"And Haldane hated her for it."

"Then I'm glad I could carry on my mother's legacy."

"So am I. Of course, I never liked my daughter much either. So it seems you're carrying on *my* legacy as well." She held up a plate. "Biscuits?"

Izzy took the plate from her and threw the whole thing against the wall. Biscuits and all.

"Oy!" Éibhear snapped. "I was going to eat those."

When Izzy glowered at him, he quickly added, "Well . . . they did look a bit dry."

"Don't worry," Elisa said with a smile. "I have more." She stood and went to a small cabinet in what Izzy assumed was her study. There were books from floor to ceiling and crates filled with witch supplies. At least that's what she guessed they were since the materials looked like the kinds of things that she'd seen her mother and Morfyd using every full moon.

Elisa came back to the table and placed another plate of biscuits in front of Éibhear. Once done, she sat at the table, her smile still in place.

"So," Elisa said, acting as if Izzy's temper hadn't snapped like a twig, "you want us to take little Rhianwen in."

"She's not an orphan I'm trying to palm off on you lot."

"No. She's a powerful being that you have no control over."

Izzy studied her great grandmother. "Maybe."

"But you think we can help with that?"

"My mother thinks you can. I have no idea what you can do."

"We can teach your sister to control the power within her. We can make her safe to be around those she loves."

"And you know all this . . . how?"

"Your sister's power radiates for thousands of leagues. Even the mages as far off as the Eastlands feel her power—and fear it."

"So you're going to try to make her a Nolwenn then?"

"That's the one thing I can assure you will never happen."

Feeling slightly insulted, Izzy had to ask, "And why is that?"

"I was born to this life, Iseabail. So were Haldane and your mother. And, if Talaith had stayed, she'd be a Nolwenn. Trained in the arts from birth. But your sister, like you, can't jump in now. She's sixteen winters, past her first blood—"

"And trained to be a free-thinking human being who can make her own decisions?"

Elisa smiled. "Some might say. Really, Iseabail, it's about preparing your sister for something beyond these grand walls. That is . . . if we decide to help her."

"Why wouldn't you help her? Because I'd happily cut your daughter's thro—"

Éibhear suddenly coughed, pointed at his throat. "Biscuit went down the wrong way." He glared at Izzy and practically snarled between clenched teeth, "Sorry."

"Your feelings about my daughter, Iseabail, are expected and, I'm sorry to say, quite natural. She was abhorrent to my grandchild, but Haldane has always been stubborn."

"*I'm* stubborn. She's a twa—"

Another cough cut into her words. "Another biscuit struggling down your gullet?" Izzy asked sweetly.

"They're a little *dry*."

Izzy focused on Elisa. "What do you want? Because I know you want something."

The witch rested her arms on the table and leaned in. Her smile reminded Izzy of her mum but without that warmth Izzy had always taken comfort in. "I'll take your sister in, ensure her safety, and have her trained, but there's a task."

"Of course there is." Izzy sighed loudly. "Who do I have to kill?"

"This task isn't for you." Elisa focused on Éibhear. "It's for you."

"Me?" Éibhear said around another biscuit. How many was that now?

"This has nothing to do with him."

"Isn't he Rhi's uncle?"

"I am definitely *Rhi's* uncle."

Izzy's eyes crossed. "I see we're not letting that go."

"Nope."

Elisa offered Éibhear more tea, which he readily accepted. Did he think this was some kind of tea party? It wasn't!

"So do you need *me* to kill someone?" Éibhear asked.

"You two seem kind of focused on that. Do many ask you to kill?"

Izzy and Éibhear shrugged. "Sometimes."

"Well, I hate to disappoint you both, but this isn't about killing. This is about rescuing."

"Rescuing?" Éibhear was surprised. No one had asked him to rescue anyone. Ever. "I can do that."

Izzy looked at him. "Do you really have time?"

"Why wouldn't I?"

"Your mother gave you a task, Éibhear. To find out about Vateria."

"Well then," Elisa cut in. "That makes this much easier."

"You need me to rescue someone from Vateria?"

"No. Before the last night of the full moon, you need to *rescue* Vateria before she's sacrificed."

"Huh," Éibhear grunted, truly surprised. "I really didn't see that coming."

Chapter 38

One of the Nolwenns led them to the doors that Éibhear had kicked in. "When you're done," the witch said before they walked out, "you may return. But not before."

Not liking the cow's tone, Izzy pulled her arm back, but Éibhear caught hold and dragged her out the doors.

"*Why do you keep doing that?*" she demanded.

"Must we repeat what just happened?"

"Forget that, Éibhear. We need to talk about—"

"Izzy!" a voice called out.

Izzy looked at the street and grinned. "Brannie!" She ran down the stairs and met Branwen halfway. They threw their arms around each other and Éibhear looked past them to Aidan, Caswyn, and Uther. All four of them rolled their eyes at each other. One would think the two females hadn't seen each other in years rather than a few days.

"Are you all right?" Izzy demanded of her friend. "Were you hurt?"

"Iz, I'm fine." Brannie hugged her again. "I figured this was the most likely place to find you. We have word from Rhiannon."

"I'm sure you do, but that'll have to wait." Izzy smiled. "I have people for you to meet."

"People?"

Izzy took Brannie's hand and led her down the steps to her birth father's family, who were still waiting at the bottom of the stairs for her.

"Who's that?" Aidan asked, the four of them watching Izzy introduce each family member to an overwhelmed Branwen.

"The family of Izzy's birth father."

"Really?"

"Aye."

"How are they?"

"Ever so nice. All soldiers and blacksmiths. I think my father will like Izzy's grandfather."

"How does Izzy's grandfather feel about you?"

"Oh, he hates me."

Aidan shrugged. "He knows you're defiling his granddaughter. What do you expect?"

"I hate you."

"Only when I'm right."

"So now what?" Caswyn asked.

"You sound eager."

"He's met some long-tailed royal," Aidan explained. "And hopes to spend time with her at the human's harvest festival."

"I hope to buy a prostitute at the harvest festival," Uther announced. "Just for a night or two. Not to keep."

"Especially since Annwyl outlawed slavery of any kind."

"Did she?"

Éibhear walked around his idiot friends and headed toward Izzy and her family. "You ready?" he asked.

"What's going on?" Maskini asked.

"Well," Izzy said, "I beat up my grandmother, which was weird because she looked just like Mum, but she did start it, and I found out that all the times I've used a shield to protect myself from Magicks was apparently a vast waste of effort. I also met my *great* grandmother who said she'd help my sister but only if Éibhear does something *incredibly* stupid, but it seems he won't listen to me about it. Plus, Brannie, it looks like Macsen is descended from battle dogs, and as far as Éibhear's concerned, tea can soothe anything."

Aidan smiled. "Now aren't you glad you asked?"

"Gods," Layla sighed, "you really are like your mother."

Chapter 39

Éibhear held up a map that Zachariah had dug up for them. Normally, they'd place a map on a table, but at the moment, there wasn't enough room around the table for that. There was Izzy, Izzy's family, Éibhear's comrades, and Brannie all packed into this small, fourth-floor family room.

"Are you just going to hold that?" Maskini asked him.

"Unless you have a better option."

Maskini took the map from Éibhear's hands and walked over to the far wall. She held it up against the cool brick. "Layla."

Layla walked over to her mother and pulled out two blades from her boot. Lifting the daggers, she rammed one in each of the top two corners. "There," she said, pleased with herself. Her smile just like Izzy's.

Stepping back, Éibhear studied the map.

"What did the witch tell you?" Aidan asked.

"That they'll have Vateria near a source of power. Most likely here," he said, pointing to a mountainous terrain less than a half day's flight outside the city walls.

"They weren't more specific?"

"They never are."

Éibhear felt a tug on the back of his shirt and he saw that it was Izzy sitting on the table behind him. He stepped back until his ass rested against the table and she handed him something. He stared at it.

"What is this?"

"I got it from Zarah. She took two slices of bread and put meat in the middle. It's good and you can eat it without a knife."

Éibhear took a bite.

"It's good, yeah?"

He nodded his head in approval while Uther sidled up next to him. "What's that you got there?"

Éibhear glared at his comrade. "It's *mine*. That's what it is."

"You can't share?"

"No."

"Are you two done?" Maskini demanded. She pointed at the map. "We've got work to do."

"But we're hungry," Uther replied.

"Are you whining?"

"Maybe. A little."

Rolling her eyes, Maskini pushed past her family and walked out.

"Maybe?" Izzy teased Uther.

"I'm hungry!"

"Okay!"

Éibhear stared at the map and ate his meat and bread.

"All right," Izzy said next to him, her voice low. "What's bothering you?"

"Who says something's bothering me?"

"I do. I can see it on your face."

"Know me so well now, do you?"

"I've always known you well, dragon. You just never wanted to see it. Now what's bothering you?"

"Can witches be lied to?"

"Anybody can be lied to. The question is whether they believe the lie or the liar. Why?"

"How many converted does this cult have?"

"Heru didn't say. Enough for him to be nervous and for them to feel confident enough to attack your mother's troops at the salt mines."

"Right. But they didn't strike right at us. They came under cover of dark, nice and quiet. If you hadn't alerted us, they would have had you and been gone long before we'd realized you were missing."

"Which means what to you?"

"That they're not at full army strength yet, and they're not ready for direct attacks."

"So?"

"Then why would they put themselves here"—he pointed at the map again—"out in the open, where they'd be unable to stop a full onslaught?"

"Because they need the power that's there."

"According to my mother, there are power sources everywhere. She can get power from a bloody vegetable patch if she needs to." Éibhear walked closer to the map, studied it. "There has to be a place of power that makes more strategic sense."

"Who says they're strategic?" Uther asked, grinning when Maskini handed him, Caswyn, and Uther two slices of bread each, with big chunks of meat in the middle. "Ta."

"Just because they're zealots doesn't mean they're stupid."

Izzy studied him for a moment, then asked, "What would you do?"

"What would I do about what?"

"If it was you."

"You mean if I was a crazed zealot?"

Izzy chuckled. "Right. How would crazed-zealot Éibhear handle this?"

Éibhear glanced at his fellow Mì-runach, then walked over to the double doors that led out to a balcony. He stood out there and looked over the beautiful city. He was sure Rhi would like it here. It was large, had amazing architecture, and strong walls surrounding it. Lots of things for her to sketch.

He walked back into the study. "I'd want to stay within the city walls. Once those gates are closed, they could hold off a sustained attack if they had to."

"How can they be in the city and we not know?" Layla asked.

"Especially when their top people blind themselves in some kind of solidarity with their god." Izzy added.

Éibhear stared out at the city again. "There must be a way for them to stay out of sight and be near a power source that helps them with whatever they're doing."

"What about this god?" Aidan asked around his food. "We know anything about him?"

One of Izzy's cousins stepped forward. "I went to the library like Izzy asked and spoke to one of the sisters. Chramnesind is called the Sightless One. He has no eyes. He's the god of earth and pain."

Izzy scrunched up her nose. "That sounds awfully unpleasant."

"The god of earth?" Uther asked. "You mean like dirt?"

"That's unimpressive," Aidan sighed, his food now gone. "You might as well be the god of grass. Or the god of cow shit." Aidan blinked. "What?" he asked Éibhcar. "What did I say?"

Éibhear went back out on the balcony, looked out and down.

"Do you lot have a sewer system here?" he asked.

"Yes," Maskini replied. "Don't you?"

"No," Izzy answered.

"Ew."

Éibhear scratched his chin. "Do the sewers run under all the temples?"

"Of course."

Izzy walked out on the balcony and stood by Éibhear. She

stared up at him until he looked out over the darkening city. She followed his gaze and cringed. "Oh, no."

"It makes sense."

"I know." She put her hands to her face and rubbed her forehead. "But we both know this can't end well."

Maskini gazed at her beloved son's child. The grandchild she never thought she'd get to see, much less meet. And to find out that her son's only child had become a beautiful, intelligent, and powerful warrior brought nothing but great pride and satisfaction to Maskini.

So Maskini gazed at her beautiful grandchild. She gazed and asked, *"Have you lost your fucking mind?"*

"That's still up for debate."

"You want me to unleash the Imperial Guard into the sewer system under all the temples? Because this fire-breathing lizard thinks—only *thinks,* mind you—that the Cult of Chramnesind might be somewhere down there? Don't you think someone would have noticed them by now? Wandering around? A cult?"

"Maybe she's right, Izzy," the lizard said.

"I know I am!"

"No. I think Éibhear's right," Izzy pushed.

"How could you think he's right?"

"Because it's the perfect place for them."

"How could the witches, magi, and sorcerers in these temples not know they have some cult leeching off their power?"

"Perhaps they're part of the cult," the lizard with gold hair suggested.

"No," Izzy said. "They can't afford pissing off the other gods by just choosing one."

"Especially this Chramnesind," Maskini's granddaughter, Rachel, explained. She'd been the one to talk to the sisters at the library since she already had a good relationship with them. "The other gods hate him."

"Bit of a prat?" Izzy asked.

"You could say. He wants to be the one god. The one we all bow down to."

"Then for his acolytes to quietly use the power of other gods for their rituals would be quite the insult."

"Plus the shit."

They all looked at the brown-haired lizard. Uther, maybe?

"What?" Izzy asked.

"The shit."

"What about it?"

"It makes sense they'd use the sewers to get around."

Maskini glanced at Rachel. "Because of the shit?"

"He's blind, yeah?" the brown-haired one went on. "Their god? And so are some of the acolytes. If they consider the sewers home . . . it must be easy to get to if they can smell it, especially since they can't see it." When they all just stared at him, he went on. "When you're blind, you use your other senses. We have a few Mì-runach who've been blinded in battle. Not just lost one eye, but both. But just because they're blind, don't mean we can't use 'em. We just give 'em some time to get used to being blind; then they come back in with us. They use their sense of smell and their hearing to get around. They're bloody brilliant in battle."

"You use the *blind* in battle?" Maskini demanded, unused to this sort of barbarianism in her own home.

"We don't force 'em, do we, Éibhear? But if they want to fight, we let 'em fight. They're damn good, too."

"A Mì-runach would rather die in battle," the blue-haired lizard explained, "than sit around a cave waiting for death. So missing limbs . . . missing eyes . . . doesn't really stop a Mì-runach."

After staring at the fire-breathing lizards for several long seconds, her mouth hanging open, Maskini faced her grand-daughter. "Iseabail?"

She gave a small shrug. "It makes a bizarre kind of logic, doesn't it?"

"You want us to check out the sewers?"

"It couldn't hurt. Besides, Éibhear and the others are here for a reason."

"And who told you that?"

"Rhydderch Hael."

"Who's that?"

"The father god of dragons."

"The father god of dragons . . . talks to you?"

"Made her his champion," the brown-haired lizard tossed in. "Didn't he, Iz?"

"He did."

"Why?"

"It's a bit of a long story," Izzy admitted. "Just know I really had no choice at the time."

"And you trust this god?"

"Oh, gods, no. No, no, no," she laughed. "Never!"

Maskini glanced at Rachel again, but the girl could only shrug.

Poor Izzy. Being raised among the barbarians in the Dark Plains had made her . . . uneven. Desert Landers were all about cold logic and precise planning. None of this insane guessing and ruminating and talking to gods. Who had time for all this?

"You don't trust him, and yet you're going to believe him on *this*?"

"Rhydderch Hael wants something. No. He *needs* something. Something he can't do himself. So, yeah, I trust Éibhear and the Mì-runach on this. Besides, sneak attacks are what they do. And they do it well."

"I guess if you're sure . . ."

"It couldn't hurt to look, Gran," Rachel suggested. "We'll

call in a few of the Guard who are off for the night. Put the others on alert. By tomorrow we'll have a good idea what's in those sewers."

Maskini looked over the group, then at Layla. Her daughter nodded. "It couldn't hurt, Mum."

"All right. We'll do it."

"Thank you . . . um . . ."

She saw the girl struggling with what to call her. And Maskini understood. The girl had a mighty loyalty in her, and it must be confusing to think about her family—or kin, as she liked to call them—back in Dark Plains. Although they weren't blood, they'd helped raise her, loved her, taught her to care for herself in battle and life. They'd done what Maskini and her clan had been unable to do. For that alone Maskini would be eternally grateful.

"Maskini, child. Just call me Maskini."

"Maskini. Thank you. Now, Bran and I can get started tonight and check out—"

"No." The blue-haired dragon shook his head at Izzy.

"No, what?"

"You need sleep. We'll get started tomorrow."

"Éibhear—"

"After what happened between you and Haldane, you need your sleep."

"I'm fine. I don't need—"

The dragon put his obscenely large hand over Izzy's face. *Completely* over her face.

"Hush, now. I'm doing what's best for you."

That seemed to irritate Izzy because she began swinging and trying to pry his hand off her face. Maskini glanced across the room at her husband. Zachariah didn't believe this disturbingly large—when human; as dragon he was horrifyingly large—blue-haired "uncle" was any sort of proper uncle. But like her mother, Izzy seemed a bit clueless when it came to the true feelings of males.

The dragon pulled Izzy into his body, one arm around her waist, the other still over her face while Izzy continued to swing and curse behind that hand. "Poor Izzy is always so eager to work. I often have to remind her that she's merely human and needs her rest."

"It's not a problem," Maskini told him. "We can send my troops out tonight to do some recon around the city. We'll have more information for you in the morning so you won't have to waste any time."

"Excellent! Hear that, Izzy? This is just what we need."

Although Maskini couldn't quite make out the words, she sensed that her granddaughter was not agreeing with the dragon.

"My lady—"

"General."

"Right. Well, General, will you be able to fit my comrades and Branwen in your beautiful home for the night? Or should I find them accommodations in the city?"

"They can stay here."

Rachel looked at her. "They can?"

"Of course. The three males can stay with you, dragon. And Branwen can stay with Izzy."

She saw the immediate disappointment on the dragon's face. "Oh. Branwen won't get her own room?"

"We just don't have the space. Sorry. But I'm sure the, uh, *cousins* would like to share a room together tonight. Eh, ladies?"

"Oh, yes, General," the lady dragon crowed. "Thank you!"

Now those two, Branwen and the blue-haired dragon, were definitely related and viewed each other as such.

Izzy finally pulled herself from the dragon's arms, spun around, and slapped at his chest and shoulders with her hands.

Rachel leaned in and whispered in Maskini's ear, "I certainly hope she's better in battle than this."

"That makes two of us."

* * *

"Maybe we shouldn't wait. We should go looking tonight," Izzy pushed.

Brannie pulled on a loose, white cotton shirt and soft cotton leggings. Her usual clothes for sleeping whenever humans were around.

"Maskini already sent out her troops. You gave them detailed instructions. I don't know what you think we can do. We don't even know this city." Brannie looked over her shoulder. Izzy stood on the other side of the bed they'd be sharing, dressed in the same style as Brannie but her shirt was blue. "You're anxious, Iz. Why?"

"Don't know."

Bran settled on the bed, her legs crossed. Izzy always got like this when she had to wait to go into battle. Like Annwyl, she wasn't good with the waiting. Unlike Annwyl, however, Izzy could go ages without a good war to keep her busy. As long as she got in her daily training and spent time with her troops, she was fine. But when she knew a battle was imminent, Izzy hated the occasional delay that happened before she could dive in and start the killing. That's when Brannie had to be careful because it was easy to start fights with her cousin.

"Don't worry, Iz. We'll get this cleaned up, get Elisa's agreement about your sister, and take it from there."

"Right. Of course."

Bran knew her cousin had given up that fight much too easily, which made her think there might be something else going on. Something beyond all the doings of witches and sand.

"Are you going to tell me what's going on?" Brannie demanded quietly, so as not to disturb the rest of the house, which had settled down for the evening.

"What are you talking about?"

"You. You're anxious. Practically crawling the walls."

"I've got a lot on my mind."

"Does what's on your mind have really big hands and blue hair?"

"Let it go, Bran."

"You fucked him, right?"

"So? It's not like he's the first."

"There's fucking, Iz, and then there's something more. Or at least that's what I've been told."

"And?"

"And, it looks to me like you've got something more."

"With Éibhear? Lord I-Can't-Get-Too-Close?"

"He doesn't seem to mind getting too close now. Doing it in front of your human kin, too. With all of them glaring at him. The fact he hasn't run off screaming I find admirable."

Izzy chuckled and sat down on the bed. "They probably don't like him because he's dragon."

"They tolerate me well enough. Not an unkind word or terrified scream of panic yet." Bran studied her friend. "You falling for him, Iz?"

Izzy snorted, shook her head, and said, "Come on, Bran. I fell for that idiot when I was sixteen. Now I'm in love with him!" Izzy grabbed a pillow and began to rip it into shreds, feathers flying all over the room. "*Because apparently my life isn't ridiculous enough!*"

"Well," Brannie reasoned, stopping to blow a white feather off her nose, "as long as you're handling it well . . ."

When the knock came, Uther scrambled across the room—ignoring the fact that he was stepping on actual chests in the process—and snatched the door open.

One of Izzy's aunts held a tray piled with food and drink. Although she looked ready to bolt at the sight of Uther's overeager face.

"Is that for us?" he asked; then he smiled.

That didn't seem to soothe her.

"Uh . . . thought you all might be hungry. And my father wanted to make sure you wouldn't turn on us in the middle of the night because you hadn't been fed enough."

"Good plan!" Uther said, taking the tray from her.

Éibhear quickly stepped to the door and gave his warmest smile. "Thank you so much for this. We appreciate it. And you can tell your father he need have no fear of us."

"Yeah." She looked them over. "Right."

Éibhear watched the woman walk away before he closed the door and rounded on his comrades. "Is there something wrong with all of you?" he demanded.

"Now that we have food . . . no."

"You're an idiot." Éibhear stomped back across the room and, still fully clothed, dropped facedown onto the bed.

"What's wrong with you?"

"I'm trying to ease the discomfort of these people, but you lot aren't helping."

"Why bother?" Caswyn asked around a mouth full of food. "It's not like we're staying here forever."

"They're Izzy's kin."

"She seems to get along fine with them."

"Yeah, but . . . I'm just saying . . ." Éibhear growled. "Forget it. I don't know why I bloody bother."

"I have no idea what you're trying to tell us, but you sound particularly pathetic."

"What he's trying to say," Aidan offered, "is that he wants Izzy's human kin to like him. Unlike his own kin, who can barely stand the sight of him."

"Thank you for that. That was very nice."

"What do you care if they like you or not?" Uther asked.

"Because it matters."

"Why does it matter?"

"Because."

"Because why?"

"By the gods of piss, blood, and death!" Aidan exploded. "Because he loves her!"

"Oh." Uther stared at Éibhear. "Why didn't you say that then?"

Éibhear pulled the linen bedsheet over his head and he was quite proud of himself for not tearing Uther's head off when the idiot pushed, "Well . . . why didn't you?"

Chapter 40

It was the blade sliding under her chin that woke Izzy up. Otherwise, she didn't hear a thing.

With the blade resting against her neck, she slowly rolled onto her back. A Sand dragon in human form stood above her. She could tell by the hair and that bronze overlay. With the curved sword under her chin held in one hand, he raised the forefinger of the other and placed it against his lips.

It wouldn't have mattered to Izzy. She'd risk a cut throat before she'd let someone drag her anywhere. But the Sand dragon wasn't alone. He had another dragon, also in human form, with him, and that one held a sword over a snoring Brannie's chest.

And that was something Izzy wouldn't risk. So she slowly got up, that blade never far from her throat, and let the Sand dragons lead her out into the city.

Éibhear sat up and as soon as he was awake, the other Mì-runach woke up as well.

"What?" Aidan asked.

"Thought I heard something." He slipped off the bed and eased the door open. He listened again, but this time Éibhear didn't hear anything. Yet he knew what he was feeling. Threatened. He just didn't know why.

Stepping out into the hallway, Éibhear listened again. Still nothing, but he decided to check it out. He eased down the hallway, heard a creak, and stopped. Holding his hand out, Aidan placed Éibhear's short sword in his hand. With a nod, he proceeded forward. As he reached the turn into the next hallway, he readied his weapon before he strode around that corner—and ran right into Brannie.

"*Gods.*" He lowered the sword he'd almost skewered her with. "What the hells do you think you're doing?"

"Looking for Izzy, and, Éibhear—"

But Éibhear didn't wait for his cousin to finish, simply pushed past her and stalked down the hall to Izzy's room. He threw the door open and went in.

Izzy was gone, but her weapons were still there. Izzy wouldn't even go out to take a piss without a weapon. Suddenly Éibhear realized the true value of that damn dog that was still at the Imperial Guards dog kennels—Macsen would have alerted them all to any threat near Izzy.

Éibhear sniffed the air. He scented Izzy, Brannie, and . . .

"Éibhear?"

"Sand Eaters. They were here." He turned and walked past Aidan. "Get everyone up. Now."

Éibhear had been right. The Cult of Chramnesind was in the sewers but not living in the shit-covered tunnels. They'd built chambers directly off the tunnels, burrowing far into the center of the city. But Izzy still didn't know what they could possibly want from her or why they hadn't killed her yet.

Izzy was pulled into a chamber and her wrists bound behind her. With a hand against her back, she was shoved forward.

She could tell the zealots right away. She knew this even though some were dragon, others human, some neither of the two; some from the Desert Lands, others clearly from different territories. But what identified them as the most devoted to their god was the fact that the zealots had blood-and-dirt encrusted bindings around their heads, where their eyes had probably once been, and wore witch's robes. Some carried wands or staffs.

Those with eyes still in their heads were the converts, she suspected. And, like the zealots, they came from a wide range of species and territories. Some on their knees in supplication, others standing guard. She didn't know why because they didn't seem to be paying much attention to her.

"So what do you want?" Izzy asked the room.

"Who is that?"

Izzy turned toward the voice coming from behind her.

"Vateria," Izzy sneered.

"I asked a question," Vateria snapped, ignoring Izzy. "Who is this?"

"The one you wanted. Daughter of Talaith."

Vateria put her talons to her temples and rubbed them, sighing dramatically. "I said she was sixteen winters. Does she look like sixteen winters to you?"

"You said Daughter of Talaith," the dragon insisted. "*She's* Daughter of Talaith."

"The older sister, you idiot." She threw her claws into the air. "I am surrounded by stupidity!"

Vateria gestured at Izzy. "This bitch has no power. Her sister has the power. She's the one I want."

"Well, she's not here. So what do you want us to do with this one?"

"Kill her." She started to turn away, but then stopped. "Wait. Stop."

"They hadn't actually started."

"Shut up, human." She faced Izzy, looked her over. "Yes. Your sister is powerful. She'll feel your pain. Know your suffering. She'll come to protect you."

The Sand dragon behind Izzy sighed deeply. "I guess you're torturing this one too."

Izzy had to chuckle. "You sound so bored."

The She-dragon's eyes narrowed. "You don't fear me, do you, human?"

"I already know what you can do. What you're willing to do. To your own family, if need be."

Vateria leaned in to get a better look. "Why do I know your face?"

Izzy smirked. "Because I was there when my queen killed your lover—and you couldn't stop her."

The She-dragon's back snapped straight, eyes fierce. "I remember you. Annwyl's little pet whore who fought the ogres to distract me."

"It worked, didn't it?"

"Excellent point."

Vateria turned away, her tail lashing out. It hit Izzy full on the side of the face and she immediately felt blood drip down her jaw to her chest, but she didn't fall. She wouldn't.

The She-dragon looked at Izzy over her shoulder, her eyes widening a bit. "My, my. You are strong."

Izzy grinned. "You have no idea."

Éibhear stalked behind the humans, allowing them to lead the way toward the sewers. Izzy's kin had moved like lightning as soon as they'd heard she was gone, calling in the Imperial Guards and readying them for combat. Now they would take the information that they'd gotten from the scouts Maskini had sent out earlier and track down Izzy.

He refused to think beyond that. Of what might be happening to Izzy. He had to believe she'd be okay because he needed her to be okay.

The Mì-runach were with him, keeping their distance but still, in the most important sense, by his side. They would always be by his side, as he would always be Mì-runach. And knowing that kept him focused because he knew he wouldn't have to fight alone to get Izzy back.

"You know, you might be going in the wrong direction." Éibhear slowed down and stopped, slowly facing the owner of the voice. A male. A dragon male in human form. But not a Sand Eater. Nor a Southlander. In fact, Éibhear didn't know what breed this dragon was. He couldn't scent anything specific about him, but rather *all*. Although that didn't make sense, did it?

"Really?" Éibhear asked.

"Hhhm. Just a thought really."

"Do I know you?"

"Not that I'm aware."

"Éibhear?" Aidan walked back toward him. "You all right?"

"Yeah. I'm fine." He looked at the other dragon. "So you think I'm going in the wrong direction."

"Just a thought."

"So you said."

"Éibhear—"

Éibhear shook his head to silence Aidan. "So what's the right direction?"

"*Éibhear.*"

"What?" he snapped.

Aidan shrugged a bit, Caswyn and Uther now standing behind him also looking concerned. "Who are you talking to?"

"I'm talking to—" Éibhear blinked, looked at his comrades. They stared at him like he'd lost his reason. Because they couldn't see the other dragon, could they?

He faced the god, stared hard at him. "Where is she?" he asked flatly.

"They've always underestimated you, haven't they? Big, sweet Éibhear with the heart of gold. They thought you'd be like that forever."

"Where is she?"

"But Izzy . . . my little Izzy always had faith in you. Even when you were breaking her heart. Even when you were accusing her of all manner of beastly things. Tell me something, little blue dragon, when you find her body, will you feel guilty?"

Éibhear swallowed past what felt like definite panic. "Are you trying to tell me you won't keep protecting her? That you don't have plans for her?"

"Is that what you think? That I protect her? Do you have so little faith in my Izzy?"

"She's not *your* anything. She's never been yours. Izzy doesn't belong to anyone."

"Perhaps. Then again . . . if that's true, why should I bother helping her?"

Chuckling, Rhydderch Hael turned to walk away.

Éibhear's mind scrambled and he quickly called out, "What about your precious Vateria?"

"What about her?" the god asked, walking away, his long hair dragging in the sand-covered cobblestones.

"You still need me to find her, don't you? The word the Nolwenn used was 'rescue,' I believe."

The god stopped. "What about your poor Izzy?" he asked, not bothering to even look at Éibhear.

"Izzy can take care of herself."

"What the hell are you doing?" Aidan snapped.

Éibhear raised his hand, silencing his friend.

"You still need me to do that, eh?" Éibhear pushed the god.

"Try where you started," the god cryptically told him.

"What is going on?" Aidan asked.

Brannie ran toward them, her arms spread out from her body. "Oy! You lot? What are you doing?"

Éibhear looked at his cousin. "Go with the Guard into the tunnels."

"And what are you going to do?"

"Just do as I say, Brannie. Protect them. There'll be Sand Eaters all over that tunnel. Now go."

Brannie let out a frustrated growl, spun around, and ran back toward the others.

"And what are we doing?" Aidan asked.

Éibhear looked in the direction the god had walked. "What we're supposed to do."

"Which is?"

"Rescue that bitch, Vateria."

"But Izzy—"

"Isn't our problem. I made a commitment to the Nolwenns."

Caswyn stared at him. "Are you kidding?"

"No."

Uther stepped closer to him. "You want to rescue Vateria over finding Iseabail?"

"I'm Mì-runach. I made a commit—"

"*For the love of the gods, shut up about that!*" Uther bellowed.

"Wait, wait." Aidan stepped between them, faced Éibhear, studied him. "You sure about this, mate?"

"I'm positive."

Aidan blew out a breath. "Then let's go."

"Yeah, but—"

"Stop asking questions," Aidan barked at the others, "and let's just move. Now." He looked at Éibhear, nodded. "We're with you, Éibhear. Mì-runach to death."

"Uh-oh," Vateria said. "You poor thing. You're bleeding. It must hurt so."

Izzy laughed. She couldn't help it. And Vateria laughed with her, but Izzy knew there was no real humor in it.

"What's so funny?" Vateria asked her.

"I was just thinking how strange it is."

"How strange what is?"

Izzy leaned in a bit. "I'm supposed to be rescuing *you*."

"Rescuing me? From what?"

"The crazed zealots." Izzy glanced over at the eyeless ones. "Isn't that right?"

"Darling girl," Vateria said, slowly moving around Izzy. "Why would you need to rescue me from this? I'll admit," she went on. "It's not what I'm used to. I do prefer the comforts of my homeland. But this . . . this will lead me back there. This will be my army. And after I claim what's rightly mine in the Sovereign Provinces . . . I'll be coming for your bitch queen. And she will know pain."

"The woman's been dead. Then brought back. And then went about raising children referred to as the Unholy Ones by many priests—and surviving said unholy children. So you really can't believe that *you* are going to scare *her*. Do you?"

"And you're not going to scare me."

"But I already have. Because you know I'm right."

"No. You're not."

"Then prove me wrong," Izzy suggested. "Leave."

"What?"

"Leave. Walk out. It's not like I'm going anywhere."

"You don't really think this will work, do you? Trying to convince me that—"

"You're a prisoner? A prisoner in a very comfortable cell? Or a calf they've been fattening up for the kill."

Determined now, Vateria headed toward the chamber exit. But a dragon stepped in front of her, blocking her way.

Vateria tried again, moving around the dragon. But another dragon cut her off.

"Move out of my way," she ordered.

Izzy smirked. "But you've been so comfortable here."

"*Shut up!*"

Vateria stormed back into the center of the chamber.

"You can't keep me here," she argued. "I'm Chramnesind's chosen one."

"Really?" Izzy pursed her lips. "Huh."

"What does *that* mean?"

"It means why would Chramnesind make you his chosen one? It's not like you're truly loyal to him. Look at these others. Vateria, this lot gave up their *eyes* for him. The others kneel in supplication. And they've all given up their families and friends in honor of his blessings. And you . . . you want an army. To win back land you never had a right to. Oh, yes. You are *so* the chosen one."

"This isn't working."

"Fine. It's not working."

"They're just keeping me here for my own safety."

"Fine. It's for your safety."

"Well, what other reason could they be keeping me for?"

Izzy shrugged. "Well, I'm sure we can safely rule out virgin sacrifice."

"Bitch."

"But they could be planning to rip you open, clean you out, and fill you up with someone or something else. It's kind of what happened to my mother."

"Fill me up with what, exactly?"

"Whatever's behind that wall."

Vateria looked over her shoulder. "There's nothing behind that wall except . . . sewage."

"Fine. There's nothing behind that wall."

"Stop doing that!"

"I'm just agreeing with you."

"Well stop it!"

Vateria sat back on her haunches, front claws twisting together.

After nearly a minute, she pointed at the wall. "Show me," she ordered the others.

"Lady Vateria—"

"Do it! Show me what's behind that wall!"

One of the dragons looked at the zealots, nodded. A wand was raised and, slowly, the rock wall separated and slowly opened.

Stifling a scream, Vateria stumbled back.

Izzy leaned over to the dragon standing next to her and asked, "Are those tentacles?"

The Sand dragon looked at her . . . and smiled.

Chapter 41

"Are you sure about this?" Aidan asked him, the four of them staring up the stairs at the badly repaired doors Éibhear had just ripped open the previous day.

"I think so."

"And I *hope* so. I'm not in the mood to suffer. Even for you."

"What about when we get in there?" Caswyn asked. "Then what?"

"I don't know," Éibhear admitted. "We'll figure it out as we go."

Damn gods, he thought. Damn gods with their damn centaur shit. He hated them all, but he especially hated bloody Rhydderch Hael.

"I know. He can be a bit of a prat."

Éibhear sighed and looked to his left. She stood there, tall and strong, brown of skin, arms covered in runes. But she was no mortal being. He could tell because of what should be the mortal wound on her neck. Her throat had been slashed from one side to the other and yet she was still . . . strong. Powerful. Breathing.

"It's not his fault really. He has so many things on his mind. My focus is very clear. Always has been. But he's involved in so many things. And after eons of dealing with those who don't truly appreciate him, he just got a little . . ."

"Bitchy?"

"I was going to say cranky. And you're no better."

"Look, I don't have time for—"

"Where the hells did you come from?" Aidan asked.

And that's when Éibhear realized that his friends could see her, too. It was a relief to know he wasn't actually going insane.

"I come from blood and death and good quality steel. Battle makes up my organs and war makes up my soul."

"Uh . . ." Uther leaned in. "Are you sure you're all right? You've got a bit of . . . uh . . . well . . . a scratch on your throat?"

She laughed. "Aye. A scratch. Don't worry. This scratch will heal."

Needing to know, Éibhear asked, "Why can they—"

"As warriors, when you leave this life, you'll come to me. All the Mì-runach come to me. So I allow you to see me when I choose."

"You're Eirianwen," Aidan gasped. "The goddess of war and death."

"I thought you'd be a She-dragon," Caswyn said. "But I don't think you are."

"That's because I'm not."

"What do you want?" Éibhear asked, unable to keep the tiredness out of his voice.

"My mate, he sometimes forgets that balance is necessary in this world. Without it, I don't exist. But Chramnesind doesn't want balance. It's of no use to him, you see, because he wants it to all belong to him."

"He'll bring you war and death."

"Only for a short time. A few decades perhaps. Maybe a century or two. But to me . . . centuries are like seconds in a short day. So I need you, Éibhear the Blue, to stop what's to happen. What's already begun."

"You mean rescue Vateria."

"Exactly. Because if she dies here, in this spot of great power, at the hands of Chramnesind's acolytes . . . there will be dark times indeed. Her soul is a deep well of hatred. Combine that hatred with what they actually plan to do to her . . . what they'll have her become—and none of you will survive. Not human. Not dragon. Not your Izzy. Vateria, here and now, cannot die. For if she dies here, she will be reborn—and then gods help you all."

"So how do I stop this?"

"Do what you do best. The Mì-runach are my greatest creation, the idea given to your forefathers millennia ago."

"We'll still have to get past the witches."

"Let Aidan do the talking." She threw a ridiculously large hammer at Éibhear's feet, the sound of it clanging against the marble stone steps, ricocheting through the quiet of the sleeping city. "You do the hammering." She walked around them. "And good luck to you all."

Éibhear picked up the hammer. It was heavy even for him, but he rested it on his shoulder anyway.

"You know, Éibhear," Aidan said as they walked up the steps to the Nolwenn temple, "I'm starting to see why you don't go home very often."

"I tried to tell you. . . ."

Vateria turned to run, but a tentacle shot out and wrapped around her back leg, yanking her to her stomach. She screeched and dug her talons into the stone floor. Smoke came from where the tentacle held her leg, a sizzling sound and the smell of burning scales causing Izzy to shudder.

The cultists moved forward, all of them chanting, calling

out to their god. While they did, Izzy stepped back. And, while their attention was focused away from her, she did something she'd only done willingly once before when she'd been very drunk and Brannie had dared her in front of all her men.

Gritting her teeth, Izzy dislocated both her shoulders. Something much easier to do once she'd had them broken in a battle. Yet easier didn't mean any less agonizing. She bit back a cry of pain, and maneuvered her arms down and her legs over her bound wrists. Then she brought her arms up.

She panted, working hard to control her pain. Then, making sure she still had no one's attention, Izzy moved back to the wall behind her and faced it. Taking another deep breath, she rammed first one shoulder, then the other against the hard rock, snapping both joints into place.

"I have *really* got to stop doing that," she muttered.

She turned away from the wall and faced one of the Sand dragons. Without a word, he raised his sword and brought it down. Izzy rolled forward, out of the way of the blade, but as she came out of the roll, she brought her bound arms up. The weapon slashed through her bonds but, thankfully, only scraped the inside of one palm.

Shaking off the rope, she got to her feet just as the dragon's tail came at her face. She caught hold of it and the dragon picked her up. Something she'd realized long ago that all dragons did when something was hanging from their tail. She took the short trip until she could land on the dragon's back. He tried to shake her off, but she caught hold of his hair and held on. He spun in a circle, his tail coming at her again. She dodged first one way, then the other, never losing her grip on his hair.

Frustrated, he began using his sword as well, trying to swipe her off. When the sword came at her a third time, she waited until it was near her legs before she jumped to the side and rammed her foot down on the blade, pinning it to the dragon's back.

He roared in anger and released the weapon, using his tail again to try to stop her. Most likely assuming she couldn't lift the sword. But Izzy had been playing with dragon swords since the night she'd stolen Éibhear's from his room when she was a teenager. She grabbed the leather-bound grip, raised the extremely heavy weapon, and swung it once. The blade, sharp, cut through the end of the dragon's tail. Izzy dropped the sword, no longer needing it, and caught the tail tip before it hit the ground. Taking firm hold of it, she charged the rest of the way up the dragon's back, ignoring his screams of pain and the blood flying everywhere from his whipping tail, until she was at his neck.

Izzy dropped down, her legs going around his shoulders. She leaned over to grab one of the scales, but then remembered that the Sand dragons' scales were different from all the others.

Cursing her stupidity, she scrambled back up, kicked the bleeding tail that was now trying to grab her, and charged up the rest of the dragon's neck and right to the top of his head. She dropped to her knees, raised the tail tip over her head and brought it down into the dragon's eye.

He screamed in pain and sand exploded out of his snout and mouth. He went back on his haunches, forearms flailing out.

Izzy, losing her grip on the tail tip, flipped back, rolling down the dragon's spine until her head hit the ground and everything went black.

Fed up with arguing with her daughter, Elisa stormed away. But Haldane followed her, still arguing, as was her way. And yes, it did cross Elisa's mind to turn her daughter into something that slithers but she fought the urge. It would be a very bad precedent to set.

She did, however, stop, spin around, and yell at her daughter to, "*Shut the fuck up, Haldane!*"

"*I will do no such thing!*"

"Elder Elisa!"

Sighing, "What is it, Akila?"

"The dragons are back."

"Tell them to come back tomorrow. I don't have time—"

"They're ripping up the floor of the Great Hall!"

Elisa locked eyes with Akila. "They're *what?*"

Éibhear raised the hammer again and again, ramming it into the thick marble floor. With each piece he loosened, one of his comrades tore out the marble and tossed it aside.

"What the holy hells do you think you're doing?" Elisa yelled up at them. The Mi-runach had all shifted to their natural form so that they could do this as quickly as possible.

"He's doing what you asked him to do," Aidan explained calmly.

"What are you talking about?"

"He's rescuing Vateria."

"From under our floors? Is he insane? Are *you?*"

"I wish he was," Aidan sighed. "But I assure you, we're not here to harm you. Trust me, my lady. You *want* us to do this."

Éibhear brought the hammer down again, hit the marble, and lifted it away.

"Éibhear!" Caswyn said, digging harder. "I think we're through."

"Through?" Elisa demanded. "Through to where?"

"To the Cult of Chramnesind's hiding place," Aidan told her.

"I told you before, you big oaf. They're in the desert."

"No. They're not."

"And you know this how?"

Éibhear looked down at Elisa and answered, "From the goddess Eirianwen." When the witches only stared at him, he added, "Beat that."

"You mean they've been under us all this time?"

"Leeching your power to increase their strength," Aidan explained.

Éibhear focused on Haldane. "But know this, witch, if Iseabail dies because you were a bitch to her, I'll be coming back for *you*." He nodded at Elisa. "Call your witches from their beds. Anything that comes out of here that's not us . . . kill it."

Éibhear focused on the pit his comrades had dug. "Move," he ordered. They did.

Unfurling his wings, Éibhear took to the air, going up to the tall ceiling. He flipped over and raced toward the floor. As he neared it, he unleashed his flame, and burst through to the chamber beneath.

Izzy woke up when she felt someone shaking her shoulder.

"Izzy. Wake up."

Looking up, Izzy smiled. "Rhi."

"You need to get up. Now."

"Just let me sleep a little longer."

"Please, Iz!"

"Ssshhh."

Izzy rolled to her side and tried to get back to sleep, but someone strong grabbed her shoulder and rolled her to her back.

"Oy! Cousin!"

"Talwyn?"

"Time to wake up, bitch." Then her cousin slapped her. Hard.

Izzy sat up, the sword that had been aiming for her head, ramming into the ground instead.

Raising a brow, Izzy snarled at the human acolyte over her, "Missed me." Then she swung her fist, knocking the bastard out. Getting to her feet, she yanked the sword from the ground. The thing with the tentacles, which Izzy was beginning to believe was once something human, had drawn an hysterically screaming Vateria close to its gaping maw, blood, drool, and shit pouring onto the floor around her.

Disgusted but not having much choice, Izzy charged forward, ducking under dragon tails and Minotaur fists and centaur hooves in an attempt to reach the bitch she absolutely hated.

She was nearly there when she saw dirt and rock pour down from the ceiling. It distracted her for a moment, a moment she desperately couldn't afford.

A dragon tail swung out and rammed into her, sending her flying to the side. She waited to hit a wall but instead flew into one of the zealot dragons.

It sniffed and smiled. "Aaaaah. Iseabail," it whispered as she dropped to the ground in front of it. "Daughter of Talaith, favored among Rhydderch Hael's worshippers."

Crawling backward, Izzy tried to get to her feet. But she was weakening fast. Losing her strength from the battering her body was taking. She feared she wouldn't last much longer if she didn't find a way to . . .

Thinking fast, Izzy recalled something she'd heard her mother chant once. She got to her feet and raised her hand.

"I call upon the powers of . . . um . . . Rhydderch Hael," she screamed up at the zealot, shrugging at invoking that idiot's name.

"You?" the zealot snarled. "You dare try to put a spell on me? You have no power here. Among us. With our god!"

"Oh . . . uh . . . Rhydderch Hael. Bring destruction down upon these . . . uh . . . bad people."

"Kill her, Vincent," another zealot ordered. "Show her what real power is."

The dragon raised his fist, chanted something, and Izzy watched a ball of power shoot from the center of his claw and ram right into her.

Éibhear punched through the last bit of stone and metal and into the chamber beneath. As he crashed through, he saw what could only be Izzy flipping across the stone floor.

Changing course, he raced toward her, but he heard Vateria scream and remembered what he needed to do.

He wanted to go to Izzy. He wanted to rescue her. Take her out of here. But something, he didn't know what, something told him that would be the exact wrong thing to do. He knew it with every fiber of his being. So he changed course again, spinning around in midair to face Vateria and . . . and whatever had hold of her.

Good gods . . . are those tentacles?

Éibhear shook off his disgust, lifted his hammer, and raced toward the enemy Iron that needed his help.

Brannie, having heard the fighting, screaming, and roaring nearly a mile away, charged into the chamber once she reached it, her sword and shield at the ready. As she did, she saw two things at the same time. First, she saw Izzy fly by her, heading into the far wall. Then she saw Éibhear crash through the ceiling and rush toward Izzy.

But then her cousin stopped. He stopped and instead of going for Izzy, the woman she was sure he loved, he turned and faced Vateria and . . . and whatever *that* was that had hold of the bitch.

Brannie had no idea what was going on, but she'd be damned if she'd let Izzy die because her cousin didn't have his gods-damn priorities straight.

"In here!" she called out to the humans following her. "Hurry!" They could help with all this. She'd help with . . . with . . .

"Izzy?"

Izzy was no longer flying but walking with purpose back across the floor toward what Brannie was guessing were the zealots Iz had told her about. And even though those zealots didn't have eyes, one of them still cocked his head like he could see. Like he was looking right at Izzy.

"You?" the zealot said in a raspy whisper. "You still live. How is that possible?"

"Kill her, Vincent! Kill her now!"

The zealot lifted both claws and unleashed a flash of powerful Magick that even Brannie with her non-Magickal existence could easily see.

And that Magick rammed right into Izzy, but this time, she didn't fly anywhere. She just stopped, shook her head, cracked her neck, and moved forward.

"Combine our powers!" Another zealot screamed. "Now!"

"No! Use something else. Kill her!"

While they were busy arguing, debating, Izzy kept moving forward. She swiped up a dragon's short sword that lay on the floor. One of the soldier dragons ran at her, but she dodged his weapon and him, then dragged the blade she held against his back leg, severing the tendon. The dragon dropped to the ground with a scream and Izzy kept going.

Someone else threw more Magick at her. And this time Izzy didn't even pause. Instead, she suddenly sped forward and right at the first zealot. When he saw her, he panicked and swiped at her with his claw. Izzy caught hold of it and went with it when the zealot's arm swung up. Iz pulled back the dragon sword she held and rammed it forward, slamming it into the side of the zealot's neck, bypassing his hard scale and tearing open a main artery. Izzy flipped her body up onto the zealot's head, yanked out the blade, and charged across, leaping to the dragon beside him, seconds before the first zealot crashed to the ground, dead before his head hit the floor.

"Oh, that's right," Brannie said, laughing a little. "Iz doesn't need my help."

But, she realized, looking down at the humans Izzy was descended from, who threw themselves into the battle with a gusto any Cadwaladr would appreciate, Izzy's kin did need her help. And with great pride, she gave it.

Using the hammer he was beginning to appreciate more and more, Éibhear battered at the tentacles that had hold of Vateria.

"Éibhear!" he heard Aidan bellow.

"Get Vateria!" he ordered. "Pull her out!"

A tentacle slapped across his snout, acid from it leeching past scale and into flesh. Snarling—because he knew that would scar—Éibhear battered the tentacle away.

"Éibhear! Axe!"

Éibhear lifted his claw and caught the axe Uther threw at him. He brought it down, cutting off three tentacles at once, but another three slithered out from . . . well, he didn't want to think about where they slithered from.

"We've got Vateria!" Caswyn yelled.

"Get her out of here! Now!"

Knowing Caswyn would take care of Vateria, Éibhear moved forward. He needed to cut off something more important than a tentacle. But before he could get close enough to anything important, tentacles slipped around his throat and arms, pulling him away. Holding him tight while what he assumed was a really vile-looking tongue slithered out from what he was guessing was a mouth, across the floor, and headed right for him.

Éibhear struggled against the tentacles. But as soon as he yanked one forearm or leg free, another tentacle caught hold again, holding him in place. The tongue neared him, slithering across the floor, blood, slime, and shit spreading from it as it did.

Gods, the smell alone made him want to vomit.

Éibhear opened his mouth to unleash flame but the tentacle around his throat tightened, choked him. Still, he didn't stop fighting. Uther dropped onto the thing's back, raised his second axe above its head, and began hacking away, but still it didn't release Éibhear. Aidan came at it from the side, using a broadsword to stab it through its thick skin. And still, nothing.

But Éibhear didn't care. He only fought harder. As did his comrades. He knew they wouldn't stop until they all took their last breath . . . which they might be very close to doing.

That tongue was close now, nearly under him. *This* Éibhear wasn't looking forward to. Especially when the tip of the tongue slowly began to lift up, too close to the important parts of him. Blood, shit, and death dripping off it and onto the floor, the smell making Éibhear gag. But still he fought. Still he—

A bare foot rammed down on that tongue, holding it in place on the floor, and a sword lifted up and plunged into it, pinning it to the ground with one hit.

The thing screamed out and released Éibhear so that it could attack the new threat.

Éibhear hit the ground, his sword still in his front claw. He looked down at the one who'd pinned that disgusting tongue—and smiled.

"See how I have to protect you?" he demanded with a smirk. "What if I wasn't here? To . . . you know . . . protect you?"

Izzy rolled her eyes. "Oh, yeah, you're right. Don't know what I'd do without ya." She motioned to the thing with a tilt of her head. "Look, you lot kill . . whatever that is. Me and Bran will take care of the rest. And then I'll see you after."

"Aye," Éibhear promised her. "You will."

They smiled at each other, knew the truth in those smiles. And, with love in their hearts . . . they proceeded to kill absolutely *everything* in the chamber that wasn't a loyal friend, kin, or Imperial Guard.

Chapter 42

"So I'm a prat?"

"No," Eirianwen corrected her mate while she stepped over the bodies from the recent battle in Sefu's sewers in search of souls she could use. "I said you were a *bit* of a prat. A bit."

"It's all about semantics with you, isn't it?"

"Semantics, my darling mate, is what makes war gods' lives full and wonderful. Destruction of entire territories has been based on semantics."

Rhydderch Hael leaned against a wall. He was in his human form today. She didn't mind. She loved seeing him in any form he chose. "You interfered again, Eir."

"I didn't go near Izzy. Not once."

"You know what I mean."

She faced him, waved her forefinger at him, only to realize she'd lost it at some point to someone's battle axe. In fact, she'd lost half her hand.

It didn't help when her mate chuckled.

Quickly lowering her hand, Eir said, "Éibhear is mine, Rhy. *Mine*. We agreed. The Mì-runach come to me upon their deaths.

To me. So stop acting like I stepped over some boundaries only you can see."

"First Annwyl," he reminded her.

"You'd already given her up to the Minotaur. She was mine to take."

"Then Talaith."

"She wasn't yours in the first place and her human gods had deserted her long ago."

"Now Éibhear . . ."

"Also not yours. But Izzy . . . she's all yours. I haven't touched her." Although Eir liked the human female and the clan she came from. A warrior breed Eir had begun before she'd been tossed from the human pantheon of gods. "She'll serve you well."

"Well, she's clearly so open to that," he said with great sarcasm.

"What do you expect when you're a bit of a prat? She's loyal and you keep fucking with those she's loyal to."

"Whatever."

Seeing that her mate was about to fly off in a pouty dragon rage, Eir walked toward Rhydderch Hael, crushing a few skulls beneath her feet. Using her unmarred hand, she pressed her palm to his cheek. "Don't ever think for a moment, my love, that the games we play change how I feel for you. How I'll always feel. I love you with all of my hardened warrior heart."

"You'd best. My feelings for you, Eirianwen, have not and never will change. If I thought any of this truly angered you, that I might lose you—"

She pressed her body against his, kissed his chin. "Never. Haven't you realized that yet? Besides, what we do now dictates what happens with Chramnesind later."

"I've noticed he hasn't been around."

"He starts things, then flitters away," she said off-handedly. "His lack of vision has always bored me."

Rhy gazed down at her, one eyebrow raised in that oh-so-handsome face—and Eir gasped. "No, no! I mean his lack of *creative* vision and how it affects the universes we rule. Not his lack of actual . . . *vision*. I don't mean that! I'd never say that!"

Rhy laughed. Not a chuckle or a mocking laugh, but a true laugh, from his gut. It was so very good to hear because he did it so rarely. And although horrified at what she'd just said, Eir joined in, hugging her mate tightly while she laughed into his neck.

Éibhear glanced up at the ceiling. "Thunder?" he asked Aidan.

"I don't know. Do they have thunder here? Do they have rain?" He looked at Maskini. "Do you lot get rain?"

"We have a rainy season. It makes the rivers overflow."

"Oh. That's unfortunate."

Éibhear stepped around his friend, watching Izzy mount Brannie's back, his cousin taking to the air.

"Oy!" he called after them. "Where are you two off to?"

"We'll be back in a bit," Izzy promised.

"Is it me or does Izzy always sound like she's up to something no good when it involves your cousin?" Aidan said.

"No," Éibhear admitted. "It's not just you."

Vateria tore across the Desert Lands, ignoring the growing heat from the suns above her head. She wanted to put as much distance between her and this cursed territory as she could manage.

Gods! Could no one be trusted these days? Damn zealots and their damn gods!

But this setback wouldn't stop Vateria. She would get her birthright back if she had to destroy the damn world to do it! Nothing would stop her. Not Southlanders. Not zealots. Not gods. No one.

Vateria heard the flap of wings behind her and she sped up, trying to get away. She'd slipped away from that dragon who'd freed her from that . . . that thing back in the sewers but he'd been a big bastard. No way he'd be faster than she in open skies like this.

Yet no matter how much faster Vateria went, she couldn't seem to outpace the dragon following her. She didn't stop, though. She kept moving, kept dodging. Even when the dragon was over her.

Vateria was about to dive again, hoping to get the dragon to smash face first into the hard ground, but before she did, something light landed on her back.

"Hello, Vateria. Remember me?"

Vateria looked back. That human female from earlier? The one whose sister she had coveted?

"What do you want, human?"

"Didn't think we were done."

"Thought you were to rescue me. I've been rescued. Now go."

And to help her along, Vateria spun three hundred and sixty degrees. But the human clamped her thighs down around Vateria's neck and easily held on. Dammit!

"Is this about your sister?" Vateria wanted to know when she realized the human wasn't going to give up easily.

"No. This is about your cousin."

"My . . ."

Of course. Agrippina. That bitch.

"Well, you can tell my cousin to go fu—"

"Why don't you pass that sentiment on to her when you see her again? Here," the human offered, "I'll help you with that."

And that's when a blade rammed between the scales on

her back, severing the muscle that controlled her wings. Like that, her wings stopped in mid-flap and suddenly Vateria was heading fast toward the ground with no way to stop.

She fought for control, tried to keep herself up. It helped, but barely. She landed hard on the ground, her belly skidding across the harsh sand, scraping away some of the protection of her scales.

When Vateria's body finally stopped, the human on her back easily slid off and walked around until she was face to face with her.

Panting, Vateria asked. "You're going to finish me off now?"

"No, no. I have no intention of finishing you off. That's not why I'm here. Just like I wasn't the one who finished off your father. But I did stop him from running. Like I just stopped you. Now . . . when Agrippina's ready it'll be much easier for her to track you down and finish what you began in your dungeons with her."

"Your cousin," some low-born black dragon appeared, sighing dramatically and shaking her head. "Your own bloody cousin. Sick bitch," she hissed before she spat at Vateria's claws. "Let's go, Iz. I can't stand to look at the twat a second more."

"Good luck to you, Vateria," the human said. "May Agrippina have mercy on your worthless soul. I certainly wouldn't."

The human mounted the low-born dragon and the pair flew off, heading back toward Sefu.

At that point, Vateria dropped her head to the ground and tried to cry. But, to be quite honest, she just didn't have that kind of weakness in her.

So, instead, she plotted and made plans while she waited for the bleeding in her back to stop. And that plotting . . . gods, that plotting felt so very good.

* * *

Izzy found her Desert Land family back at their house, a healer helping with any wounds that had been sustained during the battle in the sewers. When Izzy and Branwen walked into the yard at the back of the house, Zachariah immediately came to her side.

"There you are. You all right?"

"I'm fine. Just had to take care of something."

"Well, that *uncle* of yours seemed awfully worried when you didn't come right back."

Brannie snorted and Izzy elbowed her cousin in the side.

"Um, Zachariah, about Éibhear and me—"

"There you are." Éibhear strode across the yard until he was in front of Izzy, and her grandfather was forced to move quickly out of the dragon's way. "Are you all right?"

"I'm fine." Why did everyone keep asking her that?

"I thought you were coming right back."

"I told you I had something to do."

"With Vateria? Because if you killed her—"

"I didn't, but I don't report to you, Squad Leader."

"Could you say that with any more disdain?"

"Actually I could."

"I see our spoiled-brat side has not changed in the last two decades."

"And I see that our know-it-all, thinks-the-world-should-bow-at-his-feet side is still a bit of a bastard!"

"Fine! I won't bother worrying about your tight ass again!"

"Good! Because my tight ass doesn't need your tight ass doing anything!" Izzy stopped, thought a moment. "Now we're just flinging compliments at each other."

"It's not my fault we're amazing."

They laughed and Éibhear stepped a little closer, his hands reaching up and gently sliding across her jaw, his gaze locking with hers. "I'm just glad you're all right, Izzy," he admitted. "You had me worried."

"I'm fine. Now just kiss me."

Éibhear leaned in, big fingers framing Izzy's face, and he whispered, "When we get back, Iseabail, we have much to discuss."

"Gods, more conversation?"

"You can't avoid it forever."

"No. But I can try." Then she leaned up and kissed him instead. But as soon as she did, Éibhear's hands tightened on her jaw, his tongue slid boldly into her mouth; teasing, playing. Izzy wrapped her arms around his waist, gripped the back of his shirt tight. Gods, she was tempted to rip it off right here and now!

Izzy had no idea how long they stood there, kissing like that, lost in each other, but Zachariah roaring, "*What the hell kind of uncle are you?*" snapped them right out of it.

They stepped away from each other, both of them looking around at the group of people, kin, who were staring at them. That's when Izzy knew she and Éibhear were in deep. Too deep. One did not start passionately kissing someone in front of their entire family unless they were just rude, and Izzy considered herself a very polite person. But Éibhear had her all confused and desperate and, to be blunt, damn horny.

The bastard.

Zarah, standing near several of her daughters, shook her head at the embarrassed couple and chastised with a smile, "Someone's a very dirty uncle."

"And a very naughty niece," Maskini added.

Éibhear's head snapped around, and he glowered at Izzy, his jaw tense, his hands in fists, and Izzy immediately jumped back before black smoke poured out of his nose. She hated when that happened.

When the dragon kept glaring at her, Izzy demanded, "What are you looking at me for? I didn't tell them to say that!"

Chapter 43

Rhi hummed to herself and sketched a beautiful tree several hundred yards away. She was in a very good mood. Her sister and uncle, both quite safe, were heading home. Should be back any time now. What Izzy would have to say, though, Rhi still didn't know. And if her mother knew, she wasn't telling her yet.

That was okay, though. She could wait. Because right now, all that mattered was that her sister and uncle were safe. And, she was guessing, very much in love.

Rhi stopped humming so she could smile.

"Lady Rhianwen?"

Rhi looked up, her grin growing wider. "Hello, Frederik! And please, call me Rhi. Everyone else does."

"When I do your father glares at me."

"Don't take it personally. My father glares at everyone except me and Izzy. Even my mother. Although she thinks it's cute." She studied the Northland male. "That's a rather large stack of books you have."

"Oh, yes. Auntie Dagmar has given me reading assignments."

"How much time do you have to read all that?"

"Quite a while. Until dinner."

Rhi blinked. "Oh. All right." She gestured to a corner of the fur covering she sat on. "Would you like to join me? I'm just drawing, and I promise not to bother you while you read."

"Are you sure? I don't want to interrupt you."

"No, no. Not at all. We're kind of family now, so we should be acting like it. Please. Sit."

With a nod, he placed his books down on the grass and sat on the far corner of the fur covering. He didn't have to sit so far away, but she didn't blame him either. Her father had been saying things in front of poor Frederik to make it clear that his daughter was off limits.

Rhi went back to her sketch, enjoying how it was working out while appreciating the quiet company of the male with her. They worked like that for nearly thirty minutes when a shadow fell over her. Using her hand to shield her eyes from the two suns high in the sky, she looked up and immediately smiled at Albrecht. Their time in the village the other day had gone really well; Uncle Brastias was not nearly as brutal as her father when Lord Pombray's son moved too close to Rhi.

"Hello, Lord Albrecht. How are you?"

The boy didn't answer, and she instantly saw the distress on his face.

"Albrecht?"

"I'm . . . I'm so sorry."

Strong hands grabbed Rhi and yanked her to her feet. Lord Pombray's guards had moved up behind her and she'd not seen a thing.

"What is this?"

"Don't blame the boy." Lord Pombray walked around his guards and looked down at Rhi. "It's truly not his fault."

"What are you doing?"

"You'll be coming with us."

"You don't really think my kin will let you get away with this, do you?"

"If they want to get you back alive . . ."

"Father—" Albrecht began.

"Shut up!" He smiled at Rhi. "Now, your father, uncles, and all those other dragons are away from here today, so there won't be any flying lizards to help you. So let's not make this difficult. All right?"

"Please don't do this," Rhi begged.

"We won't hurt you, girl. I promise."

"It's not herself she's worried about, I'm afraid."

Pombray glared down at Frederik.

"What do you know of it, barbarian boy?"

"I knew what you were planning. Your men are chatty when they're drunk in the pubs. And I like wandering around pubs . . . because of drunks who are too chatty." Frederik stood. "My Aunt Dagmar already knows of this. Even now Rhi's dragon kin are heading this way."

"You little bastard."

"But even if they're not quick enough, I've already learned that Lady Rhianwen is never truly alone. Not really."

"And what the hells is that supposed to—"

The sword tore through Pombray's back and out his stomach, blood spraying across Rhi's face.

The blade was yanked out and the twins walked around Pombray. Talwyn's sword dripped with blood. She, like most of her dragon kin, was a fan of the sneak attack. While Talan was more like his mother. He hefted a battle axe and swung it, removing Pombray's head from his body.

"*My lord, no!*" one of the guards screamed.

Rhi looked at Albrecht. "Run," she told him. "Run and don't look back. *Run!*"

The boy took off, tears coursing down his cheeks as Talwyn kicked Pombray's head aside.

"Now which one of you is next?" she asked, smiling.

"Don't do this, Talwyn," Rhi implored her cousin. "Please."

"Don't be weak," her cousin snapped. "The line was crossed. They die."

The guard holding Rhi grabbed her hair and yanked her head back. "But not before this bitch dies first, monster."

Fear and panic swept through Rhi like a firestorm and, before she could stop, the power of it exploded out of her like an active volcano.

When the sky suddenly darkened Izzy pulled her horse to an abrupt stop as her father dropped to the ground in front of her.

"Daddy?"

"Izzy! Your sister! Where is she?"

"I don't—"

Éibhear's head tipped to the side. "Iz . . . what's that sound?"

"Oh, gods," Izzy whispered as a terrible roaring sound reached her ears. Though she'd never heard the sound before, she could easily guess where it had come from.

"Éibhear," Briec ordered. "Take Izzy out of here. *Now!*"

But Izzy grabbed Éibhear's arm before he could shift to dragon and watched as Elisa and the other Nolwenns they'd been escorting dismounted their horses and focused their collective attention deep into the forests.

Chanting, they all raised their hands, and Izzy felt the power they unleashed explode from them into the forests. The roaring coming from inside rammed into the power coming from without. The powers collided, the ground beneath their feet shaking, the sky above them darkening. Their horses began to panic and Izzy released Éibhear so that they could both get control of their animals.

The war between those powers raged, then abruptly . . . died.

The shaking stopped. The sky returned to its brilliant blue.

Elisa lowered her hands but then stumbled back, the Nolwenn sisters catching her. Izzy's great grandmother had been weakened by all this, but she and the Nolwenns had been able to do what no one else had managed. Stop Rhi before she destroyed all that she loved.

"I'm fine," Elisa said weakly. "Or I will be. I need food. Wine."

Izzy held her arms out. "Give her to me."

She lifted her great grandmother from the witches' arms and easily hauled her onto her saddle. "Hold on."

Then Izzy took Elisa straight to Garbhán Isle.

Once the shaking stopped, Talaith picked herself up off the floor and charged down the stairs, through the Great Hall, and out onto the hall steps. But before she could make it down the stairs, she saw her daughter riding into the courtyard. A woman in witch's robes sat in front of her.

"Izzy?" Knowing her daughter was alive and well, versus *seeing* her in the flesh alive and well was something that could not be compared. "Thank gods, Izzy."

"I'm all right, Mum. So's Rhi, I think. Daddy went to get her."

"Good. Good." Talaith started down the steps but stopped, her eyes widening. "Elisa?"

Exhausted from what Talaith now realized was an unleashing of immense Nolwenn power, her grandmother nodded at her. "Talaith. You're looking very . . . Southlander."

"What are you . . ." Talaith took a step back. "Is Haldane with you?"

"Did you really think she'd let me come here to meet you alone?"

Her grandmother had a point.

Once on the ground, Elisa pushed Izzy's hands away. "I can walk without you, child." She made her way up the steps. "Is there food inside?"

"Aye. And wine."

"Good." And, without another word, she walked into the Great Hall.

"Izzy . . . what the battle-fuck?"

"I'll explain everything. Later. Just . . . prepare yourself."

"Prepare myself for what?"

"Well, from what I can tell, your mother hasn't changed."

"Sweet girl, *I* could have told you that."

More horses rode into the courtyard. Talaith saw some of the sisters she'd grown up with, but she had no desire to speak with them.

"I'm going in," she told her daughter. "I'll deal with this later."

"Mum . . . wait."

"Izzy, please. I just don't want to deal with my mother—"

"Forget her," Izzy cut in. "This isn't about her."

"Then what is it?"

Izzy stepped back and Talaith watched the protective guard that had ridden with the Nolwenns. Not surprising. One of the duties of the Sefu Imperial Guard was to provide protection when necessary for the Nolwenns.

Several of the guards dismounted and strode toward the stairs. Helms were removed and heads lifted to look directly at Talaith. She blinked, her head tilting to the side. Something seemed . . .

"Talaith?"

Talaith took in a breath and looked past those younger guards to the powerful older man behind them. A feeling she hadn't known for more than three decades now hit her in the chest, her hands covering her mouth.

"Zachariah?" she asked when she had her voice back.

The blacksmith walked up the stairs, those light brown eyes that were so like his son's sweeping over her. "Still a beauty, I see."

Unable to wait for him to reach her, Talaith ran down the stairs and right into the blacksmith's big arms.

"Zachariah," she whispered before sobs racked her body. She held him tight, remembering how kind the man had always been to her. And now, she realized, how kind he'd been to Izzy. Otherwise Izzy would never have brought him or any of Sethos's kin here.

"Talaith, thank you so much," Zachariah whispered back. "For sacrificing so much for my grandchild. This amazing warrior you've bred. You've managed to give me my son back. Thank you. Thank you."

And, holding the old man close to her, Talaith finally allowed herself to mourn the first love she'd ever known, the man who'd managed to give her one of the two greatest gifts she'd been allowed by the gods to receive.

Chapter 44

The most entertaining thing for Éibhear was watching Rhianwen hug her grandmother and great grandmother over and over again, even though they clearly detested being hugged and truly felt it was an inappropriate display of emotion for a Nolwenn witch. Or any witch who planned to study under them.

They sat at the dining table in the Great Hall. Talaith, Briec, and Izzy on one side. Elisa and Haldane on the other. Éibhear at the very end and sweet Rhi constantly moving around the table. What probably could have been the worst day of her life had turned into the best because of Elisa and Haldane. So she was willing to overlook what she'd begun calling "their unfortunate past mistakes regarding my mother."

Izzy and Talaith however . . . not so much on the forgiving.

"So," Talaith began, "heard about the welcome you gave your first granddaughter."

"I was trying to protect myself. I'd assumed you sent someone to kill me," Haldane tossed back.

"Of course, I didn't send someone to kill you. Because I'd planned to come and kill you myself. At least that was my dream."

"Mum," Rhi said. "Please."

"It's all right, Rhianwen. Your mother was always a ridiculous whiner."

"What's ridiculous," Talaith shot back, "is how wide you let your ass grow."

"Mum!"

"Quickly, Rhi," Izzy gleefully urged her sister. "Hug grandmother before she gets too angry! Your hugs soothe her so."

"No, no, Rhianwen, I—" Haldane gritted her teeth, glowering across the table at Izzy while her younger granddaughter hugged her around the neck.

"I'm so glad we're all together!" Rhi cheered, kissing Haldane's cheek.

"So am I!" Izzy clapped her hands, her smile bright.

And when Izzy saw Éibhear watching her, she winked at him. That's when he knew he had to get her alone. Just for a little while. For days they'd been traveling with an entire entourage of humans and dragons, so there had been no time for them to just talk or do anything else they'd enjoy that might involve their being naked.

Éibhear tried to think of a good excuse to get Izzy away from this table, but he never had a chance as Gaius, the Rebel King, and his twin sister Agrippina entered the hall, Uncle Bram behind them. It had been decided that he'd be the one to inform the Irons about their cousin since he was known among the family as the peacemaker.

"You let her go?" Agrippina demanded when she finally stopped at the table, her eyes on Izzy.

"Aye. And I'm sorry, but it wasn't my choice."

"What do you mean it wasn't your choice? I was told you had her. In your grasp."

"We did."

"And?"

"And we could not kill her there. I assure you it was not my or Éibhear's decision. Rhydderch Hael made it quite clear what he wanted and there are times when it's too much trouble to go against him."

"Why didn't you just bring her back here alive then?"

"I felt confident she wouldn't have survived the trip," Éibhear admitted, and the smirk on Izzy's face told him he was right. "And after what had happened to Vateria in the Desert Lands, it would not have looked good for her to die at the hands of Southlanders. I'm sorry. I know that's not what you want to hear but—"

"Did she do that to you, Izzy?" Gaius asked. He was staring at the wound on the lower left of her jaw, his brow pulled down in concern.

"It's just a little thing."

Agrippina closed her eyes, let out a breath.

"Izzy, Éibhear . . . I'm sorry," she finally said. "I shouldn't be blaming you for any of this."

"Do not trouble yourself so," Izzy said." I understand hating someone who treated a family member so cruelly that you dream of killing them with your bare hands." Izzy looked right at Haldane. "Dream of it every damn day." She focused back on Agrippina. "And, if it helps, I did incapacitate the bitch."

Gaius grinned. "You mean like you did Vateria's father?"

"Well . . . she did love him so. And Rhydderch Hael just made it clear she was to be left alive. He didn't say she needed to be able to fly."

"You—" Haldane suddenly stepped in—"keep mentioning Rhydderch Hael in such a way as to suggest you speak to him as a friend. Do you expect us to believe *that*? That the father god of all dragons bothers with someone like *you*?"

"Our Izzy," Briec stated with great pride, "is Rhydderch Hael's chosen warrior."

Haldane snorted. "Her?"

That's when Talaith scrambled across the table, her hands almost around her mother's throat. But Briec caught his mate, yanked her back, and tossed the cursing, screaming woman over his shoulder. "Well," he stated calmly, "I'll see you all at dinner."

They watched him walk up the stairs with Talaith, then to Éibhear's surprise, Izzy apologized.

"Gods, I'm so sorry, Haldane. Are you all right?"

"I'm fine," Haldane practically snarled, while Elisa rubbed her own mouth to hide her smile.

"Are you sure? That was horribly awkward, wasn't it?" Izzy clapped her hands together. "I know! Rhi . . . hug your grandmother! Soothe the moment!"

"Okay!"

"Rhianwen, no—"

Her grin wide, Izzy asked Haldane, "Now don't you feel better?"

With her arm around her sister's shoulders, Izzy stood on the top step outside the Great Hall entrance. Together they ignored the near-violent arguing coming from inside.

"Dinner wasn't bad, eh?" Izzy said, gazing into the courtyard.

"No. Not bad at all." Her sister looked at her. "We're still leaving day after tomorrow, though, yes?"

Izzy laughed. "We'll miss the harvest festival."

"I don't care."

"It'll be fine, Rhi."

"Mum is just so angry."

"You need to accept the fact that she will never be friends with Haldane."

"But—"

"Never."

"But maybe if—"

"Never. Say it with me, Rhi. Nev-errrr."

Rhi sighed deeply. "All right."

Izzy kissed her sister's temple. "Want to stay the night at my house?"

"No."

Surprised. "Really?"

"Really. You go on."

Izzy narrowed her eyes. "What's going on?"

"Nothing. You're so suspicious."

"Because in this family I have to be."

Rhi laughed and hugged her. "See you in the morning."

"All right." Izzy whistled. "Macsen! Come on!"

Her dog charged out of the hall and tore off into the darkness. He'd been in great spirits since his brief time playing stud at the Imperial Guard dog kennels.

Izzy followed the dog down the steps, lifting the skirt of her gown so that it didn't drag on the ground. She briefly stopped at the bottom of the steps though and debated about spending the night in her old room until she heard her mother yell, "You were a bitch when I was sixteen, and you're a bitch now!"

Followed by Rhi's plaintive, "*Mum!*"

Izzy shook her head and headed into the forest. It was dark in these woods, but when Izzy saw light in the distance, she knew she was near the group of homes that made up her little neighborhood.

She had almost cleared the trees when Macsen charged past her heading the other way. Izzy immediately pulled out the sword Zachariah had given her and turned, barely blocking the weapon aimed right for her. Izzy shoved the weapon—another sword—away and spun to give herself momentum, slashing at the attacker. But her opponent blocked the move, their weapons locking. Izzy, fed up, stepped close to see who the hell would attack her here, so near her home.

Shocked, Izzy roared, "*Éibhear! What the bloody hells are you doing?*"

"I've come to Claim you as my own, Iseabail, Daughter of Talaith and Briec."

"Oh." Izzy lowered her weapon at his dramatic announcement. "Why didn't you say so?" She stepped back. "I'll go home and get naked." She turned to head to her house.

"That's it?" Éibhear asked, sounding disappointed.

Izzy faced him again. "What were you expecting?"

"For you to fight me."

She re-sheathed her sword and placed her hands on her hips. "Éibhear, I've been waiting since I was sixteen for you to get it through your excessively large skull that we would be together forever. And now that we're here and you're finally dragon enough to Claim me as your own . . . why would I fight you about that?"

"Because that's how it's done."

"Well, what would I have to do? Because to be quite honest, I'd like to get this moving. My patience is waning."

"Well . . . do you have any chains?"

"Brannie left a set once—"

"I don't ever want to know why."

"Trust me when I say it had absolutely *nothing* to do with sex or having a good time."

"Do you still have them?"

"I did for a while, but Macsen ate them."

"He ate chains?"

"And the cuffs. He was shitting metal for weeks. And yes," she hissed before he could say it, "he really is a dog."

"If you say so."

Izzy stepped into Éibhear, wrapping her arms around his waist. "You know, Éibhear. I thought that the Claiming could be anything we wanted it to be."

He nodded. "That's true."

"And let's be honest. The two of us . . . we could really hurt each other if we went toe to toe."

"That's a good point. And I can't afford to have my beauty marred any more than it already has been. I mean, look at what that thing did to my face."

"It's small." She reached up and stroked the scar on the bridge of his nose. "I think it's sexy."

He laughed, his arms tightening around her waist, pulling her closer. "So tell me, beautiful Iseabail…what do you want for your Claiming?"

"For me to be yours and for you to be mine," she told him, no longer teasing. "I want no more doubts, Éibhear."

The dragon lifted his hand, stroked her cheek. "Never doubt. Ever. I love you, Izzy. I'll always love you."

"And I love you, Éibhear the Contemptible. Since I first met you and your blue hair—that you wouldn't let me touch."

"Not letting that go, eh?"

"No and I never will. But I can overlook it, except when I bring it up during arguments I'm losing."

Éibhear laughed again and kissed her. As always, it started off soft and sweet, both of them still laughing. Then it changed to passionate and demanding.

"Take me home, Éibhear," she whispered when she finally managed to pull back. "Take me home and make me yours."

With his hands under her ass, Éibhear lifted Izzy up. As a naturally tall woman, she now felt like one of the old trees of the forest, so very tall, giggling as she pushed Éibhear's hair off his face and kissed his nose, cheeks, and forehead.

"One thing, Izzy."

"Of course."

Éibhear looked down and Izzy followed his gaze. Macsen sat on his haunches watching them, drool pouring out of his mouth and onto the ground, creating a little mud puddle. It was, in a word, vile.

"We'll drop Macsen at my neighbor's for the night," she offered, knowing he didn't want to have to fight her dog for Izzy's attention on such an important night.

"That's all I ask, Iz," Éibhear said with a smile while he easily carried her home. "That's all I ask."

Chapter 45

Briec walked down the stairs into the Great Hall. He stopped at the dining table, yawning and reaching for one of the warm loaves of bread the servants put out every morning. Although he wasn't looking forward to another day of fighting between Talaith and her bitch mother, he didn't know what he'd do once his Rhi left. It was hard enough when his Izzy left, but he knew she'd be back more often than not. However, Rhi and even those despicable twins that he'd secretly grown fond of . . . he had no idea when they'd return from their training.

Tearing a piece of bread off the loaf, Briec wandered over to the partially open Great Hall doors and looked out into the courtyard. It was extremely early and things were just beginning to stir as the two suns rose. But Briec saw them easy enough. Gods, how could he miss them standing there, saying nothing—and staring at the castle.

Briec slammed the doors shut.

"Briec?" Fearghus asked as he walked up behind him. "What's going on?"

"Where the hell is that idiot?"

"Gwenvael?"

"No."

"Dad?"

"No. The big blue idiot."

"I don't know. Why?"

"The Mì-runach are outside."

"So. They're probably looking for the big blue idiot."

"Not the three he brought with him. *All* of the Mì-runach. They're standing in our courtyard . . . waiting."

Fearghus nodded. "All right. We'll kill all the females first and then kill ourselves."

"What's going on?" Brannie asked as she came down the stairs with Celyn behind her.

"The Mì-runach are outside."

"They're probably looking for Éibhear."

"But we don't know where he is," Fearghus said.

"Have you checked Izzy's house?" Celyn asked.

Briec looked at Fearghus, then back at Celyn.

"Why would we look at Izzy's house?"

"No reason," Brannie quickly said.

"Why do you think?" Celyn asked.

"Shut up, Celyn," his sister told him.

"Brannie, they're not children. Éibhear and Izzy can do as they like."

Briec walked over to his young cousin, grabbed him by the throat, and yelled, "Are you saying that bastard is doing what he likes with my perfect, *perfect* daughter?"

Sighing, Brannie shook her head. "You are such an idiot, brother."

Izzy turned over and stretched, but immediately regretted that particular decision. Groaning, she slipped out of bed and stood, going across the room to the full-length standing mirror she kept there. She turned to the side and lifted her arm, examining the brand Éibhear had placed on her the night before. She cringed a little. True. She loved it, but she knew when her mother saw it . . . she would not be happy. The brand stretched from the base of her right foot and up the right side of her body until the tail of the dragon brand wrapped around her right breast.

Aye, she adored it, but her mother . . . oy.

Deciding not to deal with it right now, Izzy pulled on leggings, a cotton shirt, leather boots, and her two favorite weapons, strapping them to her back, before stepping outside. She smiled at one of her older neighbors. "Good morn to you, Mistress Sally. Any problems with Macsen?"

"Oh, no. He's asleep in my rosebushes."

Izzy winced. "Sorry. I'll make sure to have some new rosebushes sent to you to replace what he may have destroyed."

"That's fine, dear. Just fine."

Looking around, Izzy asked, "Did you happen to see my friend from last night? He was gone when I woke up."

"Oh, yes, dear. He was dragged out of here about half an hour ago by your father and his brothers. Kicking and fighting all the way," she added cheerfully.

Izzy, in the middle of a yawn, nodded. "Great. Thanks so much."

Heading back inside, Izzy decided to get the tea started. But as she held the kettle in her hand, she suddenly realized what the woman had just told her.

Izzy ran back outside, startling Mistress Sally. "You saw my father do *what*?"

"Pull that young man out of your house. Bit of a scary one that boy, so I don't really blame your father. He's always been so protective of you and your—"

"Which direction did they go?"

"Down toward the river but—"

Izzy didn't wait for Mistress Sally to finish, she just ran, charging around her neighbors and some Garbhán Isle guards,

Annwyl's troops, and even a few relatives. She ran until she hit the road that would take her to the river.

She heard Brannie call out to her, but she ignored her as well and kept going. Kept going with visions of a bloody and limb-missing Éibhear dancing through her head. Gods! What if they cut off his wings? Or removed his scales? Oh, by the gods, what if they shaved his head? What if they shaved his head? *Nooooo!*

Izzy had known her father wouldn't be happy about any of this, neither would Fearghus and Gwenvael, but she'd planned to put it all out in the open once they got Rhi squared away in the Desert Lands.

But for them to find out this way . . . oy!

Izzy cut off into the woods and ran down the hill. But as she neared the river, she stumbled to a stop. Standing there, lifting a battered Fearghus off the ground was some . . . well, she'd guess, Northland dragon scum. Ragnar and his kin might be welcome in the Southlands, but Lightnings who come to beat up Izzy's family were not. Pulling her sword and axe, Izzy silently charged forward. She was no more than a few feet from the Lightning when he caught sight of her. He dropped Fearghus and reached for his weapon, but Izzy was already swinging at him with her axe. She didn't make contact, though, because a heavy hammer slammed into her weapon, forcing it to the ground. The power of that hit radiated up her arm and she had to drop the axe. But she still had the sword. She spun and slashed the sword. The Lightning blocked it, but Izzy forced him back. Another Northlander came at her from behind, so Izzy went low, cutting the back of the hammer-wielder's leg. He cried out and dropped to one knee. Izzy quickly stood and brought her knee up into the Lightning's face. Her opponent fell back and she snatched the hammer off him. Now brandishing two weapons again, Izzy turned and . . . stopped dead. The Lightnings had multiplied rather quickly, going from about four to forty or so. They all stood watching her with the hoods of their fur capes covering their faces, their weapons out and ready to use.

Izzy took a step back, briefly studied the Lightnings—then she attacked. Charging at the closest one. But before she reached him, she sensed someone behind her and changed direction, running toward a small boulder. She ran at it until she could place her foot against it, shoved off to give her some height, and spun in midair. Which was about where that big arm snatched her out of the air and held her.

"Izzy!" Éibhear's voice practically screamed at her. "What the bloody hells are you doing?"

Realizing it was Éibhear, Izzy relaxed. "These Lightnings attacked Fearghus."

Éibhear rolled his eyes. "No. *I* beat up Fearghus, along with Briec and Gwenvael. And before you say anything, they started it. And these aren't Lightnings. They're the rest of the Mì-runach. Mum wants them to escort Rhi into the Southlands."

"Oh! Oh." Cringing, Izzy looked at the dragon whose leg she'd cut. "Sorry."

"It's all right." The dragon got to his feet. "It'll heal."

Éibhear put her on the ground. "Lads, this is General Iseabail. Iseabail . . . these are the lads."

"Nice to meet you," she said, returning to the dragon whom she'd not only cut but whose hammer she'd stolen. She handed it back to him. "Nice. Rhona's work?"

"Aye." The dragon shook his head. "I can't believe you lifted it on your own."

"Well, that was . . . Daddy!" Izzy ran over to a tree no more than twenty or so feet away, where her poor father hung over one of the lower branches. "Éibhear the Contemptible, you get my father down from there!"

"He started it!"

* * *

"Oy—" Gregor the Appalling motioned Éibhear over. "That her then? That your Izzy?"

Aidan had been filling the rest of the Mì-runach in on what had happened in the Desert Lands, somehow managing to mention Éibhear's change in status as now mated. Éibhear wasn't sure how far the details had gotten before his three brothers had dragged him down to the river, not far from the rest of the Mì-runach. His brothers didn't know the Mì-runach had set up camp here, but it didn't matter. His comrades wouldn't interfere in a sibling fight anyway, not that Éibhear needed them to. Not once he knew that the four brothers were far enough away from Izzy's house that he didn't have to worry about her protecting Briec.

"Aye. That's her."

"She carried my lovely girl." Gregor held up his "lovely girl"—his hammer. It was not a healthy relationship Gregor had with his favorite weapon. No. Not healthy at all.

"I saw."

"I bet that thing ain't even that heavy," a new, untested recruit challenged. "If some girl can pick it up."

To see if the lad had a point, Gregor threw his hammer at the recruit's head, splitting his skull open, and leaving the lad moaning in pain on the ground.

"Guess it's heavy enough then," Gregor reasoned.

"I think so," Éibhear agreed.

"Hey." Gregor smiled at him. "Why don't we take your girl to find something to eat? So she can get to know us a bit."

That actually sounded like a good idea. These were the kind of warriors Izzy was most comfortable around anyway.

"Izzy," Éibhear called to his mate. "Let's go get something to eat."

"What about Daddy and the others?"

"They'll live." Éibhear tilted his head. "Come on."

Her lips pursed, Izzy briefly debated, but after less than a minute, she ran to Éibhear's side. "I am hungry."

He put his arm around her. "Mì-runach!" he bellowed so they could all hear him. "We go to eat!"

The Mì-runach cheered and headed toward town. Éibhear started to follow, but Izzy pulled away from him and ran back to his brothers.

"Sorry, Daddy," she said to Briec before she put her hand against his forehead and shoved him off the tree limb he'd been hanging off.

Once done, she ran back to Éibhear's side and put her arm around his waist. "Sorry," she said when they began walking again. "I just couldn't leave him like that."

"It's all right. It's nice that someone cares about those mean bastards."

"I won't say it's easy . . . but they are family."

Chapter 46

Éibhear watched his kin say good-bye to Rhi and the twins. It tore his heart, knowing how hard it was. But they all knew it had to be done. Although it wasn't clear yet what the future held for the three, he knew they had to get ready for whatever was heading their way.

The plan at this point was quite simple. They'd all leave together, but once on the main road, Éibhear, Izzy, the Mìrunach, and Izzy's birth family would head to the south, while the Kyvich would take the twins north. Talan would split off from his sister and meet the monks somewhere in the Northlands and then take a secret route to their monastery far past the Sovereign Provinces. The rest of Éibhear's kin, including his brothers, sisters, parents, and Cadwaladr Clan, would stay in Dark Plains. They all seemed to know that for them to stretch this good-bye out any more would only make it more painful.

What Éibhear and Izzy would do after that he didn't know. They were now mated for life, and no other female would ever be able to fill his heart the way Izzy did. But they were still warriors and the need for battle and blood would last for a long time. Still, Éibhear knew that his Aunt Ghleanna and

Uncle Addolgar had managed life with their mates just fine over the centuries, so why couldn't he and Izzy?

Haldane, sitting on her horse, sighed again loudly. "Can we please get on the road?" she said over the wailing of Rhi and Talaith, who were clinging to each other while Briec patted their backs and rolled his eyes.

Izzy pulled out her sword and started down the stairs toward her grandmother, but Éibhear quickly caught her and pulled her into his arms.

"You have to calm down," he warned her quietly.

"I kill her now, my worries are pretty much resolved."

"We have a bigger issue."

"Which is?"

"Annwyl."

Izzy glanced over at her queen. "She is being a little quiet."

"A little?"

Finally, Rhi pulled away from her mother. "I'll miss you, Mum."

"You, too. But I'll be coming to visit. I promise. And don't let those horrid bitches turn you against your kin."

"Of course I won't! Never!"

The sobbing started again and the pair started to throw themselves into each other's arms, but this time Briec stepped between them and led Rhi down the stairs and to the horse Izzy had picked out for her. He helped his daughter mount the mare, then kissed her cheek.

"We're only a thought away, my sweetest girl. Please don't ever forget that."

"I know, Daddy. And I won't."

Now that Rhi was safe on her horse Talan hugged the women of his family. Rhiannon, Morfyd, Keita, Talaith, and Dagmar. Finally, he stepped in front of his mother. "I love you, Mum."

"I love you, too."

He hugged her, kissed her cheek. "You'll hear from me soon."

"Good."

He went down the stairs toward the mare waiting for him. Éibhear had picked out a stallion for him, but it kept throwing the boy, so they'd finally settled on one of the big battle mares. The situation told Éibhear a lot about his nephew.

"Talwyn!" the boy called out. "Let's go."

Talwyn walked out of the Great Hall. She hugged her father, grandfather, and Gwenvael, nodded at her aunts, grandmother, and her mother. Then she went down the stairs and hugged Briec. But instead of getting on the horse Izzy had chosen for her, she went to the Kyvich and waited for her next orders.

The Nolwenns snorted in disgust—it was official, the Kyvich and the Nolwenns really did loathe each other—and Annwyl's hands curled into tight fists.

Izzy glanced at Éibhear and then went right to her queen's side, Aidan moving next to Éibhear's.

"Mount up, Kyvich!" ordered Bryndís, second in command to Ásta.

"Wait," Annwyl called out. She walked down the stairs, Izzy right behind her. The Southland Queen went to her daughter and wrapped her arms around her. At first, Talwyn just stood there, her arms at her sides. But then, after a moment, she hugged her mother back. The pair held each other tight.

Annwyl stepped back, pushing her daughter's never really combed hair out of her face. She kissed her forehead and smiled. Then, without another word, Annwyl released her only daughter, turned, and walked away.

"There's no need to worry, Queen Annwyl," Ásta said to her. "You're doing the right thing. Talwyn will finally be where she belongs. With the Kyvich."

"Ásta really thinks this is a good idea?" Aidan asked Éibhear.

"Apparently."

Annwyl faced Ásta. "She's my daughter. She'll always be my daughter."

"No one said that would change. But you have to know this is for the best. You have to know that—"

Éibhear and Aidan cringed when Annwyl's fist collided with Ásta's face. Bone shattered and blood spurted, the warrior witch stumbling to the side but not falling.

"I feel better now. Thank you." Annwyl looked at her daughter. "I love you, Talwyn."

Her daughter smiled. "I love you, Mum."

Turning away, Annwyl headed up the stairs until she reached Fearghus. She took his hand with her own and he kissed the back of her bloody and bruised knuckles.

Wiping the blood from her nose with her forearm, Ásta nodded at her second in command and headed toward her horse.

"Kyvich!" the second in command called out. "Mount up!"

The oversized travel party headed out of the courtyard and toward the main road. Éibhear signaled the Mì-runach to follow the party while he went up the stairs to Talaith.

"We'll watch out for Rhi. Make sure she gets there safe."

"I know."

"When we get her settled, I'll bring Iz back."

Talaith went up on her toes, her arms open. Éibhear crouched so that she could hug him, his brothers behind her sneering. In answer, Éibhear took the middle and forefinger of his left hand and flicked them at the bastards.

And without even turning around, Talaith snapped, "You three! Leave your brother alone!"

She pulled away, patted his arm. "Go on, Éibhear. Don't let them bother you. They're just jealous."

"Of what?" Briec asked. "His giant head?"

Éibhear moved toward his brother, but Talaith stepped between them.

"What is wrong with you?" she demanded of her mate.

"Why are you yelling at me?"

"Why do you think?"

Knowing this might go on for a while, Éibhear walked over to Frederik and Dagmar.

"Good travels, Éibhear."

"Thanks, Dagmar."

He looked down at Frederik. "You'll be all right until I get back?"

"He'll be fine." Dagmar answered for the boy while wrapping her arms around Frederik, squeezing him tight. "I'm just so glad he's here. He fits in well, don't you think?"

"Well—"

Dagmar released the boy. "You know what, Frederik? Why don't we adopt you?"

"Uh . . ."

"I'll write my father," Dagmar insisted. "Right now!"

She went back inside and Frederik looked at Éibhear. "That probably isn't necessary. I doubt my family will be back for me."

"That's good, because I'm guessing she's not giving you up without a fight."

Gwenvael pushed himself away from the wall he'd been silently leaning against and patted the boy on the shoulder. "*We're all very glad you're here!*" he yelled before he followed Dagmar inside.

"Is he going to keep yell—"

"Yes. He is." Éibhear sighed. "Just . . . deal with it."

"Will you be gone long?"

"Not too long. I'll make sure to bring you some books from the Desert Lands. Okay?"

"Okay. Safe travels."

With a wave, Éibhear headed off, mounting his horse and catching up with everyone else. Weaving his horse through the crowd, he tried to find Izzy. He finally rode up to Aidan, Caswyn, and Uther. "Seen Iz?" Éibhear asked them.

"Uh-huh."

"Well?" he pushed when his friends said nothing else. "Where is she?"

Aidan pointed . . . up.

"Gods of piss and fire!" Éibhear roared, wondering what else this woman could do to drive him insane.

Izzy charged up Addolgar's neck and over his head, and leaped off his snout. The wind this high up was harsh, knocking her off balance, so that she missed Celyn's back. She rolled and flipped in midair, the ground below rushing forward. She saw Ghleanna not far away and knew she could reach her with a bit of effort. She simply needed to—

A tail wrapped around her waist and tossed her up. Izzy flipped again, laughing the entire way until she landed hard on Éibhear's back.

"What is wrong with you?" he snarled, sounding just like her mother.

"Just a bit of fun."

"Can't you do something a little safer? Like ride into battle against demons, naked and without weapons or go swimming in molten lava?"

"You sound angry."

"Because you seem determined to make me insane."

"That's a cruel thing to suggest," Izzy stretched her arms across the length of Éibhear's neck. "You know I simply adore you."

"What you adore is being irritating—and stop writhing around back there."

"Sorry," but she didn't remotely mean it. "You know, Éibhear, I still love your hair."

"Thank you."

"Can I put warrior braids in it?"

"No, you may not. We are on a serious mission to deliver

a Southland royal to the Desert Lands. We don't have time for your obsession over my hair and whether it's in braids or not."

"Do you think Aidan will let me braid his hair?"

With a snarl, the bastard spun in midair, Izzy screeching and tightening her thighs around his neck until he'd righted himself again.

"*You evil bastard!*" she laughed.

"That's what you get! Taunting me with another dragon, you cruel, vicious female."

"That you love more than the suns."

She felt his deep chuckle spread through her, wrap around her. "That's very true. My tragic weakness."

"But a weakness I'm going to allow."

"That's good. Because I do love you, Izzy. I truly do."

Resting her cheek against his scales, her face buried under all that blue hair being whipped about by the wind, Izzy wrapped her arms around Éibhear's neck and said the only thing she could possibly think of at this moment.

"Well, it's about gods-damn time, Éibhear the Blue. Because I've been waiting a bloody lifetime for you."

Epilogue

They reached the main road that cut through Dark Plains and the one large group split into two distinct parts. One turned south toward the Desert Lands, the other north toward the Ice Lands.

While the two groups headed off on their separate paths, three held back, two on horses, one standing.

The three didn't speak. They didn't have to. Since they were babes they'd never needed words to know what the others were feeling or thinking. But this would be the first time they would be apart from each other. It wouldn't be easy, but they all knew that it wasn't forever. No matter what the witches or monks or anyone else thought or said or believed, the truth was that the connection of these three beings was stronger than anything anyone would ever understand. They were only separating now so that when they were together again, they'd be even stronger, even more powerful, and most importantly, even more ready.

Ready for when the dark times came and they were needed.

Because those dark times were coming. They were coming fast. And what had happened in the Desert Land city sewers had only delayed their problems—not ended them.

With a nod, Talwyn walked off first. Rhi, still crying from

when she'd said good-bye to her parents, headed south, the Mì-runach that Uncle Éibhear had hidden in the nearby forests following her.

Then Talan took one more look around, turned his horse north, and went off to prepare for his future.

The males, never good with emotions, had gone off to steal cows from the local farmers for a quick meal while Annwyl sat on the stairs leading into the Great Hall with Ta-laith, Dagmar, Keita, and Morfyd.

Thankfully no one felt the need to speak. Instead they just sat and stared off, the loss of the children felt by all of them equally.

"Excuse me."

Annwyl looked up. A pretty woman with a young child stood in front of them. "Can I help you?"

"Aye. I was trying to find someone who could help me get an audience with Queen Annwyl."

"I'm Queen Annwyl."

The woman's jaw visibly tensed. "Can't you just say I can't meet with her? Do you have to mock me?"

"Actually," Dagmar said, "she *is* Queen Annwyl."

Frowning, clearly not believing any of them, the woman looked Annwyl over.

"What do you need?" Dagmar prompted kindly when the woman just kept staring.

"I need help," she said tentatively. "And I was told you were the one who could help me."

"Help doing what?"

"You see, my lady, I was driven from my village. Because of my son."

Annwyl studied the child. He was a beautiful boy. Tall with golden blond hair and big green eyes. "Is he ill?" He looked well enough but perhaps he carried something. . . .

"No, my lady. He's . . . uh . . ." The woman wrapped her arms around the boy like she was protecting him. "He's my son. *My* son. And I'll do what I must to protect him."

"Has someone threatened him?"

"The elders of our village say that if I try to bring him back, they'll kill him."

Annwyl fought her urge to crack her neck or turn her hands into fists. She'd discovered over the years that those who didn't know her well found those reactions threatening.

"Why would they say that?"

She hugged her son a little tighter. "Because . . . because of his father."

"Who's his father?"

"Not who, my lady." Slowly, the woman turned her head, then looked up into the sky. Annwyl and her sisters followed suit, looking up. And, over their heads, dragons flew.

"A dragon?" Morfyd finally said. "The boy's father is a dragon?"

The woman nodded. "Yes. I don't understand it myself. The one I was with . . . I didn't know he was"—she cleared her throat— "a . . . a dragon until my son was nearly two. But by then it didn't matter. He's my son."

"But the village elders wanted you to give him up?" Talaith asked. Of them all, she had the most experience with small village life.

"I couldn't do it. I didn't know what I was going to do, but a temple priest said to come here. That you might be able to help. That at the very least, we'd be welcome since you're not averse to dragons. So here we are."

Annwyl scratched her head. This hadn't been the way she'd planned to spend the rest of her day, but perhaps it was for the best. It would not be a good idea for her to sit around and brood over her children.

She began to stand. "I'm sure there's something we can do for you and your son."

"And the others," the woman said.

Annwyl again sat down. "Others?"

Pulling her boy with her, the woman stepped back and Annwyl let out a hard breath.

"Annwyl?" she heard Talaith whisper.

"By all reason," Dagmar sighed out as what appeared to be about fifty *families* made their way into the courtyard, some of them clearly carrying all their belongings with them.

"All this time," Keita said, "we thought that the twins and Rhi were the only ones."

"Clearly, sister, we were wrong." Morfyd shook her head. "Very, very wrong."

Annwyl stood, the others following suit. She looked at the females of her family. "Dagmar, we need to find some place for these people to stay. Talaith, round up healers and make sure everyone is healthy. If any are sick, let's find some place for them where they can get better. I don't want anyone here getting ill as well. Morfyd, get your mother and the Elders—and manage them. Please. Keita, find out what you can. And call your brothers back here."

With her orders given, Annwyl walked down the stairs and stopped by the woman and her son. "What's your name?"

"Diana. And this is my son, Camden."

"Well, Diana and Camden, why don't you introduce me to your friends?"

"Of course, my lady." Taking her son's hand, Diana walked toward the growing crowd.

Annwyl watched them for a moment, noticing how around her everything looked the same but nothing really was.

"And so it begins . . ." the Southland Queen whispered before heading off to face this new future.